Marion Lennox has written over one hundred romance novels and is published in over one hundred countries and thirty languages. Her international awards include the prestigious RITA® award (twice!) and the *RT Book Reviews* Career Achievement Award for 'a body of work which makes us laugh and teaches us about love'. Marion adores her family, her kayak, her dog, and lying on the beach with a book someone else has written. Heaven!

Alison Roberts has been lucky enough to live in the South of France for several years recently, but is now back in her home country of New Zealand. She is also lucky enough to write for the Mills & Boon Medical line. A primary school teacher in a former life, she later became a qualified paramedic. She loves to travel and dance, drink champagne and spend time with her daughter and her friends. Alison is the author of over one hundred books!

Also by Marion Lennox

A Rescue Dog to Heal Them
A Family to Save the Doctor's Heart
Dr Finlay's Courageous Bride
Healed by Their Dolphin Island Baby

Also by Alison Roberts

The Doctor's Christmas Homecoming
Fling with the Doc Next Door

Morgan Family Medics miniseries

Secret Son to Change His Life
How to Rescue the Heart Doctor

Discover more at millsandboon.co.uk.

HER OFF-LIMITS SINGLE DAD

MARION LENNOX

THE ITALIAN, HIS PUP AND ME

ALISON ROBERTS

MILLS & BOON

First published in Great Britain 2023
by Mills & Boon, an imprint of HarperCollins*Publishers* Ltd,
1 London Bridge Street, London, SE1 9GF

www.harpercollins.co.uk

HarperCollins*Publishers* Macken House, 39/40 Mayor Street Upper,
Dublin 1, D01 C9W8, Ireland

Her Off-Limits Single Dad © 2023 Marion Lennox

The Italian, His Pup and Me © 2023 Alison Roberts

ISBN: 978-0-263-30617-0

09/23

This book is produced from independently certified FSC™ paper
to ensure responsible forest management.
For more information visit: www.harpercollins.co.uk/green.

Printed and Bound in the UK using 100% Renewable Electricity
at CPI Group (UK) Ltd, Croydon, CR0 4YY

HER OFF-LIMITS SINGLE DAD

MARION LENNOX

MILLS & BOON

CHAPTER ONE

THIS SEEMED LIKE a job for Air Rescue. The nearest helicopter base, though, was South Sydney, and their only available unit was caught up on another job.

They were on their own.

The crashed truck, on its side well below the road, seemed to have caught on a straggly coastal gumtree. From where Jenny stood it was a good ten metres down to the truck, then another ten to the rock-strewn surf beneath. The truck seemed to be balanced across the tree trunk. It looked like it could slip further at any minute and there seemed no way they could safely climb down.

'Are we sure someone's inside?' she asked, and Gary grimaced.

'We're pretty sure.'

Jennifer Roden and Gary Drummond, Willhua's only two paramedics, had been called to this crash by Chris, Willhua's sole police officer. Chris, though, was caught up with a break-in and assault. He'd taken the frantic call from a member of the public, but could do nothing but pass the message to the ambulance service. That meant Gary and Jen were first on scene. First things first—they needed to check this wasn't just a vehicle pushed over the cliff to avoid dumping charges.

From where they stood the truck looked old and rusty, and if it was worthless it'd be costly to get rid of. How much cheaper to drive it here, release the parking brakes and give it a push into the sea?

That'd be the easy scenario but it didn't fit here.

'Deirdre McConachie saw it go over.' Gary, Jenny's partner and Willhua's senior paramedic, was staring down at the truck and looking grim. 'Deirdre didn't have her phone—she had to drive into town to call Chris. She told him the truck was weaving all over the road in front of her—she thought the driver might be drunk. She said it went straight down. Going over here... Well, Deirdre assumed it'd ended up in the sea and there'd be no hope of survival. She was too scared to look— she just headed fast into town for help—but by the look of the truck she guessed it might be Charlie Emerson.'

'Who's Charlie?' Jen had only been in this job, in this town, for two days. Gary had worked here for thirty years and knew everyone.

'Retired farmer. Hell, I'll ring Chris back. We need urgent help. More cops. The State Emergency Service. They'll have to come from Whale Head—and the chopper from Sydney.'

But as he spoke a gust of wind slammed across the face of the cliff and the truck seemed to shudder. And Jenny saw something in the side window facing upward. A face.

A dog? Definitely. Fawn-coloured, with oversized white ears. Staring straight up at them?

Surely no one would drive a truck over the cliff with a dog inside.

Unless it was a suicide attempt?

'How old's Charlie?' she demanded. 'He must be inside the truck as well. Or thrown out and in the sea?'

'He's eighty if he's a day. Dammit, Jenny, Charlie *must* be behind the wheel.'

'I'll go down.'

'Are you kidding? We need to wait for help.'

'By which time the truck might have fallen. You have ropes in the back of the ambulance. I can abseil down.'

'You? Abseil?'

'It's what I do for a hobby,' she said, and she managed a smile. 'You didn't read my résumé, huh? That bag I tucked into the back of the truck yesterday—it has my abseiling gear.'

'You're kidding.' He shook his head, staring down at the truck again. Its movement had them both almost mesmerised. 'Jen, we've been desperate,' he said as he stared. 'Pete'll be out of action for months, and that's left me with just Chris and Doc. Pierson to help in an emergency. The first page of your application confirmed you had a pulse and qualifications. You were therefore hired.'

She managed a chuckle at that. 'Wow, I'm flattered.'

It was Saturday evening. Jenny had arrived in Willhua on Thursday, planning to start work on Monday, but Gary had spent time with her the day before. So far she'd liked what she'd seen. Gary was in his sixties, he had the beginnings of arthritis in his hands which held him back, but he seemed skilled, sensible and friendly.

He was a far cry from the last man she'd worked for. Bottom-feeding toerag.

Now, however, was not the time to dwell on the humiliation she'd walked away from in Sydney. Now was the time to focus on the guy in the truck. It was late and the light was fading. If she was going down she had to go now.

'I can't abseil,' Gary said. 'Not when it's this steep, and as your boss, I'm not sure I should allow it. Pete always does the climbing stuff. I'll ring Doc Pierson. He'll know what to do.'

'Call him by all means,' Jen said. 'But I'm going. If Charlie's had a heart attack, if he's bleeding out...' Already she was seeing this Charlie-the-farmer as a real person, not just a random accident victim. 'There's no choice.'

'Can you do it without risk?'

That was a fair question. Safety was drilled into paramedics from their earliest training—*Do not put yourself in danger*. The last thing you wanted was to add yourself to the roll call of dead or injured. But still, almost every paramedic eventually faced situations where risk had to be weighed.

She was weighing risk now. It looked a simple abseil. The driver's side of the truck was facing upward and the door looked clear. She couldn't see the driver, but the dog was looking out of the window. She was assuming the driver had slumped sideways.

Deirdre had said the car had been weaving all over the road. So…drunk? Stroke? Heart attack? Diabetic hypo?

And at any minute the truck might fall.

Yes, there was a risk, but it was a risk worth taking.

'I'll push back if the truck moves,' she told Gary. 'But I might be able to clear an airway, or stop bleeding, at least do the basics. If you could lower the stretcher, maybe I could attach it to the tree, get it steady, even get him out.'

'By yourself? In your dreams. But could we stabilise the truck?' Bob sounded doubtful. 'With the bushfires down in Victoria and the amount of rain we've had here, our local fire crew figured they were needed more down south. They left as part of the interstate response. We need a crane, but Jodie Adams has the only crane in Willhua, and her family has dinner with her mum in Whale Head on Saturday nights. She won't be back yet. Could we use the ropes to attach the truck to…?' But then he paused and stared around him. There were no trees near the road. It was a narrow strip of bitumen and the cliff rose steeply behind them. 'To the ambulance?'

'We could try,' she said. 'But that's a heavy truck. I doubt the ropes'd hold—or they'd pull our truck over.'

What had she got herself into? she thought. She'd just come from a huge paramedic service in Southern Sydney, and her team had been multiskilled. Here there was no one but herself and Gary.

Willhua was a tiny coastal town that attracted retirees, plus people who liked out-of-the-way places—scuba divers, surfers, a paragliding community who used the wind to fly along the lonely but spectacular cliff faces. It had a tiny hospital that existed only because the place was so remote.

Pete, the paramedic she was replacing, had smashed his foot while surfing off the rocks a few weeks ago. With him out of action, the little town had been desperate for a replacement. The temporary job had seemed an ideal solution, a place to come and nurse her broken heart—or at least her shattered pride—but right now what she wanted was her huge metropolitan rescue team.

'We could use a tractor,' she said now. 'Or something else heavy to hold things firm. But with this wind there's no time to wait till they arrive. Once it's dark I can't abseil. But ring everyone you can think of. Meanwhile I'm going down.'

'Jen, I'm your superior. What'll people say if I let you go?'

'They'll say I have every certificate available in advanced abseiling skills,' Jen said, with only an inward qualm at the slight…deception. As far as she knew, there were no certificates available for advanced or any other level of abseiling. 'It's only sensible.'

'The risks…'

'I won't go into the truck,' Jen promised. 'And we have gear in the ambulance.' She did have her abseiling kit—one of the things that had attracted her to this place had been the opportunity to practice her climbing skills, and she'd guessed, given the popularity of this place for windsurfers and para-gliders, that she might even get to use her skills for profes-sional reasons.

But to help someone in a truck in this position...

At least she could get to him, she reasoned. 'I will take care,' she told Gary. 'We can't just stand here and do noth-ing. Agreed?'

Gary stared at her for a long moment. 'I should go myself,' he said at last. 'But...' He shook his head. 'I can't.'

'What, thirty years in the service and you've never learned how to clamber down cliffs like a rock crab?' Jenny said, and tried a smile. 'But isn't that the reason I was employed, to add to the skill set your service offers? Are you happy to help me?'

He stared at her again, thinking. 'I'd like you to wait for Doc. And for Chris. Either of them might know what to do. We need more people than me to control things.'

They both stared down at the truck again and another gust shook the tree holding the vehicle.

'Yeah, but Charlie can't wait,' Jenny said. 'Let's go.'

It was eight o'clock on a Saturday night and Dr Rob Pierson had just disconnected from his nightly call to the hospital at Brisbane Central. The response had been pretty much the same response he'd had every night for the last four years.

'No change at all, Dr Pierson. Your wife's as comfortable as we can make her.'

Dammit, why wouldn't they let her go?

He stared into the empty fireplace—it was cool enough to light a fire but he couldn't be bothered. He'd have a drink and head to bed in a minute. Or maybe he'd check on Jacob again, then head through and do a fast check on his patients.

Willhua's official doctor's residence had been built to make a doctor's life easy. There was therefore a door in the hall that led through to the rear of the hospital's nurses' station. Rob had also rigged up a video and monitor. If four-year-old Jacob called out, or if he moved from bed, Rob or one of the nurses on call could be through here in seconds.

It wasn't a perfect system—Rob's parents-in-law had raised it in court as yet another reason why Rob shouldn't have custody—but the judge had come down on Rob's side. Willhua was desperate to keep its doctor. Not only the nurses, but almost every local was only too ready to drop everything and take on Jacob's care in an emergency, so somehow the system worked.

Willhua wasn't all that prone to emergencies anyway, apart from the occasional paraglider or windsurfer who did something stupid. Such casualties were mostly airlifted to Sydney. The hospital was thus pretty much a glorified nursing home for the retirees who made up half the population. But Rob had a local farmer in tonight who was recovering from snakebite, plus he'd admitted a young mum with mastitis. She wasn't desperately sick, but she was exhausted, and admitting her might force her lazy husband to step up and take care of the other two kids for a couple of days.

It wasn't cutting-edge medicine but he liked it, though the ongoing conflict with his in-laws was doing his head in.

Maybe he should give in, he thought grimly. Head back to Brisbane. Sit by Emma's bed for the how many years she might live like this?

He couldn't do it, to himself or to Jacob. But his thoughts were bleak, and when the phone rang it was almost a relief.

'Doc?' He knew Gary's voice well, and the single word conveyed trouble.

'What's up?'

'We have a truck near the bottom of Devil's Pass. We think it's Charlie Emerson. Deirdre McConachie called it in, said the truck was weaving like he was drunk. It went straight over. It's caught halfway down but not stable. Chris is caught up on the far side of the valley, you know the fire crew's still down in Victoria and Jodie's tow truck's unavailable. Meanwhile we think Charlie's stuck halfway down the cliff.'

His heart sank.

Safety had been drilled into him since medical school, and safety would be on the line here. There was a time when he'd have taken risks almost without thinking, but being sole parent to a four-year-old changed things. With Emma's parents seemingly watching every move, almost paranoid in their need to protect their grandson, his appetite for risk was pretty much nil.

Pete, the paramedic who'd injured his foot, had been adept at cliff rescues, but Gary had reluctantly agreed some years back that he couldn't do it. And this new woman they'd just employed? Gary had done the interview. Could she help or would he be forced to intercede? On his own?

'Ring South Sydney Air Rescue,' he said bluntly. 'Get a chopper.'

'I already have, but they're caught up on another job and there's no time to wait.' There was suddenly an odd note of pride in Gary's voice. 'But our Jenny…the new lass…damned if she's not an abseiler. She's rigging herself a harness and she's about to head down.'

'She can't!'

'She says she can, and I believe her. Truck's about to fall, Doc. She says she won't take stupid risks and Charlie must be bad. Can you get someone to ring round for tractors? A few guys with decent ropes. Just in case. Then come?'

So there was no choice. 'I need to hand over Jacob's care but I'll use the car phone to do the rest,' he told him. 'Stop her until I get there and that's an order.'

'The lady's got a mind of her own,' Gary said, and the pride was there again. 'And you know what? The way she looked at the whole set-up…the way she's acting… I'm thinking she knows what she's doing a lot more than the pair of us put together.'

The abseil down the cliff had been relatively straightforward. The tricky part now was to reach the person inside the truck without adding to its instability.

There was also a dog, and the dog wasn't helping one bit.

The driver's door was almost horizontal, a flat plane, and as soon as she reached the truck Jenny could see down inside the cab.

Charlie—or at least she assumed it was Charlie—was slumped across the seats. His legs were still almost in the driver's seat position but he'd slide sideways so his head was on the passenger side. There was blood on his chest and on his face. The left side of his shirt was ripped and she could see a jagged wound on his upper arm.

The dog was clambering over his body, seeing Jen, desperate to get to this newcomer. A corgi? This was a complication she didn't need. The dog, too, looked bloody, but she had no idea whether it was Charlie's blood or its own.

As a trained paramedic Jen had been in situations before where a dog had been protective of an injured owner. Her heart sank, but she couldn't get to Charlie without dealing with the dog.

She had ropes. There were light lines in the gear kit attached to her back.

First priority dog?

'What's happening?' Gary yelled from up on the road.

'I'm getting the dog out,' she called back. Gary would understand the situation.

'Hey,' she said, turning back to the cab's occupant, not sure if he could hear her but talking anyway. 'Hold still there, Charlie, rescue's happening.'

She hoped.

First things first. She steadied herself as much as she could, finding leverage for her legs, almost stability. And then she attacked the door.

Opening a truck door when it was the right way up was relatively easy, unless it was damaged. This door wasn't damaged but, the way it was lying, it needed to be hauled up to open, a dead weight. Jen was fit, but even so it was a challenge, more so because the minute she got it open the dog was in her face.

'Stay,' she said firmly as she struggled. 'Good boy. Stay still!'

And, amazingly, he did. He was on Charlie's body, and he was leaning out to greet her, his tongue lolling. It was an impossible situation but at least he wasn't vicious.

She hauled the door up further until finally its own weight caused it to slam back against the truck tray. Okay, she now had a clear entrance, but her access was still blocked by the dog.

She grabbed one of the cords she had in her kit and reached in, then gave herself a moment to steady, reassure the dog.

'Now, mate, come on out,' she told him and tugged.

And he did. The position of the truck must have given him a false sense of security, its side forming a flat surface. He scrambled out, and Jen saw grazing along his side—a lot of grazing. Blood. Lacerations. He whimpered as she hauled, but she had no choice.

'Sorry, mate,' she told him. 'But we need to get your master safe first.'

She moved herself further along the tray and dragged the dog with her. The side of the truck formed part of a rusty crate. As she pulled, the dog lurched off the door onto the crate's wire sides. There was a yelp of pain, but she had no time for further reassurance. Once the dog was stable she tied him fast and left him. If the truck fell, the dog would go too, but there was no choice.

And now Charlie. With the corgi out of the way she could get into the truck, but she had to be so careful. Her weight could easily make the difference, causing the truck to slide.

She steadied herself, fighting to find a decent toe-hold, allowing the ropes to hold all her weight when all her instincts were screaming at her to use the truck to balance herself.

Finally she leaned in.

Charlie looked grey. In his eighties, small, almost wizened, his face looked ghastly. 'Pain,' he gasped. 'I can't…bear…'

Pain from where? In this situation it was impossible to tell.

But stopping the bleeding had to be her first priority. How much blood had he lost? Was it his blood or the dog's? In the fading light it was impossible even to guess.

'Are you Charlie?' she asked as she gloved.

'I…yeah.'

'I'm Jen, Willhua's new ambulance officer, here to get you out of here,' she told him. 'But let's get you a bit tidier first.' She was forming a pad and applying pressure as she spoke, assessing, thinking fast.

She had to get him out, but to pull him out when he was already grey with pain…

'Hey, you'll be okay.' They were easy words, but how to make them true?

By the look on his face, the pain he was feeling was excruciating. In the back of her mind was the description of him weaving on the road and then driving straight over. Heart problem? It had to be a possibility, but aspirin was out of the question here. She had no way of assessing internal bleeding. Risks, though, had to be weighed and tugging him out of the truck without pain relief might well kill him.

But giving pain relief in this situation was risky, too. Even finding a vein would be hard. Respiratory depression was problematic and pain might be coming from anywhere, but somehow he had to be dragged out.

Okay. Decision made. Low dose morphine.

'I'm giving you something for the pain,' she told him. 'We'll wait for a couple of moments to let it take effect and then get you out of here.' When she'd figured out how.

The injection went home. Charlie was still staring at her with eyes dilated with terror and she grabbed his hand and held, hard.

And then, despite the slight tremors of the truck, despite the knowledge that the tree could give way at any minute, Jen forced herself into the space her training had instilled. She took a long look at the truck, at the guy's position. The passenger side seemed damaged. The door must have been bashed open as it slid or tumbled down the cliff. Where the door should have been, she could only see broken glass, torn metal and rockface.

She didn't want Charlie to talk any more than he must, but this was vital.

'Charlie, was anyone else in the truck with you?'

And his terror seemed to grow. His eyes swivelled to see, and he made himself whisper.

'My...dog?' His voice faltered and he looked pleadingly up at her, as if trying to say something more but there was no strength. 'My mate, Bruce?'

'Is Bruce your dog?'

'He was just...just here.'

And Jenny relaxed just a touch. 'He's safe,' she told him. 'I got him out. Now, let's get you out too.'

But how? His legs weren't trapped—thank heaven for small mercies. He must have been cut in the fall, she thought. Maybe there were crush injuries, but underlying everything...what? There was no smell of alcohol. Had a medical event caused this? Was there an underlying heart attack?

She pulled back so she was leaning out of the cab and grabbed her radio. 'Gary?'

'Reading.'

'He seems alone apart from his dog. You'll have seen me tie the dog to the tray? Nothing's holding Charlie in the cab but we need to get him out fast. Bleeding, lacerations, severe pain, possibly internal injuries, possibly prior, maybe a heart attack?'

There was a sharp intake of breath as Gary processed the implications, but he was professional enough to move straight to the practical. 'Doc's here, on his way down now. He's bring-ing the stretcher'

Yeah? That was like a shot of adrenalin all on its own. Gary had organised the ambulance floodlight, so the deepening dusk was now alleviated by the artificial light. She swivelled to look up the cliff and yes, a figure was near the edge, leaning back, his feet finding a foothold on the cliff face. The ropes around him, the way he held himself, told her that here was someone else who was capable of abseiling. And by his side Gary was lowering a stretcher rig, lined up for a vertical rescue.

She'd spent yesterday browsing the ambulance set-up, familiarising herself with what this service could offer. Because Willhua was remote and a lot of its retrievals were from the beach, they carried a stretcher rig. It consisted of a light metal frame with webbing, with maximum hand holds, fastenings to secure a patient if they needed to cross rough ground, with the rigging needed if the patient had to be hauled upward.

Such a rescue should wait for the specialised chopper team from Sydney, but Charlie's breathing said they didn't have the luxury of waiting. She swung herself back to the cab.

'Charlie,' she said and lifted his hand again and held. Shifting him before they had the stretcher in position seemed fraught—any movement could send the truck down. All she could do right now was reassure, reassure, reassure. 'Doc's on his way. Doc Pierson—you know him? They say he's good. He's bringing a stretcher so we can get you out.'

'But…' The man's eyes were wild with fear, searching the cabin.

'We have your dog safe,' she repeated. 'Everything's okay except you seem to have broken some ribs. We'll get you to the hospital.'

He closed his eyes and for a sickening moment she thought he'd gone into cardiac arrest. But her fingers found his wrist and his pulse was still there, weak and thready but constant.

'Here.' The voice came from above her and she almost jumped. She swivelled and here he was, the doctor she'd met for a brief moment when she'd arrived for her interview.

She'd come to Willhua a week ago in answer to the job advertisement, and Gary had organised an interview. This doctor had been there. They'd therefore met—just—but two minutes after her introduction there'd been a call. Someone had arrived at the hospital having sliced their hand while cooking.

'It's bleeding like stink and I can't stop it,' she'd heard the woman say via the speaker phone. The doctor—Rob Pierson—had apologised and left in a hurry.

'You gotta get used to that here,' Gary had told her. 'It's a small town, so any drama we all stop everything. Luckily dramas don't happen all that often.'

Like on the first day of her first shift? The local policeman was caught up with an assault, and now, what had the doctor had to abandon to get here?

Regardless, she was blessedly glad to see him. What was more, he was moving as if he was accustomed to this type of situation. He'd swung down the cliff fast, with the stretcher attached by harness and the blue lines she recognised. He was now almost at eye level. With black hair, tanned, sun-weathered skin and a long, lithe body, he looked superbly fit, the type of guy she'd met during her climbing training. Now he was meeting her gaze, with eyebrows raised. Questions were in his dark eyes though, not in his voice.

But she knew what he was asking. Condition? Urgency? There was no room in the cab for him to take her place to examine, and no time either. Demanding a condition report within the patient's hearing was also problematic. But that one questioning glance contained trust. One professional to another.

Her gaze met his and held, and she saw that he got it. The urgency.

This guy wasn't so old, mid-thirties maybe, and in her work

Jen had often found that younger doctors were suspicious of paramedics' ability. Rob Pierson, though, glanced in at Charlie—a cursory glance, given the lack of light in the cab—then looked at Jen. Jen nodded and the decision seemed to be made.

'Harness coming in,' he said briefly. 'Attach the line. Two minutes.'

Right. Deep breath.

Pulling a grown man out of a truck in this position seemed impossible. She didn't think she could do it. But they had to get him out of here, and the harness was a godsend. It was hard to get it fitted, but somehow she did, and with that came a slight lessening of tension. Now he was harnessed, the blessed safety lines fixed, all she had to do was shift him upward so if the truck plunged he wouldn't follow.

All she had to do? Shifting a dead weight was easier said than done.

'Swap.' Rob's order was a curse snap and she obeyed instinctively. If she knew how to achieve this she would have fought him, but she was only hoping he might have more of an idea than she did.

She backed out, using her climbing ropes to steady her, conscious all the time of not putting weight on the truck.

She risked another glance at Rob as she emerged from the cab. The unspoken message, one medic to another. Situation dire.

'On my signal, tell Gary full strength on my ropes,' he told her. 'You control Charlie's line, using it to help pull as much as you can.' And then, as he moved closer, he spoke to Charlie.

'Charlie, mate, this is Rob Pierson. Dr Pierson—you know me. We need to get you out of here, but we need your help. I'm going to link my hands under your shoulders and pull, but do you reckon you can push a bit with your legs? I know it'll hurt like hell, but a nice comfy stretcher's waiting.'

Could he do it? It was almost a vertical lift. Jen shifted a little on her ropes, ready to grab what she could if—when— he emerged. The safety lines attached to Charlie would help, but not much. She couldn't see how...

But he did. One moment Rob was bent over- all she could see was his back. The next he was pulling back and, miraculously, Charlie was in his hold.

What sort of Herculean strength...?

But there was no time for questions. As Charlie emerged she grabbed his thighs and helped manoeuvre him. Rob had set the stretcher up so it was hanging just above the tray. In less time than she would have believed possible they had him fastened, and Rob was calling upward.

'Bring us up!'

There must be more people on the clifftop by now, Jen realised, because the ropes tightened instantly. Rob moved into position beside the stretcher, attaching himself, stabilising it as it moved. Then, with the utmost care from those above—that'd be Gary, she thought, even if he couldn't abseil he'd know the drill—Rob and the stretcher were on their way upward.

The whole process had been so fast she felt dazed. She let herself hang for a moment, using her feet to steady herself, but taking a moment to let her breath subside to normal.

And then the dog whined.

She'd almost forgotten him. Bruce, the dog. He was crouched low, flattened on the wire crate. Another gust of wind hit and the truck shuddered again. She couldn't leave him.

'Another harness,' she yelled upward.

'Someone else?' She heard alarm in Gary's voice.

'Dog,' she called. All attention up on the road had to be on

Charlie, but she'd promised. 'He's too big for me to carry but I reckon a harness might work.'

And Gary must have agreed because a rope came down, with a harness.

It was a stupid fit—a human harness—but the dog seemed almost paralysed with pain and fear. She hooked the harness around his rear and the corgi looked up at her with limpid trusting eyes that made her melt.

'It's okay, boy,' she said softly. 'Let's get you to your master.'

And somehow she managed it. She had whoever was up the cliff pull gently, she swung on her rope with the dog in her arms, the harness took her weight from her rear, and she steadied Bruce and herself by finding footholds as she rose.

And, moments later, she and the dog were on the road.

This was a very different scenario than the one she'd left, what, half an hour back? There were people everywhere. Gary and Rob were crouched over the stretcher. A guy in a policeman's uniform—was this Chris?—was in charge of the rope pulls, and there were at least half a dozen locals looking desperate to help.

Thank heaven. She let herself slump on the road for a moment, cradling the dog, letting herself believe that the drama was over. Then she rose and carried the dog across to the stretcher.

If anything Charlie looked even worse than when she'd last seen him. Rob was setting up a syringe. Gary was trying to fit an oxygen mask, but the old guy was fighting him.

'Bruce,' he gasped.

'Hey, we have him.' She knelt by the stretcher, holding the corgi so he could see him. 'Here he is. Bruce.'

The old man's eyes widened in hope. He stared wildly— and then he looked straight past her.

'Stumpy,' he stammered, and he tried to raise his hand to pat his dog. 'I knew she... But where's...where's Bruce?'

'Who's Bruce?' Rob snapped, his voice urgent.

'Best...best mate,' Charlie whispered—and stopped breathing.

CHAPTER TWO

AFTER THAT THINGS got a bit blurry. Someone took the dog from her, and the three of them went into overdrive. Full CPR, defibrillation, the works. There was total silence from the on-lookers as they worked; maybe every one of them was doing what Jen was doing. Pleading. Please...

And, blessedly, on the third shock there was a pulse. Thready, weak but glorious. He was still unconscious, but with a pulse anything was possible.

'We need to get to the hospital, fast,' Rob snapped to Gary. 'I need equipment, lights, sirens—Gary, can you give us an escort? I need—'

But... 'Bruce,' Jen said out loud. She was leaning back on her heels. This had been so close. She'd been feeling relieved but now...

'Bruce?' They were suddenly all looking at her.

'Down in the truck,' she said, trying to figure things out as she spoke. 'Charlie was calling for Bruce and I assumed he was worrying about his dog. He said, "My mate, Bruce. My dog." I'd already pulled the dog out. I asked if Bruce was his dog and he seemed to agree but...' She closed her eyes for a millisecond, then she rose and crossed to a guy who was hold-ing the dog she'd hauled up the cliff.

The corgi was lying passively at the guy's feet, its sides bloodstained, eyes wide with fear.

'Hey,' she said softly as she approached. She knelt and raised her hand to let the dog smell her, then gently fondled the spot most dogs loved, right behind the ear. And as she did she manoeuvred the dog's collar so she could read the faded rusty disc.

It said 'Stumpy'.

And Jen's hands did a fast check in the fading light and found confirmation.

Stumpy was a she.

'What gives?' The doctor—Rob—was suddenly by her side. He must have seen the colour drain from her face. 'Jen?'

'I assumed Bruce was this dog,' she whispered. 'But this one's a bitch and her name's Stumpy. And...and Charlie didn't actually say Bruce was a dog. He said...my mate.'

And he got it. 'So that leaves Bruce, dog or man, unaccounted for?' Rob's hands gripped her shoulders. 'You saw the inside of the truck,' he said in a voice that steadied her all by itself. It was firm, emotionless, demanding that she become professional again. 'Is there any way someone could have been thrown out?'

'I... Maybe?' she managed. 'The passenger door looked to be ripped off.' She closed her eyes, hauling the visual of the inside of the truck back into her mind. 'There was a seatbelt though. Undone.'

'If he wasn't wearing it...'

'I guess.'

And they both stared out over the cliff, into the deepening dusk.

'Okay, moving on. Let's leave the self-blame for later, Jen—and there's no need anyway. Even if we knew someone else was down there, we couldn't have done any more than we've done. Chris!' Rob called to the policeman. 'There's a possibility of someone else down there. Dog or man, we're not sure, but we need to assume it's a man. Name of Bruce. It's too dark for anyone else to climb down, and no use at all if they're in the sea. Can you get onto neighbours, anyone who might know who this Bruce is? Meanwhile, we need to get Charlie to the hospital. Come on, Jennifer, let's go.'

'Doc, I'll put the dog in the truck.' It was the guy who'd been holding Stumpy. 'Front seat? I assume you guys will be travelling in the back. Charlie'll want his dog when he wakes up, and that cut on its side…it'll probably need stitches. Doc?'

'Because I'm doctor for everyone?' Rob said bleakly. 'Macca, we can't take the dog.'

'Limp as a biscuit, not causing any trouble,' the guy— Macca—told them. 'And she…she's gotta go somewhere. I don't know what to do with a bleeding dog.'

'Fine,' Rob said wearily. 'Gary, if it's okay by you…'

'I'll need to clean the truck out anyway, and the only alternative's your nice, clean car,' Gary said. 'Someone else'll bring that in, but who knows when? We can hardly leave the dog here.'

Rob sighed, but there was no time to argue.

Gary drove. He knew the curves of this cliff road like the back of his hand, and the ambulance moved as fast as he could while still allowing Jen and Rob to work in the rear. Rob worked on Charlie, monitoring his every breath. Jen knew she'd be needed if that breathing stopped, but it faltered on, and she had time to catch her own breath.

This was her first job, and she felt that she'd failed spectacularly. Rule number two, after personal safety, was to ascertain number of casualties.

The radio crackled into life and Gary called back, 'This'll

be the chopper update. There was no availability when I called. Can you take it, Jen? Concentrating here.'

He must be, Jen thought. The curves here were almost hair-pin.

She flicked her radio into life and switched it to the main channel.

'South Coast Emergency Response Centre to Willhua First Response, do you copy?'

South Sydney Air Rescue. Her crew.

That was where she should be now, but this wasn't the time for regrets. She was needed just where she was.

'Willhua Paramedics, copy, loud and clear,' she said now into her radio. 'Status?'

'Hey, it's our Jen.' She recognised the operator and Donna obviously recognised her. 'You down a cliff already?'

'Transferring critical care to Willhua hospital,' she said.

And Donna got it—the tension, the unspoken need for ur-gent action. 'Crew's still half an hour away,' she said. 'We have co-ordinates of the crash scene. You want them to change route and pick up from the hospital?'

'Tell them he'll need transfer,' Rob told her. He was adjust-ing Charlie's oxygen mask and his face was grim. They both knew that if Charlie was to survive he'd need the specialist treatment of a major city hospital. 'But priority needs to be this Bruce.'

Jen nodded. He didn't have to go further.

'Donna, there's a strong possibility there's someone else on the cliff, on the rocks below or in the sea,' she told her. 'Our guy—Charlie—was calling for someone called Bruce before he lost consciousness. The police are making enquiries, but for now we need to assume Bruce is someone missing. The truck's on its side. Possibility someone's trapped underneath? We don't know, and it's too dark to climb down again.'

'Roger that,' Donna said, efficient and businesslike. 'I'll get the chopper there as soon as possible. You take care of your guy and stop worrying about the rest.'

'We'll also need transfer for Charlie,' she said.

'He'll need stabilisation first,' Rob said, loud enough for Donna to hear. 'There's probably time for the crew to search the cliff.'

'Roger that,' Donna said again. 'Good luck.'

What followed was an hour of futile fighting. A fight where everything Jen had ever learned in her medical past was called into play.

An hour where she learned that Rob Pierson was almost as skilled as the best emergency physicians she'd ever worked with.

When she was fourteen, the grandma Jen had loved and lived with had had a major stroke. Her parents, adventurers, wanderers, pretty much selfish to the core—they still were— had reluctantly flown home, but after a month they'd decided that Jen could cope.

And Jen had. During the next few years she'd juggled schoolwork with living with and caring for the frail old lady, and during that time she'd seen the best side of nursing. The medical care given to her grandmother by the district nurses had been amazing, and the teenaged Jen had never had a doubt that this was where her career lay. Her grandma had died just as she'd started her nursing training.

But during her parents' sporadic visits she'd also been introduced to other skills. Abseiling, speed climbing, bouldering— she was enough her parents' child to learn and love them all.

So as she'd finished training and started working as a nurse in a Sydney hospital emergency department, another desire had come to the fore. She'd watched the paramedics come in and out of the emergency rooms, she'd seen the care they gave, and she'd thought…why not?

She'd been accepted into paramedic training and she'd never regretted it.

But her nursing training was still there, and now, as they arrived at Willhua's hospital, as she realised there was only one nurse on duty and Cathy was already overloaded, and as Charlie's heart faltered yet again, it made sense to tell them her qualifications and offer to help.

So for the next hour she assisted Rob as best she could. She watched and worked as Rob put everything he could into saving this old man's life.

But it was no use. When finally Charlie's injuries, or Charlie's heart, or the combination of everything the old man had gone through, finally overwhelmed his frail body, when Rob finally stood back from the table, his face blank with defeat, she felt like weeping. And she felt like hugging him—this doctor who'd worked so hard.

Of course she didn't. She didn't even know him, but she'd seen how hard he'd fought and she wanted…what?

The emotions of the past weeks plus the tension of the day were suddenly threatening to overwhelm her. She didn't know what she wanted.

For there to be a world where the sky didn't fall? Where toerag bosses didn't betray in the worst possible way? Where Charlie wasn't dead? Where the unknown Bruce was safe and well.

'I'm so sorry,' she said, and he closed his eyes and his shoulders sagged.

'Useless, useless, useless,' he muttered and the urge to hug him was even greater.

What was it with this man? She'd watched him swing down the abseiling line and thought he looked like some sort of hero in a movie—tall, lithe, dark-haired and dark-eyed, abseiling with ease, a man in charge of his world. But now he looked shocked and numb—like this was personal? Had Charlie been a friend?

And then she remembered something Gary had said, at that interview when he'd been called away.

'Doc works too hard. We're lucky to have him, he's a damn fine doctor. Bloody tragedy about his wife, though. He and the kiddie… Well, life kicks you around, that's for sure.'

Had his wife died in an accident as well?

'What a waste,' he said now, heavily, and then opened his eyes and looked at her. 'But his rescue was down to you, Jen. You got there when he was conscious, you got pain relief into him and he knew he was being cared for. Heaven knows if that truck's still in place—it could well have plummeted by now. And now, assisting with this… You've done great, Jen. Willhua's lucky to have you.'

Willhua was lucky to have *him*, she thought, but she didn't say it. The memory of Darren showering her with compliments was still fresh and raw, and something inside her cringed.

'It's my job,' she said a little too curtly. 'I just wish…'

She stopped and looked down at Charlie's face. In death he looked peaceful and there was something about him… An old man. Had it been his time?

And as if he knew what she was thinking, Rob reached out and placed a hand on her shoulder. He did it lightly, almost a casual contact, but something made her feel that right now he needed the touch as much as she did.

'Charlie's been a loner almost all his life,' he told her. 'I have no idea if he has any relatives around here. Or friends. I've seen him twice in the five years I've practiced here. The last time he came in was a year ago, for an infected leg. He'd ripped it on barbed wire and hadn't bothered to clean it. While he was here I insisted on basics, including a blood pressure check. It was through the roof, but he wouldn't have a bar of treatment. I sent him home with prescriptions, instructions and an appointment for follow-up but I suspect he ignored the lot.'

And then his grip on her shoulder tightened—a reassurance, a certainty? 'All I'm saying, Jen, is that we fought damned hard, but some choices were his.'

'But this Bruce? I should have…'

The pressure remained. 'You made decisions based on the information you had, and you did really well. The chopper's doing the rest now.'

By silent consensus they moved out of the room. Charlie's body needed to be dealt with, but there was no rush. They could give themselves—and Charlie—space while they talked of the future. As they closed the door behind them, Rob glanced at his watch.

'Surely there'll be news by now,' he said softly. 'This Bruce… But meanwhile, what happened to the dog you rescued?'

She managed a rueful smile, trying to shake off the desolation of what had just happened. 'Stumpy? Our next patient? Gary put her on the passenger seat of the ambulance. He couldn't take her home—he tells me his wife's allergic—but he's popped her into the hospital laundry. She'll need treatment. In the morning, I guess? Does Willhua run to a vet?'

He sighed. 'It does not,' he said heavily. 'If there's any emergency vet work, the locals call on me. I'll take a look at her now, but she can't stay here.'

'What, not prepared to admit her under your bed card?' They'd moved on, but the presence of death was still around them. 'I'll… I'll take care of her until someone claims her,' she said. 'I could use…some company.'

'What, you're lonely? Do you know anyone here?'

'Not a sausage.' She tried summoning a smile she was far from feeling. 'My landlady seems crabby but my studio at the back of her place has a garden which she says I'm free to use. Stumpy might help me settle in.'

He was looking at her curiously. 'Just like that?'

'Just like that,' she agreed. 'So…moving on?'

He nodded, taking her lead. 'Okay. We need to find out what's happened to this Bruce, and we need to check out Stumpy.'

'Gary told me you have a little boy,' she said, looking at his strained, tired face. 'Is he okay alone?'

'He's not alone. We have a great system,' he told her. 'We have video and alarms set up for sound and movement in his room—it's linked to monitors at the nurses' station, which is almost just through the wall, and if it's likely to be for any more than a few minutes I have Minnie.'

'Minnie?'

'Mrs Minnow. She a retired nurse and she lives next door,' he told her. 'And she's Jacob's and my own personal angel. My place is the original doctor's residence and when this place was built the doctor had five kids. So we've set up one of my spare rooms as Minnie's home away from home, right down to spare knitting. Minnie cares for Jacob during the day, but also during the night when I need her. She put on her moccasins and woolly robe, filled her hot-water bottle and pottered across the front lawn before I even left. Jacob's so used to it now I suspect he's delighted when he wakes to find her there.'

'It sounds ideal.'

'Some would think so,' he said, and strangely his voice suddenly sounded heavy. 'Others...well, there are some who'll never concede I can care for my own son.'

They split up then. He and Cathy needed to cope with the aftermath—the moving of Charlie's body to the morgue, the paperwork, the effort of finding relatives. Jen shouldn't even be here—she was officially off-duty. Actually she hadn't even officially started work yet, but who was noticing?

She needed to head back home, or where home was right now. It was a couple of blocks to Lorna's, but first...the dog.

She made her way to the hospital laundry, but paused as her phone rang. Frankie.

Frankie had been her best friend while she worked for the chopper service. She was still her best friend. Frankie had stood by her while her life had felt as if it was being ripped apart, had even pushed her to try and get her boss sacked instead of walking away. Even if he had been sacked though, the humiliation would still be with her, and in the end Frankie had accepted that decision.

Was Frankie with the retrieval crew? If so, she must have decided to make this call private, and part of her relaxed. If it was bad news Frankie would have made it official.

She stopped mid corridor and leaned against the wall. 'What gives?'

'You're not going to believe this,' Frankie told her. 'Bruce is a dog.'

'A dog.' Her body seemed to sag with relief. She'd been haunted by the vision of an injured man on the rocks below the cliff, someone who, if she'd asked the right questions earlier, could have been saved. Okay, she was being hard on herself—there'd been no time to do any more—but she'd still been haunted.

'A great big hairy dog,' Frankie was saying. 'I'm no expert but Mozzie's spent time on farms and he reckons he might be a bearded collie. He and Nico are trying to dry him off a bit.'

She knew Mozzie, but Nico? Was Nico her replacement in the crew?

'I'm not really surprised,' she said. 'We already rescued one dog that was with Charlie. Where was this one? Why didn't I see it?'

'He was curled up in a tight ball, hiding amongst rocks and scrub not far from that tree that the truck was initially caught on. He must have been thrown clear when it first went over the cliff. He's black and white—it was only because I caught a glimpse of the white hair that we found him. He would have been totally hidden from view when you pulled that guy out. Speaking of whom… Condition?'

'He's just died.'

It was a stark statement. Her voice seemed to echo in the corridor and there was a sharp intake of breath from her friend.

'Oh, no… I'm so sorry, love, and on your first day!'

'My first day's supposed to be Monday.'

'And you wanted a quiet life.' There was a pause and then Frankie went on. 'Our reports were that a fatality was likely,' she said, obviously deciding that professional brevity was the way to cope. Wasn't it always? 'Jen, we still have a problem. 'The Serious Crash Squad got mobilised when your local cop pinged this as a possible fatality. They're here now, but they don't want anything to do with the dog. They suggested we drop him off to you so the local vet can check him out.'

'Is he injured?'

'Not sure. Nico's having a look now, but I'd be surprised if he wasn't hurt. Pretty rough ground for a fall.'

'Who's Nico?' She had to ask.

'You're replacement on Red Watch.'

Ouch. That definitely hurt. She'd loved working with this team.

It couldn't matter—but there was something in Frankie's voice that piqued her interest...

'Is he nice?'

'He's Italian.'

Yeah, like that told her a lot. Sadly, however, they both needed to move on.

'Do you know if the local vet will be available?' Frankie was asking.

'There's no vet in Willhua.'

'Can he go to Charlie's family?'

'I have no idea who that might be. Frankie, can you take him on to Sydney? I seem to be stuck with the other one— Stumpy—and I can't cope with two injured dogs.'

And then she paused as Rob appeared in the corridor. 'Just a moment,' she told Frankie. 'Rob, Bruce turned out to be a dog. He's safe.'

'Well, that's a bit of good news.'

'Frankie, I need to go,' she told her friend. 'Stumpy's got lacerations and grazes, and Rob's going to help me sort her out.'

'Who's Rob?' And she heard a lightening of interest in her friend's voice. Which would be a lot more intense if she could see Rob, she thought. The guy was standing in the doorway, looking weary but also...hot? Definitely hot. A doctor who'd climbed down the cliff to rescue a dying man, who'd shown as much, or more, abseiling skill as she had, who'd fought with skill and desperation to save the life of an old man...

There must be a better descriptor than hot, she thought, but right now hot was all she could come up with.

'Cut it out,' she said, but it was as much to herself as it was to her friend. Dammit, Frankie was incorrigible—though she thought of how her own interest had pinged at the mention of the unknown Nico and she almost smiled. She and Frankie knew each other so well.

Now, however, was definitely not the time for an inquisition. Or thinking of the man standing in the doorway. 'But can you take Bruce?' she managed.

'I'll see what I can do.' There was a moment's hesitation then, 'There's already a discussion about having a dog in the chopper,' Frankie told her.

'But that would be a yes?' Jen said quickly. 'That's great. If and when we find relatives we can tell them he's in the best of hands and to contact you.'

'Jen...'

'I need to go,' she told her friend hurriedly. 'Love you.'

CHAPTER THREE

AFTER THAT THEY went straight back into work mode, only this time their patient was a dog.

Looking at the corgi from one side, it appeared there was no damage at all. 'She's just like the Queen's,' Cathy, the night nurse, said as she saw Rob carrying the injured dog through from the laundry to the theatre. The dog looked relatively young, with lovely fawn and white colouring and a gorgeous bushy tail. But her tail was hanging downward and her over-sized ears seemed almost drooping. That, and the expression in her eyes, were a giveaway that something was badly wrong.

And as soon as the strong overhead lights went on they could see why.

She must have been hurled against the shattered side window, Jen thought. Her side was a gory mess. Most of the fur was torn away, her skin was grazed and bloody, and a long laceration ran almost from shoulder to the base of her ribs. It was still sluggishly bleeding.

In any other circumstances this dog should have been a priority, Jen thought, horrified. Instead she'd been tugged ruthlessly out of the truck, tied to the crate, hauled up the cliff—and then left alone in the hospital laundry. All of them had been too concerned with the drama around Charlie's survival to take more than a cursory interest.

But even injured, in pain, in a bewilderingly strange environment, she seemed passive, looking up at Jen and Rob with something that seemed almost like trust. She stood quietly on the bench as Rob examined her. Jen stood by her head, fondling her ears, speaking gently to her, and the dog seemed to almost melt into her hands. Her head sagged, and as Jen bent a little she lifted her snout and gave Jen's face a long, trusting lick.

And Jen's heart almost broke. 'Oh, she's lovely,' she breathed.

'Not from this angle, she's not,' Rob said grimly. 'This side's a mess. I can see embedded glass.'

'The nearest vet?'

'At Whale Head, and that's over an hour's drive along the cliffs. Even then, Ross is elderly and overworked. This'll be up to me. He will help by phone though. If I ring he'll give me anaesthetic doses and talk me through—he's done it before.'

'There's no one?' she asked, horrified.

'Do you know how hard it is to get any sort of medics to work outside the cities?'

'That's why you got me,' she said with an attempt at lightness, her hands still fondling the dog.

'And aren't we lucky that we did?' Cathy had followed them and was standing at the door, watching. 'Rob, Mike O'Connor's woken and his leg's bad. He was bitten by a snake yesterday,' she told Jen. 'He's recovering but his leg's very swollen.' She turned back to Rob. 'Could I have an order for pain relief?'

'I'll check him before we start here,' Rob said curtly. 'Hold the fort, Jen.'

And Jen was left…holding the fort…and wondering what sort of place she had landed herself in.

She thought briefly of her job with South Sydney Air Rescue. There her role had been clearly defined. Go with the ambulance or chopper to call outs. Treat at the scene and on the way to hospital. Maybe wait a while at the hospital—ramping, being stuck on the hospital ramp because of lack of hospital staff, had become common during the recent pandemic—but as soon as space was available the patient was wheeled through the doors and became Not Her Responsibility.

And her hours… She'd usually been rostered for eight-hour shifts, which occasionally had stretched a little longer, but nothing like this. To be called out when she wasn't even on duty, to do a traumatic retrieval, to be needed to assist in a hospital setting, and then to stay on to treat an injured dog… If she reported this to her union, officialdom would have a field day.

But as she stood and waited, speaking and crooning to the dog, rubbing her soft ears, she was suddenly hit by a wave of something that was almost excitement.

The last few weeks had been a muddle of confusion and humiliation. Almost every waking moment had seen her reliving the worst of Darren's betrayal, and her rush to get away had been driven by those emotions.

But tonight she'd been needed—she was still needed. Her skills had been tested. Her nursing training had mostly receded to the point where she'd thought it had almost been a waste, but tonight, even though Charlie had died, her skills had been front and centre again.

And this doctor…

He was skilled, empathic and…gorgeous?

Down, girl, she told herself, but a part of her was smiling ruefully at herself. After Darren she'd promised herself she'd never look at another male again—yeah, that was never going to happen, but now, after only weeks…

Right now it didn't exactly hurt, the feeling that as a paramedic she'd be working with Rob over and over again. Instead it seemed to have lifted something that had felt, for the last weeks, like it might take years to lift.

Because he was gorgeous? Her mind was back on that *hot* descriptor again.

'You can cut that out,' she told herself severely, but still…

She could hear him now. He'd obviously returned from his snakebite patient and was standing in the corridor talking on his phone. To someone called Ross.

The vet in Whale Head?

Yes.

She listened as Rob described Stumpy's condition, as he repeated instructions out loud, as he confirmed and reconfirmed.

This man was good, she thought, incisive, careful—caring?

He must be. To stay awake after midnight to treat a dog…

She thought of Cathy's request for pain meds for the snakebite patient. That'd be a normal thing for Rob, she realised, phone calls in the middle of the night. Call outs. With no backup… When was he ever off-duty?

Would the same apply to her? She was starting to realise that life in Willhua wouldn't be eight-hour shifts either but, rather than being dismayed, the thought filled her with a sense of anticipation that had somehow pierced the conflicting emotions of the last few weeks.

And then Rob was back, standing beside her, crouching a little so he was almost nose to nose with the injured dog.

'Okay, girl, let's get you fixed,' he murmured. 'You trust us to get you feeling better?'

And the corgi's tongue slipped out again and Rob also received a slurp, jaw to nose.

Rob grinned and Jen thought, *I agree. I'm with Stumpy.*

* * *

The surgery took over an hour.

Jen was *not* an anaesthetist, but, 'It's you or no one,' Rob told her. 'Ross has given us instructions and dosages and we can't leave glass in her side.'

So she worked way past her skill level, monitoring depth of consciousness, breathing, heart rate, while Rob worked on the dog's side.

It was lengthy, meticulous work. The shattered glass was clear, making it almost invisible, and individual puncture marks had mostly been obliterated by further damage—the dog must have crashed hard against her side. But if this had been a child Rob couldn't have been more painstaking. He searched and cleaned, searched and cleaned, and when the kidney dish held every shard he could possibly find he washed and washed and washed the entire area until he was almost satisfied.

'She'll need constant checking over the next few days,' he said grimly as finally he set about stitching the worst of the lacerations. 'If I've left any behind...'

'You've done your best,' she said, and he flashed a look at her.

'You know as well as I do that best is sometimes not good enough.' He sighed. 'Okay, let's get this dressed.' And then he hesitated. 'Jen, she can't stay here.'

'I know that.' She'd already accepted it. There was no way a dog could stay in a hospital setting—no way this man could be expected to do the obs an injured and sedated animal would require. 'She's coming home with me.'

'And home is?'

'At Lorna Dumet's. I'm renting a studio in her back garden.'

'Mrs Dumet.' He frowned. 'Um... Lorna... I'm not sure...'

'I'm not sure either,' Jen said and managed a rueful smile. Her impression of Lorna was that of an officious, controlling matron, but the studio was self-contained and separate, with its own small garden.

'Will having a dog be okay with her?'

'There wasn't a no pets clause in my lease,' she said. 'But I'll run things past her tomorrow, just to keep things sweet.'

He cast her another doubtful glance. 'I guess it solves the problem for tonight at least,' he said slowly. 'You're happy to take her home now?'

'Of course.' And then she hesitated. Lorna's place was four or five blocks from the hospital, too far to walk with an injured dog, and her car was back at the ambulance station. The station was just as far as Lorna's. 'I guess… I can walk back and get the car and come and pick her up.' It was, though, two in the morning and the prospect wasn't exactly appealing.

'I'll take you,' Rob told her. 'If you're taking on Stumpy's care it's the least I can do. Give me a couple of minutes to check in on Jacob and Minnie, and I'll be right with you.'

They drove across the silent, sleeping town in near silence, with Jen cradling the drowsy Stumpy on her knee. This was hardly professional conduct, she thought, a medic carrying a patient in the front seat. No seat belt for Stumpy.

'Please don't crash,' she told Rob as the thought hit. 'We should have her in the back, properly secured. And do you have insurance for patient transport?'

'I wouldn't worry,' he said dryly. 'Anyone sues me—or you too, for that matter—then Willhua loses medics it can't do without. There are advantages to being irreplaceable.'

'Do you have no help at all?' she asked curiously and she saw his face relax a little.

'I do,' he told her. 'Willhua's last family doctor is still living here. Angus is over seventy, he's retired and wants nothing more than to spend his time growing vegetables, but in an emergency or when I need to have time off, he covers for me.'

'When you need to have time off?' she ventured, hearing a strange note in his voice. 'You mean holidays?'

'I wish. I need to spend time in Brisbane. My...' He hesitated and then seemed to change tack. 'Jacob needs to spend time with his grandparents—my wife's parents—and I...' But he didn't finish the sentence and she saw his hands tighten on the wheel.

There was obviously something behind that story, Jen thought, but there was no time now to unravel it, even if it was her business—which it wasn't.

They were pulling up outside Lorna's. The house was a fastidiously manicured ode to pseudo-Georgian. Not a blade of grass ventured higher than its companions on the pristine lawn. Pansies and petunias lined up like well drilled soldiers along the driveway, and standard roses guarded the front fence. They were all in bud because as soon as the roses bloomed—and risked shedding a petal—they were clipped and delegated to the trash.

Not even the compost. The day she'd arrived, Jen had found Lorna dead-heading roses that clearly weren't dead. Intrigued, she'd offered to carry her cart to the compost heap—and snaffle a few on the way to put in her kitchenette.

'The bin, you mean,' Lorna had snapped. 'Why would I want compost? Filthy, smelly stuff.'

Now Lorna's front lights were blazing, and as they pulled up Jen could see two of the nearer rose bushes had buds that were daring to unfurl. She pretty much expected Lorna to dart out and be off with their heads. She grinned at the thought, and saw the query in Rob's eyes.

She explained and he chuckled as he lifted Stumpy out of the car.

'Yeah, I can imagine. You know, Lorna has…issues of her own. She can be a bit volatile. If you have any trouble, let me know.'

'I intend to keep out of the lady's way. I need to use the side path to get to the studio, but I'm thinking I'll slink.'

That brought another chuckle. 'Okay. Let me help you slink, though. I'll carry Stumpy.'

She accepted with a certain amount of relief—the idea of carrying Stumpy while she fiddled with unfamiliar locks and door handles presented problems. So Rob followed with Stumpy as she led him down the side path.

They'd almost cleared the main house when the security lights blazed on. Thirty seconds later, as she fiddled with the lock of her front door, Lorna, resplendent in a flowery oriental bathrobe, banged out of her back door and surged across the lawn towards them.

'What do you think you're doing?' Her voice was a high-pitched screech. I said no men! It's in your lease. No men, young woman! I will not have it.'

Oh, for heaven's sake. Jen sighed. Her first impression of Lorna—that being her tenant was not going to be easy—suddenly multiplied by ten. But, before she could answer, Rob intervened.

'Good evening, Mrs Dumet,' he said pleasantly, and Lorna stopped in her tracks.

'Dr Pierson! What are you doing here?'

'Just helping Miss Roden home,' Rob told her, his tone still pleasant. 'She's caring for one of my patients overnight.'

He'd been standing back a little, waiting for Jen to open the door. She succeeded and flicked the light on, a porch light which, inconveniently, could only be activated from the inside. Light flooded the trio on the porch, and Lorna's jaw dropped.

'A dog,' she breathed.

'It's Charlie Emerson's dog,' Rob said mildly. 'Charlie died earlier this evening and Stumpy was injured. Miss Roden has kindly offered to care for her until we can locate Charlie's relatives.'

If he'd hoped to gain sympathy he was sadly mistaken. Jen, standing in the doorway, saw her landlady's face turn from indignation to downright anger.

'And you thought you could just bring it here. At two in the morning? Disturbing my sleep with your goings-on! I thought you'd be a quiet single woman who'd keep to herself, and that was the only reason I agreed to let my dear mother's studio. It's been empty since she died and I will not have goings-on...'

'By goings-on, do you mean living?' Rob asked, his voice still mild. He'd stepped forward a little, his body between Jenny and the woman who was stalking over the lawn. 'Lorna, we've talked about this before—reacting with anger. There's no need for anger tonight. Jenny's our much-needed ambulance officer and she's been doing her best to save a life tonight.'

'It's two in the morning! All the security lights came on. Outside my bedroom window!'

'If you want Jenny to stay, you may have to do something about that,' he told her. 'Jenny's an ambulance officer, so there will be out of hours calls. We all know how much the town needs another ambulance officer. It's been great that you've been able to give her somewhere to live.'

But his placatory tone didn't seem to be helping. Lorna was totally focused on Jenny and the dog. 'Well!' She put her hands on her hips and glared. 'Of all the effrontery... But to come here... With you... And a dog... There's no way she can have a dog here.'

'Mrs Dumet, I have my own yard on the other side of the studio,' Jen said, stepping forward. It was all very noble of Rob to stand between them, but this was her battle. 'I know I didn't ask about pets when I applied—I didn't intend to have one—but there's no pet ban in my lease and Stumpy's hurt. Her master's dead and she needs short-term care. If there are real problems, if you're allergic, if you really hate dogs, then I'll figure something tomorrow.'

'You figure something now.' She glowered at the two of them. 'And bringing a man here... Dr Pierson, you should be ashamed of yourself.'

This was escalating to the point of being ridiculous, Jenny thought. What was the lady suggesting—that she and Rob were heading indoors to have a spot of red-hot sex? She opened her mouth to speak, but Rob sent her a warning glance and spoke himself.

'We're sorry we've woken you, Lorna,' he said mildly. 'I'm dropping Jenny and the dog off now—I need to get back to Jacob—but could we talk about this in the morning?'

But Lorna Dumet was clearly nursing her grievance and had no intention of letting it go.

'I should never have let you have the studio in the first place,' she snapped. 'It's been empty since my dear mother died, and I don't want you sullying her memory. Charlie Emerson's dog... It'll be full of fleas, it'll bleed and heaven knows what else. Get it out of here or I'll call the police.'

'I hardly think Chris will be sympathetic,' Rob told her. 'He's dealing with Charlie's wrecked truck.'

'That's nothing to do with me. Get it out of here! And you

too,' she screeched at Jen, indignation turning to rage. 'Pack your bags and go.'

'Jen…' Rob said in a low warning voice and Jen got it. This woman was out of control, at the point of hysteria, but both she and Rob had been trained in the art of de-escalation.

Sense said back off and let her calm down.

'I'll take you both home,' Rob said softly but urgently, watching Lorna's face turn from purple to puce. 'I'm sorry, I should have said something earlier, but I hoped… Jenny, Lorna has mental health issues and tonight's obviously not one of her good times. I'll see her and sort things in the morning, but for tonight… I need to sort this out, but not at two in the morning. Grab your overnight gear, you're coming with me.'

'Do you have room?' she asked. She, too, was watching Lorna, realising this wasn't something that could be sorted with a few soothing words.

'I have room,' he said grimly. 'There are reasons…well, my little boy…the dog…'

'I'll keep them apart.'

'I know you will,' he said gratefully. 'There's a bedroom with an en suite at the end of the house we don't use, and the laundry's nearby. Go inside now and grab any gear you need, but do it fast. We both need to sleep and in her current state Lorna isn't going to let anyone sleep here.'

Then he turned to Lorna. 'It's okay, Lorna,' he said, gently though, doctor to patient. 'I'll take Jenny and her dog back to the hospital for the night.'

'Strumpet,' Lorna hissed.

'She's no such thing,' Rob said, his voice still gentle. 'Jenny's a part of our medical team and I think she's just what this town needs.'

CHAPTER FOUR

JEN WOKE AND there was a small child standing in the door-way, looking at her.

Well, so much for keeping boy and dog apart, she thought, and her hand dropped instantly to Stumpy's collar. *Whoops.*

They'd arrived back at the doctor's house after two a.m., silent, both weary almost beyond belief.

'Gary should have warned you,' Rob had told her when they were all back in the car. 'Lorna's been treated for schizophrenia for years—occasionally she needs to be hospitalised. If she stays on medication she can function, but when she comes to me as a patient, I always have a nurse present. If ever a patient's likely to sue me for all I'm worth, it'll be Lorna. She sounds like she's on the edge now—her medication might need to be tweaked.'

Jen had sighed, feeling mortified and more than a bit confused. The studio had seemed perfect.

'When I came for the interview there was a note in the general store advertising the studio,' she'd told him. 'Your local realtor said he could offer no alternative. Lorna seemed pleased to have me as her tenant and I didn't even ask Gary.'

So now she was temporarily homeless—except it seemed she was sharing with Rob, at least for one night.

And Rob's house didn't exactly feel like home. She'd walked into it in the small hours and had been hit by how big it was—

and how empty. She'd walked through the cavernous living room to reach the bedroom Rob had suggested and thought it looked like a show home. Rigid furnishings, soulless pictures on the walls, the only personal items being photographs on the living room's marble mantel. There were many photos, all of one person—a young woman.

Rob's wife? The tragedy?

But Rob hadn't paused long enough to explain. He'd carried Stumpy into the laundry. They'd set up a pile of towels on the floor and organised heating so she'd stay warm. Then he'd ushered her to a bedroom—also clinically sterile—and said goodnight.

An hour later Stumpy had started moaning, a low, distressed howl. She'd gone to check and fondled those extraordinary ears—and then Rob had arrived.

He'd been wearing boxers and nothing else. What was it about this man that made her want to gasp?

Pure testosterone, she'd told herself. Any woman would feel it.

'I'm sorry,' she'd told him. 'I didn't want her to wake you.'

'Not your fault,' he'd said and knelt beside her. 'Poor pooch. No dog should go through what she's been through today.'

'I'll take her to my bedroom, if that's okay with you,' she'd told him, almost expecting resistance. She hadn't got it. Instead he'd gathered Stumpy and her bedding against his chest and carried her into Jen's bedroom.

'Can you put her right by the bed where I can touch her?' Jen had asked, and he'd cast her a strange look—a look that was almost puzzled. But he'd obliged, said a simple goodnight and then disappeared. And Jen had drifted back to sleep with her hand dropped down to rest on Stumpy's soft coat.

They'd both slept, woman and dog—and now Rob's son

was standing in the doorway. He looked a miniature version of his father. Dark-haired, dark-eyed, his small face serious. He was wearing cute blue pyjamas with dinosaurs all over them, and he was carrying a battered…what looked like a toy scarecrow?…by one disreputable leg.

'Why do you have a dog?' he asked.

He hadn't talked to his dad yet?

'Her name's Stumpy,' she told him. 'She was injured last night. Your dad and I bandaged her side and brought her here.'

'Why did you come, too?'

'Someone has to look after Stumpy,' she said, and he thought about it and nodded, gravely accepting.

'My dad's in the clinic, seeing someone who got stood on by a cow,' he told her. 'Minnie's making pancakes. She told me you were here and I wasn't to wake you, but I thought you'd like pancakes.' He took a couple of steps into the room but, before he could go further, Jen was out of bed, crossing to stoop before him, blocking his way.

'Jacob…you are Jacob, aren't you?'

'Yes,' he said, clearly a bit confused at the way she'd deliberately put her body between him and Stumpy. He held out the battered stuffed toy. 'And this is Eric-the-Scarecrow. Minnie says you're Jenny and you drive ambulances. With sirens and everything. And you help Daddy.'

'That's right,' she told him, squatting before him. 'Jacob, Stumpy isn't very well. We might let her wake up by herself.'

But Stumpy was awake. Her nose poked out from the bundle of towels she'd been lying among, and as she saw Jenny and Jacob her bushy tail gave a tentative wag.

How much did she remember of last night?

Jen had hurt her—she'd had to. Hauling her up the cliff in such a way when her side was so injured must have been excruciating. But there'd been no sign of aggression, no sign of anything except distressed acceptance. And with Jen's hand gently stroking she'd slept in this strange place, with strange people.

Now...that tail lifting in a tentative wag made something inside Jen's heart lurch.

'Can I pat her?' Jacob said. He'd also seen the big ears, the huge brown eyes and the wag of the bushy tail. 'She looks like she'd like a pat.'

But Rob had clearly said... What?

'There are reasons...well, my little boy...the dog...'

An allergy? That was the most obvious reason.

'Jacob, sometimes dogs make kids sneeze, a lot. I need to check with your dad that you don't have an allergy before you can pat her. I think we need to go find your Minnie while Stumpy wakes up.'

'Dogs don't make me sneeze,' Jacob said scornfully. 'Dad says that's an allergy, and my friends Ella and Toby have allergies. Cats and dogs make Ella sneeze all the time, and Toby can't eat peanut butter sandwiches or anything. Dad says I'm very lucky not to have them 'cos they sound pesky. Minnie has a cat at her place and I pat her all the time. Can I pat Stumpy now?'

'We'll see after your dad's checked her,' she temporised. There must be some reason... 'I'll take her out in the garden now—I think she'll need a wee—and then I'll come to the kitchen. Will I meet you there?'

'Me and Eric will watch her have a wee,' Jacob said definitely. 'But we won't touch her. I don't want to hurt her.'

And I don't want to hurt you, Jen thought, deciding, allergy or not, it was totally reasonable for Rob to worry about his kid and a strange dog.

'Okay, will you tell Minnie that I'd really like some pancakes too? Then you can come out to the back veranda and watch, but you're not to come close until your dad says you can.'

'Okay,' Jacob said happily and grinned and left, with Jen thinking… *This kid has a smile just like his father's.*

A gorgeous smile.

A smile to melt hearts?

There was a pyjama-clad woman and a dog on his back lawn.

Rob had spent an hour coping with a messy foot injury. A decent-sized heifer had stood on Rebecca Ireland's foot, and Rebecca hadn't been dressed for the occasion.

At sixteen, the kid fiercely resented having to work in her parents' dairy. She had to do so every Sunday morning or she'd get no allowance, her parents had told her—they struggled dealing with their large herd alone. But the thought of wearing decent boots had added insult to injury in Rebecca's rebellious teenaged mind. The dry weather meant there was little mud so she'd defiantly worn her trendy new runners. With subsequent consequences.

'It's broken,' she'd sobbed as her mother had helped the limping girl into the hospital clinic. 'And it's all your fault. You shouldn't make me milk.'

Fault. The mere word had made Rob wince, and he'd watched the mum's tired face and seen her flinch before he'd set about fixing the damage.

It wasn't broken but it was bruised, lacerated and filthy.

'Why didn't your boots protect you?' he'd asked, almost conversationally. Then, suspecting he already knew the answer, he added another question. 'Mrs Ireland, why haven't you bought your daughter decent boots?'

'She did,' Rebecca admitted sullenly. 'They're dog ugly and I wouldn't be caught dead in them. Mum finally bought me the trainers I like and now they're ruined.' This was clearly her mother's fault too.

'I guess not wearing boots in the dairy is like not wearing a helmet on a motorbike,' he said, pseudo-sympathetic. 'That messes with your hair—and your image—but people really are caught dead without them. And I do mean dead. You're going to end up with a small scar on your ankle, Rebecca. I'll do my best to make it inconspicuous, but maybe...well, you decide what makes sense in the future.'

'I won't be milking cows in the future.'

'The way I'm seeing it, you might need to.'

He'd cast a glance at her mother—he knew this family well, he knew Rhonda struggled with arthritis as well as the needs of a large family and a dairy farm that brought in an income that was, at best, marginal.

'Your parents are so tired now that they might even need to sell the farm. Your dad told me that a few days back. With no farm, no income...there'd be no money for trendy trainers—there'd be no money for new clothes at all.'

Rebecca's eyes had widened in shock.

'You've seen the kids at school whose parents can't find jobs. How many of them have trendy trainers? You might need to think about it.'

He'd left it there. He'd cleaned, stitched and dressed the foot, but as they'd left Rhonda Ireland had turned and given him a swift hug.

'Thank you,' she'd said, a little bit tearfully, and then her daughter had caught her hand and he'd watched as mother and daughter made their way back to their car.

Thinking...*fault*.

And now… He'd walked out to the back veranda and Jen and Stumpy were on the back lawn and Jacob was watching and he thought of the next word after *fault*.

Consequences.

He thought of Charlie Emerson, an elderly farmer, shy to the point of paranoia, dying of a heart attack. He knew of no relatives, no one to mourn.

But, because of that, on the back lawn was a slip of a girl. She was wearing faded flannel pyjamas. Her hair had been tightly hauled into a knot the night before, but was now cascading to her shoulders as a mass of tangled brown curls. She was tall but slight, or should that be…wiry? Built for service rather than style? That was the sort of comment Emma used to make about herself, he thought, and smiled at the thought. *'I'm a failure,'* she'd wailed. *'Put me in haute couture and everyone'd guess there'd be a khaki chest warmer underneath.'*

Emma. For the thousandth time he demanded of the world: *why won't they let her go?*

And with that thought…consequences. He just knew there'd be consequences of inviting Jenny and Stumpy to stay.

But then Jenny saw him and grinned and waved, and grim thoughts changed to an inexplicable lightness. There was a woman in his backyard in cute pyjamas. There was also a dog, obviously trying to figure the best spot to honour with her ablutions. And Jacob was there, seeing him, squealing in pleasure and bounding along the veranda to join him.

'Daddy, Jenny's got a dog and her name's Stumpy, but Jenny says I can't pat her until you come home. *Please*, Daddy…'

'Pancakes are ready,' Minnie called from the kitchen, and there was another inexplicable shaft of pleasure. And then came the thought…

I've come home.

* * *

They ate breakfast together, the cheerful, motherly Minnie supervising, beaming that her pancakes were being appreciated, and joining them at the table so she could boss them to eat more.

Jenny should be dressed, but there'd been no time. She'd taken Stumpy outside fast because…well, when a dog woke from sleep and seemed agitated one couldn't mess around getting dressed. She'd taken her out to the lawn and then Rob had come home and the pancakes were ready…and who was going to waste time dressing when there were pancakes to eat?

And Stumpy…

'I'll take her back to the laundry,' she'd said tentatively, but the dog had whined and rubbed her head against Jenny's pyjama-clad leg and Jacob had looked pleadingly at his dad.

'We could give her a pancake too. Daddy, she wants to be with us, I know she does.'

So the reservations Jenny had heard from Rob the night before seemed to have disappeared. Maybe he'd been worried about the possibility of an aggressive dog, Jenny thought, as she'd watched Rob kneel with his little son and show him just the right way to rub behind Stumpy's soft ears. And Stumpy, wounded, shocked but still dozy and pain-free, courtesy of the drugs Ross had told Rob to give her, had almost purred with pleasure, and as Rob had agreed to let Jacob give her a nibble of plain pancake, the dog's devotion seemed complete.

Stumpy was now lying under Jen's chair, her unwounded side brushing Jen's leg as if she needed the reassurance of touch. But Jacob's chair was just beside Jen's, and his little hand was surreptitiously dropping pancake nibbles to the dog below.

It felt good. No, it felt great.

The night before, Jen's impression of this house was that it was huge and empty. The living room she'd walked through to access her end of the house had looked almost unused. But this room... Well, the kitchen was also large but it was clearly more than a kitchen.

There was a big fire stove at one end—an Aga—set in a cavernous fireplace. At this time of the year it would have heated the room unbearably—Minnie was using a smaller electric hotplate to cook her pancakes—but the Aga gave a sense of age and domesticity that felt good. As did the scrubbed and worn table, the chairs with red gingham cushions and the comfy, faded sofa that took up one end of the room. A small television was mounted on the wall. Books, adult and kids' variety, were scattered on almost every available surface, and an obviously mid-construction building block edifice lay on the rug.

And the kitchen was domestically...muddled? The mantel above the fireplace held a mish-mash of domestic trivia. She could see a kid's attempt at pottery—was that supposed to be a unicorn? A pile of seashells, some broken. A partial bird's nest, obviously used. A rat trap.

A rat trap?

Rob, sitting opposite, was obviously following her gaze, and as she turned to him he grinned.

'Yep, a rat trap,' he told her. 'Minnie took Jacob to a Father's Day stall at the local market, full of assorted bric-a-brac. Jacob had saved up just enough to afford it and he decided it was the thing I needed most. The lady on the stall helped him gift wrap it with bright blue ribbons. He thinks we might have rats any day now, and it's best to be prepared.'

'Of course it is,' she agreed. 'Great choice, Jacob.'

'I knew Daddy would like it,' Jacob said, pleased, also looking at the mantelpiece. 'And I collected all those shells, and the bird's nest fell out of the tree after all the little birds flew away. And that's my daddy and mummy,' he added.

For, tucked between shells and bird's nest, was a photograph.

She'd seen photographs of this woman before—the living room was full of them. Life-sized portraits, montages of a girl turning to a woman, professional debut and wedding photographs. The living room seemed almost to be a shrine to her memory.

This, though, was different. It was a casual shot of a couple, a small photograph in a simple wooden frame. Rob and his wife? They'd obviously been hiking—they each had day packs on their backs. They were standing next to a creek, surrounded by trees, the water seemingly rippling along at their feet. The woman was looking up at Rob and laughing and he was smiling, holding her close.

She looked lovely. She looked pregnant.

'I'm in that picture,' Jacob said importantly. 'I'm the bump in Mummy's tummy. Daddy said she patted me all the time when I was in her tummy but she never got to cuddle me when I got out. We feel sad about that.' Then, moving on, 'Daddy, do you have to work this morning or can we take Jenny to the playground? And Stumpy? Stumpy would like the playground.'

'I'm so sorry about your wife,' Jenny said to Rob, because something needed to be said.

'She's still very much a part of who we are,' Rob said simply. 'And I bet if she were here now she'd say, "Get you to a playground."'

And then he hesitated. 'One of us might need to run Stumpy over to Ross in Whale Head later on,' he said, obviously planning his day in his head. 'She'll need antibiotics and I'd like a vet to check her. I talked to Chris earlier—he's having trouble locating anyone related to Charlie so it seems we're the fall-back Stumpy carers. But I just rang Ross, and he's caught up at a tricky calving right now, so we'll let Stumpy sleep for a while. That gives us time to head to the playground.'

He hesitated again, and as if going against his better judge-ment he added, speaking directly to Jacob, 'But maybe Jenny has other things to do.'

'I need to figure out my housing,' she said. 'But I doubt I can do anything on a Sunday. Would it be okay if Stumpy and I stayed for another night?'

'Yes!' Jacob said, and Minnie beamed as she rose to flip more pancakes.

But then she saw the crease deepen on Rob's forehead. There was a pause, and then he sighed, as if his planning for the day had become even more complicated.

'Sure you can,' he told her. 'Sorry for the hesitation. I was thinking...you'll have so few options.'

'I can go back to Lorna's,' she said doubtfully. 'I've paid a month's rent in advance. It's just... I don't think I can take Stumpy.'

'You can't. Her medication obviously needs adjusting, but even so... There has to be another option.'

She nodded. 'I hope so. But if you can let me stay for an-other night I'll worry about it tomorrow. Isn't that the best way to approach life? Never worry about something today which can be equally fretted about in the future. Meanwhile, I'd love to come to the playground. Why not?'

'Why not, indeed?' he replied and gave a rueful smile. 'So, a plan. Pancakes and playground. Does that sound okay to you, Jacob?'

'Yes!' Jacob said, and smiled at his father and then smiled

at Jenny, as though including her in some wonderfully exciting scheme.

A walk to a kids' playground? Another night with this man and his little boy?

There was nothing exciting in that at all—was there?

But as she looked across the table and saw Rob's lazy, caressing smile aimed at his small son she thought...yep, there was a reason for the weird tingles she was feeling.

Oh, for heaven's sake... It was hardly more than a month since that appalling night with Darren. But Darren had messed with her life enough, she thought savagely. She was darned if she'd let him mess with...the idea of heading to the playground with a little boy.

And his really gorgeous father.

CHAPTER FIVE

WHY WAS HE thinking this woman—and this dog—could somehow interfere with his life? Surely it was the simplest thing. She needed short-term accommodation and the dog needed short-term care. His house was big, Jenny seemed a cheerful addition, the district needed her skills and there were so few housing options.

Lois and Paul would have kittens.

But his parents-in-law were prone to having…kittens… at a whole lot less provocation than this. Their grief for their daughter had left them almost blinded to everything but the need to preserve her life—and everything and everyone in it. For them, time had stood still since Jacob's birth. Rob's life was supposed to mirror that need.

The path to the beachside park meandered along Willhua Creek. There'd been an unseasonal amount of rain this summer, and the creek was flowing fast enough to make him wary of letting Jacob too close, but the little boy's hand was confidingly tucked into Jenny's. He was giving her a running commentary on the local birds.

'That's a little egret—you can tell 'cos he's smaller and his neck's not bendy. The giant egrets have really bendy necks. And those ones are plovers. They've had their babies now so they don't swoop, but when they're swooping we don't use this path. Their babies are really cute but they're really hard to see. Mum used to take pictures of them—I can show you when we get home if you like.'

He'd been right to bring Jacob back here, he thought, not for the first time. Willhua was their home, and the idea of living in Brisbane, of an indefinite future of mourning, mourning and mourning, was enough to do his head in. It *had* done his head in, and he couldn't allow Jacob to spend any more of his childhood immersed in that grief. Here he was among people who loved him. He was happily surrounded by the sea, the beach, the birds, the nature that Emma loved.

Had loved.

Dear heaven, would they ever allow her to die?

But she *had* died, he told himself, as he'd told himself for four long years, as so many specialist doctors had told him, as they'd also told Lois and Paul.

'There's a Nankeen heron!' Jacob's shout caused the said Nankeen heron to rise in fright from where it had been wading in the shallows. 'It's still a baby—see its spotty wings? When it's grown up it'll be shiny brown all over. Will I draw you a picture when I get home?'

'Yes, please,' Jen said, watching the heron circle a couple of times, cast them what seemed to be baleful glances and then settle to feed again a little further away. 'I like birds.'

'Me too,' Jacob said, and his hand slipped into hers again and he recounted a silly joke. 'What do you give a sick bird? Tweetment.'

Jenny chuckled and Rob found himself grinning.

They'd found that joke among a stash of kids' books Emma had started building the moment they knew she was pregnant. If only…

Enough.

Today, walking in the sunshine, listening to Jacob's happy

chatter, suddenly the need to be free of grief and regret and worry about the weird time-lock he found himself in was almost overwhelming. What harm would there be in asking Jenny to move in with them? Why not?

But then they reached the playground and he saw the long black sedan sliding to a halt in the car park.

'Tony's here,' Jacob said happily, and waved frantically towards the car. 'Hi, Tony!'

There was no response from the car—the tinted windows stayed firmly closed.

'Tony?' Jen asked curiously as Jacob whooped across to the slide.

'Jacob's minder,' he said. 'Or... Lois and Paul's minder.'

She frowned. 'Minder?'

'Courtesy of my in-laws,' he said briefly. 'He's not here all the time but they arrange sporadic checks. They worry about Jacob's level of care. They'd like custody, but there's no way.'

'Of course not,' she said, astounded. 'You're his dad.'

'But they're Emma's parents,' he said simply. 'And I never have been—never will be—good enough for Em.'

There was a moment's pause while she let the preposterousness of this statement sink in—but finally she asked, really, really cautiously, 'Did Emma think you were good enough?'

The question caught him off-balance. He stood still, thinking about it.

He and Emma had met in med school and had been friends from the start. Their social circles, though, were hugely divergent. His mum was single. She worked in their local fish and chip shop, and he'd needed to work there too, every spare hour, to get through medicine. Emma was the only daughter of parents who were wealthy, influential and adoring. They'd been politely tolerant of him when he'd been Emma's friend. When she'd announced she wanted to marry him they'd been appalled.

'She did,' he said softly now, thinking of Emma's reaction to their hostility. 'I remember their questions to me when they objected to us marrying. "What does your mother do for a living? She does *what*? And do you even know who your father is?" Em was furious, gutted by their reaction, but in the end it didn't seem to matter. We were in love, and Emma clearly *did* think I was good enough.'

'Good for her,' Jen said roundly. 'So…they didn't change their minds when they found what an all-round good guy you are?'

He grinned at that, and his mood lightened a little. But still he had to answer the question. 'They never changed their minds. We had a quiet wedding rather than the lavish event Emma said they'd always planned for her. They didn't contribute, but that was okay by us. They came, but they looked like they were attending a funeral. Over the next couple of years we did our best—we threw out olive branches, over and over, but the fact that both of us wanted to practise medicine in the country seemed to them to be the last straw.'

And with that the lightening of his mood ended. 'Maybe, given time, they would have softened,' he said. 'We certainly hoped so. But then Em fell pregnant, and at thirty-two weeks it all turned to horror.' He stopped, his voice turned bleak.

What had Gary told her? *'Bloody tragedy about his wife…'*

'Oh, Rob, I'm so, so sorry,' she said softly, sensing the bone-deep pain. 'But surely…' She hesitated. 'Surely they couldn't blame that on you?'

'Of course they could. I wasn't here,' he said heavily. 'It was eight weeks before her due date and I drove to Sydney for the day to listen to an expert discussion on peripheral neuropathy. I left Em gardening, happy, but Minnie popped over mid-afternoon and found her unconscious on the veranda. Eclampsia. The rest...' But he didn't go on. He shrugged and fell into silence.

'So Mummy didn't get to say hello to me,' Jacob interjected. He was sitting on the top of the slide, but he must have had half an ear on what they were saying. Despite the tragedy behind this, he sounded happy, imparting what was obviously a well-known story.

'Gran says she still watches me, all the time. Gran and Grandpa say they can still talk to her, and they send Tony to tell them everything I'm doing so they can tell her. Daddy says maybe she does watch us, and when we have fun then she's happy. We can talk to her here too, in bed at night, when we close our eyes and think about her. Daddy says we don't really need Tony, but Daddy says he makes Gran and Grandpa feel better, so that's okay. He waves to me. Catch me!' he ordered his father, and Rob did.

Jen watched Rob snag his little son in his arms, swing him into his chest and hug, laugh at his delight and then let him go and watch as he ran to the swings.

'I can push myself,' Jacob said importantly as his father stayed beside him. 'You can go away.'

But Rob didn't go far. Jen saw him cast a glance at the black car. There was so much about this situation she didn't understand. It wasn't her business, she told herself, but she was too intrigued not to ask.

'So...the minder?'

'Lois and Paul worry about Jacob,' Rob told her. 'They'd like Jacob to live with them, but Jacob and I think we're fine together.'

'And I don't want to live with Gran and Grandpa,' Jacob said sternly, wiggling onto the swing. 'They cry about Mummy all the time.'

'But surely they have no rights...' Jen started.

'They have rights.' Rob sounded weary, as if this was a conversation he'd had many times before. Changing his mind, Jacob set Eric-the-Scarecrow on the swing and proceeded to swing him high enough to scare the stuffing out of any self-respecting soft toy. Rob watched for a while, and then stepped back a little to stand beside her. Decision made to talk?

'The problem...well, one of the problems when we married was a house, a solid old home in a good part of Sydney,' he told her, his eyes still on Jacob. 'It belongs to Emma's grandmother. Pre Emma meeting me, her grandma made a will, leaving her house to Emma and her brother, Colin. In turn, at their grandma's request, Colin and Emma wrote wills leaving everything to each other. They were both young at the time and it even made sense. Then the old lady was diagnosed with Alzheimer's. She lost the capacity to change her will, but she was still alive when we married—she's alive still.

'But part of Lois and Paul's worry over Em marrying me was around the house. Colin is...well, he has some mental health issues and he struggles. He's living in the house, and he loves it. Em had almost forgotten about the will. But her parents hadn't, or maybe the moment we were married they remembered and panicked. They knew marriage invalidates any previous will.'

'Ouch,' Jen said dubiously, not sure where this was going.

'Okay, long story, but bear with me,' he said. 'Because it turns out it was important. We had lunch with them the day after we were married and they brought it up—if anything happened to Em then Colin would lose the place he loved. Em told them she'd change her will as soon as she got back from our honeymoon, but we were going skiing and we could see they were panicked. And of course Em still wanted Colin to have the house—we both did.

'So they brought out the documents and she signed a codicil saying marriage hadn't invalidated her intentions. It was done in a rush. She had no intention of dying and she thought we could fix things up properly in the future. All we wanted was to get out of there and get on with our honeymoon. And we never realised that what she was signing was not only a will, it was also medical and legal powers of attorney.'

He sighed. 'So that was that, and afterwards…well, to be honest, we forgot about it. Our lives were too full, too happy, to think about changing our wills again, so when Em became… not capable of making decisions herself, her parents took control. They have full power over almost everything.'

'Oh, Rob!' The ramifications of what she was hearing were appalling. 'Oh, no.'

'Their control over Em's medical care when she was so gravely ill was bad enough,' he said grimly. 'But they wanted more—they still want more—and they've used those documents to say they have rights to ongoing influence over Jacob's care.' He sighed. 'In a way…to be honest, their loss has left them unhinged. They have every influential lawyer in the land at their disposal, but so far they haven't been able to win custody. The bottom line is that I'm Jacob's father. They argue though, that I can't be a full-time doctor and take care of Jacob, and they hate that this place is remote. They think I should employ a qualified nanny instead of Minnie—in their ideal world I'd have a staff of nannies on shifts. And then last Easter we had an accident…'

'I got bitten,' Jacob said from behind the swing. 'Wendy

O'Hara fell off the slide, right here, and hurt her arm. She was crying and Wendy's mummy was crying too. So Daddy had to take care of Wendy's arm. And Wendy's dog Fred was tied to a tree and he started crying too, so I went over to pat him. And he bit me. But Tony was here and saw from his car and he came over and kicked Fred and broke his leg. Gran and Grandpa say it was Daddy's fault, and Minnie told me that Daddy paid the vet, and Minnie said it was…un…unfair, but Daddy said Fred was just upset 'cos everyone was screaming.'

'Whoa.' There was so much in that statement to unpack. 'So that's why no dogs?' she asked cautiously.

'You got it,' Rob said. 'But you know what I thought this morning?' He was still watching his son, but his voice was suddenly a little unsure. 'I've decided—enough.'

'Enough?' She didn't understand half of this story—surely, as sole parent, Rob's control couldn't be questioned—but standing in the sunshine with this man and this little boy… Maybe she didn't have to understand. Maybe she should just enjoy the sunshine—and the sensation of being…a friend?

'Maybe it's time I drew a line in the sand,' he said.

'Sorry?'

'I imagine you understand how gutted Em's parents are,' he said, sounding as if he was thinking things through as he spoke. 'I've been immersed in my own sadness, but I can still understand theirs. But their demands…the fact that Tony turns up unexpectedly and hovers, just to watch…the fact that they arrive themselves, to visit, unannounced… You've seen the living room—they set that up themselves so Jacob can always see his mum. I've let it be because it was too hard not to. But today…'

He glanced over at the black car. 'Today Tony will report back that I'm here with a woman, and I'm betting that within hours he'll have sniffed out that there's a dog staying at the house as well. They'll be down on me like a ton of bricks.'

He paused but then, slowly and deliberately, he started talking again. 'So here it is. If you can cope with a visit from my in-laws—and I warn you, it won't be pretty—I wonder if you're interested in sharing our house?'

She'd been listening in a certain amount of horror—the idea of in-laws holding such sway seemed inconceivable—and his last statement caught her unawares. 'Sharing?'

'It's a hospital house, so why not?' he said, obviously moving on from in-laws discussion. 'Accommodation in this town is tight but you've seen that our house is huge. We'd need to share the kitchen but nothing else. What's more, because the house is deemed part of the hospital, I pay minimal rent. It's called the doctor's house, but this doctor doesn't need all of it. The hospital board is made up of three sensible locals and they know how much we need a paramedic. I wouldn't be the least surprised if they agreed to your staying and set you a minimum rent as well.'

She frowned, turning it over in her mind. The idea might be good, but there did seem to be complications. Complications she didn't understand, but she glanced across at the black car and winced. 'I won't...cause problems?' she ventured.

'With Paul and Lois? I try very hard to avoid confrontation, but enough. I'm Jacob's father. There needs to be an end to this constant battle.'

'Would having Stumpy make things worse?' Not having to return to Lorna Dumet's was appealing, but this man had obvious issues. And so did she. When she'd settled Stumpy the night before, the dog had raised her soft paw and put it on her arm, and she'd thought...

'Rob, I do like dogs,' she told him. 'And I've sort of fallen for Stumpy. If no relative comes forward to claim her, with her side looking so awful it'll take a month or so for her to look presentable enough for adoption. I've been thinking I'll look after her until that happens, but if I'm to look after her for that time I might…get attached.'

'You think that's a risk?' he asked, bemused.

'I'm not bad at getting attached,' she admitted and then gave a rueful shrug. 'A couple of hopeless exes spring to mind. Stumpy's complications look a doddle in comparison.'

He gave her a curious look. 'So… Stumpy instead of exes?'

'You got it.'

'You're not suffering from a broken heart as well?' he asked, but the way he said it, it wasn't intrusive. It was simply a comment from…a friend?

This man *could* be a friend, she thought, and it was like a frisson of pleasure, bursting through the muddle she'd been in for the last few weeks.

'It's not exactly a broken heart,' she said, knowing suddenly that it was true. In comparison to what he'd gone through, her story was surely nothing. 'Humiliation though. Falling for a toerag.'

'I'm sorry.'

'Yeah, well, yet another life lesson learned. Don't they all come at us when we least need them?' She shrugged and then she gave a wry smile. 'And I did, sort of, leave my mark.'

'What, you bit him, like Fred?'

She chuckled. 'Ugh! Biting toerags would be like voluntarily biting into tripe—not in my life's plan.' But then she paused, thinking of that last night with Darren, the anger, the humiliation, the pain. And then she thought, why not tell someone?

Tell Rob? This man with the smiley eyes? This man who knew real tragedy, as opposed to her sordid story?

Jacob was busy pushing Eric-the-Scarecrow on the swing. The sun was on her face and there was nowhere to go. If this man was to be her new housemate...why not tell him?

'Darren was my boss,' she said. 'He was hired eighteen months ago to head South Sydney Air Rescue. He had all the qualifications in the world, and the world was his oyster. He was too good-looking for his own good, sexy-as-hell and... Am I boring you?'

'Not at all,' he said faintly, and she grinned.

'Hey, if you're my new housemate, maybe we get to tell each other things. Anyway, he arrived and swept me off my feet, or as much as anyone can sweep someone my height off my feet. He said he'd been married, but things hadn't worked out. She'd taken some bigwig job in New York and their marriage was over. So romance, romance, romance, blah-blah-blah. I won't bore you with the soppy bits. Or how much I made a fool of myself.'

'But then our service was nominated for this huge award, and as its head Darren was due to accept the award at a black tie gala dinner. Politician celebrities, you name it. And of course I was to be his significant other. "Let's make a week-end of it," he said, and I was so excited. I bought the most gorgeous dress. He booked us a suite in the fanciest hotel in Sydney, overlooking the harbour, just dream stuff—and then it all fell apart.'

'Uh-oh.'

She managed a rueful smile. 'Yeah, uh-oh. Idiot me. So come Saturday night, we'd had a lovely lunch, then we'd come back to the room to dress for the presentation dinner. But he got a phone call, and halfway through making ourselves pretty he went outside to take it. And it was his wife. He'd told her about the award and it seemed their marriage wasn't exactly...

over. She'd flown back to surprise him, rung from the airport to ask which hotel he was in and she was on her way. And that was that. "I'm married," he said. "And my wife is here. You need to leave."'

'Um...' Rob said mildly. 'Ouch?'

'You could say that,' she muttered. 'Bottom-feeding, two-timing toerag. When he came back to the room after the phone call I was half dressed, and I felt humiliated to my socks—if you could categorise the gorgeous lingerie I'd bought specially for the occasion socks. So I stood there with my mouth open while he said calmly that he'd organised another room for me and changed the dinner seating arrangements. He'd see me at dinner, and would I please remember that we were just acquaintances. After all, he said, it wasn't as if our affair was serious, but now he needed to take a shower. And then he walked into the bathroom and closed the door.'

'Oh, my... I'm so sorry. Jen...'

'Don't be too sorry,' she said, and somehow she managed to smile again. 'You know the saying—don't get mad when you can get even? I stood there staring at the closed bathroom door, and then I stared at his gorgeous bespoke dinner suit laid out on the bed. And my suitcase was on the floor and I'd packed nail scissors.'

'What...you cut it up?' he demanded, appalled, and she chuckled.

'No such thing,' she told him. 'I'm no vandal. I simply...improved it. It was a hot night in Sydney and surely long trousers would be uncomfortable. So I carefully converted them into zigzag-edged shorts, surely much more appropriate than formal attire in the heat. I zigzagged his lovely Italian silk tie to match. Then I packed my stuff and walked out and went home. The next day I started looking for a new job—and here I am.'

'Did he…did you hear what happened?' he asked, horrified but fascinated.

'Of course I did. I gather my friend Frankie had to accept the award on his behalf, because Darren seemed to have come down with a sudden illness. Maybe there was a dearth of dinner suit hire places open at seven on a Saturday night? Anyway, Frankie apparently made a very nice speech and everyone cheered. And thus endeth an affair.'

Only it hadn't ended—at least not like that, though. Not with an insouciant shrug and moving on. There was still enough tension in her voice to tell him the hurt and humiliation had been bone-deep.

He had a sudden urge to find the bastard and do more than rip his pants.

'He's gone back to New York,' she said, watching Eric-the-Scarecrow being swung higher and higher. Her voice was carefully neutral. 'The award was a biggie and it seemed he used it to get himself a great admin job in the States. Head of some city paramedic service where he'll get to sit behind a desk all day. Right up his alley.'

There was a long silence. Eric-the-Scarecrow fell off the swing a couple of times and was retrieved and sent sky-high again. *Get up and move on*, Jen had told herself that first morning, when all she'd wanted to do was move on. And she had.

'So it seems to me,' Rob said at last, cautiously, into the stillness, 'that we're both in the mood for moving on.'

And there was only one answer to that.

'Indeed I am. Why on earth not? Housemates? Dog? Onward and upward, I say.' She glanced at Jacob, who'd suddenly abandoned Eric and was clambering up a chain tepee. 'Jacob, do you mind if I join you at the top?'

'Will you come up?' Jacob said, sounding startled. 'It's very high.'

'But I'm good at climbing,' she told him. 'Very good. So maybe it's time I climbed right out of the funk I've been in and come up to join you.'

Frankie rang that afternoon, while she was moving her stuff out of Lorna's to Rob's. Because, just like that, she now had a new home.

Of course she was copping invective from Lorna and sacrificing two weeks rent, but she'd be living with Jacob and Rob. Friends? Surely they could be. There was also the possibility of keeping a very nice dog.

And…a guy who made her smile? Whose own smile made her…

'Hey!' Frankie's voice down the line was welcome—they'd been friends for a long time. 'How goes it?'

She'd just finished stowing boxes into her car. She stopped and leaned on the bonnet and felt the sun on her face. The smell of the sea was everywhere, plus the eucalyptus from the giant gums overhead. Three blocks away was her new home. With Stumpy and Jacob. And a very nice man called Rob.

'It goes pretty well,' she told Frankie and filled her in.

'Um,' Frankie said at last as she finished. 'Jen?' And Jen heard doubt.

'What?'

'Can I remind you how fast you fell for Darren?'

'I'm not falling,' she said hotly. 'I'm just… He could be a friend, that's all. Stumpy's messy but she's recovering. We haven't found any relations yet, but there's still time. If no one comes forward though, I might just adopt her myself. So tell me about Bruce.'

'He's okay,' Frankie said, abandoning the inquisition. 'He's got a bruised leg that's been all bandaged up by the vet, but nothing's broken. I'll let Nico know that you haven't found any relatives.' There was a huff of laughter from Frankie. 'He might be happy about that. I think they quite like each other. Like you and Stumpy.' Then there was a sigh. 'Just be careful, won't you? Falling for a dog…falling for a man…'

'I'm not falling for a man.'

'No, twenty-four hours isn't long enough to fall for anyone,' Frankie said darkly. 'Neither, in my opinion, is falling a good idea at all. Do your homework, my friend, so you don't end up getting a nasty surprise down the track. You know as well as I do that if they want something from you, they can hide stuff you should know about. Like a wife. Or a new, better girlfriend? Just remember that.'

'I'll remember,' she said and disconnected and tried for a whole five minutes to feel sober and reflective and careful.

And then she thought of Rob and Jacob and Stumpy and her new job and her new life—and she decided she didn't need to feel sober and reflective and careful at all.

CHAPTER SIX

WHAT FOLLOWED WERE a couple of weeks where Jenny decided the job of paramedic at Willhua could well turn out to be a very fine career choice. She loved it.

The service was busy, but not usually with casualties. The main medical service for the district was at Whale Head, and infirm patients without their own transport options needed to be ferried back and forth.

The service's second vehicle was a minibus. One of the retired locals was the usual driver, but for that first week Harold was down with a heavy cold and Jen had to step in. She'd been dubious, but the end of the week, instead of feeling like a glorified taxi service, she was starting to realise what a great little community this was.

Sam Dutton was going back and forth for kidney dialysis. Marianne Carmichael was halfway through radiotherapy for breast cancer. Timmy Loden, six years old, had lost a leg to sarcoma and needed to visit Whale Head twice a week for rehabilitation physiotherapy. They were a motley set of patients, but somehow they gelled.

Timmy's parents were passionate surfers, and their shock was still palpable months after their son's surgery. The elderly Sam was an ex-surfer as well, so there was stuff to talk about—but Timmy's missing leg made initial conversations constrained.

The second time Jenny drove the truck, though, Sam produced photos of a mate of his who'd lost his leg to a shark some twenty years ago and was surfing still. Sam had pictures of his mate surfing one-legged—he even had pictures of the shark! Marianne oohed and ahhed, then borrowed the pictures, enlarged them overnight and the next day brought the essentials for Jen to stick them up in the truck.

'You want me to draw teeth marks on your stump?' Sam had asked. The next trip Marianne had produced indelible markers and the teeth marks looked...real enough for Timmy to love them.

The power of community in the little truck seemed almost breathtaking, Jenny thought, and this power extended beyond the patients they were transferring.

'You're staying with Doc Pierson?' she was asked, over and over. She was looked over with interest, but again there was warmth. The common consensus? 'Well, that's wonderful. They rattle around in that great big house. You'll look after them, won't you, love?'

But right now *they* seemed to be looking after her.

There'd been an emotional call from Charlie Emerson's daughter, still reeling from the loss of her dad. 'I'm so sorry, but I can't take the dogs. I live in an apartment in Sydney. When I sell the farm I might be able to buy something bigger, but that'll take ages. Besides, I really like my apartment. Is there anyone who can take them?'

Jen still wasn't sure what the fate of the dog Frankie had rescued—Bruce—would be but she knew he was being well looked after for the moment, and she had enough support from Rob and Jacob to give her own promises.

'Stumpy's safe with me,' she'd promised. The dog's side was healing. She still looked appalling, with little hair and scabbing on the left side of her body, but her personality was already showing. She was gentle, inquisitive, answering to her name, sitting when requested—and when Jacob surreptitiously offered her toast crusts she practically turned herself inside out in a display of gratitude that made them all laugh.

And they did laugh. The arrangement was supposed to be independent living but that had lasted a whole two minutes. With Stumpy at one end of the house and Jacob at the other... yeah, well...

'This house is starting to feel like home again,' Minnie said in satisfaction after the first week. 'You and your blessed dog seem like magic.'

Jen and her dog seemed to have transformed his life. Just like that. One slip of a girl—okay, maybe slip was the wrong word, she was almost as tall as he was, but she was slim, lithe, tanned and fit. Wearing her paramedic uniform she looked ready to face down the world, and that was what she seemed to have done for his world. She giggled at Jacob's corny jokes, she admired his weird artwork and she kicked the footy round the backyard with him. She sat with him on the back veranda with Stumpy between them, gently teaching Jacob how to stroke behind those big soft ears to give Stumpy maximum pleasure.

And she gave *him* pleasure. For the first time since, well, since Emma, the house seemed to be alive again.

She was an appalling cook—she admitted that. 'There's nothing wrong with egg on toast and an apple,' she'd told an appalled Minnie. Minnie cooked the basics for them when Rob was busy, but he'd always enjoyed cooking. There'd seemed little impetus, though, when it was just himself and Jacob, and Jacob thought pasta, pasta and pasta—with the occasional hit of sausages—was all a four-year-old required.

But with Jen here—when the afternoon ended early enough—he found himself hauling out cookbooks that had been ignored for years, and heading into the supermarket on his way to and from house calls to check out the 'international' shelves.

His triumph so far had been his *Chiles en nogada*. Jacob had refused it on the grounds that, 'It has ingredients! Yuk!' They'd given him spaghetti instead, but Jen had raved. He'd gone to bed that night feeling smug and light and...happy.

One woman, one dog, two weeks...

He was due to take Jacob to Brisbane this weekend—the agreement was once a month—and no doubt that'd bring the fog back again, but for now...

For now things seemed okay. The way Jen made him smile...the way he felt when he looked at her hugging her disreputable dog...the way she made his little son chuckle...

He wouldn't look into the future. For now...well, for now things seemed great.

Thursday night—or was it Friday morning?—Jen's phone buzzed into life and she was instantly awake. That was what medical training did for you—there was never any time to yawn and stretch and bring yourself back to consciousness with ease.

'Jen?' It was Gary. 'Call. Pick you up in three minutes? I'm ringing Doc now to expect us.'

Even after only two weeks they had this down to a fine art.

She didn't ask more—the tone of Gary's voice said there was urgency and he could fill her in on the way. Three minutes later she was uniformed and heading for the back door. Rob was already awake, dressed and in the kitchen.

'Teenager,' he said briefly, 'Anna Windsor. Gary says

sounds like appendix, but her parents are panicking. If you decide to take her on to Whale Head pick me up on the way. I'll contact Minnie.'

She nodded and left him, heading out into the dark to wait by the kerb for the flashing light of the ambulance.

She slid into the seat beside Gary and saw his face was set.

'What are we facing?'

'Hysterical parents first off,' he said as he hit lights and sirens. Willhua's tight cliff roads made it almost essential to give as much warning as they could to oncoming traffic.

'Anna's eighteen. She went to bed without eating, saying she had a tummy upset. Now she's curled up in bed, her parents say she's screaming with pain but she won't let them near. She's yelling at them to get out every time they go near. Heaven knows why. Her mum's bleating appendicitis but, by the sound of it, blocked bowel? Gallstones? Your guess is as good as mine.'

'Tell me about the family.' They had time before arrival, and if they were faced with hysterical parents, background could help.

'They're do-gooders,' he said, in a voice that wasn't exactly full of admiration. 'In the worst possible way. Marjorie and Graham Windsor think their role is to keep the town nice. They run the local pharmacy, Windsor and Son—it's been in the town for generations. Graham considers himself pretty much Willhua's founding father, and Marjorie concurs. If one stray tumbleweed wanders down the main street they'll be out looking for the source, and woe betide the owner of the garden they think it comes from.'

As a character description it took some beating. Jen gave a wry smile. 'And their daughter?'

'Anna. Only child. Nice kid, clever they say, but incredibly quiet. Kept on a tight rein. They've been telling the town she's going to be a doctor since she was seven. Imagine if she decides to be an accountant. Oh, the shame.'

She chuckled at that, and then settled, putting herself into the quiet zone she tried to move into before she faced a job.

Two minutes later they were at the front door. The house and garden were almost rigidly perfect, the brass bell-pull at the front door so shiny it hardly needed the outside light.

But as they approached a scream split the night, a scream so primeval, so full of pain that Gary opened the front door without knocking. Her parents, Marjorie and Graham, were outside a bedroom door, Graham looking wild-eyed and desperate, Marjorie crouched on the floor, holding her knees as if she herself was in pain.

'She won't let us in,' Graham said hoarsely. 'Marjorie tried, she went in but Anna screamed even louder and told her to get out or she'd kill herself. My Anna. My little girl.'

Gary and Jen exchanged glances. They were both experienced paramedics. They'd both been in situations where parents were the last thing a kid needed. Drug use? Alcoholic poisoning? The one that sprang to mind now though—they'd both heard that primeval scream—was also one they'd both faced before.

'By the sound of that pain she'll need hospital,' Gary said firmly.

'But what…?' Marjorie said wildly. 'What…?'

'Possibly a kinked bowel. Possibly gallstones. Doc will examine her.'

'She won't let you in.'

Gary nodded to Jen. If what they were both thinking was right…

'Let Jen try,' he suggested. 'She's nearest to Anna's age.

Sometimes pain makes you feel like a trapped animal—weirdly, a complete stranger might be more effective.'

And, before they could answer, Jen slipped quietly into the room.

The room was pink. Very pink. Fifty shades of pink? Pink pile carpet, pink curtains, a pink four-poster bed. A huge desk under the window was piled with impressive texts. A girl was crouched almost in a foetal position under the pink duvet.

The squirrel-shaped bedside lamp cast the only light. Jen hesitated, then went and crouched by the bed, finding the girl's hand. The thin hand she found gripped like death. Then came another scream, this time muffled. Fingernails dug in so hard Jen would later find scratches. The foetal position changed to arching. Pressure, pressure, pressure...

And then the pressure eased. The girl looked wild-eyed at Jenny—and then she folded back into herself.

'Don't tell. Don't tell!' she whispered.

Gary had slipped in behind her. Jen looked back at Gary—and their shared look said they were both guessing what this was about.

'Anna, I'm Jenny and I'm an ambulance officer,' Jen said gently as she bent close to the girl's head. 'You can't cope with this pain alone. Gary and I are here to take you to hospital. Doc Pierson—you know Doc Pierson?—he's waiting for you, but I need to check your tummy first. Will you let me?'

There was a wild nod—the girl was obviously too far gone to argue. 'But not...not Mum and Dad,' she managed.

'That's your choice,' Jen said, still gently. 'But we can talk about that later. Your mum and dad are staying outside while we help you. Now, I'm going to feel your tummy.'

Gary moved silently into position and helped her move the bedclothes from the girl's convulsive, covering grip. Even through the bedclothes they could feel the hard swell of her tummy. She lay limp while Jen did a fast examination.

Suspicion confirmed. A baby. Coming soon.

Another contraction. Another terrified grip and muffled scream.

'Anna, do you know your baby's coming?' Jen asked, as Gary moved to the side of the room and spoke softly into the radio. It seemed impossible the girl didn't know, but terror could sometimes make it possible to block out the most obvious of pregnancies.

'Of course I know,' Anna sobbed. 'But I can't...'

'You can,' Jen told her. 'Your body's doing exactly what it needs to be doing—and you have the strength to help it. Do you know...' She hesitated at this, not sure if it was right to push the girl further, but it was important information. And Gary had said this girl was bright. 'Anna, do you know how long you've been pregnant?'

'Thirty...thirty-seven weeks,' Anna moaned. 'But I can't...'

'You can,' Jen said again, more strongly. 'You're a strong, capable woman, Anna, and you now have all the help you need.'

'But Mum and Dad...'

'We'll be with you when you tell them,' she told her. 'You're not alone any more, Anna.'

Okay. Enough talking. It was time to get her to hospital. Time to bring Rob and his skills into this scenario—and Jen suspected it'd be more than medical skills that were needed tonight.

'Anna, first things first. We need to get you to hospital. Doc Pierson is waiting.' She thought, not for the first time, how awesome was the responsibility facing family doctors. Rob would be facing more than just a simple birth tonight. 'For now let's get you shifted to where we can ease the pain and help you with what's to come.'

Rob was waiting at the hospital entrance. Minnie was already installed in the house. Gary had briefed him while driving—it seemed Jen was in the back with Anna.

'I can't imagine how she's hidden it,' Gary had told him. 'From the whole town? I've seen her myself, walking to and from school. I thought she was putting on weight, but she's been wearing T-shirts about three sizes too big. Well, they all are, seems it's the latest thing, baggy, baggy, baggy. But how her parents didn't know… Or maybe they did, in a way. I'm thinking it must be that thing, you know, where the mind can't take in the bleeding obvious because it's too big. Anyway, when her mum tried to get in the truck with us Anna started screeching again, said, "Stay with Dad, stay with Dad." So they're coming behind, but fair go, Doc, you have a right drama to face.'

So by the time the ambulance doors were opened and Jen emerged, seamlessly helping Gary move the stretcher and roll it into their small theatre, he'd pretty much prepared himself for hysterics to come.

But not from Anna. The moment the stretcher's wheels were down and Jen could be at her side again, the girl's hands clutched hers, but she seemed to be in as much control as a woman nearing her time could be.

'Jen says you won't tell Mum and Dad…unless you have to… I mean…'

'Anna, you're eighteen, an adult. I need your permission for anything I talk to your mum and dad about,' he told her. Then he turned to the night nurse. 'Cathy, could you deflect Mr and Mrs Windsor? Ask Kita to make them a cup of tea.

Put them in my consulting room—it's the furthest from Theatre so they won't hear as much. Then I'll need you in Theatre. You too, Jen, if you'll stay.'

He wanted Jen as well as Cathy. Kita was the backup night staff, with basic training only, and she wasn't much older than Anna. Possibly not mature enough to hide her shock.

'I don't think you'll disengage Jen anyway,' Gary said dispassionately, looking at the death grip on Jen's hand.

'Another contraction,' Jen said. 'That's less than two minutes. It's okay, Anna, grip as hard as you like, harder if you want. Someone's looking after Mum and Dad. Now, we need to look after you.'

'They'll guess,' Anna whispered. 'They'll kill me. I can't...'

'Yes, you can.' Rob took her other hand as the contraction eased. He knew this girl. He'd treated her for acne, for menstrual pain, for a consultation eight months ago when her mother had brought her to him for 'depression'. She'd said sullenly that it was just drama at school, but it was sorted and she didn't need help. He hadn't been able to take it any further but, thank heaven, he hadn't prescribed the antidepressants her mother had insisted she needed.

'You're a strong woman, Anna Windsor, and strong women rule the world,' he told her. 'Isn't that right, Jen? Jen's our newest ambulance officer and you know what she did on her first day here? She abseiled down Devil's Pass to save a life. She even managed to climb up, holding a full-sized corgi. If she can do that, you can push out a baby.'

'I can't...'

'You can,' Rob said again, softly but with total authority in his voice. 'You're not alone now, Anna. With our help, you will.'

'You won't leave me?' But the girl was talking to Jen.

'We're with you all the way,' Jen told her, because there was nothing else to say. She was thinking of what this girl had endured—months of fear, months of hiding what to her must have been a terrifying secret. 'What Dr Pierson says is the truth. Now, during the birth and afterwards, we promise that you won't be alone again.'

Which was how, for the next two hours, Jen found herself acting as a birth partner.

Medically she wasn't needed. Cathy and Rob did everything they could to ease the pain, to ease the panic, to ease the terror. She simply sat and let Anna grip her hand as much as she needed. She wiped her face with a damp towel, which sometimes Anna wanted, though sometimes her hand was slapped away. She listened to swearwords, to curses, to pleas, to rants directed at someone called Tyler, to cries for her mother, but desperate pleas saying no when Cathy offered to fetch her.

And, through it all, Rob's gentle voice. 'You're doing great, Anna. I know it hurts like hell but it'll soon be over. Breathe through the mask—Cathy's holding it for you. You can do this. I know how strong you are...'

Most doctors would disappear at this stage, Jen thought, leaving the waiting for the midwives. There was no urgent need for him to stay—Cathy could call him back at the end. But Anna's eyes kept flying to him as she surfaced from each contraction, and Jen knew that his presence was important. Rob was her family doctor. She knew him. Jen and maybe Cathy as well were strangers. Even though it was Jen's hand the girl was gripping as if she were drowning, Rob seemed her anchor.

And he made a great anchor, Jen decided as the labour progressed. Big, solid, infinitely reassuring, he was the teenaged mum's rock, her link to her parents—her link to reality?

And when that final push came, when a tiny, mewling baby finally emerged into the glare of the overhead lights, when Cathy lifted the little boy onto his mother's breast and Anna sobbed and cradled her baby and looked up, she looked to Rob. Her eyes were filled with tears and fear—but also wonder.

'He's mine,' she whispered, and unconsciously her hands tightened around her little one. 'They'll kick me out. They'll kill me, but he's mine.'

'He is yours,' Rob said infinitely gently as Cathy took over midwife duty—cleaning away the afterbirth, the detritus of the last two hours. He sat on the bed beside Anna and used his finger to trace a feather touch on the tiny downy cheek. 'Your son.' And then his voice softened. 'Anna, your mum and dad are going crazy with worry out there. What would you like me to tell them?'

'Tell them to go home.'

There was a long silence at that. Jen thought she should go home too—surely she was no longer needed—but the moment she walked out of this door she'd have to walk past the room where the Windsors waited. What would she say? Whoever walked out of this room first had to have their ducks in a row. To walk out and say nothing—impossible.

And Rob knew it. This whole situation was impossible. The best thing for Anna now was to be left in peace with her baby, with Cathy in the background to help, if help was needed. But how possible was that?

As a paramedic Jen had been present at births before—they usually got their mums to hospital in time, but she'd seen babies born at home, babies born in the ambulance, once even a baby born on the side of the road before the ambulance reached them. But in every single case there'd been someone. A partner, a mother, a sister, a friend. Someone to hold and love and share the awe. This frightened child—for that was what she seemed—appeared to have no one.

'Have you told anyone?' Rob asked gently, and Anna shook her head.

'One night. And he's not even my boyfriend. The school dance. We got together beforehand, us girls, and Georgie Lewis had vodka. We drank it with cola. Dare, she said, and we all did, or at least I thought we all did, but maybe she put more in mine. And then Tyler...' Her eyes filled. 'He'd been nice to me but it was a dare. I don't...please...don't even say his name. I'm the goody two-shoes at school and the next day...they were all pointing and laughing—Tyler must have given Georgie the vodka. It was a set-up. He was dancing with me and he's so popular, so good-looking... I remember feeling dizzy and great and like I was one of them! But I wasn't. Then we sneaked out and it was only the once and I couldn't... I didn't...'

And Jen saw Rob's face darken. He'd know these kids. He'd be seeing the whole picture, she thought. An overly protected kid, a *goody two-shoes*.

'That's enough,' Rob said, infinitely gently now. 'That's past, done with. There'll be ways we can sort out what needs to be sorted out with Tyler, but for now all that's important is you and your little boy. Anna...'

'I want to keep him.' Her eyes, desolate while telling her appalling story, suddenly flashed fire. Her arms tightened on her little one. 'I was so scared and then he started moving inside me and I could feel him and I knew... I knew I'd feel like this. He's mine. He's nothing to do with Tyler, nothing to do with my parents. But I don't know...'

'You don't need to know,' Rob told her. He was still sitting on the side of the bed, his finger was still stroking the tiny baby's cheek.

'You know, Anna, my mum was seventeen when she had me. She was just like you, a scared kid, but she knew what she wanted. She wanted me. And somehow she managed. Her parents weren't there for her, but someone at the hospital was. Someone helped her to find somewhere to live, how to get government help. She and I had fun—she was a great mother. She died of cancer two years ago, but she told me, over and over, the two biggest things she learned. The first was to face down those who judged her—she was proud of herself and she was proud of me. The second was to ask for help when she needed it. So what's happened in the past…it was no fault of yours, Anna, but what's come out of it is something wonderful. Something you can be proud of forever. Your son.'

And the girl's gaze, drowning in the wonder of her baby, moved up to his. 'I can do that?'

'If you want, you can do anything. There are people who can help you. I can help you and Cathy can help you. We can hook you up with services that'll keep you and your baby safe. But first…' He hesitated and then went on.

'Outside, your parents are going out of their minds with worry. They've probably guessed what's happening—or maybe Gary was forced to tell them. Once upon a time they looked down at you just like you're looking at this little one. Will you let them come in and see you?'

There was a flash of terror at that, and then she closed her eyes and when she opened them again something had changed.

'You said,' she whispered, but there was a subtle difference in her voice now, the determination to move forward. 'You said…to ask for help when I need it.'

'I did say that and I meant it.'

'Could you…' She hesitated. 'It's just… I've been trying for all this time and I can't… Can you tell them about the vodka and the dance and…and what happened? Only not names, please not names. I don't want…'

'You don't want anger tonight,' Rob said and smiled and snagged a couple of tissues from the bedside table and wiped her eyes. 'Of course you don't. Tonight is your son's birthday. It's a day of joy and wonder and welcome.'

'And you'll come in when they come? You won't leave me alone until…'

'I'll stay as long as you need me.'

'So will I,' Cathy said roundly. 'Anyone upsetting my patients tonight will have me to answer to.'

'But I need to go home,' Jen said simply. Her place was no longer here; Cathy and Rob were all the girl needed. She'd backed away from the bed, leaving the tableau to doctor, nurse, mother and baby. 'Congratulations, Anna. You did magnificently and I know you'll keep on doing the same.'

'But…you helped me.'

'I'll come back to see you tomorrow,' Jen told her, 'I promise. You're calling the shots now, Anna. We're all here to help, for whatever and however long you need.'

CHAPTER SEVEN

ROB FOUND JEN an hour later, in the laundry.

For four years Rob had been accustomed to nights of solitude, of reheating dinners Minnie had left for him, sitting in the darkened kitchen/family room—because who'd want to go into that mausoleum of a living room?—and staring at nothing until tiredness overcame him.

Minnie would still be here—she had a room next door to Jacob's that she slept in on nights like this. The slightest sound from Jacob would have her springing up in full childcaring mode, but she was so used to Rob coming and going that his movements didn't disturb her. Jen's room was at the far end of the house. He assumed she'd be long asleep as well, so the night was his, the demons to be faced alone.

He washed, he headed into the kitchen and flicked the kettle on—and then he heard a voice—Jen's voice—coming from the laundry. Soft and gentle, a murmur only.

'You're doing great, Stumpy. I know I woke you up, but you can go to sleep again now. And I know you're missing Charlie and Bruce, and your side still hurts, but we'll figure a way to get you through that. You and me together. Friends for life. How does that sound?'

It sounded okay to him. He headed to the laundry and stood in the doorway and watched.

She didn't see him at first. She was wearing pyjamas and

sitting on the floor, legs out in front, Stumpy's boofy head on her knee. She was stroking her over-big ears, still murmuring.

'Tomorrow I reckon we might dawdle down to the park, not fast, not far, just far enough to find a few interesting smells. Rob and Jacob say lots of dogs go to the park, so there'll be great smells all over the place. Maybe we might even make a doggy friend or two.'

She bent and gave the dog a kiss on the head and then lifted her back onto her pile of bedding. The dog looked adoringly up and then nuzzled back into the soft wool.

Was this a nightly occurrence, chatting to Stumpy in the small hours? The way Stumpy was settling, he suspected it was.

This woman... He thought about the way she'd responded to Anna over the past few hours, the way she'd sat and let the girl cling, the soft things she'd said to her. 'I'll come back to see you tomorrow,' she'd said as she'd finally left. 'I promise.'

This was a woman who kept her promises.

This was a woman who made his heart twist.

But now she was looking up, seeing him. There was no start of astonishment though, just a warm smile, as if he was simply a part of her world. And right now it felt like that was the way it was. Her flannel pyjamas were oversized, and her dark curls were tousled—she usually had them pulled back but now they drifted to her shoulders. Her face looked scrubbed. She was obviously ready for bed.

So why did he say, 'Hey, well done on settling your patient. I'm making tea and toast. You want to share?'

'I did have tea with Minnie when I got home,' she confessed and then she beamed. 'But drama makes me hungry and I could definitely use more.'

* * *

Uh-oh. What was she saying?

This was not sensible—not sensible in the least. There was no need at all for her to stay with Rob for a moment longer. She was this man's tenant and a colleague, and that was all. She lived at the far end of the house. She needed to keep some distance.

But distance had never been Jen's strong suit.

Maybe it was her childhood, absent parents who'd appeared sporadically, causing her to cling fiercely, to take what she could because she'd known they wouldn't be there the next day.

Maybe that was why she'd jumped into all sorts of disastrous relationships—okay, Darren hadn't been the first. Jump first, ask questions later. Take people at face value because looking forward didn't change a thing.

And here it was, happening again. This man had so much baggage—impossible baggage—yet here he was, looking down at her, smiling, and here was that longing again—for closeness, for warmth, for connection.

Her friend Frankie might have poured a bucket of cold water over her, she thought, demanding, 'Will you ever learn?' But right now…

Right now Rob was reaching down to help her up. His hands were strong and warm, and his smile was oh, so lovely.

Maybe this time…

What was she thinking? It was too soon—way, way too soon.

But that smile… She had no hope of fighting the way his smile made her feel.

And he tugged her a little too strongly, or maybe she rose a little too fast, and all of a sudden she was very, very close.

Here comes another catastrophe! She could almost hear Frankie's inevitable warning.

But Rob was right here, and she could feel his warmth, his strength… His lovely hands were steadying her, and he was still smiling.

She was lost.

Here I go again.

She could hear her brain almost sighing in exasperation, but did she care?

Not tonight. Not when he was so close.

So, she thought blindly as she felt the warmth of his chest, felt his hands steady her. Catastrophe, here I come.

This felt risky. Really, really risky.

Why risky? Wrong word. If not risky then what was the word for the way he was feeling?

There was no one word, he decided. Meanwhile, he needed to release her, but just for a moment his steadying turned to something more.

What?

Suddenly it felt as if his world was changing. Doors that had slammed shut four years ago were suddenly inching open.

But nothing was said. There was a loaded silence as finally his hands dropped away. There was silence as they moved to the kitchen, put the kettle on, concentrated on the minutiae of toast-making. Settled at the kitchen table as if nothing was between them.

He should make this fast and head to bed, he told himself, fighting to escape sensations he wasn't sure how to deal with. Sensations he had no right to be feeling. Tomorrow would be a heavy day. The repercussions of tonight's baby were going to be far-reaching—and he and Jacob were due to fly to Brisbane in the evening.

Brisbane. The thought made his heart sink. Over and over, they made the journey, with Jacob objecting every step of the way.

'I don't like them crying,' he'd say. 'I don't want to stay in that room any more.'

Neither did he. The thought of his lovely Emma...

No. He wouldn't think of that tonight. He couldn't, because emotions seemed to be heightening by the minute.

Right now he was sitting across the kitchen table, sharing tea and toast with a woman who almost seemed to glow with life. Who made him feel...alive.

She'd been superb tonight. A trained midwife could hardly have done better. That level of support for a woman in labour was surely not in her training, yet she'd stayed, unasked, and he'd felt Anna taking strength from her presence.

'So what's happening next door?' she queried, coming back to the prosaic as she watched him butter her toast. 'More,' she added. 'There's a school of thought that says you should butter your toast lavishly while it's hot, wait until it all melts and then put another butter layer on top. I like that school of thought. Oh, and peanut butter on top of that, please.'

'You're kidding.'

'I would never kid about anything as serious as toast.' She'd made tea and brought mugs to the table, then sat and watched as he followed her toast recipe. Her first bite seemed pure sensual pleasure. 'What?' she demanded. 'You've never watched a woman eat toast before?'

He grinned, but suddenly, through all the other sensations crowding in, there was a jab of memory. Emma. She'd never have layered toast like this—she'd been too health-conscious. A lot of good that had done, though.

'What?' Jen said suddenly. 'What did I say?'

'Nothing.'

'It's your wife, isn't it?' Her voice became gentle. 'You must miss her so much.'

'Four years is a long time.'

'I don't think counting's helpful,' she said, still gently. 'Missing is just…missing.' She watched him for a moment and then obviously decided to return to the events of the night. As a way of alleviating the tension?

'So the Windsors now have a grandson? How did they take the news?'

'Like stunned mullet,' he told her. 'But in a way, subconsciously, maybe they already knew. She's been withdrawn, wearing baggier and baggier clothing, spending time with her books and not her friends. Maybe pregnancy was something they couldn't bear to face, couldn't possibly confront her with. But when you left, when Master Windsor decided he liked his mother's milk, when Anna was almost euphoric with post baby bliss—plus the lingering effectiveness of the drugs—we talked and decided there'd be no better time to bring them into the equation.'

'Primed?' she queried, but sounding like she already knew the answer. 'You talked to them first?'

'Of course. Just to tell them the outline of what she'd told us—she gave me permission. I told them that "How?" didn't come into the equation tonight, and also that I'd promised to stay. The moment I sensed any distress then I'd call a halt.'

'Kick them out, you mean.'

'If I needed to.' He gave a half smile. 'But in the end I didn't. At first they were so shocked they could hardly speak. I could practically see Marjorie summoning the force of her judge-mental ancestors as she headed in, but then she saw Anna, she saw the distress—and then she saw the baby.'

'She folded?'

'She just crumpled,' he said in satisfaction. 'I'd forgotten Marjorie's patient history—two stillborn babies. She looked down at the little one, and then she looked at her own Anna. I could almost see the moment she remembered that this girl was her own baby—and then she started to cry. And the moment she did, Graham caved as well. He, too, crumpled at the sight of the baby in his daughter's arms, and when I left he was muttering, "A son, my Anna has a son!" I could practically see him in the main street tomorrow, up a ladder, repainting the Windsor and Son sign on his shopfront. Tomorrow I suspect they'll also find out all about Tyler. Anger will kick in, but I suspect that anger won't be directed at Anna.'

'You mean, all that secrecy for nothing?'

'Not for nothing.' He'd been thinking it through as he'd watched them. 'If Anna had announced she was pregnant early on, I'm pretty sure their puritanical instincts might have meant anything could have happened. But now…'

'Now they're learning some instincts are stronger than oth-ers.' She beamed. 'Yay for instincts.' She rose to carry her plate to the sink. He rose as well, a bit too fast. She swerved a little and caught her foot on the leg of the chair. He reached out to steady her.

And then let her go?

Well, that was what he should have done. That was what any sane, right-minded male would have…

Um…not. Any sane, right-minded male right here, in the small hours, looking down at this lovely pyjama-clad girl, might have frozen. As he did. His hand stayed on her arm and she looked at it, as if questioning.

And back came all those emotions, all those sensations—or maybe they'd never gone away, just been suppressed.

How long had emotion been suppressed?

She was looking up into his face and, amazingly, she was smiling. Almost laughing.

'Instincts,' she said again. 'They get in the way all the time. Or maybe they don't get in the way. Maybe they just tell us when we're right. Did you know that you're a very nice man, Dr Pierson?' There was a moment's pause and then she said, 'Did you know that right now, also, you're amazingly, astonishingly sexy?'

The room seemed to hush. The whole world seemed to hush. There was a long, long silence while they stood, with his hand on her arm, while she smiled up at him, her teasing smile fading to a slight question.

And then she seemed to collect herself, lifting her arm away, dodging so she could put her plate in the sink. 'Just saying,' she said, almost airily, but there was a sense of breathlessness about her. 'My instincts right now mean I'm probably risking all sorts of rental agreements and putting housemate status at risk. But...'

'But it's only weeks since...'

'Since the Greatest Zigzagged Dinner Suit Incident of the Century? I know.' She had her back to him now, rinsing her plate, even though it surely didn't need rinsing when it was headed for the dishwasher. 'I should still be a soggy heap of humiliation, but somehow I'm getting it in perspective. Or maybe this isn't perspective, the way I'm feeling.' She took a deep breath and turned back to him. 'It's just...this night, the way I'm feeling… You, Rob Pierson, are one amazingly sexy doctor.'

Sexy? The word seemed to take his breath away.

When was the last time he'd felt…sexy?

Testosterone had had no place in his world for four long years. He couldn't let it. He was still Emma's husband, Jacob's father, son-in-law to Lois and Paul.

But right now the adrenaline from the night's drama was still with him, and it was shifting barriers he'd had no intention of moving. He should turn away, get himself to his end of the house, remember that he was Emma's husband, Jacob's father, Lois and Paul's son-in-law.

But he was something else. Someone else. A someone he'd almost forgotten.

He had to steady himself. He had to remember who he really was, who circumstances had forced him to be.

But right now, conscience, sadness, loss were all fading in the presence of this vibrant, smiling woman. She was looking at him with teasing, questioning eyes.

She was looking at him as if…as if he was a man, she was a woman and the night was theirs to do with as they wanted.

And he did want.

So why not? It was surely just…this night?

They both knew the facts. She'd told him of her past, of her humiliation, and she knew his story as well. The whole world knew his story. Every woman he'd ever met looked at him with sympathy, sadness—even sometimes horror.

But not Jenny, at least…not on this night.

This night…

Her face had changed now. The teasing had gone and there was understanding.

'Rob, four years is a long time,' she said, gently into the

night. 'And Rob, I won't intrude. Tell me to back off. It's just…
we're both adults. What I'm feeling now seems pretty right
to me, but I won't be hurt or offended—even not too disap-
pointed—if you tell me the feeling's not reciprocated. I'm not
expecting commitment here, Dr Pierson. I just thought…fun?'

'Fun?'

'Well, maybe a bit more than fun,' she confessed. 'Maybe
warmth and closeness and a bit of human contact we both
seem to be missing at the moment.'

'I…' He closed his eyes.

And in that moment something stirred. Anger? Rebellion?
No.

Fun.

The word was suddenly front and centre. *Fun!*

Maybe that was what this night could be about, he thought.
To take this lovely woman into his arms, to feel her body, to
smile into her laughing eyes…

Fun and so much more.

'You know what?' she managed, and now she sounded almost breathless. 'Your in-laws aren't in my bedroom.'

'Your bedroom?'

'It's the furthest away from Minnie and Jacob,' she said, a
trace of insouciance surfacing again.

'Jen…'

'Don't you dare sound shocked,' she said, her eyes flashing
with anger again. 'It's just… I've watched how lovely you've
been with Anna tonight, how skilled, how gentle, and I've been
thinking of how damned sexy you are. And I just thought, suddenly, in between mouthfuls of toast, that if you and I wanted
to exorcise some demons together it might be fun. So… If a
guy thinks a woman is sexy and interested and free, he might

proposition her. No force, just a gentle enquiry. Does it work both ways or have I offended you to the core?'

Sexy and interested and free? As simple as that.

Was he available? Here, in this house echoing with memories, in this night filled with charged emotion, in the silence where Jacob and Minnie lay sleeping and in this world where Emma still lived, but only her body, not her lovely mind...

Here was this woman. Sexy and interested and free.

Jenny spoke again before he could begin to form a response, but now she sounded as if she was struggling to get the words out. He realised that she'd put herself in an impossible position. The words she'd said couldn't be unsaid.

'So back to our separate ends of the house, Dr Pierson?' she managed. 'That's okay. But you know what? I'm not even going to feel vaguely humiliated. I might go back and cuddle Stumpy a bit more until I'm over it, but there's an end. Don't you dare judge me. If you could kindly move to one side, I'm going to bed.'

He should let her. He should simply stand aside and let her pass.

But she didn't move. She was watching him, her eyes wary, her very stance shouting of defiance. And then he thought... *no. It's not defiance. It's courage.*

He knew her well enough now to have seen through the sorry tale of the zigzagged dinner suit and realised the shattering effect it would have had on her. She'd left her job, her friends, her community because she'd needed to get away. He'd have expected her to curl into a ball of self-protection, yet here she was, exposing herself again. To pain?

To judgement? To yet more humiliation?

She was wearing oversized pink pyjamas with blue penguins on them. She was wiry and tough and defiant. She was competent and...and beautiful.

Soul-searingly beautiful.

She was offering fun. For both of them.

'I think,' he said, slowly now, as if every syllable needed to be carefully considered, 'that I might just have reacted all wrong to your...your very interesting idea.'

'Idea?' she queried. 'So not proposition?'

'Idea,' he said, feeling a little more sure of his ground now. 'Or maybe...ideas.' And then he finally allowed himself to voice the idea that had been in his head from almost the moment he'd seen her inside that damned truck, from the moment he'd seen her risking her life to save one old man and his beloved dog. 'Jenny, I think...the moment I saw you I thought... I felt...'

'Desire?' she ventured when he stopped, because he couldn't figure a way to say what he was feeling without it sounding chauvinistic, primeval, inappropriate.

'I guess,' he said helplessly, and then more strongly, 'yes, desire. Jenny, you're so damned beautiful. But I won't hurt you.'

'Eyes wide open,' she said. Her voice was now a husky whisper and he knew without asking that desire was building in her as well as in him. The very air seemed charged with something he didn't understand—or something he'd forgotten existed. 'We both know that if it's good it might lead to something more, but I'm only here until Pete gets back to work.'

'In three months.'

'Less than that now,' she whispered. 'So...so if things get messy we simply go to being formal housemates.'

'If things get messy?'

'Well, if you fall madly, passionately in love with me it

might happen,' she said, sounding thoughtful. 'I'm not looking at a long-term relationship here, Dr Pierson, and I imagine neither are you.'

Long-term...

He was over long-term, he thought. Four years of grief, of
heartache, of living with the unbearable, and also of facing
the massive judgement of his in-laws, had locked something
deep inside. That was long-term.

But maybe that long-term lock was disintegrating. This
woman in her crazy pyjamas, with her smiling eyes, her voice
saying no strings, her words saying she understood...maybe
she could help him try.

She was so...

'Jenny,' he managed, and his voice felt so thick he struggled
to get the word out.

'I'm here,' she said. And she stretched out her hand and
laid it on his arm.

It was enough. That one gesture was enough to break
through the grief-stricken barriers of the past four long years.
He felt them dissolve, crumple away. He loved Emma, maybe
he always would, but with the crumpling of barriers a new
truth was suddenly there.

This woman was beautiful and she wanted him. Simple as
that. She was standing before him and what she was offering...

A gift beyond price?

Life.

His hand took hers, locking fingers, feeling the warmth,
the firm grip of her decision. His free hand came up to cup
her face. His gaze met hers and locked.

'I'm not sure about you,' she whispered. 'But right now
I'm over over-thinking. I just need to go to bed. You want
to come?'

And how was a man to answer that?

'Jen, are you sure?'

And in answer she stood on her tiptoes. She cupped his face in both her hands and she kissed him. And it was such a kiss... It was deep, warm and sure. It was a kiss of desire, of certainty, an affirmation of something he couldn't even begin to understand.

'I think we're both sure,' she managed when the kiss finally ended, a kiss that had somehow become not her idea, not under her control but somehow something that seemed to have changed something deep within him. So it was no longer Jen kissing and him being kissed, but it was a joining of two passionate people. A man and a woman with mutual desire, mutual need.

Somehow it seemed that things had shattered inside. The future was suddenly gloriously his. His, with this woman before him.

And he laughed, a deep, rumbly chuckle that seemed to come from deep within, a chuckle he'd forgotten he even had. And with that, he swung her up into his arms, this lovely woman with her crazy pyjamas and her glorious hair and her heart so big, her generous wonderful heart...

'Then that's amazing,' he managed, and he kissed her again, deeply, strongly, and then he whirled her around in his arms so that she put her arms around his neck and clung. 'That's truly, fantastically splendiferous, like a dream come true. So speaking of dreams... You're right. Let's go to bed.'

She woke spooned in his arms, her naked back cradled against his chest, and she felt perfect. This was what bliss felt like, she decided, and then she thought no, bliss wasn't strong enough to describe what she was feeling.

It was as if she'd come home.

The night had been long and languorous and wonderful. At some stage, early on, he'd said, 'Four years, you think I might have forgotten?' but even then, as their bodies had found each other, as skin touched skin, as sensations burned, the thought of skills forgotten were...well, forgotten.

She'd thought the intensity might be too much, that the mating might be fierce and needful for them both, but instead there'd been wonder. A slow exploration of emotion as well as physical need. Touching, tasting, savouring. Lovemaking that had her feeling right now that she was where she was meant to be, where she wanted to be more than anything in the world.

And that thought had to be crazy. This was surely a one-night stand, or at least a temporary pleasure. For heaven's sake, she'd practically seduced him. Maybe she *had* seduced him, using his body as a way to finally rid herself of the humiliation of Darren.

In her mind, in the beginning, that was what she'd told herself what she was doing. Lovemaking as a cure for them both. She knew he was hurting and she hated that he was.

But there was more. She'd seen his skill, his gentleness and his empathy with his small son, with his patients, with Anna— and added to those admittedly very desirable attributes, she'd unashamedly admired the sheer physicality. There'd been desire there, she admitted to herself, and now...rather than that desire being sated...

She wanted to stay where she was for the rest of her life!

But then her phone buzzed into life and she could have cried. They both had their phones by the bedside—of course they did—they were both medical professionals and calls didn't necessarily stop because...well, because both medical professionals were thoroughly sated after a night of pure, un-adulterated lust.

Rob woke and sighed as she pulled away, and as she answered the call his hands stayed on her waist. Not breaking the connection.

Please don't let it be a callout, she told herself. Please...

'Jen?'

Frankie.

'Hey,' she said, thinking she should have looked at caller ID before she'd answered. A call from a friend could have been put off.

'You busy?'

'Sort of.'

There was a moment's hesitation. Frankie knew her well.

'You sound half asleep. You're not at work?'

'Um...no. Is this urgent? Can I call you back?'

But maybe Frankie knew her too well. 'You're with someone!' she said in a tone of delight. 'Aren't you?'

'Frankie!'

'Hey, I'm going. But you have to ring and tell me everything. I wanted to talk dog, but it can wait. Eight o'clock in the morning, huh?' She could hear the grin in Frankie's voice. 'There's no urgency, I just had a moment and thought I'd check in. Now I'm very glad I did. You go, girl, right back to what you were doing.'

And the phone went dead.

Yikes. She was now in for an interrogation that'd be no holds barred. She slumped back on the pillows and Rob's arms tightened.

'Sprung,' he said, and she could hear the smile in his voice. He was so close he'd have heard what Frankie had said. 'But... did she say eight?'

'She did.'

The arms were withdrawn a little and he pushed himself up. 'What the...?'

But she was still holding her phone, and on the screen was an unread message. Almost subconsciously, she flicked it through. It was from Minnie.

Jacob and I are heading out for donuts and hot chocolate, and then I'll drop him off at childcare. Stumpy's been out to the lawn and fed. I just popped through to the hospital and everything's peaceful. If I'm right, Rob doesn't have clinic until ten so I'm praying neither of you gets a callout. Enjoy yourselves.

She held it up for Rob to see. He stared at it in bewilderment and then reached for his own phone.

A matching message.

'Did you and Minnie...?' he said slowly as he stared at the screen '...set me up?'

She chuckled at that, because there was no anger in his voice, not even a trace. Instead she heard the beginnings of laughter.

It made her feel...delicious?

'No such thing,' she declared. 'But maybe...well, she did seem to sense that I thought you were sexy.'

'You thought that?' Their phones were tossed aside. He rolled over so he was looking down into her eyes and the desire she could read there was unmistakable. 'You didn't know for sure?'

'Okay, now I'm sure.' She was feeling so good, so lucky. This man was beautiful, and this seemed so right. 'And maybe she did just mention that it's been four long years since your wife died, so maybe it's time...'

And then she paused. His expression had changed. 'What?' she said, bewildered.

'Jen?'

He was still above her, looking down, but the desire had gone. What was in his face now—what? A blankness? Something she had no hope of recognising.

'Mmm?' Something was really wrong. What had she said?

He rolled away and sat up, putting distance, even if only half a pillow's length between them.

'Jen,' he said again, and his voice dragged.

'What?'

'I don't know how... I have no idea. But Jen, Emma isn't dead.'

He told her then, sitting up in bed, a pillow's length apart, the covers pulled up over her breasts because distance suddenly seemed desirable. There'd been a lurch at those first words, the sickening recognition of the feeling she'd had, what, only a couple of months back, when Darren had walked into their hotel room and said, 'My wife is here. You need to leave.'

The sensation was different now, but the emptiness was the same. Only moments ago her world had felt steady and right and wonderful, but now... There was no steadiness here.

'Four years.' Rob's voice was deadpan, expressionless, telling a story that seemed like a recording in his head. 'The haemorrhage caused by the eclampsia was catastrophic, causing irreversible brain damage. Jacob was born at thirty-two weeks and Emma never saw him. For weeks we held onto a desperate hope that there might be something—anything...

but nothing. Finally we removed the tracheostomy tube—and then she breathed.'

'By herself?' Her voice was tiny.

'Just for moments.' Still his voice was dead. 'And then…' He closed his eyes. 'Then it ceased, but suddenly Em's mother was screaming at them to put it back in, to help her, to not let it end. And her dad joined in and all I could do was stand back while they made the decision to let their daughter live.'

'You mean…keep their daughter breathing?' There was a difference. She'd been a medical professional for long enough to recognise the scenario. An almost perfect life—perfect apart from one thing. The lack of brain activity. The decision to turn off life support must be soul-searing. 'Oh, Rob…'

'But that was four years ago,' he said, still in that blank, withdrawn voice. 'There's been nothing since, no life, no stimulus response, peg feeding, clear evidence of massive brain damage. But they won't accept it. Lois and Paul are incredibly wealthy, both professional lawyers at the top of their game, and in their grief they can't accept that she's gone. They moved her into a private hospital, they arranged round-the-clock nursing and they've moved heaven and earth to keep her alive. So for almost two years I stayed, caring for Jacob but surrounded by grief and loss and a waiting that could go on for ever.'

She couldn't speak. There seemed nothing she could find to say.

'They wanted Jacob there all the time,' he said, and it was as if repeating a story he knew by heart. '"Jacob's our daughter's baby," Lois kept saying. "If anything can bring her back, the feel of him, the sound of him will do it. She's not dead and her baby needs to be with her." And when I fought it they fought me. Because of that stupid moment when Em signed over medical power of attorney, they applied for her guard-

ianship. I've had to fight to get that reversed—and also fight
to reverse the half and half custody arrangement they put in
place between me and Emma.'

She stared up, confused and stunned. 'So that's why...'
Things were starting to make sense now. Sort of. 'They demanded half and half custody when she's...'

'In this country equal shared custody is normal when parents split,' he told her. 'They simply formalised it when I was
too grief-stricken to realise. When I finally surfaced, when I
realised Jacob could never have a normal life unless I fought
for him, I had to take them to court. I won but they hate me
for it.'

He sighed. 'So...the arrangement now is that I take him
to Brisbane once a month. That's okay because...well, I still
need to see Em myself. I would have built our life there until
she...well, I would have liked to be closer. But there's no half
measures for Lois and Paul. They take Jacob and sit in that
dreadful room and tell him over and over that Mummy loves
him, that Mummy will wake one day. But hush, they tell him,
and don't touch Mummy, except maybe stroke her hand, but
no playing here, nothing. Her room is filled with medical paraphernalia, but it's a place of reverence.'

'But for a baby?' she whispered, horrified, and he grimaced.

'Yeah, not appropriate, or not long-term. By the time he
was old enough to register where he was being taken, Jacob
was sobbing every time we got near, but if Lois and Paul had
control that'd be every day. In the end the only way forward
seemed to be to bring him back here. Em and I both loved
Willhua, and here he has the chance to be...just a kid.'

Whoa. She felt as if her breath had been sucked right out
of her. Their lovemaking had been light and free, but now
the ghost of a not-dead wife was suddenly all around them.

The idea of a little boy being forced to sit in such a vigil. The thought of Rob with such a load to bear.

The joy of the night had disappeared as if it had never been, and there seemed no way it could come back. This was too heavy. Too much.

And all at once she thought, *I'm not old enough for this. Not wise enough. I don't have the courage to face this.*

'I thought you knew,' Rob was saying. 'Everyone here knows. I just assumed…'

'People talked about your tragedy,' she whispered. 'I guess… I assumed…death.'

'And it makes a difference,' he said—and it wasn't a question.

But it was a question to Jen. It shouldn't make a difference, she thought. Or should it? Part of her wanted to turn now, take this man in her arms and assure him that it made no difference at all. That the sex and laughter and the pure, free joy of the night could be resumed, just like that.

But this was too big. Too huge.

Maybe it was the shock, the echoes of Darren's betrayal. Maybe it was some sort of inexplicable moral barrier, the thought of Emma lying in a coma while she lay with her husband.

Maybe it was cowardice?

Whatever, all she knew right now was that she needed space. This was doing her head in.

And Rob knew.

'Jen, I'm so sorry,' he told her. 'If I'd guessed… But even if you'd gone into it knowing, I should never have…'

'You think it's wrong?' she whispered, watching his face. 'There's part of you that thinks being with me is…a betrayal?'

'No. I…' He paused and shook his head, as if struggling

to find words. 'Jen, I don't know what to think. I loved Em. I still do. When I see her now there's grief, but it's like visiting a shrine. The difference is that instead of a monument there's a living, breathing woman.'

'I can see that.' She put her hand on his face and said gently, 'Rob, I'm sorry. I'm so, so sorry.' But her feelings were threatening to overwhelm her. She was close to tears, but the last thing Rob needed was weeping. She had to get away. 'Rob... I... I need to take a shower. I need...'

'To back off? Of course you do.'

And there was nothing she could say to deny it. There was just...nothing.

'I'm so sorry,' she whispered again. 'But I need to go.'

CHAPTER EIGHT

SHE FELT SHATTERED.

There was a part of her, the cowardly part, that wanted to do exactly what she'd done after Darren's betrayal. Pull up stumps and leave this whole complicated mess. Deal with the confusion in her heart by running. To do so, though, would be hurtful, a declaration that somehow she'd been betrayed.

And she hadn't. She stood under the shower and forced her mind to replay every conversation she'd ever had with anyone about this man, everything he'd ever said to her.

About the tragedy that was Emma.

Those first days on the job had been frantic. The first time she'd worked alongside Gary had been the night of the truck accident. It had been intense, tragic, lurching her from knowing little about her working partners to being involved up to her ears.

Gary had spoken to her briefly about Rob, but in those first meetings there'd been no opportunity to delve into Rob's personal life. To do so then would have seemed…creepy? Certainly less than respectful.

If she'd started work on the Monday to normal activity, if things had been less frenetic, Gary would probably have given her the lowdown on the town and its inhabitants. He surely would have told her then about Rob's background. But that first night had catapulted her from being an outsider to being

Rob's housemate. From that night on, Gary would simply have assumed she knew.

And Rob? Same thing. This was a small town. Everyone knew everyone's business. He'd spoken briefly about the tragedy. She'd wondered why his in-laws had such ongoing influence, she'd been astounded that he'd worry they could apply for custody, but he'd never lied. He'd just assumed...

Stupid, stupid, stupid, she told herself. To assume that here was a gorgeous, sexy man with a perfect little son who was...

Ripe for the taking?

She'd practically seduced him.

She felt herself cringing as she stood under the steaming water. Her actions the night before now seemed totally inappropriate.

Why? Because Emma wasn't dead.

Because Rob was still legally married.

Maybe this was Darren's legacy, she told herself. Maybe the humiliation of finding out about her boss's wife was still with her.

Or maybe she was imagining Emma.

The walls seemed to be closing in on her. She was being stupid, she told herself. No one had lied to her. She'd thought Emma was dead, but wasn't she? Brain death was surely death, even if the body kept functioning. There was no need for shame or humiliation, or even regret.

But she did feel these things.

Finally she dried and dressed and headed for the laundry. Stumpy was fast asleep—she was healing nicely but she was quite happy to be woken and hugged.

'Dogs are safer,' she whispered into her overlarge ears. 'Dogs are far less complicated. If your bed here was a little bit bigger I might even be tempted to join you.'

* * *

And Rob?

He headed back to his end of the house and did exactly the same thing. He hit the shower.

He felt ill.

Last night had been almost miraculous. A magic sliver of rainbow in a life that for the last few years had seemed an unbroken grey. Jenny's smile, her laughter, her body, her unadulterated joy in their joining—for a while during the night he'd thought this could be what life might be like. There could be a future without this overwhelming sense of loss and betrayal.

Because betrayal was all around him now. Emma was still a warm, living being, his wife, the mother of his son. He hadn't made it clear to Jenny that she was still alive. He'd just assumed.

How could he possibly have assumed something so important? He had no right. He'd seen the shock on Jenny's face and he'd thought…*she's feeling betrayed.*

Had he betrayed Em? Had he betrayed both women?

When could he let go? Never.

Last night, as he'd held Jenny in his arms, the years of bleakness had faded. He'd…loved.

Loved? It was a strong word, surely too strong after only two short weeks, but she was gorgeous, clever, strong, funny—a way forward?

A way out of this grey fog he lived in?

Was it no accident that Jenny hadn't realised Em was still alive? Taking her to bed, loving her, had that been a lie on his part? A betrayal to both women?

This was doing his head in. He needed to get out of the shower and go talk to her. Damn that he and Jacob were due to fly to Brisbane tonight. It was the worst possible timing.

Or maybe it was the best. It'd give them both time and space to come to terms with…

With reality. That he was still married. That he couldn't move on, that he was trapped in a life he couldn't begin to understand.

So much for rainbows, he told himself as he dried and dressed and readied himself for the day.

Rainbows were fleeting, an ephemeral illusion.

So was the idea of loving Jenny.

They met over breakfast. Jen was wearing her paramedic uniform. She looked clean, fit—lovely. She was sitting at the table spreading marmalade on her toast when he entered.

'Good morning. There's coffee in the pot.' As a first approach into a morning-after conversation it wasn't exactly helpful, but it was something.

'Jen, I'm so sorry.'

'There's nothing to be sorry for,' she said. 'Or maybe there is. I'm sorry for you, sorry for Jacob, sorry for this whole situation, but you don't need to apologise to me.' And then she looked up from her toast and attempted a smile. 'I had a very nice time, thank you, Dr Pierson. You make a great lay.'

He hadn't known what to expect, but it wasn't this. The teasing laughter was back in her eyes. Maybe it was a shield, he thought, but if so it was a very good shield. And it was a shield she was asking him to share.

'Thank you,' he managed, mock modest, and she chuckled. And then she looked ruefully down into the jar she was holding. 'I appear to have finished your marmalade. Sorry, Dr Pierson, but you're on Vegemite. I should have saved you some but…' she sighed, mock theatrically '…but I didn't. So now you know. I'm not good at sharing. Bed for one night is great, but any more than that... Not a good idea.'

And she met his gaze and held. There was a long silence while all sorts of things were unsaid but present for all that.

'Not?' he said at last.

'Not,' she repeated, and was it his imagination or did her voice tremble a little? And then she shrugged and her voice became serious. 'Rob, this isn't a situation I can face. I don't have the courage. A one-night fling might be great—it was great—but let's leave it there.'

He nodded. Courage... It'd take more than that to move into a relationship with him, he thought.

A relationship?

He was married. Emma still lived. What had he been thinking?

'But don't you dare feel bad about it,' she said, the bounce returning to her voice. She stood up, toast in hand. 'You know, I'm betting your Emma wouldn't begrudge you last night one bit. I wouldn't if I was her. So no guilt, from either of us. You're going to Brisbane tonight?'

'I...yes. We drive to Sydney and then fly.'

'It's a pain of a trip.'

'We're used to it. Angus is on call while I'm away. Have you met him yet? He's great—he was the family doctor here for thirty years. He's in his seventies, but trying to retire to potter in his veggie garden. He took over again during...in the years after Jacob was born and he looks after things now when I need to be away.' He was talking too fast, he thought. Trying to drive away the emotions of the morning.

The feeling of shame?

Shame. Was that what this was? Shame for loving this

woman last night. Shame for enjoying her body when Emma was still…

'Don't!' What was it about her that made her guess what he was feeling? She put down her toast and stepped forward so she was standing right in front of him, hands on hips. 'Don't you dare analyse last night, make it something it wasn't. It was two adults having fun, nothing more and nothing less. So put it behind you and go to Brisbane.'

'How did you know…?'

'Let's call it a good guess,' she told him and then she put her hands on his shoulders, raised herself on her toes and kissed him on the mouth, but very lightly, a feather touch, no more.

'You're a very nice man, Dr Pierson,' she said as the kiss ended. 'And, as I said, you're a very good lay. It was a lovely night, but that's all it was. Now, I'm thinking you need to eat your breakfast and go see some patients. I hope Anna and her little one are okay this morning. Meanwhile, Gary and I are scheduled to bring Moira Gardner home from Whale Head. Apparently her hip operation was a resounding success—you know she's booked in here for a couple of days' aftercare? You'll still be here this afternoon to admit her? Great. So we're both busy and it's time for us to move on.'

And then she gave a fierce little nod, as if she was cementing something into her mind.

Then she picked up her toast and departed.

CHAPTER NINE

WORK WAS HER SALVATION, and she was lucky because Friday was busy.

By the time she returned to the house that night Rob and Jacob had left. 'They'll be back Monday morning,' Minnie told her when she walked in. It was almost six o'clock. Minnie was taking a lasagne to the oven, and the smell made her feel like she...well, like she was home. But this wasn't her home. This weekend was time out from a situation she didn't know how to deal with.

'You shouldn't be here,' she told Minnie. 'I can look after myself.'

'I thought you might be up for a home-cooked meal,' the older woman told her. 'By the look on Rob's face as he left... well, he always looks strained when he leaves, but this afternoon it was another level. I'm hoping you're not feeling the same.'

'A bit,' she admitted and then thought...why not say it like it was? Minnie had practically played the part of matchmaker here. It was surely appropriate to be honest. 'I hadn't realised Emma was still alive,' she said, and she knew she couldn't keep pain and shock from her voice.

'Oh, my dear.' The woman's face crumpled and she put the lasagne down on the table as if it was suddenly far too heavy. 'Oh, my dear! Oh, for heaven's sake, how...?'

'I have no idea. But it…makes a difference.'

'It does.' Minnie sat, suddenly looking every day of her seventy-odd years. 'I thought…we all assumed… I mean, the whole town knows the story.'

'Yeah,' she said bitterly, and headed for the fridge. 'Wine?'

'Yes,' Minnie said definitely. 'My dear, does it make a difference?'

'You must see that it does.'

'I can't imagine he concealed it deliberately,' she ventured. 'If that's any help. It's no secret.'

'No. He told no lies. It's just…' She shook her head. 'It makes things way too complicated in my head.'

'And those in-laws of his make things so much worse,' Minnie ventured. 'They can't get away from their grief and they expect Rob to stay in the same state of perpetual mourning. Speaking of in-laws…'

'Are we speaking of in-laws?'

'Well, parents,' Minnie said and smiled, a sort of sideways smile that said this was an obvious attempt to change the subject. 'You should see Anna's parents.'

'The Windsors? They're not giving Anna a hard time, are they?'

'The opposite.' Minnie relaxed. 'Rob had them in his clinic this morning and talked to them for ages. And when they came out Marjorie went straight to the baby shop. I hear she practically bought the place out of everything blue, and Graham drove to Whale Head to buy a cot and a pram because nothing here was good enough. And they're telling the world that their grandson has arrived, as if they've been counting the days for the last eight months, and Marjorie already has a phone full of baby pictures. Things could have gone the op-

posite way, but now…thanks to Rob…and to you…they've
decided to go with pride.'

'Well, good for them,' she managed, and she knew, she just
knew, that Rob would have told them of his own background.
Despite her confusion, the muddle in her own heart, she found
herself smiling. Feeling…pride? Pride in Rob?

She had no right to feel pride, she told herself. He was nothing to do with her. A colleague. A landlord. A one-night stand?

'So what will you do now?' Minnie asked tentatively and
she thought…what?

'I'll go and see Anna.'

'That's lovely. Rob said to tell you she's been asking for
you. But after that?'

'I have no idea.' She sighed and sat down. 'Lasagne first.
Anna second. And then…maybe a weekend on my own to
figure where to take things from here?'

And then the weekend seemed to take on a life of its own.
Angus took over in the hospital. She met him on Saturday
morning and instantly liked him, an elderly doctor who looked
more like a gardener than a medic.

'I keep my registration current, just to give Rob a break,'
he told her when she met him finishing a ward round. 'But I
miss my garden. Just lucky the ground's waterlogged after all
this rain, or I'd be suffering withdrawal.'

She and Gary were at the hospital to collect Olivia Hoffman
and take her home. Olivia had had a fall a couple of days back.
The ninety-six-year-old had been waiting until her daughter
could clear her schedule to come and stay with her, but her
seventy-five-year-old daughter wasn't confident about driving
her mum along the winding cliff road to her farm.

'They look about as old as each other,' Jen commented as Gary finished tucking both women into the ambulance.

'It's this place,' Angus said. 'You don't age, you just sort of pickle. The salt wind does that to you, like herrings.' He motioned to Olivia's daughter. 'Hildy's on the hospital board, she's a volunteer at the charity shop and she takes part-time care of her three grandchildren. Olivia's only just retired from the charity shop as well. That's what I intend to look like at ninety-six too,' he told her. 'This is such a great place to grow old. So you've been here for two weeks. Ready to put down roots yet?'

With that he met her gaze, his look kindly but a little quiz-zical. And Jen wondered just how much talk there was already about a young female paramedic moving into the doctor's house.

'It's far too soon to tell,' she said, a bit too brusquely, and he nodded, his look a bit too understanding for her liking.

'It takes courage to move into a whole new situation,' he said gently. 'But they tell me you abseiled down a cliff to try and save Charlie Emerson. A woman like that…she'd have courage for anything.'

'Not anything.'

'Maybe not.' He hesitated. 'It's women,' he said slowly, as if he was thinking it through. 'I've just been talking to Anna in there, holding her baby but declaring she'll sit her exams because she's darned if she'll waste all of the study she's been doing this year. And when her dad said, "Why not wait a year, let things settle?" Marjorie flashed at him, "Let what settle? Everything's settled already." Women,' he said again. 'Cour-age in spades. And you…abseiling, taking on the role of Will-hua paramedic…' His voice softened still further. 'And maybe you and Rob?'

'Has Minnie been talking to you?' she demanded, hands on hips.

'Maybe,' he said. 'Minnie and I go back a long way, and Minnie's feeling bad.'

'She shouldn't feel bad.'

'She's worried that you'll leave.'

She sighed, thinking that'd be the easy option. But she'd signed up for the three-month stint. To leave now...

'I'll stay working,' she told Angus. 'But...'

'But the rest is none of my business?'

'I wish it wasn't *my* business,' she told him and then she thought of Rob and Emma, and the situation with Jacob and his in-laws, and the whole tragic mess. 'From now on... I can't see how it can be.'

The call on Sunday morning was to Ruth Corben, a sixty-year-old woman who bred alpacas on a small farm a couple of kilometres inland. On her distressed call she'd said she'd suffered a fall and had struggled to reach her phone. She was still on the floor.

'She's been suffering from myelofibrosis,' Gary told Jen on the way there. 'She was diagnosed about four years ago. It's a bugger.'

Jen knew the condition, a rare form of chronic leukaemia that caused disruption of normal production of blood cells. Left unchecked it could cause severe anaemia, with associated weakness and fatigue. It could simmer for years, but flare-ups had to be treated fast to avoid the leukaemia transforming to acute.

The thought of Ruth lying alone on the farmhouse floor, was enough for speed, lights and sirens, and when they got there they both wished they could have got there faster. Ruth was crumpled on the kitchen floor, weeping with pain and with frustration. By the look of her face, she'd been weeping for a while.

'I tripped on the back step,' she told them. 'And I couldn't get up. It took me so long to crawl back in here and get the phone off the table.'

'Which is why Rob asked you to wear the alarm,' Gary scolded, his tone not hiding his anxiety. He was feeling her pulse while Jen did a fast visual examination. 'What hurts?'

'Everything hurts. And I don't need it! Stupid thing.'

'You do need it, Ruth! What hurts?'

'Nothing. Everything. My ankle. I must have twisted it when I fell. But I haven't even fed the animals yet. I have ten alpacas,' she said, looking helplessly up at Jen. 'And Betty's pregnant and Bosun needs me.'

They'd already met Bosun, a gorgeous young border collie who'd raced out to meet them and then raced back to his mistress. Now he was lying flat on the floor a few feet back, crouched as if in readiness to…save his mistress? But he seemed to be almost quivering in anxiety. Did he know they were there to help?

'I'll just need another iron transfusion,' Ruth managed. 'Could you ring Rob? He'll tell you. If you could just help me feed everyone, then you could take me down to the hospital and I'll be home by dinner. Betty's almost due to give birth. I have to stay.'

'Angus's on call this weekend,' Gary told her. 'And I know what he'll say.' He gave Jen a fleeting glance that was information all by itself. He'd been feeling her pulse, listening to her heart, and they'd both seen the greyish tinge to her face that said this wasn't all about a fall. 'There's no way he'll let you come home to be alone tonight. Is there anyone you can call?'

'My daughter's overseas,' she whispered, more distressed. 'I told her to go, don't worry about me. She and her husband have been saving for years. They're in Venice and I won't let you worry her. Please…ring Rob. He knows how important it is for me to stay home.'

There was a moment's silence while Gary considered. Jen stayed in the background, organising injections for pain. Gary knew this woman, he knew the situation.

'Give Rob a call,' Gary told Jen at last. 'On speaker. Ruth, will you do what he says?' He nodded to Jen. 'Rob won't mind you ringing—he'd want us to contact him. Angus will concur. Rob's been there for Ruth…'

'Since I got this damned thing,' Ruth whispered. 'He knows how important it is that my daughter has a holiday. I have to stay here.'

So while Gary worked on, Jen rang Rob. He answered almost on the first ring. 'Jen?'

And what was there in that to make her heart clench? The way he said her name. As if he needed it to be her?

Where was he? By Emma's side? With his in-laws? This was doing her head in.

'Rob, Gary and I are with Ruth Corben,' she told him, trying to make her voice practical, professional. 'You're on speaker so we're all listening. Ruth's had a fall. The only obvious damage we can see this early is her ankle, which we hope is just twisted, but she didn't have the strength to get herself up. It seems to have taken her over an hour to get to the phone. What she wants is a quick trip to hospital, an iron infusion and to be brought home again tonight. She's listening now. Would you have time to talk to her or should we ring back when we have her down in Willhua?'

'I'm not going anywhere until I've talked to Rob,' Ruth

said, starting to weep again. The long wait on the floor must have frightened her to the stage where she was acting purely on instinct. 'Rob, please tell them. I can't go. All I need is some iron.'

'Could you wait just a moment?' Rob said quietly. 'I need to step outside where it's quiet. Jen, can you put the phone near Ruth?'

What followed was a wait, interrupted by a muted, muffled announcement…

'Could the owner of a Mercedes parked in the ambulance bay please report to Reception immediately?'

He must be in hospital, Jen thought, recognising the sound of an intercom. Emma's hospital? She closed her eyes, and when she opened them Gary was watching her. With sympathy?

Already? Had word got around so fast? Or was it clearly obvious how she was feeling towards this man?

But when Rob came back on the line he was professional, kind, firm, definite. The phone was still on speaker but he was speaking only to Ruth.

'Ruth, you had an iron infusion two weeks ago,' he told her. 'And the one before that was recent too. You know we talked this through, and we talked to Ben, your oncologist in Sydney. He said then that you'll need a blood transfusion and tests to see if another round of chemotherapy is called for. I'd like to ring him now to tell him to expect you.'

'But I can't go to Sydney,' Ruth stammered. 'You know I can't.'

'And you know the alternative,' Rob said, his voice becoming even more gentle. 'Come on, Ruth. Lorraine and Peter are overseas right now having a babymoon. Your first grandchild's due in three months. You want to miss that?'

'No, I…'

'Of course you don't. Ruth, your grandbaby needs you. Your alpacas need you and so does Bosun. So you want to live, but you need to accept what's necessary to make that happen.'

'If you tell me what to do, I can feed the alpacas before we go,' Jen offered. 'At least, I think I can. Is it complicated?'

'Just…hay.'

'Well, I can heave hay bales with the best of them. You said Betty's pregnant. Is Betty an alpaca?'

'Yes, I need to check her. And Bosun…'

'I'm already looking after one dog,' Jen told her. 'Why not two? And I'm trained in home births. How different can an alpaca be? I don't mind coming up here to check and feed them until someone else can take over. If your doctor says you don't need chemo you might be home in a couple of days.'

There was silence from all of them. Gary was looking at her, his brows raised. Ruth was staring at her as if she was… her best hope? And Rob… Who knew what he was thinking, but it was Rob who broke the silence first.

'There you go, Ruth. Problem sorted for today. Gary and Jen will take you down to Willhua, Angus will make sure you're stable and we'll organise a transfer to Sydney. I'll be back tomorrow. I'll ring you and Ben, and we'll sort something permanent then.'

'Permanent?' Ruth whispered.

'Until you're strong again,' Rob told her. 'If you accept our advice and help, I know you will be.'

He disconnected and headed back to Emma's ward. Emma's shrine. That was how it felt, how it had felt for years. He walked in and Lois had put Jacob back on Emma's bed, forcing his hand to stroke his mother's. Or what had been his mother.

The pallid, lifeless figure under the perfect bedding seemed almost a ghost of what had been his Emma.

Jacob had that stoic look. He was used to this, a ritual where his grandparents insisted he sit on his mother's bed, but he hated it. What four-year-old would sit reverently beside someone…who wasn't there?

There was a basket of building blocks and random toys in the corner. Whenever Rob was in the room he was allowed to play with them, but Lois wanted a connection between Jacob and his mother.

But the slight, still figure in the bed had no connection left to give. Rob's heart clenched, as it did every time he saw her. His beautiful Emma.

How dare they leave her like this?

But anger didn't help, and he fought it down as he'd done for years. It wasn't their fault they couldn't get past their grief, and anger didn't help. But Jacob was looking up at him and wriggling forcefully, until finally he was permitted to get down.

'I want to home,' he said fiercely to his father. 'Daddy, can we go home?'

'Home should be here,' Lois said almost as fiercely, and Rob's anger was tempered, as it always was, by the knowledge that Lois was struggling, as she always did, to hold back tears. Lois was here alone this weekend—it seemed Paul was away on business. 'He'll be back on Monday,' Lois had told them, unable to keep bitterness from her voice. 'Unlike you, he'll never stay away from our Emma for long. Rob, please make Jacob sit back on the bed.'

'We're going for an ice cream,' Rob told her as Jacob's chin wobbled toward mutiny. 'We'll be back in half an hour.'

'You know the court says we control what happens on our access weekend.'

She was right. Legally, it was Emma who had control, and her unbreakable power of attorney meant that Lois and Paul were her voice. The more Rob fought it, the more obsessive they became.

Grief did appalling things to people. He knew it and he tried his best to make allowances, but this was impossible. So far, all his legal challenges had achieved was the agreement that when Jacob was with his mother, Rob would be there too.

Right now he could insist Jacob leave with him but he'd learned there were easier ways.

'We both know that's true, Lois,' he said gently. 'But I'm about to buy an ice cream and eat it downstairs. Are you saying you want me to leave Jacob here with you and have my ice cream by myself?'

Lois looked at Jacob and had the sense to know that Rob walking out would lead to a full-scale meltdown.

'Half an hour,' she whispered.

'You could join us.'

'Not when I can stay here. Someone has to.'

CHAPTER TEN

AN HOUR LATER Jen walked through into the back yard of the doctor's residence, and unclipped Bosun's lead. To alleviate Ruth's distress they'd brought the collie back with them in the ambulance. Ruth had hugged him all the way, but now Angus had her in his care.

Ruth's ankle was being X-rayed and stabilised, and the chopper from South Sydney Air Rescue was due to pick her up in an hour. Gary and Jen would be needed then to take her the short distance to the football field where the chopper would land, but until then Jen had time to settle. And introduce Bosun to Stumpy.

This was some imposition, she thought. One dog became two in the house. But Rob had heard her make the offer on the phone and hadn't objected.

There'd be so much going on in his life that one more dog could hardly make a difference, she thought, and Bosun was gorgeous. Beautifully trained, quiet, subdued—well, of course he would be—he still reacted to a rub behind the ears with a cautious tail wag. And when Stumpy limped out of the laundry to meet him, the two dogs did mutual nose and tail sniffing and then started a slow perambulation of the yard.

It was almost as if Stumpy was showing Bosun around, Jen thought, and smiled to see them. The continued effort to find any of Charlie's friends or family who'd want her had proved fruitless, but after two weeks Jen was starting to hope they'd never find anyone. Stumpy was still subdued, but she was warm and cuddly, and more and more Jen was treating her as a trusted confidante.

'Look after each other, you guys,' she told them, and headed inside. She needed lunch before she was needed for the chopper transfer. She walked through to the kitchen—and stopped dead. A stranger was sitting at the kitchen table.

The man was immaculately groomed, in what she recognised as the casual clothes of the upper classes—crisp chinos, brand name loafers, a classy shirt with a discreet woven logo and a bomber jacket she'd seen in advertisements that fleetingly appeared on her social media forays—but only fleetingly because social media algorithms seemed somehow to recognise paramedics' salaries.

And the man himself? He was in his sixties, with silver fox hair, tanned complexion and blue eyes that seemed…cautious.

He was cautious? This man was sitting at *her* kitchen table, she told herself. She needed to remind herself of that, because she'd realised who he must be.

She paid rent. This man didn't, but he still had a place in this house. In the formal living room there was photo after photo of a baby, a small girl, a teenager growing to womanhood. Emma with her two parents, and one of them was this man.

This was Emma's father.

'Mr…' She stopped. She didn't know his surname, she realised.

She didn't know anything. She was so out of her depth.

'I've been waiting for two hours,' he said, his tone letting her know he was displeased.

Keep it light, she told herself. What use was conflict, and this man had lost…was losing?…his daughter.

'Were you waiting for me? I had no idea. Sorry, but I've been working,' she told him, making a slight gesture to her uniform. It helped, she decided, having it on. It made her feel professional, as if this guy could be just a problem patient.

'Ah, yes,' he said, still sounding irritated. 'Tony tells me you work for the ambulance service.'

'Tony?' She thought of the guy watching them in the playground. 'The guy in the car?'

'Tony Lester. He's a security agent. We pay him to keep an eye on our grandson, on our daughter's behalf.'

'Really?' She was having trouble here, but the last thing needed was escalation to anger. 'I can't imagine why that's necessary—Rob seems such a good dad, but I guess that's not my business. I'm only a tenant. Would you like a cup of tea? Lunch?'

'No, thank you.'

'But you wanted to see me?'

'Tony told me about you.'

'Really?' She hesitated and then forged on. 'Sorry, but I need to eat,' she said, and headed for the refrigerator. 'I'm on a fast break from work.'

There was method in what she was doing. If she made herself a sandwich while she talked it'd give her something to do with her hands. Also she could turn her back on him, giving her space to catch her breath. 'So what…what can I do for you?'

'Lois and I have decided you need to be spoken to without Rob's interference.'

Whoa. There was so much in that sentence that she felt winded. She didn't turn from the fridge, though, just found the sliced bread, retrieved two slices and started buttering. What would she put in her sandwich? Who cared?

'Could you look at me, please?' he said.

'I'm on my lunch break. I have a patient transfer in thirty minutes. I need to eat and run.'

'What I have to say is important.'

'So's my patient's life. Her transfer is urgent.'

'Is her life more important than my daughter's?'

That brought her around. She swivelled and stared blankly at him. 'What…what on earth do you mean?'

'My daughter's marriage is important to her.' And his voice suddenly cracked—with grief? With anger? She could hardly differentiate. 'What's happening now…if she found out about you…it could kill her.'

'Do I have it wrong?' she whispered. 'Emma's been in an unresponsive coma for four years. No?'

And his face twisted, grief and anger combined. 'You don't have permission to use her name!'

Whoa.

But, strangely, this helped, for suddenly Jen found herself slipping into medical mode.

For four years this man and his wife had kept watch over a beloved daughter, had refused to let her go. What was happening now…he sounded on the edge of sanity.

And with that realisation, professional training kicked in. There was no use escalating a conflict here. There was no use trying to reason. She had to do whatever was needed to de-escalate.

'No,' she said, meeting his gaze head-on. 'I don't have your permission. I apologise.'

'I need you to do more than that. I need you to leave.'

'That's tricky,' she said, still quietly. 'I'm not sure what Tony told you, but I rent a room here from the hospital board. This is a hospital house, for hospital medics.'

'It's my daughter's house.'

She nodded, still carefully calm. 'I can understand that's how it must feel.'

'And you have no place here. Not with my grandson, and not with *him*.' And he said *him* with such a mix of emotion that she physically flinched.

But it still wasn't her place to escalate anger. This wasn't about her. It was Rob who had to face this situation over and over. He'd have to negotiate this anger...for the rest of his life?

This situation was beyond her and suddenly she knew it. She'd known Rob for what, two weeks? The shock of finding Emma was alive was still with her and, logical or not, it had piled on the humiliation of Darren's betrayal. There could be no comparison, yet her bruised heart was struggling to come to terms with both.

She was the 'other woman'. Darren had done that to her— he'd treated her as his lover and all the time there'd been a wife, a true love, in the background.

This was so different and yet...maybe it wasn't? She was still the outsider in this mess.

'Rob and I are friends,' she said slowly. 'And so are Jacob and I. I'm here as a housemate.'

'You shared a bedroom on Thursday night.'

And that seemed to suck all the air from her lungs. 'What the...?' She couldn't find words.

'His bedroom lights didn't go on at all,' he snapped. 'Yours stayed on until after midnight and there were two people. There were two shadows behind the drapes.'

'Did Tony tell you that?' She could hardly get the words out.

'Of course he did.'

'I can't believe...'

But she couldn't make herself go on. She didn't have the words.

This man's actions were beyond reason, and she should respond with fury. Half of her did, but overriding her anger was another emotion. She just felt…smirched.

She was the 'other woman', caught up in a sordid domestic triangle that was none of her doing. She hadn't known. Rob hadn't betrayed her deliberately as Darren had but, logical or not, that was how she felt now. Betrayed.

Lost.

Somehow she had to keep calm. She put her fingers up and touched the paramedic insignia on her uniform, a gesture she used professionally when dealing with drunks or addicts throwing invective at her. Situations all paramedics had to deal with.

Her insignia reminded her to take a deep breath and stay professional. That was what she needed to do now—treat this guy as if he was ill—as maybe he was.

But, unlike an injured drunk, she had no obligation to stay, no obligation to treat. So wind this up and get out of here.

'Your…your relationship with your son-in-law and your grandson might be your business,' she managed. 'But my life is my own. Spying on my bedroom is not right. It might even be illegal. So I'm sorry you've come all this way to see me, but this conversation is done.'

Enough. She turned back to the counter, grabbed a jar of Vegemite and smeared a thick black layer on the bottom slice of bread. Then she slapped the top layer on and bit deliberately into her sandwich.

The Vegemite was so thick it almost made her gag, but she was fighting for dignity here. She didn't gag. She even managed to swallow as she headed for the door.

But what she saw there… The man's face had crumpled and he

looked close to tears. 'Please,' he said, and he almost sounded…
broken. 'This is my daughter's house. Please just leave.'

She didn't go straight back to work. There was time before the
transfer. Instead she went out into the back yard and shared
her sandwich with Bosun and Stumpy.

Or tried to share. It seemed they weren't all that keen on
inch-thick Vegemite either. It had started raining and they
came to sit with her on the veranda, but the sandwich stayed
uneaten.

My life is my own.

Those words had come from her mouth almost as a reso-
lution, something deep within telling her what she must do.
She hugged the dogs and thought of the difficulties of going
back to Lorna's—with two dogs now. Impossible. Or leaving
town. That was hardly fair. The town needed her and she'd
committed to three months.

Besides, she'd be running away. She thought of the wonder of being with Rob, of the way she'd felt in his arms, of
the pure joy.

She didn't deserve such joy. He was Emma's.

She was indeed 'the other woman'.

Dear heaven, that was twisted. That was channelling Paul
and his grief-twisted opinions. If her logic held true…if she
didn't deserve joy, then neither must Rob. For ever and for
ever and for ever?

'I don't know what to do,' she whispered to the dogs and
then her phone pinged and it was Angus. 'Ruth would like
to talk to you before the chopper comes,' he told her. 'Could
you come?'

Work. Her salvation. Hooray.

'I'm on my way,' she told him and hugged the dogs goodbye and headed across to the hospital. But as she went she knew Paul was still sitting in the kitchen. Waiting for what?

'I'm on my way,' she said again, but a part of her was thinking...

On her way to where?

Angus was waiting for her, looking worried. His face cleared when he saw her. 'I was about to come and find you,' he told her. 'I saw the Corvette outside the house. Paul and Lois always hire the same car when they fly down from Brisbane. Are they both there?'

'Just Paul,' she said briefly, and the elderly doctor looked closely at her and then reached out and gripped her shoulder.

'I'm sorry. You know they're...not stable.'

'I know it now.'

'I should have spelt it out more clearly. You've met Chris, our local cop. Would you like me to give him a call? If Paul went into the house without Rob there... Well, there have been instances before. They tried to redecorate Jacob's room a few months back and Rob finally got so angry he had them evicted. I think...well, I know that Emma's condition has left them almost crazy. They can't let her go—they can't let anything go.'

She winced, thinking of that formal sitting room, thinking of what they'd like to do to a little boy's room. Compared to that, what had just happened seemed minor. 'I can handle it,' she said. 'But Ruth?'

He gave her a searching look but moved on. 'She's frantic,' he admitted. 'Rob rang the oncologist in Sydney and they've talked it through. I gather Ruth was advised to start chemo six months ago and the oncologist says she must start now. But that means a six-week stay in Sydney. Her sister lives near South Sydney Hospital, so accommodation's no problem, but she's frantic about Bosun and her alpacas. Her daughter and son-in-law moved in the last time she had chemo, but she won't hear of asking them to come home now. But I gather you offered to keep an eye on them. Could you reassure her?'

'Of course I will.'

'Thank you.' But his grip on her shoulder tightened again. A gesture of comfort and support. 'Paul's upset you.'

'I can handle it,' she said, trying to sound light. 'This situation's horrid, but really, it's nothing to do with me.'

'Isn't it?' The elderly man's eyes were kind and watchful and she thought that a lifetime of being a family doctor would have given him insights now that were far from welcome. So why not be honest?

'I guess maybe,' she whispered. 'If it really isn't...why does that make me feel...desolate?'

The chopper landed on the football oval twenty minutes later, just as the first clap of thunder and a sweep of hailstones heralded a storm front. Which meant delay. To Jen's delight, though, Frankie was on board. The crew elected to stay with the chopper, but Jen wasn't going to miss a chance to catch up. She drove her own car out to the football field where the chopper had landed.

'We have time for coffee,' Frankie decreed, after they'd hugged under mutual umbrellas and dived for the cover of the car. 'This is happening all the time at the moment. There's flooding inland and we've been busy with patients trapped by cut roads. They're saying it'll get worse before it gets better though, and right now...this is great. Your place is part of the hospital, right? Can we head there for coffee?'

And Jen thought of Paul. What was he doing? Still sitting

at the kitchen table? Or standing in that appalling living room, feeding his grief?

'No,' she said, a bit too brusquely, and Frankie looked quickly at her face—and then nodded.

'Café it is, then,' she agreed, and then she said nothing until they were settled at the back of Willhua's only coffee shop, with a couple of mugs of pretty ordinary coffee in front of them.

'Ugh!' Frankie said as she tasted it. 'I hope you don't normally drink this stuff.'

'Rob has a great coffeemaker.' But for the life of her she couldn't keep the strain out of her voice.

'So... Rob?' Her friend sat back in her chair and eyed her with care. 'Rob was the guy with you when I phoned?'

'I...yes.'

'And you sounded lit up like a Christmas tree.'

'Maybe.'

'But now...not so much?'

And Jen met her friend's gaze and knew there was no point in lying.

'I've just found out he's married,' she said bluntly. And then she told her, the whole sad situation, ending up with Paul's close to madness demand, the impossibility of going forward... and how unutterably confused she felt.

'Oh, Jen, I'm so sorry,' Frankie said at last. 'But you really like this guy, right?'

'I...yes. But...'

'But what?'

'But it's just too sad,' she said. Then she tilted her chin, and metaphorically squared her shoulders. 'And complicated. But I've only known him for two weeks and I have no right to feel...how I'm feeling. So I think I have a plan. I'm moving out of the house this afternoon.'

'You're *what*?'

'The lady you're about to take to Sydney has given me a solution.'

And she told Frankie about Ruth.

Her conversation with Ruth had been brief and emotional, and in the end it had handed her a way out. Ruth had sounded close to desperation at the thought of leaving her animals alone, and with Paul's vindictiveness still in her head the solution had seemed obvious.

'Ruth's farm's just out of town,' she told her friend. 'She has alpacas and a border collie named Bosun, and she'll need to be in Sydney for maybe six weeks. I offered to move in and take care of them all and she fell on my offer like it was manna from heaven. I now have a place to live. So moving on...'

'Wow,' Frankie said softly and then, thoughtfully, 'So... you're running away again?'

'I am not running. I'm just...'

'Jen, you loved your job with us,' Frankie said, cutting her off. 'And yet you left. And now...do you love living with this guy?'

She flushed. Did she?

'It's only been two weeks,' she muttered. 'It's far too soon to know. And I'm not running far.'

'But still running.'

'Leave it, Frankie,' she said, more angrily than she meant to. What was Frankie suggesting? That there was an element of cowardice in what she was doing?

Well, maybe Frankie was right, she conceded, but how to be brave enough to face the situation in that sad house?

'So what about you?' she asked, desperate to turn the subject. 'Tell me about Bruce. Was that what the phone call on

Thursday was about? You know, I now have a farm big enough for all of us. If you need me to foster him...'

'Are you kidding? Nico adores him. Nico was living in a campervan when he first arrived but he found this gorgeous house near the beach—well, actually I found it for him—and he and Bruce are living the dream. They're at the beach every day. Bruce just waits on the sand, watching like a hawk while Nico does his paddleboarding thing.'

'And Bruce is okay? He wasn't as hurt as Stumpy?'

'He had a badly bruised, strained leg so he was bandaged up and limping for a while, but the main problem was psychological. He was really traumatised. If it hadn't been for the way he bonded with Nico and trusted him right from the start, I don't know how this would have played out. But don't worry. Nico's not going to let anything bad happen to him. And I don't think he'll be giving him up for adoption any time soon.'

'That's so good to hear. We never did find any relative or friend of Charlie's who could take the dogs. Now, tell me...'

But then Jen's phone pinged again and so did Frankie's. The rain was easing, the forecast looked okay and transfer was about to happen.

'Back to work,' Jen said ruefully as she gave her friend a final hug. 'Isn't it lucky we love our jobs? Sometimes it seems like work is time out for both of us.'

Rob arrived back at the hospital mid-morning on Monday, half an hour before the start of clinic. His visits to Brisbane were an established routine. He dropped Jacob off at childcare as he drove through town, then headed home for a quick shower and change.

He walked through the kitchen—and Jenny's mug was gone. Maybe it was weird, to notice it as soon as he walked in the door, but it was quite some mug. It was an elephant, large and fat and fluorescent pink, with the trunk forming the handle. The grin on its cartoon-like face was one of pure glee.

'One of my patients gave me this,' she'd told Rob when she'd first produced it. 'Malcolm's nine years old now, but when he was seven he had non-Hodgkin's lymphoma. His mum was single and struggling, she didn't have a car and Malcolm was immunocompromised. We transferred him back and forth to hospital so many times we became friends, and the Christmas they announced he was clear he and his mum gave me this. There's no way this baby's going near any dishwasher.'

It had sat in pride of place next to his state-of-the-art coffee machine, and both he and Jacob had decided they liked it. A lot.

And now it was gone. Why did that make his heart sink?

Maybe she'd left it in her room. Instead of heading to his end of the house, to his room, he went to hers. Knocked.

Nothing.

It was mid Monday morning. Of course she wouldn't be here. He had no business looking.

But he looked—and there was no mug. Not only that, the room looked exactly as it had looked before she'd arrived.

Clean. Neat.

Empty.

There was a note on the bed addressed to him. He walked forward and picked it up.

Rob,

Angus will probably tell you that Paul came to see me while you were away. Even before that, though, I was realising how impossible this situation is. So I guess I've decided that this is all getting too heavy, too fast. It might seem cowardly, and maybe it is, but Ruth needs someone to look after her farm and it seems a sensible solution for us all.

I don't want to upset Jacob though, so maybe you could bring him to see the alpacas at the weekend? He'll like the farm.

Welcome home, Rob, and take care of you.

He stood and stared at the note for a long, long time and then slowly he crumpled it between his fingers. *How impossible this situation is.*

She had it in one. Impossible, impossible, impossible.

He thought of Paul coming to see her and he felt ill. The last four years of unrelenting grief had seen a once sensible, urbane lawyer inch closer and closer to the edge of reason. Rob understood, but what was happening now was past irrational. He could only guess what sort of anger had been thrown at Jen.

How could he hope that she withstood that? How could he ask her to?

He couldn't. He stood in the empty bedroom and he thought of their night together, what, only four nights ago? That night had felt like the heavens had opened, light, freedom—a future!—had suddenly seemed possible.

But it had been an illusion. The weekend, this note, was his reality. It was what it was, and he had no right to ask Jen to share.

What had she said in her note? *It might seem cowardly...* It wasn't cowardly, he thought. This grim reality was his, and he had no business to ask her to share.

He closed his eyes and for a moment he let despair wash over him. Emma was still a part of his life, and her parents' anger and distress were part of his life as well. To move on...to let the embryonic concept of Jen sharing his life when Emma was still real, still…loved?…what was he doing? What right did he have to want Jen to share?

He was feeling ill—the emotions in his head were so knotted that he had no chance of unravelling them—but a knock on the door brought him back to the here and now. Minnie stood in the doorway, her face a picture of concern.

'Oh, Rob,' she said miserably. And then, 'Let me make you a nice cup of tea.'

He raked his hair and then almost visibly braced.

'That'd be great, Minnie,' he told her. 'But I need to move fast. Clinic's in twenty minutes.'

'Pop in to see Anna before you go to clinic,' Minnie suggested. 'It'll make you a tiny bit late, but it'll be worth it.'

'Why?'

'Because Anna's happy and her baby's gorgeous,' Minnie said softly. 'Sometimes we all need to remind ourselves that happy ever after is possible.'

As if. But she gave him a hug as he passed, and somehow it helped.

So he showered and had his tea—and then he did what Minnie had suggested. He ducked into the hospital, to find Anna surrounded by soft toys, flowers, baby paraphernalia. Cuddling her baby. And when she saw Rob she smiled shyly and held out her son.

'Would you like a cuddle?'

And he would. He stood in the sunlit room and held a tiny newborn in his arms and remembered holding Jacob four years ago. And with that came memories of grief, of shock, but, superimposed, was the wonder and the surge of protectiveness and hope that had filled him at the sight of his little son.

This was what it was all about, he told himself. He loved Jacob so much and he still had to fight for him.

And what he felt for Jenny?

'It's not about me,' he whispered to this tiny scrap of snuggling infant. And then he looked at Anna and smiled.

'You're doing so well. He's beautiful, Anna.'

'He is, isn't he?' Anna told him, her smile shy but happy. 'Mum and Dad have said they'll help and that's wonderful— unbelievable even—but as soon as I saw him I knew... I can cope, even by myself if I have to. I'll do whatever it takes.'

'I know you will,' Rob told her. 'Don't we all?' And then he handed back her precious baby and headed to work.

Knowing he'd accept...whatever it took.

CHAPTER ELEVEN

THANKFULLY, AT LEAST for Jenny's state of mind, after that life got busy. Put simply, the heavens opened. The creek rose, flooding parks and playground. The sea became a swirling brown mass of foam as the inland water surged outward from the creek's mouth, creating a dirty brown bloom instead of the gorgeous sapphire surf Willhua was known for. The district became swathed in mud.

And that meant medical problems. The muggy heat meant beachgoers were tempted into the water regardless of warnings. There were cuts from debris, and infections caused by contaminated water.

There were minor car accidents as vehicles slipped on muddy roads. Two farm accidents where tractors had slid and rolled left one farmer with crushed ribs, another with a badly fractured leg. The mud in the farming community meant falls. Sodden boots led to infections, and a landslip between Willhua and Whale Head meant that Willhua's two doctors were coping with problems they'd normally have referred on to specialists in the larger town.

Jen and Gary were working flat out as well. The ambulance was four-wheel drive, bought with just such weather conditions in mind, and it was increasingly needed for almost trivial transfers. Olivia Hoffman's leg needed dressing, her intrepid daughter wasn't brave enough to face the winding road, but the filthy conditions meant that Hildy wasn't the only one to admit that they didn't feel confident and asked for the ambulance to collect them.

Rob and Jenny therefore saw each other only in passing, as patients were transferred in and out. Finally, though, the Saturday after he'd arrived home, the skies cleared a little.

'Please can we see Jen and Stumpy today?' a tearful Jacob pleaded. He'd been unutterably distressed to get home and find them gone—though Rob thought it was Stumpy he missed more than Jen. Maybe he should get a dog himself, he thought, but then he thought of Jen and Stumpy and thought, *One without the other?*

The thought was illogical, and it left him feeling desolate. Just do what comes next, he told himself. It was Saturday morning and for the first time all week he had time.

'Sure, I'm home.' Jen sounded cautious when he phoned, as well she might. But then she seemed to catch herself and her voice became enthusiastic. 'We have a baby alpaca. Jacob will love him.'

So he drove up to the small farm and Jen met them at the gate, swinging it open for them to drive through.

She looked like a farmer, he thought. She was wearing faded jeans, an oversized T-shirt and muddy gumboots. Her hair was flying every which way in the wind, and a large smear of mud lay across her cheek. She was smiling a greeting and waving to Jacob, and as Rob waited for her to swing the gate wide he was hit by a wave of longing so great it was all he could do not to groan out loud.

There was a sudden vision… A small farm, just like this. A big farmhouse kitchen. Dogs, kids, mess.

Family.

Jenny.

'Hey, are you awake in there?' She was holding the gate wide, he realised, waiting for him to go through, and he'd paused too long. He managed a grin and drove on. And then he had parked and Jacob was fighting to get his seatbelt undone, then clambering out of the car, across the muddy yard and into Jen's outstretched arms.

She stooped to catch him. She hugged and swung and laughed with his little son and there it was again. That surge of longing so great he could hardly bear it.

'Welcome to mud city,' she called to him. 'I hope you brought gumboots.'

He had. Luckily Jacob was already wearing his. That meant Jen's thighs were now liberally smeared with mud, but she didn't seem to care.

'Stumpy first, or alpacas?' she asked and motioned to the back door. There stood two dogs, Ruth's gorgeous collie, and Stumpy. They were both looking at Rob and Jacob, and looking dubiously at the mud.

'Smart dogs,' Jen said, chuckling at their expressions. 'They've learned every time they go out I put them in the outside shower and wash off their mud. It's either that or they stay outside for the day. Neither of them enjoys the experience, so they head out in the morning, get their running out of their system and then figure out whether any future excursion is worth the consequences. They're looking at you now and hoping if they wait long enough you'll come to them.'

'And they've fallen for each other,' she added. 'I reckon most of the reason Stumpy was miserable was that she was missing Charlie and Bruce. But now she's found Bosun and she has a new love. Fickle, thy name is Stumpy.'

She smiled again and swung Jacob around and set him on his feet, and Rob looked at her face, marred with mud but clear and open and happy, and he thought…he'd only known her for three weeks.

How could he fall so hard in three weeks?

But Jacob had met the dogs' expectations. He'd raced across to them and had his arms around Stumpy's neck and Stumpy was doing her best to lick every part of the small boy she obviously thought was her best friend in the world.

It was only three weeks since Stumpy had lost her owner, he thought, and then he thought that it wasn't just Stumpy who was fickle.

'Let's check out these alpacas before it starts raining again,' Jen was saying, and Jacob gave a final hug to Stumpy and came back to join them. The little boy took Jen's hand and held it like…like Jen was family.

'I've missed you,' Jacob said simply.

Jen said, 'I've missed you too.'

Gut wrench.

He followed the two of them into the stable. Most of the alpacas were in the adjoining paddock, soaking up the first glimpse of sun they'd seen for a week, but in one of the stalls was a white and tan-gold alpaca, and by her side was a new-born…foal?

'She's a cria,' Jen told them. 'That's what baby alpacas are called, Jacob. She was born last night and we're very excited. I was up at midnight. I had to video call Ruth,' she told Rob. 'Ruth's already started chemo and she's very tired but there was no way she was going to sleep while this was happening. So Ruth supervised via video link and I followed her instructions, but in the end Betty did it all herself. Ruth's named this one Pamela. So meet Pamela, people. You're the first outside people she's met.'

'She's littler than me,' Jacob said, awed. 'Hi, Pamela.'

'When she's a little bit older you can pat her,' Jen told him.

'Not yet?' He looked up. 'Would she bite?'

'Alpacas don't bite,' she told him. 'They don't have any top teeth so they can't, and Betty's very tame. But Betty's only just met Pamela herself and this is her first baby. She's only just learning to love her baby herself, so we have to give her time and space.'

'Like me when Minnie gave me Eric-the-Scarecrow at my birthday party,' he said thoughtfully. 'I had to go into my bedroom all by myself 'cos I wasn't ready to share yet.'

'Exactly,' Jen said. 'But you know what you could do for her? See her water container? It's getting low. There's a trough outside but she's not ready to use that yet. There's a yellow bucket under the tap over there. Could you fill it, not too full, just enough for you to carry, and bring it over to tip into her bowl?'

'Yes!' Jacob said enthusiastically. 'Then they can both drink.' Then he looked doubtfully at Pamela, who was showing in a very elementary way her preferred beverage. 'But Pamela's drinking from her mummy.'

'And that's why Betty needs lots of water,' Jen told him. 'Mummies turn water into milk and that's how babies feed.'

'Yes,' Jacob said again and carefully handed Eric-the-Scarecrow to Rob and headed for the tap.

They watched as he trudged back and forth, taking his task very seriously. He filled the bucket to about a quarter, tested it, figured it was heavy enough, and carried it over. After the first careful trip Betty was obliging enough to drink. 'Yes!' Jacob crowed again and turned and high-fived Jen and then headed back, determined to fill the whole bowl.

Which left them alone—apart from Eric-the-Scarecrow.

What to say?

'I'm sorry you had to meet Paul,' Rob said at last, because it had to be said. And he could say it now, when he wasn't looking at her. They were both determinedly looking at Jacob.

'I'm sorry you need to cope with Paul,' she told him. 'I can see... I can see just how dreadful it is...for all you.'

'It is,' he said and went back to watching Jacob.

Where to take this from here? In her note she'd described this situation as impossible. It surely was.

'Jen, does it have to be all or nothing?' he asked at last, feeling that every word was somehow loaded. 'I know you've moved out and I can understand that, but could we... I don't know...have dinner, meet sometimes...?'

'We're meeting now.'

'You know what I mean,' he said, and then spread his hands. 'Hell, Jen, I know it's impossible, I know I have no right to ask, but I want more.'

'Rob, you're married.'

It was said almost in a whisper, but it sounded so loud it seemed to resonate, echoing almost up to the rafters and back. And then she turned and looked at him and what he saw there...he didn't know...but her face creased in distress.

'I'm sorry,' she said, her voice wobbling a bit. 'That sounds so hard, so unfair. You're married but not married. You're caught in an appalling bind, but me being with you... Rob, it can't help. It can surely only make things worse.'

'We could try. Face it down together.'

'It's too soon.' Then she shook her head. 'No, that's a lie. It's not too soon. And before you ask, I wasn't talking about the four years since you lost Emma. I was talking about the three weeks since I met you. How can I feel about you...the way I do...after three short weeks? Being honest... I have no idea. I only know that I do. But Rob, long or short, timely or not, I don't have the courage to take this further. I just...can't.'

And what was he to say to that?

Nothing, he thought bitterly. He had no right to ask anything of this woman. This was his tragedy, his world, and there was no justification to ask her to share.

Because it would be sharing, he thought. If Jen was to stand by him, then Paul and Lois's grief would be magnified a thousandfold. He knew it'd be directed at Jen, and there'd be no way he could stop it.

'Jacob, I've made scones,' Jen said, her voice carefully lightened, redirected into neutral territory. 'They're a bit wobbly but if we cover them with jam and cream maybe we won't notice the wobbles. But I'm trying to remember—should you put jam on first or cream? What do you think?'

'Jam,' Jacob said definitely. 'And then cream and then more jam. Can Stumpy and Bosun have one?'

'Yes,' Jen said. 'You know, there are so many things in the world we can't have that I can't see that one scone will change a thing.'

They ate scones while Jen and Jacob talked and Rob said what was necessary, but only just. Then they drove away, and she was left with half a dozen wobbly scones and two dogs who'd like to eat more. As if on cue, the moment they drove out of the gate the rain started again in earnest.

Dammit. She almost wished her phone would ping, that there'd be a call from Gary. She didn't need time to think.

'Let's go for a walk,' she told the dogs, who eyed her dubiously. Yep, they knew about the shower. But once she was in her wet weather gear they decided enthusiasm was called for. So they headed out across the paddocks, checking on the outside alpacas, telling them they'd be much more comfortable in the stables, but a bit of rain didn't seem to be worrying them. Then they headed further.

The farm bordered the creek on its north side—or the river as it now was. The dogs headed off on a rabbit hunt and Jen was left staring at the swollen water. Calling herself all sorts of coward.

But how not to be?

Unbidden, thoughts of that awful night with Darren were flooding back. Frankie had told her she'd met his wife at the farewell function the service had put on before they'd returned to the States. According to Frankie, Darren's wife was a corporate high-flyer, but Frankie had said, the way she'd looked at Darren... Whatever arrangement they'd made where one worked in Australia, the other in New York, it was clear she adored him.

Two marriages. Two women married to men Jen thought... thought she loved?

'I can't cope with this.' She was talking out loud but the torrent of water rushing past was drowning her speech, making it personal. As it was meant to. Her conscience talking to her heart?

'I have to stay strong,' she whispered. 'I'm only here for two more months. I need to do what I came for and then get out of their lives.

'You *are* a coward.'

'I might be,' she said bleakly and then, 'Okay, I am. But the alternative...the vitriol I'd bring down on all our heads... the hurt...'

She couldn't do it.

She turned and headed back to the house, and if the rain on her face was mingling with tears there was no one to see.

'Which is just as well,' she whispered. 'The last thing Rob needs is more hurt.'

CHAPTER TWELVE

IT RAINED. IT rained and it rained and it rained, which pretty much suited Jenny's mood.

It also meant that she and Gary were as busy as they were likely to be. Their well-equipped ambulance—four-wheel drive, built with a high chassis to cope with the rough inland roads—became almost a normal mode of public transport.

Angus was called back in from his veggie garden—it was too sodden to work there anyway—and he and Rob were run off their feet. Many of the district's elderly residents were too fearful to face the appalling weather conditions. If they lived close by, either Rob or Angus did house calls. If not, Gary and Jen brought patients to the surgery.

Between work and the demands of the dogs and the alpacas, Jen scarcely had time to think—except she did think. The week that followed Rob and Jacob's visit she felt probably more desolate than she'd ever felt in her life.

'But there's nothing I can do about it,' she told herself, but a little voice nagged back... *If you had courage...*

It was doing her head in—and then there was a drama that pretty much drove even heartbreaking thoughts from her mind.

High in the hills, almost fifty kilometres from Willhua, was a dam, a massive man-made holding pond for millions of litres of water. It had been built to supply almost all of Southern Sydney with drinking water. An unseasonably wet summer had seen it fill to almost capacity, and now, with these unrelenting rains, it was close to overflowing.

The powers that be had been monitoring the situation, allowing enough water to escape to alleviate pressure on the dam walls. But on the Thursday and Friday after the farm visit a weather front passed that was so severe the water topped the dam wall.

The wall wasn't built for such pressure. The authorities panicked and set release to maximum but, with the water already at flood levels below the dam, the scenario was disastrous.

There was nowhere for the water to go. The colossal discharge probably avoided a greater catastrophe, the bursting of the dam wall, but even this... It meant a massive wave of water surged along the already water-soaked valley, sweeping all before it.

Jen got the call at midnight and Gary sounded terrified. 'Every boat, every kayak, every able-bodied person who can man them... Jen, heaven knows what we're facing.'

What followed was a massive community effort to reach outlying properties, to make sure people were safe. There were also casualties, people taking risks to move stock, to save belongings, to cope with a situation none had envisaged. There were fractures, lacerations, hysteria and paralysing shock as residents saw their homes filled with debris-laden water.

As Jen worked throughout the night and well into the next day, she was aware that her former crew, with Frankie on board, was in the skies helping with evacuations. There was no time for chat, though. Neither was there time for talk with Rob—patients were handed over fast so she and Gary could get out there again.

She would have preferred some other way of giving herself some head space from the personal.

'It puts things in perspective,' she told herself as she and Gary treated a young mum who'd sliced her foot heading back into a flooded house trying to find her kid's beloved teddy.

As she worked, she was reminded of Jacob and Eric-the-Scarecrow. Rob would have done the same, she thought, if Eric had been at risk. He loved his son so much. He'd do... whatever it took.

He had done whatever it took. He'd accepted a life of isolation.

But then the next call came in, and she had to abandon the pointless thoughts that kept drifting into her head at unwanted moments. There was only flood and drama, and if that meant a little time out from the way her head was working...well, she'd accept it.

She just needed to get on.

And then, mid-afternoon, came drama that almost drove everything else out of her mind.

The call was to an outlying farm. The road there was still clear, but only just. Access to the property was via a narrow track, a raised strip of gravel surrounded on all sides by lakes that would normally be bushland or paddocks. In parts, the water was sloshing over.

The call, passed on by emergency services, said simply that a woman was in labour. As they drove they could see why the couple had elected to call the four-wheel drive ambulance rather than risk driving to hospital themselves.

But when they reached the farmhouse they found a young man alone, standing on the veranda, looking frantic. He looked soaked to the skin, he was wearing shorts and T-shirt and had bare feet, and on his leg was a long, jagged cut, bleeding sluggishly.

But he wasn't worried about his leg.

'I wanted a boat,' he screamed at them as they pulled up in the driveway. 'I told them, I need a boat. Or a helicopter. The wind's coming up. It's getting worse and my wife's stuck. Where's the boat?'

'Mate, slow down a little and tell us where she is.' Gary's voice was calm and authoritative, imbued with years of experience in times of crisis.

'She's at our place.'

'And where's your place?'

'Along the creek.' The man was sobbing with fear and frustration, but Gary's gaze held his and he managed to choke back his terror enough to talk. 'The water came. That was okay, our house seemed high and Skye said she didn't want to evacuate. She wants a home birth. We've got it all organised, a birth pool set up in the living room, two midwives booked to come. And she's not due till Saturday. So we stayed put and then this wave hit. The water's all through the bottom floor, almost to ceiling height. Everything's flooded. We have kayaks, just little ones, but the water's crazy. And then...then Skye started having pains.'

'So she's still at your house?' Gary's voice was calm, refusing to buy in to the young man's panic.

'My phone wouldn't work. The electrics are out. I dunno how that's affecting transmission but I knew Gareth...he owns this place...has a landline and he has a decent boat. He takes it out fishing from Willhua. I thought I'd get here and call for help and we'd both go back and get her. But Gareth's gone and so has his boat. I guess he'll be using it to move stock—I dunno. At least I could ring though, but they put me through to the ambulance. But I didn't want the ambulance. I want someone to reach Skye.'

Gary nodded. 'Okay, mate, let's see what we can do. Jen, you contact headquarters. Meanwhile...' He looked down at the man's leg. 'Let's get this seen to.'

'My wife!' The guy backed as if they were about to arrest him. 'Don't you understand? She's by herself. In that house. And the water's getting higher.'

But Jen was already on the radio, and what she heard there made her heart sink. With evacuations all across the valley there was no one close enough to help. No boats. No choppers. The control room dispatcher sounded close to tears herself.

'I'll get a crew there as soon as I can,' she promised. 'But honestly, I don't know when that'll be.'

'A woman alone in labour surely takes precedence.'

'We have people on roofs of houses that seem in danger of collapsing. Is there no way you can get there yourself?'

While Gary tended the young man's leg, calming him, gently questioning—Were there any other children? How far advanced was his wife's labour? How far apart were the pains?—Jen looked out of the window at the driving rain. The water seemed to be rising while she watched, and so was the wind. She thought that if the ground floor of the house had been flooded hours ago, how much worse would it be now?

We have people on roofs of houses in danger of collapsing... A woman alone in labour...

But, pulled up under a dry patch of land under the picture windows of the house she was in, lay a kayak, bright crimson, built for one.

There lay a possibility.

She turned back to Gary and the man—Douglas—Gary had got that out of him. 'Is that your kayak?' she asked.

'I…yes. That's how I got here. We have two but there was no way Skye could use hers.'

At nine months pregnant? Thank heaven she didn't try.

'So where's your house?' she asked. 'Upstream or down-stream?' If it was upstream, with the ever-increasing strength of wind and water, she wouldn't have a chance.

'I…it's downstream. That's why it took so long to get here. I had to fight the current and it was getting stronger by the minute. I'm strong but this was something else. I went through the bush at the water's edge to avoid the worst, paddled and waded when I had to. That's how I ripped my leg.'

And you were wearing shorts and thongs, Jen thought, but she didn't say so. She was thinking ahead, thankfully, of the tough cloth her uniform was made of, and of her workman-like boots.

'But the bush wasn't so dense to stop you getting through?' she asked.

'Jen…' Gary said uneasily, seeing where she was going. 'You can't.'

She met his gaze head-on. 'A woman alone, in labour… If you were thirty years younger, would you do it?' she asked.

They stared at each other for a long, long moment. Then Gary said at last, heavily, 'Don't tell me. You've used kayaks since you were two?'

'I used to compete in white-water rafting.'

'Of course you did.'

She chuckled. 'There you go, then. You really should have read my résumé.'

But Douglas was staring from one to the other, his face ashen. 'What are you suggesting? If anyone tries to get back it has to be me.'

'Jen has a satellite radio, plus medical equipment, plus medical skills,' Gary said. 'Mate, there's no contest. You called us for a reason. But Jen, you know how dangerous...'

'I won't take risks,' she promised, untruthfully but they both knew that. 'If I stay in the bush as much as possible, I'll just be fighting my way from tree to tree. I promise I won't try and ride the current. Douglas, where exactly is your house?'

'You can see the roof.' He pointed downstream and they saw the glint of a metal roof, far off through the rain.

'Then I'm wasting time being here. Worst case scenario is that I get stuck, climb a decent tree, radio for help and wait for a chopper to come get me. But if that happens tell them to reach Skye first, because I'm good at clinging to trees and these gums are solid. I could stay there till morning if need be. Gary, if I get stuck, talk to Frankie at South Sydney Air Rescue. She'll give me an earful but she'll rescue me.'

'I'll contact Doc Pierson,' Gary said uneasily. 'He'll...'

'This is nothing to do with Rob,' she told him, almost harshly. 'He'll be up to his ears in his own work.'

'Oh, Jen...'

'Hey, don't fret,' she said and on impulse she leaned forward and hugged him. 'He travels the fastest who travels alone.'

'That pronoun should be *she*,' Gary said morosely. 'Bloody independent women!'

Dusk.

The South Sydney Air Rescue chopper landed on the stretch of land behind the hospital. Normally they used the oval but it, too, was underwater. Frankie helped the little family down. They'd been perched on a rooftop for hours, they were cold and wet and traumatised but Willhua had organised itself. Volunteers received them with blankets, warmth and reassurance, and within moments they were heading into the security of the school hall-cum-evacuation centre.

But Frankie was heading into the hospital at a run.

Rob met her in the entrance. He and Angus had worked steadily all day, but the stream of medical events seemed to have eased. One look at Frankie's face though, and he knew there was more.

'You're Dr Pierson, right?' she demanded, wasting no time.

'Right.'

'I'm Frankie. South Sydney Air Rescue. Friend of Jen's. Doctor, is it possible for you to leave here?' she asked. 'Do you have cover? And before you answer, would you be prepared to be dropped into a home visit? Jen and Gary were called out earlier to a woman in labour. Skye Robbins—do you know her?'

He did know her, and his heart sank. Skye had been seeing him for antenatal care, but she'd come to him reluctantly, only at the insistence of her midwives. She'd been intent on a home birth from the start, and now... He thought of the isolation of their small farm and he felt ill.

Frankie was watching his face—guessing his reaction? 'So you know her? She's alone, trapped in a house with a flooded ground floor. Her husband kayaked out to get help, but now the water's risen further, leaving her isolated. When the ambulance couldn't reach her Jen kayaked in by herself.

'No, don't look like that,' she said as he stared at her in dismay. 'I know you're a friend of Jen. Yes, she's crazy, but that's why we love her, and she's one of the most capable women I know. She told you she's a trained nurse? Anyway, she and her expectant mum have been waiting on evac for hours, but there's been so much need. There's still need. Now Jen's radioed in saying she's worried about progress, but there's nowhere we can land. She needs… well, to put it bluntly, she needs you. I'd have to take you down in a harness attached to mine, but I'd make sure you're safe. Could you come?'

Could he?

Angus could cope here, he thought, his mind in overdrive. Minnie had been staying with Jacob for the last two days, so that was fine, but what would he be facing? He was no obstetrician. Willhua's mums usually went to Whale Head to deliver. Even Anna's birth had been unusual.

'What does she say about progress?'

'Second stage, but no progress for hours—Jen's worrying about obstructed labour. Without obstruction, the birth could happen at any minute but she's becoming more and more distressed.'

And with that came a flood of possible diagnoses. He thought of what he knew of Skye. She was a small woman, finely boned. He'd done an ultrasound six weeks ago and things had looked normal, but the baby's head grew fast in the last weeks of pregnancy. Cephalopelvic proportion couldn't normally be diagnosed before the thirty-seventh week because the baby's head wouldn't have reached birth size. If Skye's pelvis was simply too small… What a nightmare.

'We have to get her out,' he said flatly. 'If she needs a Caesarean…'

'Let's hope it won't come to that,' Frankie said grimly. 'This weather's getting worse. There's no second-floor balcony, no easy way we can lift from the house, and it's possible that she'll be too close to delivering to be moved by the time we get there. The crew's consensus is the best we can do is provide additional medical assistance, but we need to do it now. Jen thinks the woman's in real trouble and she wouldn't say it lightly.'

'She needs an obstetrician.'

'We've looked at options. Even if we manage to find one willing, the nearest specialist is at Whale Head. With the dark and rising wind it'll be impossible to get anyone but you there. You could talk to them via satellite phone but that's the best we can do. Please, can you help?'

His mind was almost spinning. With no power, with no theatre equipment, there was no possibility of a Caesarean. If she'd been in second stage for hours...if the pressure stayed on...the prospect was hellish. Even if the baby died, the threats wouldn't end. There could be rupture, maybe even maternal death. He'd be fighting for Skye's life as well.

'We can drop gear with you,' Frankie said diffidently. 'Lanterns, equipment, you name it.'

'You know I can't do a Caesar in the conditions you describe.' Even if he had expert advice via the satellite phone, in this situation he knew his limitations.

'We figured that,' Frankie told him. 'So the situation's grim but we don't want it to be...' She stopped, unable to voice the unthinkable. 'Doctor, we don't want Jen to be on her own, so the more medical expertise we can get in there, the better. We said we'd try. Jen's had a look and suggested a dry place where someone—you?—can be dropped, and she's figuring a system to get you into the house.'

'Of course she has,' Rob said, and Frankie managed a wry grin.

'You know our Jen, then.'

'I surely do.'

He thought of her, kayaking into floodwaters on her own. Stranded with a woman giving birth. Facing obstructed labour, knowing the ramifications but moving to the practical. Figuring out systems to get gear into a flooded house.

Yes, he knew Jen.

He would have gone anyway. There was no choice—but this was Jen.

And with that thought came another, so heavy and strong and sure that it almost blindsided him.

Somehow he had to know her better.

'Rob's coming.' Frankie's voice on the radio seemed a life-line all in itself.

'Who?'

'Your Doc Pierson, of course. Can I put you through to the boys to tell them where we can set him down?'

'Yeah,' she said, dazed. 'But... Rob?'

'You said you needed help,' Frankie told her and, for heaven's sake, she heard a trace of humour in her friend's voice. 'A trained obstetrician's our first choice, but that's impossible. Second choice should surely be me,' she added with mock modesty. 'You know I'd be brilliant, but I'm needed with the crew. So, for some reason, the crew and I decided your Doc Pierson would be better.'

'*My* Doc Pierson?'

'You should have seen his face when I told him you'd kay-aked in,' Frankie said. 'If he's not your Doc Pierson, I'm a monkey's uncle.'

Maybe he should have spent all the time he had during the short flight to keep reviewing everything he knew about ob-structed labour. Those thoughts had been front and centre back at the hospital, while he and Angus had swiftly put to-gether everything they could think of he might need. Now, in the back of the darkened chopper, he had moments to take a breath, ready himself for descent...and think of something apart from medical need.

His thoughts were of Jen, on her own, fighting for a woman's life, doing what she did best. But then, as he watched the swirling mass of floodwater below them, illuminated by the chopper's floodlights, he also thought...what about Jacob?

Minnie was caring for him. Right now Jacob was fine, but if something happened...

He was being winched down to a tiny area of dry land above a flooded house. Frankie had described it to him—apparently they'd flown over it on their way to drop the little family they'd just rescued. Fully loaded, they hadn't been able to do anything, but they'd had time to look.

'The house is two-storey,' she'd told him. 'The bottom level's underwater, but the second storey's still above water level. There's a rise at the back of the house, where they usually park an old tractor which, fortunately, isn't there at the moment. It's too small to land but it looks safe enough to winch you down. It's a short distance to the house and Jen says she's organising a rope system from the other end to get you safely across.'

She'd hesitated, and then added, 'Rob, there are risks. We shouldn't ask this of you but...'

'But lives are at stake,' he'd said, and he'd known there was no choice.

But, sitting in the darkened chopper, reminding himself of the instructions Frankie had given him, the choice he'd made was suddenly not so clear.

This crew was incredibly capable. He knew that, but a night descent in the wind...appalling things could happen. And if anything happened to him, where would that leave Jacob? Up until now he hadn't had room for the thought, but now it was like a wave of black, a terror that left him almost immobilised.

But then, suddenly, weirdly, into this kaleidoscope of racing need, he was thinking of Emma. He was remembering

Em's laughter, her love, her joy in her pregnancy, her antici-pation of her coming baby. This was another baby he was fighting for. Em had trained as a doctor for a reason, and he knew what she'd say:

A mum and a baby? What's the risk compared to the out-come?

And then he was thinking again of Jen, who'd kayaked alone into a flooded house. Jen was doing what she must to help a woman in labour, a terrified woman.

His thoughts were so tangled, but superimposing themselves in his mind now were other images. Jen hugging Stumpy, de-claring she'd keep her. Jen climbing the chain tepee with Jacob at the playground. Jen in his kitchen, making Jacob laugh, making him laugh.

As Em would have made Jacob laugh.

Emma and Jenny.

Two women he loved.

What's the risk compared to the outcome?

And, for some reason, as he sat in the noise-filled rear of the chopper, readying himself to descend, the fog of grief and anger and helplessness of the last four years seemed to clear.

For all these years he'd been grieving for Emma, but at the same time he'd felt as if he'd been walking on eggshells. He'd been trying to placate Lois and Paul, trying to do everything he could to ensure they had no legal means of contesting custody.

And now… If he died tonight they'd gain custody, but he'd faced that risk almost without thinking—because lives were at stake.

And then he thought—what was at stake if he didn't fight for Jen?

He thought of Tony, driving his appalling black car, con-stantly watching them. He'd accepted it as just…what was.

He was thinking of his living room, a place both he and Jacob hated. A shrine to Emma. Emma would have loathed it.

And now there was Jenny—or the chance of Jenny. He thought of her courage, her sheer love of life. Of the way she'd lifted the fog of grief that had shrouded his home. Of the way she'd seamlessly accepted the responsibility of Stumpy. Of the way she'd made his little son laugh.

And then…of the way her body had melted into his, of the way she'd shown him the vibrant, passionate woman she could be.

Why had he calmly accepted her decision to move out? The answer was simple.

Because what was left after four long years was dreary acceptance of reality.

But then…tonight? Tonight he was risking everything because he could save lives. But by not risking…what sort of lives were he and Jacob to lead?

'We're ready to move to the door.' Frankie was checking the carabiner that attached Rob's harness to her own. 'You want me to go through things one more time?'

'No, I have it.'

'You're sure?'

'I'm sure,' he told her, shaking off introspection and centring himself on what had to be done. The door of the chopper was open. Rob was securely attached and would be until his feet were safely on the patch of ground now illuminated by the powerful light beneath the helicopter. Then he would be unclipped and remove his harness and Frankie would be winched back to the hovering aircraft. It sounded simple. It didn't feel simple.

But now, strangely, the perils of descent were overshadowed by thoughts of risks of another kind.

Risks...

Paul and Lois loved Jacob—he knew they did. If anything happened to him he'd have to trust that love would finally bring sanity to their care.

And there was another bottom line. He loved Jen, it was as straight and simple as that.

Maybe some risks had to be faced.

CHAPTER THIRTEEN

JEN HEARD THE approaching chopper above the wind, and she'd never been more grateful. Skye had been gripping her hand so tightly that she couldn't move, but the moment the contraction passed Jen was hanging out of the window, waving the torch that hung habitually on her equipment belt, to show the chopper where she was.

And then she saw them, two figures harnessed together, swinging down onto the top of the slope above the flooded house. The scene was lit by the chopper's searchlight. A gust of wind caught them and they swayed so close to the trees that she felt ill, and when they reached the ground she was almost dizzy with relief.

She saw the figures separate, then Frankie unclipped a back pack full of gear and handed it to Rob.

Rob...

'Skye, the doctor's here,' she told the woman on the bed behind her. 'He's brought everything we need, including pain relief.' That was the thing Skye wanted most. What Jen didn't tell her was that the bag Rob and Frankie were manoeuvring hopefully also contained other gear. She hadn't mentioned that to Skye, because what was the use in telling her what was happening wasn't normal when there wasn't a thing she could do about it? Skye had moved into second stage too long ago, and nothing was happening.

But now…

'He's coming in,' she told her, and Skye moaned.

'Be quick. Jen, please…'

But she didn't need to tell Jen to be quick—and Jen was ready.

Earlier, in between contractions, Skye had been able to answer questions, telling her what was where, and she'd had time to organise. She'd thus used Skye's kayak to get to the shed at the rear of the house, where she'd found nylon rope, luckily looped over high hooks, which meant it was above water level. 'The iron roof on the shed lifted during a storm last year,' Skye had told her. 'Douglas bought enough rope to tie it down until we could get a roofer in, and the rope should still be there.'

She'd got soaked reaching the rope and she'd decided to organise the whole thing while she was wet. So she'd waded and used the kayak, and managed to loop the rope, forming a circuit from her upper floor window to a tree near where someone could land.

When she'd got back to the house she'd attached the kayak to her makeshift pulley and sent it back to the drop site. And told Frankie. Who'd obviously told Rob.

Frankie was being winched up again. What other emergencies were Frankie and her crew facing tonight? How many other dramas were being played out across the state?

She could only focus on one.

She watched as Rob loaded gear into the kayak and started it on its way on its makeshift pulley. From above, the chopper's searchlight still lit the scene.

She had to focus. Rob had obviously figured her system, but they had to use it with care. The wind and the blast from the chopper was making the kayak sway. The last thing they needed was for the kayak to be snagged or tip halfway, and the fact that they were working in the dark didn't help.

But the gear arrived safely. She hauled it in with speed, then sent the kayak back.

Five minutes later Rob was clambering over the window-sill, into the room.

She didn't hug him. It would surely be inappropriate. They were medics on a job, and Skye, lying on the bed, recovering from her last contraction, had to see them as professionals. But as he'd stepped over the sill his hand had caught hers and held, and his grip said the idea of a hug wasn't all one-sided.

And then he was at the bed and professionalism was kicking in. 'Hey, Skye.' He caught the expectant mother's hands and Jen saw Skye's terror almost ease. 'I guess you've got your wish. Home birth after all.' His eyes were kind, his words strong and reassuring. 'Jen says you've been doing brilliantly.'

'It…hurts…'

'I'll bet it does. Mums have told me it's like pooing a pumpkin, and a big one at that. If you asked men to do that…well, women are awesome. But I can help now, and the chopper crew brought gear and drugs to give you some pain relief. We have some decent lamps. Let's get this place set up fast and then, if it's okay, I'll examine you.'

'I wanted a water birth.' Somehow Skye found the strength to wail. 'We've got a pool downstairs, all ready.'

Rob chuckled and his hand gripped hers again. 'So you told me. You said you've always wished for a water birth, but Skye, maybe you wished too hard. If we took you downstairs Jen and I would need to don snorkel and mask to deliver.'

And Skye even managed to smile back before the next contraction hit and she went back to focusing on getting this baby out.

* * *

Nothing else mattered but medical need. Skye knew Rob, he was her family doctor and his arrival seemed to give her strength, but her contractions were achieving nothing.

Rob, though, was moving swiftly. He was talking to Skye, asking permission for examination, telling her how far she was dilated, telling her that her baby's heartbeat was still steady. Not telling her what Jen had already told Frankie, and what she'd confirmed with him quietly as he'd entered—that labour hadn't progressed for hours.

And then, examination complete, he produced an ultrasound machine. Jen's knees almost sagged with relief as she saw him lift the appliance from its bag. A portable, state-of-the-art, battery-operated ultrasound seemed a game-changer. To be able to see what was happening...

But seeing wasn't fixing. One of the most common causes of obstructed labour was pelvic size, and if that was the case there was no way either of them could help, not here. And for Skye to continue labouring until first light, until conditions made evacuation possible... It didn't bear thinking of.

So all Jen could do was hold her breath and hold Skye's hand—Jen's hand was already painful from the death grip Skye had administered during contractions—and wait as Rob passed the wand over the swollen abdomen.

The silence seemed to go on for ever. The screen was so small Jen could hardly see the grainy image, so all she could do was keep on holding her breath. The world seemed to still. *Please...*

Maybe she was gripping Skye's hand too hard, returning pressure. She forced herself to loosen her hold but Skye grabbed her harder.

Both women were waiting for a verdict.

And then Rob's face changed, just a little. Just enough to give Jen hope.

'Skye, your bladder's full,' he said, calmly, as if this were an everyday occurrence, not something to shout from the rooftops. 'I'm looking at what's happening and I'm seeing your bladder's so full your baby can't get past it.'

'My bladder...' Skye whispered, confused.

'When did you last have a wee?'

'I couldn't,' she gasped. 'I mean...the toilet's downstairs. It's not working and last time... And I never even felt like I needed to.'

Dear God... Rookie mistake, Jen thought savagely. An empty bladder made for a safer delivery.

'It probably blocked early,' Rob said, cutting across Jen's instant self-blame. 'The fear from the flooding, plus early labour pains, plus no toilet...'

'But I don't think... I can't go now.'

'Because your baby's pushing so hard that everything's swollen.' He sounded prosaic but Jen heard the slight lift in his voice, a sign of hope. 'If it's okay with you, I'm going to insert a catheter. It's a simple procedure to drain the bladder and give bub room to move.'

'But I don't think I can push any more,' Skye moaned, and Rob moved so he could take her other hand.

'Women are awesome,' he told her again. 'Your baby's close and once your bladder's empty your body will take over. Skye, you have so much strength and you've done the hard yards. You have a baby in there who's aching to meet you, so let's make this happen.'

It sounded easy but it wasn't—inserting a catheter when things were so swollen and distended. Jen organised lighting, laid instruments out on sterile towels—catheter, forceps, just in case, and then set up a saline drip while Rob worked. And all the time Rob spoke to Skye gently, telling her what was happening, taking the terror out of the room.

He was taking terror out of Jen's mind as well. She'd been facing a night of Skye's continued obstructed labour, she'd known the probable outcome and it wasn't pretty. But now she was part of a capable, skilled team. Rob was here.

Maybe she'd have felt like this with any doctor—she'd certainly have been relieved—but this was Rob, with his kind eyes, his big, capable hands, his caring...

He and Emma had come to Willhua because they'd wanted to be family doctors, she thought, and it showed. Rob's compassion, his care, his skill were never more on show than they were tonight.

And, strangely, as she worked she was thinking of Emma. Until now Emma had seemed a ghostly entity, Rob's past, but their decision to be part of this community had been shared. If Emma had been here now...

For the first time she totally got the immensity of Rob's loss, his helplessness, his grief, and for the life of her she couldn't prevent her eyes welling. It was only for a moment though because...

Because the bladder emptied with a rush and almost instantly another contraction took over. The strength of it stunned them all. Skye was arching and screaming and her fingernails were digging into Jen's hand...

'Crowning,' Rob said, cutting across the scream. 'Skye, here's the head, your baby's right here, one more hard, strong push—give it all you've got.'

And in the end it was almost a textbook-perfect birth. There was even time, as Rob placed the tiny newborn infant on Skye's breast, as Skye's hands cradled her new little daughter for the first time, as her face creased into wonder and love, for Jen to blink back more tears and then find her phone and take a video.

There was no phone reception—she couldn't send this—but by now Douglas would be beyond frantic. They could radio him the news. They could organise for Skye to talk to him, but in the end she knew this amateurish shot of the birth scene might become a treasure and it was important enough to make the time to get it right. She even swung around and pointed her phone out across the moonlit water, and then back to the bed. This birth could end up as family folklore.

And then she moved back into nurse mode, making sure mum and bub were warm, assisting Rob with a swift stitching—there'd been a slight tear—clearing the afterbirth.

'We thought,' Skye whispered as they worked around her, 'that we could plant the placenta under a rose bush.'

'Hmm.' Jen glanced out again at the moonlit night. The rain had eased and she could see the swirling water surrounding the house. 'Rose bushes? Tricky. And I'm betting your freezer's downstairs and flooded as well. Don't you have a nice big houseplant we could use instead?'

And Skye giggled and it was the best sound Jen thought she'd ever heard. The best!

Then there were calls to an almost hysterically relieved Douglas, to the chopper crew, and to Angus. Jen left that to Rob—he deserved that pleasure. She had enough to do.

The linen cupboard was upstairs and Jen found clean sheets. She managed to give Skye an almost-wash—it seemed there was an uncontaminated water tank connected to an upstairs tap! Then she helped Skye's first miraculous feed, she settled her into her clean bed with her baby cradled next to her and she watched them fall into a natural, blessedly peaceful sleep.

When finally she turned to Rob her heart was full. They'd turned down the lanterns. Rob was standing beside the bed, soaking up the sight of a sleeping mum and baby.

'It's a miracle,' she whispered.

'It is.'

'Emma would be so proud of you.' Where that had come from she didn't know, but she did know it for the truth. And she watched Rob's expression change.

'I think… I hope…'

'I know,' she said, definitely now. 'And yes, I never met her, but I know she left Sydney to be a country doctor and I can see her in those lovely pictures you have in your kitchen. Not the ones in the living room—the formal ones. Just the ones that say she loved being here, she loved what you were doing, and she loved you.'

'I can't…' He spread his hands helplessly and she took them.

'I'm not asking you to,' she told him. 'I wouldn't.'

'Jen…' There was stillness in the room. Even the whistling of the wind around the house seemed to have ceased. He held her hands, just held, as if he was fighting in his head for the next words. For the right words.

'Jenny, I'm still married to Em,' he said at last. 'She and I were partners in every sense, and I vowed to love and honour her until death do us part.'

'I know that,' she said, because something about this night had made her understand in a way she'd never understood before. The sight of him being winched down in wind and rain… The way he'd talked to Skye… The way he'd touched her baby's cheek, the tenderness, the awe…

This man was who he was…and she couldn't ask him to be any other way.

'Would it be wrong though?' he asked, and she could feel some of the tension of the night's drama surge back. 'Would it be so wrong to make those same vows to you? Because I've been thinking…tonight, no, longer, maybe for a month now… Jen, could I love and honour Emma, could I care for her until the end…but still…find a place for us? Because…' He released her hands and stood back a little, as if giving her space. Giving them both space for the momentous? 'I know it's not fair on you, but Jen, I do love you.'

And then there was silence, for so long that Jen thought she'd forgotten how to breathe. Maybe the whole world had forgotten how to breathe.

And then, finally, Jen said what must be said.

'Rob, isn't there something in those vows about forsaking all others? Would that do your head in?'

'Yeah,' he said and then he shook his head. 'Actually, I don't think we said that, but never mind. Because forsaking all others…who would that include? Jacob? Angus, Cathy, Gary, maybe the whole population of Willhua? Everyone I care about? I love Em, but I love so many more. And especially I love you. Jen, you know that I'm married. I can't divorce Em—and that's not because of Lois and Paul, it's because of me. But I would be honoured, humbled, overjoyed, if you'd share my life in every other way.'

And Jen stood in the darkened bedroom, Skye and her baby were sleeping soundly on the bed nearby, water was lapping just underneath the floorboards, the rain was starting up again, and she thought…marriage.

She thought of Darren, standing in that opulent hotel

room—was it only months ago?—with his stupid, shameful belligerence. *'I'm married. And my wife is here.'*

She'd been humiliated to her socks, but yet here was another man standing before her saying, *'I'm married.'*

It was so different. It was wonderfully, miraculously different.

Because she believed him. She trusted him. This was an honourable man and part of his honour was his love for Emma.

She thought back to that appalling scene in the kitchen. Of Paul's almost irrational anger. Of her decision that she lacked the courage to face this situation head-on.

But now...would it take so much courage to face this situation together—to face it side by side with the man she loved?

Because she did love him. She looked up into his beloved face, his anxious eyes, his gorgeous, gorgeous self, and she thought—what gift is this that he's offering? To love me?

Loyalty showed itself in many guises, she thought, and this man had shown it in spades. To have such a man hold her, to give her a place in his life... What would she be thinking not to accept such a gift?

And all she needed was the courage to trust. The belief that this impossible situation was possible.

The acceptance of being loved, and loving in return.

'It'd have to include Stumpy,' she managed, because emotion was threating to overwhelm her and she somehow had to be prosaic. 'And...and Bruce too, if it doesn't work out with Frankie's mate, Nico. And I've promised to stay at the farm until Ruth comes back.'

'How could I ask you to break a promise?' His eyes were caressing her, holding her in thrall. 'Jen, I'm asking if our lives could merge, not one life dissolve into another's needs. I'll face down Lois and Paul...'

'You will not,' she said, suddenly on firm ground. 'Not by yourself. They're ours to deal with now.'

'They'll fight. They have all the legal…'

'And we have all the social,' she retorted. 'I haven't been a nurse and a paramedic for years for nothing. We don't need legal, we need social workers and psychologists and welfare workers. If needed, I could name a score who'd come into any court your in-laws choose and tell the judge just what this situation's doing to Jacob. That doesn't mean that Emma's not his mum, though,' she said. 'But maybe the Brisbane trips could be… I don't know. Different? Maybe even fun. Maybe we could take stuff there, decorate Emma's room, tell her fun stuff we've been doing. And then bookend the visits with zoo trips, or… I don't know…playing Pooh Sticks in the park? But it's *we*, Rob, because Emma's part of your life so I'm thinking she needs to be part of mine as well.'

'You've thought of this…'

'Not this minute,' she said, suddenly unsure again. 'But I've been at Ruth's for two weeks and I've been missing you so much.'

And why did that make him let go of her hands and kiss her, deeply and strongly, and then, because in this moment kissing wasn't enough, pick her up and whirl her round in the darkened bedroom? Finally they remembered where they were, that there was a sleeping new mum and her bub close by. But Skye and her baby were so deeply asleep that nothing could disturb them.

'You know,' Jen said thoughtfully as finally Rob set her down, 'there are three bedrooms on this floor.'

'Really?'

'Really,' she told him. 'And one's just across the hall. If we left both doors open…'

'We could be dutiful medics, on duty all night,' Rob said and swung her up again, cradling her against his chest as if she weighed nothing. 'I'm a very light sleeper and, after all, staying in here might eventually disturb them.'

'I can set my watch timer for checks,' she told him.

'So you can. And if she calls or bub cries we'll be here in a flash.'

'We do need to sleep,' Jen said, smiling and smiling.

'So we do,' Rob replied, and she'd remember the smile he gave her then for the rest of her life. 'Eventually.'

At eight the next morning, when the rain had ceased and the wind had eased to practically nothing, a flat-bottomed Emergency Services boat reached the house. The crew on board roped it to the upper floor, 'Ahoy' rang out—but there was no instant reply.

Finally, though, a window was thrown open and a tousled-looking doctor in a shirt that wasn't quite buttoned leaned out.

'Hey,' one of the crew called. 'You guys need rescuing?'

'If we must,' he said obscurely and grinned. 'No. You're very welcome. There's a new baby here who needs to meet her dad.'

'Douglas is climbing walls.' The burly guy in charge, dressed in filthy yellow all-weather gear, was grinning back. 'So all's well?'

'All's well. Can you give us ten minutes to be respectable?'

'Glad to oblige,' the man said. 'We're set up to receive a stretcher. Are mum and bub stable?'

'I don't want her climbing out of windows but yes, things are fine. We're even dry.'

'Great.' The whole crew was smiling. 'This is a neat change from pulling people off roofs,' the guy said.

'I'd like Skye to be taken to Whale Head,' Rob told them. 'There was a bit of intervention and I'd like her checked by an obstetrician.'

'Sure thing, Doc. We'll get them to Willhua, and South Sydney Air can take them on to Whale Head. There won't be any complaints from Douglas. As long as he has his family safe, nothing else matters.'

And as Rob turned and headed into Skye's bedroom to wake her and ready her for the move—Jen had squeaked when she'd heard the boat and was already frantically dressing—those words resonated.

As long as he has his family safe...

More than one family had been formed last night, he thought. Douglas and Skye and their infant daughter. He and Jenny and Jacob.

His family.

Awful things happened—who knew that better than him?—but they were as safe as he could make them. Yes, he was taking a risk moving in with Jen. Lois and Paul's distress would need to be faced head-on, but he and Jen and Jacob would be together, no matter what.

And today... Today the sun was shining. Jen, dressed and ready, was back beside him, giving him a swift hug before she went to wake Skye.

And for a moment Rob turned again and looked at the sun streaming through the window.

The sun was out.

It was time to move on.

CHAPTER FOURTEEN

EMMA'S FUNERAL TOOK place eighteen months later, on a cold winter's day, but with the sun breaking through the clouds enough to make the damp grass in the little Willhua cemetery glisten. There'd been a rainbow intermittently appearing and disappearing during the morning, and as the small entourage gathered around the graveside it emerged again, casting an almost halo-like effect over the scene.

It had been time. No matter what the intervention, the human body had limits. Treating recurring pneumonia had been a constant struggle during these last appalling years, and in the end there'd been no choice. With Rob by her side, with Lois and Paul fighting to the last, she'd slipped away.

And now, finally, they could say goodbye.

With Emma's death, powers of attorney, legal and medical, no longer held sway so the decisions were now Rob's. 'I'd like her buried at Willhua,' he'd told Lois and Paul, and the couple were too devastated to fight for an alternative, even if they had one. For years they'd refused to face reality and now they had no choice.

But they'd come this morning, for the simple ceremony in the small church out on the headland. And when they'd arrived they'd hugged Jacob—and they'd also hugged Rob. Small beginnings for the future?

On the other side of the grave stood Rob and Jacob—and

Jenny. A family. Not legally married, but married in every other sense. Jacob stood between them, a hand in each of theirs. At nearly six he could almost understand what was happening. Paul and Lois had been shocked at the thought of him attending, but Rob had been adamant.

'He's been with Emma every step of this journey. I think he's understood the concept of death more than any child of his age, and he needs to be with us now.'

Us.

Jen gripped Jacob's hand tighter as the coffin was lowered into the open grave. It was close enough to springtime for the wattle to be out everywhere, and they'd organised great sheaths of the soft yellow blooms to be at the graveside. They'd lain wattle on the base of the grave, and as the coffin lowered, wattle was set on top. The grave could be covered properly later, when Jacob wasn't close. For now all he saw was Emma's coffin being lowered into a cloud of gold.

A final prayer and it was done. Rob lifted his little son and hugged him, and it was time to move on.

But Jen was watching the couple on the far side of the grave, watching their pain, watching the loss they'd never allowed to hit until now. And she touched Rob's arm lightly, she glanced at him, their eyes meeting in a silent message, and then she stepped around the grave to meet them.

'Lois, Paul, I'm so, so sorry,' she said. These were the most prosaic of words, said over and over to all sorts of people, in all sorts of situations. They could hardly make a difference, but they needed to be said.

'I suppose you'll get married now.' That was Lois, and there was such distress behind the words that Jen flinched. But she'd come to talk to them for a purpose and she had to continue.

'Rob and I have already made our vows,' she said, simply

but calmly. 'We're already a family. But Emma's still Jacob's mother, and she still feels part of our family. And you're his grandparents and you could be too.'

'You don't want us.'

'We don't want your control,' Jen said gently. 'But we don't want Jacob to lose more than he already has. Rob and I have talked about it. It's early days yet, but whatever happens in the future, anger has no place. Love, though… If you think love for Jacob could let you move forward, Rob and I will be with you every step of the way.'

'We can't…' It was practically a moan from Lois.

'You can't keep loving?' And it was Rob, moving to stand beside her. He was still holding Jacob, cradling the little boy as if he was still a toddler.

But then Jacob wriggled—he'd seen someone he knew. Frankie! Auntie Frankie! Jacob's wriggle was demanding, and Rob lowered him. They all watched as the little boy weaved through the group of the locals who'd supported them so strongly over these last months and found the woman he'd learned to love. Frankie and her crew had even let him go and see her helicopter and sit in the pilot's seat. How awesome an aunt was she?

Frankie knelt and high-fived the little boy and waved to them that she had him in charge. Auntie Frankie. A loved part of Jen's life.

Jen waved back—and then she turned back to Lois and Paul. *You can't keep loving?*

That was the question Rob had asked, and it hung, unanswered.

'It just takes courage,' Rob said simply. 'For all of us.'

Then there was a whoop from Jacob and they all turned to see.

'Auntie Frankie has Bruce here!' Jacob yelled. 'Bruce! He's tied up under that tree. She says we'll take him and Stumpy to the park later and Ruth says Bosun can come too. Can we, Jen? Can we, Dad?'

'I don't see why not,' Rob called back. And then he kissed Jen because he needed to. 'It's time to leave,' he said, smiling down at her. 'Em will always be in our hearts, but she'd be the first one to say it's time for us all to move on. Together.'

A birth. A baby. A tiny girl, Stephanie Emma Francesca—because how could Frankie be left out of the equation?

Rob had been with Jen all this long night of labour. Cathy and Angus had been the medics. Rob had simply been...the dad. He was tired now, exhausted beyond belief, but there was no space yet in his life for sleep. He was perched on Jen's bedside, cradling his daughter, gazing down at this new little person and feeling as if his heart might burst.

His daughter.

Jacob had been in to inspect his new sister, but Minnie and the promise of a walk to the playground with Stumpy held much more attraction than a mere baby. Minnie had whisked him away. The medical bustle of birth and aftercare had faded and Rob was left with his wife.

His Jen.

His love.

Love... It was all around them. He could feel it in spades. It was in the way Jen was watching him, the way she was watching her daughter in his arms, the way she was blinking back tears of happiness.

It was also in the way this entire hospital, this entire community was erupting with happiness at the news. Already a small mountain of flowers and soft toys were being left at

Reception. He'd seen them in the moments when he'd had to duck out to make fast phone calls after delivery—one to Frankie—of course—one to Jen's parents, who'd answered by satellite phone from somewhere in the Himalayas—and one also to Lois and Paul, who'd responded with delight and a suggestion, tentative, almost humble, that they might meet this new addition to their family.

That could happen, he thought—their relationship had softened to the point where they'd even be welcome. But not today. Today was theirs; it belonged to Jen and Rob.

But they both knew they were surrounded by the care of those who loved them.

He'd brought two of the offerings from Reception back to Jen. One was a tiny, fluffy teddy with a note attached. It was from Anna, mother now of a chubby two-year-old. She was enrolled at online university and sharing her life with her small son and his adoring grandparents. Her note read simply— *'Thank you for my miracle, welcome to yours'.*

The other was from Skye and Douglas—a bunch of wildflowers, with a note which pretty much read the same.

He'd shown the notes to Jen. She'd blinked back more tears and then folded into his arms, their tiny daughter cradled between them.

This was his miracle, he thought. His own private miracle.

And then he thought—what was he thinking? This wasn't private at all.

Jen. Jacob. Minnie. Angus and Cathy. Frankie. Gary. Paul and Lois. The whole community of Willhua.

Love encompassed them all, he thought as he held his wife close. It filled his heart.

'I love you so much,' he whispered.

'Not as much as I love you,' she managed back. 'Oh, Rob, can I be any happier?'

'Let's work on it,' he told her, kissing her hair and then tilting her chin to kiss her lips. And then, as the kiss finally ended...

'Let's take it as our personal challenge,' he whispered. 'You and me and our family and our community—even our dogs. Take fair warning, my own sweet love. Happy-ever-after, here we come.'

* * * * *

THE ITALIAN,
HIS PUP AND ME

ALISON ROBERTS

MILLS & BOON

For Linda

With very much love

CHAPTER ONE

RULES *COULD* BE BROKEN, couldn't they?

When they were rules that you'd given yourself? And when there might be a very good reason to break them?

Like…if it seemed as if the perfect man had just walked into your life but you were not allowed to be remotely interested in him just because…

…because he was Italian?

Francesca Moretti let her breath out in a sigh that was melodramatic enough to attract the attention of the men sharing this table with her. She could feel several sets of eyes shifting to focus on her.

'What's up, Frankie?' Colin, shift manager for the South Sydney Air Rescue base, sounded genuinely concerned. 'Sounds like you just found out the world was ending. Did I miss a headline on that front page of the paper?'

'We've been on shift for too long with no action, that's all.' Mozzie, one of the Red Watch helicopter pilots shook his head. 'Interhospital transfers don't quite cut the mustard when our Frankie has such a low boredom threshold.'

'Not true.' Frankie waved a dismissive hand. 'I have no objection to transfers, even when they have an escort and we're just providing a taxi service. In theory, that is. And only in moderation, of course.' She put her empty coffee mug on top of the plate that had crumbs and melted cheese left over from her lunch toastie. 'But you're right. I've been sitting on my bum for too long and I just ate the biggest toasted cheese sandwich in the world. I'm going to go and lift some weights in the gym or something. It was windy enough this morning to bring tree branches down and it made it a bit dangerous to do my usual run through the bush reserve.'

'At least it's settled down now,' Mozzie said. 'Might still be a bit lumpy up there for a while, though.'

'Bring it on.' Frankie grinned. 'Lumpier the better as far as I'm concerned.'

She couldn't help shifting her gaze as she got to her feet. To Mr Perfect.

The new addition to Red Watch—the helicopter rescue crew she had become a part of a couple of years ago now. Thanks to a relationship that had gone bad in a rather spectacular fashion, her best friend and colleague, Jenny, had thrown in the most exciting job in the world to go and be a paramedic in a small town much further south of Sydney and her position on the crew had been filled by…

Nico.

Nico Romano.

It wasn't just his name that was so obviously Italian. He had olive skin and wildly curly black hair that was long enough to need restraining in a kind of messy man bun thing at the back of his head while he was on duty. He had facial hair that was so neatly trimmed, in contrast, that it looked like designer stubble and his eyes were as dark as sin.

As dark as Frankie's were. And they were looking straight

back at her. Frankie had to ignore the weird tingle that eye contact with this man had given her ever since they'd been introduced for the first time the other day. Now that they were working on their first shift together, she really needed to get it under firm control. She didn't actually know this man at all so this was vaguely reminiscent of a teenage crush on a movie star. Good grief…if she kept this up, she'd be putting a poster of the man on her bedroom wall and that thought was so ridiculous she could give herself the mental shove she needed to douse that tingle.

'You don't get air sick, do you, Nico?' She kept her tone light. Casual. Totally impersonal, even. 'Mozzie's quite happy to take on some pretty gnarly weather sometimes.'

'I never get sick,' he said. 'For any reason. I am…' He frowned. 'What's the expression? As healthy as a…hose?'

'That's a horse, mate.' Colin was laughing.

'That's what I said.'

'No…you said *hose*, which is what you water the garden with.'

'I thought he said *house*,' Mozzie said.

Everybody was laughing now. Except Frankie. Because Nico had an accent that was as Italian as everything else about him. He'd become a paramedic and gone on to work on helicopters in Milan and had only come to Australia to take up a position with an air ambulance in Queensland a handful of years ago but his English was as impressive as the CV that had put him at the top of a long list of contenders for the position of being part of this prestigious air rescue base.

Frankie had been born in Australia but she had grown up in an Italian community and been raised by her mother and grandmother. Both strong, independent women but they still bought into notions that should have been left behind in the old country generations ago. Frankie could actually hear an echo of her *nonna*'s voice in the back of her head.

'Why is it you want to keep doing a dangerous job like being a paramedic? In a helicopter, per amor del cielo! Find a nice Italian boy, Francesca, and settle down to have molte bambini. Give me some pronipoti before I die...'

Nico shrugged off the laughter with a resigned shrug and went back to reading the SOPs—Standard Operating Procedures—for his new base. Frankie knew he'd done an initiation protocol during her last few days off and he'd been working already with an Australian helicopter crew as a paramedic so he should fit in seamlessly with her crew, but the glue that held people together in stressful situations wasn't just about having expertise in invasive interventions in a trauma case, for example, or being skilled at winch operations.

Colin lifted his hand in a wave as he went back to his office. Mozzie said he was off to do another check on his beloved helicopter—a brand new Airbus H145 that was his pride and joy. Ricky—an aircrew officer, whose role included assisting the pilot, paramedics or doctors with medical care, looking after equipment and operating the winch—reached for Frankie's empty coffee mug and plate to take to the dishwasher with his lunch dishes.

'You don't have to tidy up after me, Ricky.'

'And there I was thinking that was the only reason you kept me around, Frankie.'

Frankie rolled her eyes but she was smiling. Red Watch

was a tight team and the reason for that was the X factor in whether a crew became tight enough for trust to be automatic. The cohesion of any group like this depended on the personalities of the people as much as, or possibly even more than any other factor.

The jury was still out on Nico Romano. Except that Frankie knew she shouldn't even be *on* the jury because she was clinging to some rebellious streak that she'd developed decades ago, thanks to her *nonna* and the community she'd grown up within. A stupid rule she'd made into a sacred vow and stuck to ever since. She also knew that it wasn't remotely acceptable to be judging someone simply on their appearance, nationality or accent. She had to give the man a chance, for heaven's sake. She didn't actually know anything about him.

Except that he was drop-dead gorgeous.

And he could do strange things to her body just by *looking* at her...

Oh, help...

Frankie had never been more grateful for the vibration and beep of the pager attached to her belt. She could see Colin coming out of the office at the same time and he had a look on his face that she could read instantly.

There was an emergency somewhere within their reach and they were about to get dispatched to where they were needed most. Frankie had no idea where it might be or how serious it was but she could feel her adrenaline levels rising fast. This was what she loved about this job. You started every single mission not knowing what kind of challenges you could be up against, but that only made it more exciting. The goal was always the same. To help people in what might be the biggest challenge they would ever face.

To stay alive.

Nico Romano was in one of his favourite places.

Sitting in the open doorway of a helicopter, with one foot balanced on the skid, trusting the strap he had hooked to the roof of the cabin as he leaned out, trying to be the first to spot their target amongst the challenging landscape below.

Finally, after a couple of trauma cases that were satisfying but pretty routine, they were way out in the Central Blue Mountains, west of Sydney, on a mission that was promising to be a lot less ordinary. They had landed some distance away from the scene location to rendezvous with the Blue Mountains Police, configure the helicopter for a winch operation and get all the details they could on the incident they'd been dispatched to. It was a mission that was already ticking a lot of boxes near the top of a job satisfaction scoresheet for Nico.

The incident had happened halfway down a canyon, which added all sorts of challenges to extract the patient. The injured hiker's accident might have only resulted in a probable ankle fracture but the sixty-five-year-old man had since developed chest pain and other symptoms that suggested he might be having a heart attack, so it could prove to be a challenge medically as well as logistically. They had hovered over the scene before landing, long enough to make a plan of action, and Mozzie reckoned he could perch a skid on the edge of a ledge, which would let the medic jump out and save the time it would take to winch them down and then back up with the patient attached to him.

Best of all, it was Nico who was going to be the one leaping out onto that ledge.

It had been Frankie's suggestion how they would decide who would take the lead in what was likely to be the last mission and the first winch operation for this shift. She'd caught Nico's glance as they moved swiftly back to the helicopter.

'Want to do the winch?'

'If you're happy, yes, absolutely.' He gave her a quick smile. 'But I wouldn't want you to get bored on your first day working with me.'

She didn't exactly smile back but there was a gleam in her eyes that looked like approval and that was a win all by itself, given the cool reception he'd noted in his new colleague up till now.

'Rock, paper, scissors, then?'

Nobody could hear them over the crescendo of the helicopter rotors gaining speed. It took no more than five seconds. Nobody would have noticed the swift hand gestures either. And Nico had won, scissors over paper, no doubt thanks to the many games of *sasso, carta, forbici* he had played with his sisters to also settle arguments about who got to have the best treat being offered or first turn at an activity they all wanted to do.

Frankie reminded him very much of his sisters, to be honest, with that long, curly black hair that was barely tamed by a braid and dark eyes beneath a heavy fringe and a luxuriant tangle of eyelashes. She might sound like an Australian but there was no mistaking her Italian genes. She was confident. A bit loud. She used her hands a lot when she was talking and…she talked—and laughed—a lot.

Nico didn't want to like that. He most certainly didn't want to find it as attractive as he seemed to be finding it. Attraction like this was dangerous and Nico knew exactly why he had alarm bells already sounding, and why he needed to shut it down before it could even start. That way, it could never escalate into something too big to resist. You wouldn't start trusting someone enough to fall in love with them and you could avoid ending up with that trust shattered, along with any shred of self-esteem.

Nico had made that mistake once before, when he'd fallen for Sofia—his first love—hard enough to marry her and it had, quite literally, scarred him for life. Emotionally *and* physically.

Never again.

It was all in the past now. That longing to find his soul mate. To be the best husband ever and to have his own children growing up as part of the beloved new generation of the Romano family. That dream, like the kind of trust he had put in the person he had chosen to share that future, no longer existed.

The yearning could still come out of hiding occasionally, however, no matter how unwelcome it was, but Nico had learned how to deflect it, if he couldn't dismiss it entirely at times. He could find a reason for its appearance that was not going to mess with how happy he was with his new life.

He missed his sisters, that was all—along with the rest of his family. Maybe this attraction wasn't sexual at all—it could be simply a comforting familiarity to have someone who shared his cultural heritage as a member of his new crew. It didn't go both ways, that was for sure. There was also no mistaking the suspicion with which Frankie had been regarding him since they were introduced a few days ago. Had she sensed that he was drawn to her and was making it very clear that she wasn't interested? It obviously wasn't going to be an instant friendship after bonding over pizza or something, but Nico was hoping that his performance on this next job might at least make him more welcome on her crew.

And that was all he wanted from Frankie Moretti—a professional relationship—no matter how attractive she might be or how easily she might be able to cure any vestige of homesickness after his years away from Italy. Even friendship could well get too close to a boundary Nico had no intention of crossing. With any woman, but especially not with someone like Frankie.

Oddio… She would be the last woman on earth who could change his mind about that, because it wasn't just his sisters that she reminded him of, was it?

It was every Italian woman.

Including Sofia.

Especially Sofia, thanks to the level of attraction that had been almost a kick in his gut when they'd been introduced.

But it was okay. It might be a bigger challenge than he was used to handling but he knew he wasn't in any danger. History was not going to be allowed to repeat itself.

Mozzie's control of the aircraft was impressive as they approached the incident scene again. So was the landscape below, with a waterfall between two rocky cliffs which were far enough apart to let the helicopter drop between them and had the advantage of protecting them from any wind gusts higher up. With one skid delicately touching the very edge of a large outcrop of rocks, Nico was able to jump out, with a backpack containing medical supplies and a winch harness for a patient. An upward glance as Mozzie took the helicopter up to hover nearby, well above the cliffs, showed Frankie leaning out to watch Nico.

His patient wasn't far away, on the ground, leaning against another member of his hiking group who had climbed down to care for him until help arrived.

'I'm Nico. I hear you've got a sore ankle and some chest pain?' Nico could already see the deformity of the man's ankle that indicated a dislocation and probable fracture as well.

'I didn't take his boot off,' the man's companion said. 'I didn't want to hurt Martin here, and I thought it might be providing a bit of a splint.'

'Good thinking.' Nico nodded. 'I'll give him some pain relief before we do anything to his foot.' There was something else that was more of a concern right now. 'Tell me about this chest pain, Martin,' he said. 'Have you ever had anything like this before?'

'No. It's right here.' He put a hand on the centre of his chest. 'And it goes into my neck and up into my jaw as well.'

'If I give you a scale of zero to ten, with zero being no pain and ten being the worst you can think of, what number would you give this pain?'

'Ten. It's worse than my ankle.'

Nico nodded. 'I'm going to put a needle in your hand and give you something for the pain and then we're going to get you up into our helicopter as quickly as possible, okay?'

'Okay…'

Martin lay back against his friend. He looked grey, Nico

noted, and he was sweating profusely. He couldn't do an ECG until he got his patient on board but the urgency to do so was high. Nico opened his kit and pulled items out rapidly.

'Are you allergic to any drugs that you know of, Martin?'

'No.'

'Do you have any medical conditions I should know about? High blood pressure, asthma, diabetes…?'

'No.'

'Okay…sharp scratch…there we go.' Nico secured the line and drew up the drugs he needed to administer. With effective pain relief on board, he removed the heavy boot and splinted the foot and ankle and, with the help of Martin's friend, he got his patient into a harness. They were able to get him standing on one leg, with the support of being clipped to Nico's harness.

'You need to get right back.' Nico had to raise his voice to a shout over the sound of the helicopter's rotors after he radioed that he was ready for pickup, and the friend began scrambling back up the cliff to where other hiking club members were huddled. The sound was deafening as Mozzie hovered between the cliffs again and a winch line was being lowered. Ricky was operating the winch and Frankie was where he'd been earlier, with one foot on the skid, waiting to help get their patient on board.

It took very little time. As soon as they were on board the door was closed and Mozzie gained altitude and turned back towards the city.

Nico and Frankie both began to work on Martin, attaching chest pads and other monitoring equipment.

'Symptoms strongly suggestive of ischaemic chest pain,'

Nico said. 'No history of cardiac problems. We're not going to get an accurate twelve-lead ECG en route but I can see significant ST elevation on the single lead rhythm strip.'

'Oxygen saturation's below ninety-four percent,' Frankie said. 'I'll put some oxygen on.'

'Blood pressure?'

'One seventy over ninety. Heart rate's sixty-two. Is he on any medication?'

'No.'

'What's our flight time to the nearest PCI unit?'

'That'll be St Mary's. At least twenty-five minutes, I'd guess. Mozzie?'

But Mozzie was busy with a call from the South Coast Emergency Response Centre that controlled the dispatch of all emergency service vehicles and aircraft. Nico could hear him telling the control room that they were unavailable for at least the next thirty minutes and that he'd update them as soon as they were free.

'How's that pain in your chest now, Martin?'

'Not so bad...'

'Can you score it for me? Out of ten like we did before?'

'About a six?'

'I can give you some more medication for that.'

'I feel a bit sick.'

'I'll give you something for that as well. Sorry, it's a bit bumpy up here today.'

Nico had to focus to be able to draw up the drugs and administer them with the sideways slipping of the helicopter in conditions that were a little turbulent again and then he had to pause to attach the syringe to the plug before injecting the drugs when they hit a sudden drop. He glanced up at Frankie.

'Lumpy enough for you?'

'I'm not complaining.' Frankie was watching his movements and her half smile suggested she was also not complaining about his handling of the conditions and their patient.

They both shifted their gaze to the monitor as an alarm sounded. Martin's heartrate had dropped below sixty into a bradycardia.

'Level of consciousness is dropping,' Frankie warned. 'Martin?' She shook their patient's shoulder. 'Can you hear me?'

But Martin's eyes were closed and his head slumped to one side. And Nico could see the ominous wide, bizarre complexes on the ECG trace that suddenly deteriorated into a pattern that was no more than an uncoordinated squiggle.

'He's in VF,' he said tersely. 'Stand clear, Frankie. I'm going to defibrillate him.'

'Want me to land?' Mozzie could hear what was being said between the crew members. He knew how urgent this was and Nico could feel the helicopter losing altitude already.

'No. We would lose too much time. I'm happy to do it now. Charging to maximum joules.'

Nico caught the startled glances from both Frankie and Ricky and he understood that they might be concerned. Defibrillating during flight was riskier than on land, especially in turbulent conditions, but he had done this before and he was confident. Trying to do effective CPR in a vibrating aircraft for as long as it took to find a suitable landing site and put the chopper down would eat too much into the time it was possible to keep heart muscle alive.

'Stay clear,' he warned the others again. 'Hang onto something in case we hit a bump.'

He pressed the shock button and Martin's body jerked but the interference on the monitor screen settled to reveal he was still in the fatal cardiac rhythm of ventricular fibrillation.

'Start CPR, please, Frankie. I will place an LMA. If that's not adequate, I'll intubate.' Nico reached for the laryngeal airway that would be much easier to place than intubating in these cramped conditions. He had to ride the movement of a downdraught before he could insert the airway and fill the cushion with air with the attached syringe to secure it. He clipped a bag mask onto the airway with a practised swiftness and a quick squeeze showed the chest rising adequately. Thankfully, they already had IV access so Nico could draw up the drugs needed and administer them before they had another attempt to defibrillate their patient. Moments later, Nico braced himself to snap open an ampoule of adrenaline and slide a needle in to draw up the drug without stabbing himself in the process. He could see that Frankie was also bracing herself and that she was doing an impressive job of keeping her chest compressions fast and deep enough to be effective. Ricky had managed to fit into a space where he could be providing ventilations and vital oxygen.

Somewhere, in the very back of Nico's brain, was a passing reminder that he'd hoped this mission would make him a welcome addition to this crew.

He hadn't expected it to be quite this dramatic. And now he had to focus completely and do his utmost to keep their patient alive.

* * *

Wow...

Just...wow...

Frankie slid yet another glance at their new crew member as they flew back to base. They were already late to finish their shift but what a way to complete a first day. Nico had shown himself to be not only confident but even more capable than any one of them might have hoped he would be. He had undoubtedly saved a man's life today. The second in-flight defibrillation on Martin had restored a perfusing rhythm and he was actually waking up as they landed on the roof of St Mary's Hospital in the western suburbs of Sydney, where he would be fast-tracked to the catheter laboratory to have his coronary arteries unblocked and prevent any further damage to his heart.

'I've never done that,' Frankie confessed. 'Defibrillated in-flight, that is. Or intubated, for that matter. I've always done it prior to transfer. Or we've touched down somewhere.'

The corners of Nico's mouth lifted a little. 'It's no different to doing it on the ground,' he said. 'You just need to be a little more careful, that's all. Especially when it's lumpy.'

'It saved so much time. It could have tipped the balance to getting him back. Not only getting his heart going again, but fast enough to prevent any hypoxic brain injury.'

'I couldn't believe it when he opened his eyes and tried to pull out the LMA.' Ricky was grinning. 'Good job, Nico.'

Nico just shrugged. 'It was a team effort.' He turned to look out of his window as Mozzie brought the helicopter down on the big cross painted outside the South Sydney Air Rescue hangar.

Frankie let her gaze rest on him a little longer this time. So Nico Romano wasn't just gorgeous to look at. He was courageous and competent and remarkably modest about his talents, and her being attracted to him had just tipped into something a little more significant.

Good grief…was she in danger of falling in love with this man already?

It was just as well they were colleagues on the same crew because that was as good as an ironclad backup rule. Getting involved with an Italian man might be the first on the list of Frankie's no-go areas, but someone she had to work with this closely was definitely a close second. She had seen all too often the damage that could be wrought in a career by an ill-advised romantic liaison and she was not about to risk any aspect of the job she loved so much. She only had to remember the reason her friend Jenny had felt forced to leave this air rescue base and that disastrous fall-out from a relationship gone very wrong hadn't even been with someone she worked with every day.

She wanted to echo Ricky's praise and tell Nico that he'd done well today but, for some reason, Frankie felt very un-characteristically shy. Maybe because she knew she'd been a little less than entirely welcoming and was now some-what embarrassed about it? Deliberately putting up a bar-rier hadn't been only because Nico was Italian and far too good-looking. Frankie had already been missing working with her best friend.

'… Jenny?'

'What?' Frankie's glance swerved towards Mozzie, who was catching up behind her. She had clearly missed some-thing he'd been saying.

'Isn't Willhua where Jenny moved to?'

'Yes…' Frankie's eyebrows shot up. Had Mozzie been reading her mind? 'Why?'

'I was just talking to Donna in Control and they're about to drop a new job on us.'

'But we're way over time to finish our shift already. It's dark…'

'There's no one else available. We got a call about this one when you lot were in the middle of saving that guy from his cardiac arrest. A truck went over a cliff just out of Willhua. The response crew got a status one patient out from the wreck and took him to the local hospital, but apparently they think there may be another person involved. Some guy called Bruce. They just want us to go and have a look. We might be able to see something from out to sea that they can't see from where they are on the road and, if there is someone down there, they'd rather not leave them until daylight when they can get climbers down.'

'Okay…' Frankie nodded. She lifted her helmet to put it back on but Mozzie shook his head.

'We might be going for just a look-see, but if we do spot something we need to be prepared. Could be a body retrieval and it might end up being a winch operation. It could be wet. We'll keep the crew minimal so Ricky can go home but at least one of you'd better get a suit on.'

Frankie caught Nico's glance. He was grinning and she saw his hand form a fist by his side. She followed his example. Mozzie was looking straight ahead and couldn't see what they were doing. Holding Nico's gaze, she pumped her fist, once, twice… On the third time she kept it as a fist. Nico had made a V sign with his fingers for scissors. It had taken only a couple of seconds this time and Frankie's rock had won. Nico conceded defeat with a single nod but held Frankie's gaze for a moment longer and, in that flick of time, she could feel…something that had nothing to do with that tingle.

The first strand of the kind of bond you wanted to have with a colleague?

The first beat of a friendship?

Whatever…

It felt good.

'Five minutes,' she called over her shoulder as her pager sounded and she broke into a run. 'Don't go anywhere without me.'

CHAPTER TWO

THE FARM TRUCK had apparently been initially caught half-way down the cliff but had since moved because it had only been a tree that was keeping it relatively stable. The tide was in and waves would be breaking over the rocks on the shoreline and probably splashing high enough to make it cold and wet if a medic needed to be winched down to a victim. It was quite possible they might end up retrieving a body from the ocean, as Mozzie had suggested, in which case the medic would actually have to be in the water.

Which was why Frankie had put on her wet suit before they even took off from the base. The section of the road where the accident had happened was already closed so the helicopter would be able to land on the road, if necessary, to prepare for a winch operation by removing any unessential equipment, like the stretcher and equipment packs, but Frankie didn't want to be trying to squeeze into a wet suit at that point.

In front of Nico…

She closed the zips on the ankles of her suit and put her wet shoes on, with their extra ankle support and the neoprene insoles to absorb the impact of climbing over rocks. She was putting on her helmet as she walked out to the landing pad, where the helicopter rotors were already gaining speed and its identification lights flashing. Mozzie had his night vision goggles in place over his helmet and Nico handed Frankie a pair as she climbed on board and slid the door shut behind her. Moments later they were lifting clear of the ground.

'Flight time?'

'Less than thirty minutes,' Mozzie responded.

'Any more info?'

'Not yet. Local cop is trying to have a good look before we get there but it sounds like he's only got a torch so I wouldn't think he'll be able to see much.'

'It's very close to Willhua Rocks, right?' Frankie was tapping the screen of her tablet to bring up all the information they had so far. 'That's where Jenny's taken that paramedic position. I know she wasn't due to start her new job for a day or two, but she might have been involved with the response effort already.'

'Jenny?' Nico raised his eyebrows.

'The medic you've replaced on the crew.'

'Why did she leave?' Nico was looking down at his own tablet. 'Looks like this Willhua's barely a dot on the map. A village. Bit of a contrast to working with air rescue, isn't it?'

'A bit of quiet time is probably just what she needs,' Frankie said. Not that she was going to divulge information her best friend wouldn't want her to share, but Nico would no doubt hear about the scandal of Jenny's relationship with the married CEO of South Sydney Air Rescue anyway. 'She had some personal stuff she needed to get away from.'

Nico's smile was wry. 'I understand. Personally, I find that keeping too busy to have time to think works better than going to quiet places.'

Frankie blinked at the idea that Mr Perfect might have found it necessary to keep super busy in order to get through the heartbreak of a crashed relationship. It was more believable that he had needed to fight off the hordes of women who would be desperate to attract his attention. Like she could be if she let herself step into that space?

She shook that disturbing thought off by turning to look down as they left the brightly lit edges of south Sydney behind them to head down the coast. The night vision goggles made the world look green and black and any lights shone like small stars. The lights from houses got further and further apart and cars moving on the coastal road made it easy to see where the land ended and the sea began.

They didn't need to wear the night vision goggles when they reached the GPS coordinates of the accident scene. Mozzie activated the 'night sun'—a searchlight attached to the front lefthand side of the helicopter that had the power of thirty to forty million candles. They hovered just above the waves at the point before they started to break, taking in the scene from the sea side. Frankie clipped a safety line to an anchor and opened the side door so she could sit on the edge above the skid and peer right beneath the helicopter. Nico had also clipped himself onto a safety line and was standing behind her, leaning over her shoulder.

The wrecked truck wasn't halfway down the cliff now. It had slipped further and was lying on its back like a dead turtle amongst huge rocks that might be well clear of the waves in low tide but had white spray cutting visibility now and water reaching the level of the wheels every time a wave washed in.

'If anyone was still in the vehicle, they would have drowned long ago,' Frankie said.

'The vehicle was cleared before the local emergency services left the scene.'

'Doesn't necessarily mean that somebody didn't try and get back to it later. What if they had a head injury and it seemed like a safe place to head for?'

'Fair call.' Nico nodded. 'Can we get the light higher, please, Mozzie, to where the truck was to start with?'

'No worries.'

The centre of the intense beam of light from the night sun moved up the cliff as the helicopter gained height.

'That must be the tree that the truck was caught on.' Frankie could see the pale scars of gouged bark and a freshly broken branch. She turned her head, trying to imagine where a body might end up if it had been thrown from this vehicle on its way over the edge of the cliff or bouncing against the rocks and sparse vegetation on its slide towards that tree.

And then she caught her breath.

'I can see something. And I think I can see it moving...'

'Where?' Nico was leaning further out of the helicopter. Frankie could actually feel the warmth of his breath on the side of her neck. Or maybe it was just his body heat?

'Behind that group of rocks at about seven o'clock. Maybe two metres down from the tree. There's a bit of scrub and there's something white...'

'Can't see a thing.'

'There...' Frankie pointed. 'It looks like... I'm not sure. A tee shirt sleeve, maybe? A bit of white clothing, anyway. I think someone's waving at us. Calling for help...' She was wriggling back into the cabin. 'Mozzie? Is the road okay to touch down so we can configure for a winch job?'

Mozzie took the helicopter higher and they all scanned the area for potential hazards like power lines or loose debris. A police car with its lights flashing was further up the road near a bend, to prevent any approaching traffic getting onto this section of the road. What looked like a tow truck was doing the same thing in the opposite direction and there was another police car beside it that was most likely the transport for members of the Serious Crash Squad who would be investigating this accident.

Mozzie put the helicopter down gently on the empty tarmac between those vehicles and they quickly set up to winch.

'You happy with operating the winch, Nico?'

'Of course. Why would I not be?' Nico's tone was slightly defensive and he was frowning.

'Just checking.' Frankie clipped a carabiner to her harness and met his gaze straight-on. It was her life that would be—literally—on the line if something went wrong. 'This is a new setup for you.'

'It's exactly the setup I was working with in my last position. I double-checked everything on my initiation.'

Frankie would have understood if Nico was offended by the unspoken concern she might have about his skills, given they had no backup by the presence of a crewman, but the way his expression softened told her that he understood exactly how much trust she was putting in someone she hadn't worked with for more than a matter of hours.

'I'll keep you safe, Frankie,' he said. 'I promise.'

Mozzie was just as responsible for keeping her safe and

he had earned Frankie's complete trust long ago. Within a short time Frankie found herself being slowly lowered on the end of a wire towards the ledge with the scarred tree and its broken branches. She was carrying only a harness that could be used to extract either a living patient or a body, but nothing else. If any treatment was needed, down this cliff in the darkness wasn't the time or place to be doing it. Mozzie could lift her straight up to the road above and put her down before landing again himself.

Frankie watched the approaching rocks of the cliffside.

'Ten metres,' she told the crew through the microphone in her helmet. 'Six…four…two… Okay…' Frankie could feel her feet were secure on the rocks. 'I'm down. Unhooking now…'

She needed to be free of the winch line quickly so there was no danger of it getting tangled with the remains of the nearby tree and she held the winch hook high and away from her body before using a signal with her other hand to let Nico know he could wind it back in. Mozzie moved the helicopter further away so that she wasn't being buffeted by the downdraught from the rotors, and that was when Frankie took a deep breath and began to scan the area.

She was alone on a steep cliff. In the dark. She could see the inky darkness of unforgiving rocks below her and the foam of crashing waves, sparkling in the light the helicopter was still providing. It should have been terrifying but Frankie knew the best way to push any fear back. She just had to focus on why she was here. She'd seen movement. Something white. Something that might be a person in very real trouble.

Except…it wasn't.

Frankie carefully climbed down past the scrub that had managed to grow amongst the rocks, thickly enough to provide both a cushion effect to break a fall and a cover to make it hard to be seen. The patch of white she'd seen from above was not a piece of clothing, however. It was the tip of a long and very fluffy tail that belonged to quite a big black and white dog. A dog who was looking straight at her as she parted the branches of the scruffy bush.

'Oh…' Frankie had never faced quite this situation before. The dog looked frightened and was trying to move. Towards her or further away? Her first thought was that if it moved too far it could quickly be in danger of falling further down the cliff onto those rocks. She reached for the thick leather collar around its neck. She could see something written on the collar, probably in permanent marker ink. *BRUCE…*

'Oh…' she said again, more loudly this time.

'What is it?' Nico's voice in the headphones of her helmet sounded like he was standing right beside her.

'I've found him. Bruce.'

'Status?'

'Um…' Bruce the dog was still looking very scared. He was damp from windblown sea spray and was probably cold and when he tried to get up in response to her focused attention she heard him whine and saw that he couldn't put weight on a front leg, but he didn't seem to be badly injured otherwise. 'Category four, I guess. Three at the most. He might have a leg injury but it doesn't appear obviously fractured.'

'So he can climb out himself? And help get the harness on?'

'No, I'll need to put the harness on him.' Frankie was thinking fast. Risking your own safety for an animal was not an approved part of any SOPs but she couldn't leave this poor dog here all night, waiting for someone to try and climb down to rescue him in daylight. 'It's okay... I can manage.'

She stroked the dog's head. 'It's okay, Bruce,' she told him. 'I'm here to help. You're going to be okay...you just need to trust me.'

And Bruce, bless him, seemed to understand. Or maybe he was just too frightened to protest as she put the dog's legs through the holes in a harness designed for humans and then strapped it tightly enough to be secure before attaching it to her own harness and pulling herself, with the not inconsiderable extra weight, back to the clearer space further up. She signalled for the winch line to be lowered again and it was then that she heard the odd pause in communication and knew that Nico and probably Mozzie were both trying to work out what was going on.

'What is that?' Nico sounded bewildered. 'Is Bruce a *child*?'

'He's a dog.'

There was another silence. Frankie clipped the winch hook to her harness and signalled that she was ready to be lifted. 'Put us up on the road,' she said. 'We can sort it out there.'

The local police officer, two officers from the Serious Crash Squad and the tow truck driver seemed to find it a bit of a joke that a multi-million-dollar helicopter and its highly trained crew had used their impressive resources to rescue an extremely scruffy-looking farm dog. They weren't, however, about to offer to take it off their hands.

The police officer walked off, laughing. 'He might like a ride in the helicopter back to the city,' he suggested. 'I better go and sort that traffic that's piling up.'

There were only two cars behind where he'd blocked the road with his police car.

'We've got a job to do,' one of the crash investigators said and went in the same direction.

The tow truck driver just shook her head and walked in the opposite direction. 'I'm not allowed dogs in my truck,' she said. 'And there's no point in me hanging around. We're not about to pull that wreck up from the rocks in the dark.'

'Can you have a look at him?' Frankie asked Nico. 'And see if he's hurt?'

'I'm not a vet,' Nico protested. 'I don't know anything about treating dogs. Are you telling me you normally take animals as patients as well as people?'

'No, of course not.' Nico's reaction was disappointing. 'But I couldn't leave him down the cliff. And we can't just leave him on the road, can we?'

'We can't just use an air rescue helicopter to take him anywhere else. I'm sure there must be some regulations about that.'

Bruce was lying on the tarmac. A bit hunched. He looked as though he was avoiding any direct eye contact as both Nico and Mozzie looked down at him.

Mozzie shrugged. 'He looks a bit cold. I'll grab a towel so we can get him a bit drier. It won't hurt to take a look at him, will it?'

'I'll try and get hold of Jenny and find out if there's a local vet or rescue centre that could come and get him.'

'Good thinking.' Mozzie nodded. 'But make it quick, yeah? It'd be quite nice to get home some time soon and I need to let Control know what's happening.'

It took only a couple of taps on the screen of her phone to call Jenny, and Frankie found herself holding her breath, realising how much she was already missing working with someone who'd been a colleague until only a matter of days ago, but so much more than that as well. Her closest friend.

The note in Jenny's voice as she answered the call made it obvious she'd been on tenterhooks, waiting for news on the missing victim.

'What gives?' she asked.

'You're not going to believe this,' Frankie told her. 'Bruce is a dog.'

'A *dog*?' There was relief in her voice now.

'A great big hairy dog,' Frankie confirmed. 'I'm no expert but Mozzie's spent time on farms and he reckons he might be a bearded collie. He and Nico are trying to dry him off a bit.'

'I'm not really surprised,' Jenny said. 'We already rescued one dog that was with Charlie. Where was this one? Why didn't I see it?'

'He was curled up in a tight ball, hiding amongst rocks and scrub not far from that tree that the truck was initially caught on. He must have been thrown clear when it first went over the cliff. He's black and white—it was only because I caught a glimpse of the white hair that we found him. He would have been totally hidden from view when you pulled that guy out.' Frankie pulled in a breath. 'Speaking of whom… Condition?'

'He's just died.'

'Oh, no… I'm so sorry, love, and on your first day.'

'My first day's supposed to be on Monday.'

'And you wanted a quiet life.' Frankie's heart went out to her friend. The silence on the other end of the line made her think that dwelling on the bad news would only make it worse.

'Our reports were that a fatality was likely.' Frankie knew Mozzie wanted to get back to base as soon as possible. She really couldn't spend too much more time on this phone call. 'Jen, we still have a problem. The Serious Crash Squad got mobilised when your local cop pinged this as a possible fatality. They're here now but they don't want anything to do with the dog. They suggested we drop him off to you so the local vet can check him out.'

'Is he injured?'

'Not sure.' Frankie turned her head to see Nico and Mozzie crouched beside the dog—dark shapes against the backlight of the police vehicle's headlights. 'Nico's having a look now but I'd be surprised if he wasn't hurt. Pretty rough ground for a fall.'

'Who's Nico?'

'Your replacement on Red Watch.'

'Is he nice?'

'He's Italian.'

'Oh…'

They both knew that was the end of a conversation they didn't have time for, anyway. 'Do you know if the local vet will be available?' Frankie asked.

'There's no vet in Willhua.'

'Can he go to Charlie's family?'

'I have no idea who they might be,' Jen said. 'Frankie, can you take him on to Sydney? I seem to be stuck with the other one—Stumpy—and I can't cope with two injured dogs.'

Frankie bit her lip. She knew how well that suggestion might go down, after Nico's reaction to rescuing a dog in the first place. She watched the men as they got to their feet to move back towards the helicopter. Nico picked up Bruce, who was now wrapped in a blanket, and he turned his head to signal to Frankie that it was time to go. He probably assumed that she had finished making the arrangement to drop the dog at Willhua hospital's landing pad.

Frankie could hear Jenny talking to someone else. Saying something about Bruce being another dog. That he was safe. She didn't want to tell her that it might not be easy to persuade her crew to take Bruce back to Sydney with them, even though there was no chance they would be dispatched to any other jobs tonight. Jenny had already had a rough day and Frankie wasn't about to make it any harder.

'Frankie, I need to go,' Jenny said. 'Stumpy's got lacerations and grazes, and Rob's going to help me sort her out.'

'Who's Rob?'

'Cut it out.' There was an understanding of why Frankie was asking. This just wasn't the time or place. 'But can you take Bruce?'

'I'll see what I can do.' Frankie didn't want to make any promises. 'There's already a discussion about having a dog in the chopper.'

'But that would be a yes? That's great.' Jen made it sound

like a done deal. 'If and when we find relatives we can tell them he's in the best of hands and to contact you.'

'Jen...'

'I need to go.' Jen wasn't listening. 'Love you.'

'Love you too,' Frankie murmured. But the screen of her phone had already gone dark. Jenny had gone and it was time for Frankie to move as well. The rotors on the helicopter were starting to gain speed and she ducked her head until she climbed in and slid the door shut behind her.

Nico was strapped into his seat, with his arms still around the big dog who was draped over his knees. Bruce had his head leaning on Nico's chest as he gazed upwards and it looked for all the world as if they were having a private conversation.

'There's no vet in Willhua,' Frankie told him. 'They've asked if we'll take him back to Sydney.'

She'd expected a flat-out refusal. A lecture on what was and wasn't acceptable for the crew of an air rescue helicopter to be using their valuable resources for. Instead, all Frankie got was a solemn nod.

'No worries,' Nico said. 'I'll look after him.'

Maybe it was something in the way he was holding the dog. Or the way they'd been looking at each other. Or perhaps it was just something in the tone of his voice that had made his words sound like a vow. He had promised to keep Frankie safe on the winch. And he had done exactly that...

Whatever it was, it felt disconcertingly as if Frankie had just stepped a little bit closer to falling in love with Nico Romano. She clipped the buckles of her safety belts together and then she leaned back as they took off—trying to remind herself that, unlike rescuing a dog instead of a human, there were some rules that she could never afford to break.

But then Nico raised his head and she caught a glimpse of the look he'd probably been sharing with that dog. Dark, dark eyes that had a glimmer of a stereotype she'd been running away from for ever, where the man was the dominant partner in a relationship and his needs came first. There was another side to that coin, though, wasn't there? That ability to be so passionate. Devoted. A keeper of promises and the protector of the most important things in the world—the people that were loved. Family...

And in that heartbeat of time Frankie had the disturbing idea that maybe she'd been wrong all along. Ever since she'd made that stupid rule.

Worse, she now had a thirty-minute flight with no patient to care for, so there was no distraction from letting her mind drift into a bit of fantasy.

What if Nico fell in love with *her*?

What if he was as ready as she was to start a family? Frankie was only in her early thirties, but the ticking of her biological clock was noticeably louder these days and she was hearing it more and more often during any job that involved children and especially babies.

She wanted a big, classically Italian kind of family like she'd never had. Frankie closed her eyes and could almost hear the noise and see the happy chaos of this fantasy family that was big enough that none of the children would ever feel lonely or left out.

Like she had...

CHAPTER THREE

'SO THIS IS GOOD. There's no sign of any broken bones. I think he's just badly bruised on this front leg and there could be some ligament damage in both joints. It's pretty swollen around the carpus, which is the equivalent to his wrist, and the elbow is sore as well. I'll put a bandage on the whole leg but he'll need to keep his weight off it as much as possible for at least a week.'

The vet's name was Phoebe. She had blue eyes and long blonde hair that was pulled back into a ponytail and she had seemed more than happy to welcome a patient at a quiet time on her night shift at the after-hours emergency clinic when Nico walked in—still in his uniform—with the large dog in his arms.

It was just the kind of scenario that Nico might have taken advantage of in the past few years—when he had finally sorted a totally new life with a career that he could focus on with a passion that made life away from work almost irrelevant. Or maybe it had just taken more time to be confident that he could *make* love and still keep himself completely safe from *falling* in love. A sex life was a physical need, after all, like eating. Fortunately, Nico had discovered that he could go for considerable periods of time without starving and any woman he'd got that close to in the last ten years or so hadn't been put off by knowing it was only ever a casual thing. An occasional treat—like a takeout meal instead of home cooking?

Phoebe looked like she wouldn't be put off either, even if it was just a one-off occasion, but Nico wasn't feeling any tingle of attraction at all, and it *wasn't* simply because she didn't have dark hair and dark eyes like Frankie. Not at all. It was because things were different right now. This was about Bruce.

'He seems well fed. I'd say he's about six to eight years old and he's definitely a farm dog.' Phoebe smiled at Nico. 'He kind of smells like a sheep, doesn't he?'

'So he's going to be okay?'

'Physically, yes. He's a bit traumatised, which is understandable after the accident, but it says a lot about his personality that he's not at all aggressive when he's this scared. I think he's a nice dog. If the owner's family doesn't claim him, I'm sure there won't be a problem finding him a good home. I'd take him myself but I've already got too many pets.'

'I can look after him for now.'

'Sure. I can sort you out with some food. Do you want to make a follow-up appointment at my clinic in a couple of days? I'm just a couple of suburbs away from here.' The look in Phoebe's eyes was one of admiration. 'I'm guessing you live near the air rescue base? You guys do such an awesome job...'

Nico wasn't about to confess that he was currently living in a camping ground that was quite a long way from his new job. Neither did he want to arrange a follow-up appointment that might give Phoebe the idea that he was interested in anything more than the only important thing on his mind right now, which was Bruce.

He'd never considered having a dog in his life before. He'd been far too busy with his career and making the most of any spare time travelling to discover the best beaches for surfing or paddleboarding and he loved the sometimes extended periods of living in his retro Volkswagen Kombi campervan, which offered no room for accommodating pets. He wasn't considering having a dog now either, but he'd assured Bruce he would look after him.

How could he not have made that promise? That look in the dog's eyes when he'd been holding him as they took off in the helicopter had been heartbreaking. More than heart-breaking, because Nico knew what it was like to have that little faith in the world.

To be at rock bottom and feel...total despair...

He'd held that eye contact with Bruce and, even before he'd said the words out loud, he'd known that the dog understood. That he was trusting him.

'I can give you a list of dog rescue shelters—just in case things don't work out.' Phoebe's glance was curious. 'Your job must mean some long shifts. That's not going to be a problem?'

'No.' Nico spoke with a confidence he was far from sure of. 'I don't think so. Thank you so much for your help. It will probably be only for a day or two and we'll be fine.'

The vet's bill was eye-watering, especially after Nico added some essentials like the food, a bowl, a brush and a blanket. He carried Bruce to his van and settled him on his own bed, before driving back to his grassy corner of the camping ground which was fortunately screened from the manager's office and residence by some thick hedges. Nico had no idea whether pets were allowed but Bruce wasn't about to go wandering with that sore leg and he'd be hidden from view when he drove in and out of the grounds. As long as he didn't start barking, his presence could remain secret for at least a few days.

Just between the two of them.

Like that feeling of connection that had already made it feel like they were a team.

When Nico finally edged into the noticeably depleted space on the mattress that filled most of the back of the van, he released his breath in a slightly resigned sigh. He only had a few hours now to grab some sleep before he was due back at work.

'It's the strangest first day anywhere,' he told Bruce.

Bruce was watching him carefully. Did he think that Nico was regretting bringing him home?

Nico touched the dog's head. 'It'll be okay,' he promised. 'Let's get some sleep.'

But Bruce's eyes were still open as Nico felt his own slowly shutting. He was almost asleep when he felt the soft warmth of the dog's body relaxing against his own. And then he felt the damp swipe of Bruce's tongue against his hand and it felt like gratitude.

Trust.

Love, even…?

Whatever it was, it felt like something that should not be broken.

It also felt like this was the end of a day when something even bigger than simply a new job had been started.

Something…important.

Sì… Nico felt himself drifting into a deep sleep with a hint of a smile curving his lips. This was *tutto bene*—all good. Maybe he'd found a door that had opened up a whole new life. If so, was he ready?

Yes. More than ready. He'd been keeping himself too busy to have time to think about some things for too long now. Maybe it was time he slowed down enough to take notice of the good things in life that had nothing to do with his work.

Frankie had, of course, noticed the bright red and white van parked in the SSAR base car park yesterday. Who wouldn't when it had surfboards tied to the roof rack and looked like it only needed some flowers painted on the sides to be a relic from the hippy era of the nineteen-sixties?

It wouldn't have occurred to her to associate something so unsophisticated with Nico Romano, however, until she arrived at work the next morning to find him standing beside the opened sliding door on the side. For a brief moment she was distracted by that rather fierce curling sensation in her gut that let her know exactly how attractive she found this man, and then she was startled by the realisation that all the men she'd ever dated in her life so far had had the streaked blond hair and sun-kissed skin of a dedicated Antipodean surfer. The only thing Nico had in common with any of them was the surfboard on top of this van and, for some reason, the idea that this was his chosen mode of transport was equally as startling.

'Is this *your* van?'

Nico's eyebrows rose at her tone. '*Sì…* Is it parked in the wrong place or something?'

'No… I just would have guessed that you'd drive something else.'

'Such as…?'

'Oh… I don't know…' Frankie was feeling slightly embarrassed now but it was too late to stop her mouth running away with her. 'A Lamborghini or a Ferrari, perhaps?'

'Why? Because I'm Italian?'

Frankie shrugged. 'Nah… Because you look kind of like you'd feel at home behind the wheel of a flashy sports car.'

He was wearing his uniform but hadn't tied his hair back yet and it was long enough for the curls to brush the collar of his dark blue shirt. It was glossy and black and looked as though it would be as soft as silk. She needed to stop looking at him right *now*, Frankie realised, but she also needed to avoid catching his gaze as she did so, because she definitely didn't want her new colleague to guess what she had just been thinking about. Or that brief fantasy he'd been included in on the way home from that job in Willhua last night. So she looked upwards.

'That's a weird sort of surfboard.'

'It's an SUP. A stand-up paddleboard.'

'Ah…of course it is.' Frankie cringed inwardly at saying something so ignorant. 'And that's something I've been meaning to try one day too. I love being near the sea and there's only so long you can keep swimming.' She was talking too much now, wasn't she? Frankie risked a quick glance to find Nico looking slightly bemused.

'So what do *you* drive, Frankie?'

'I don't drive. I ride. A Ducati. It's over there, see?' She waved to where she'd parked her sleek black motorbike between a hangar and the main buildings.

'Because it's Italian?'

Frankie pretended to look shocked. 'Because it's the best bike on the road. Normally I would avoid anything Italian on principle.' She caught her bottom lip between her teeth. She didn't want to sound rude. And part of her didn't want to burn any bridges between herself and Nico before she was sure she didn't want to break her self-imposed rule. Or that the attraction to the total opposite of her normal 'type' wasn't simply a temporary aberration.

'Except for the food, of course...' she added. 'Nobody in their right mind would avoid Italian food, would they?'

'It's a good thing that there are so many good Italian restaurants in Australia,' Nico agreed. 'It will always be *my* favourite food.' He turned back to peer inside the van. 'And that reminds me, I'd better leave some food out for Bruce in case he gets hungry. He hasn't eaten anything yet.' He picked up a bag of kibble and shook some into a bowl, but he glanced up at Frankie as he did so. 'Why do you avoid everything Italian?'

He sounded genuinely curious but Frankie pretended not to hear the question. 'Bruce is in your van?' She stepped closer. 'Hey...' She leaned in to pat the dog. 'Oh...his leg's bandaged. But not plastered. So it's not broken?'

'No. He may have torn ligaments and it's bruised badly enough for him to need to stay off it for a week or so. Which is good because he won't mind staying in the van to rest. Especially with the shade from these trees.'

'He certainly looks comfortable with that bed you've put in there for him. He's even got blankets and pillows.'

'Actually, it's my bed.'

Frankie blinked. Oh, my... Knowing that she was looking at Nico's bed had intensified that tingling sensation in her gut exponentially. What did he wear to sleep in? Or maybe he wore nothing at all…?

She cleared her throat hurriedly. 'I guess you need it for when you go camping. Or surfing?'

'I need it all the time at the moment. I haven't found a place to rent yet so I'm living at the camping ground over Bundeena way.'

'That's a bit of a drive to get to work.'

'Only forty-five minutes or so. Where do you live?'

'Lilli Pilli Point. It's a quick ride on the motorway to get to the base and, even better, about ten minutes' run from the reserve, so that's where I go every morning before work. Or after work so I can have a swim. There are some lovely saltwater swimming baths there.'

'Nice. What's the surf like there?'

Frankie laughed. 'There isn't any. There's a wharf and lots of boats moored offshore. There are some spots in the reserve where it's possible to get down to the sea but it's much easier to swim in the baths. You'll need to go to somewhere like Bondi if you want surf.'

Nico shook his head. 'Too many people,' he said. 'I prefer it quiet. And I don't need surf that often. Most of the time I prefer to paddleboard.'

Frankie gave Bruce a last scratch behind his ear. 'See you later,' she told the dog. 'I have to go to work now. In the helicopter. You had a ride in it yesterday, remember?'

Frankie certainly remembered. She could remember every detail of the entire day.

The day she'd met Mr Perfect.

The day she'd started to wonder if Nico might prove to be the exception to the rule she'd stuck to for so long.

'You've got food and water,' Nico said to Bruce. 'And the windows are open for some fresh air. And so that it doesn't smell too bad in here later. You kind of need a bath, mate. I'll come and let you out when we're not too busy, okay? And, after work, we could give you a bath. It's hot enough today and we can use the hose that Mozzie uses to wash the helicopter. You'd like that, wouldn't you?'

Frankie could see the way Bruce was listening to Nico. And the way his gaze was fixed on him as if he thought the world might end if Nico walked away. And now she was remembering the way Nico had been holding the dog last night and the way it had squeezed her heart so hard she could almost feel herself physically falling in love.

It was Bruce who'd given her a link with Nico already. This big, hairy, sad-looking dog that they'd both been involved in rescuing. Frankie had taken him to safety. Nico had taken him home.

'Why don't you bring him inside?' she suggested. 'Nobody would mind and even in the shade it might get too hot for him in the van.'

Nobody did mind having Bruce quietly sitting in a corner of the staffroom. Over the next few days everyone got used to seeing Nico taking responsibility for making sure the scruffy dog had food and water available at all times and carrying him outside to do his business on the grass by the car park when he was between jobs. It was even nicer to have him around after Nico had given him a soapy shower outside and spent most of an evening brushing tangles out of his long coat, but it was quickly apparent that, while Bruce was perfectly friendly and polite to anyone who paid him attention, Nico was his chosen person—the one he trusted in a confusing new world he'd found himself in.

Nico didn't mind that at all. He rather liked it, in fact.

'You could pretend that you like me, you know, mate.' Mozzie had crouched beside where Bruce was lying on his blanket to give him a scratch behind his ears, but the dog hadn't even wagged his tail in greeting. 'I was there too, when you were getting rescued.'

'So was I.' Frankie was making a mug of coffee. 'It was me who risked life and limb to get him off the cliff, remember?'

'Let's not make that too public,' Colin muttered as he walked past. 'Especially the bit about bringing him back to base.'

'Have you heard whether there are any relatives of the guy who died?' Ricky asked. 'People who want to take the dog?'

'Nothing,' Nico said. 'I rang the Willhua cop again yesterday. He said he'd be in touch if they heard anything but for me not to hold my breath.'

'And I've spoken to Jenny,' Frankie said. 'She hasn't heard of any relatives or friends that are interested either. She's planning to adopt the other dog, Stumpy, if no one comes forward.'

'Stumpy?' Ricky was laughing. 'What kind of name for a dog is that?'

'He's a corgi, I believe. He's got short legs.'

'That's a terrible name.' Ricky shook his head. 'But no worse than Mozzie, I guess.'

'Why *are* you called Mozzie?' Nico asked.

'His real name is Murray.' Frankie was grinning now. 'He got the nickname because there's that annoying buzzing sound people can hear when he's getting close in his helicopter. Like the world's biggest mosquito.'

Mozzie was ignoring her. 'What will you do?' he asked Nico. 'If no one wants Bruce back?'

Nico hesitated. He hadn't thought that far ahead. What *would* he do? He turned his head, knowing perfectly well that he would find Bruce watching him. Even if the dog had his eyes shut and looked like he was sound asleep, Nico knew he only had to move an inch and he would be being watched again. It was as if Bruce thought that if he didn't keep his eyes on him, Nico would vanish. At the same time, he was remembering the trust that had been placed in him. The way that being in physical contact with him had been enough to let an animal, that had to be very frightened and sore, relax enough to sleep. Already, that meant that handing Bruce to someone else—potentially a stranger who was only taking him from a sense of duty—was never going to feel right.

'I would keep him,' Nico said aloud. But then he frowned. 'But I would have to find somewhere else to live,' he said. 'I've seen a "No Dogs" sign at the camping ground and it's going to get harder to keep him hidden when he wants to walk.'

'You might have trouble finding somewhere to rent that lets you keep a pet.' Mozzie shrugged. 'I'd let you park on my lawn if I had one but all I have is a garage in the basement of my apartment block. Frankie…you've got a lawn, haven't you?'

'Yeah…and I also have a bunch of housemates who might have something to say about turning it into a caravan park.' Frankie ducked her head as though she was determined not to even look at Nico as she spoke.

'It's okay. I'll sort it.' Nico wanted this conversation to finish. He really didn't want to put Frankie on the spot. It felt like he was still waiting for her to make her mind up about accepting him as a colleague and he couldn't decide which way the balance was tipping.

On the negative side, she'd dropped comments like preferring to avoid anything Italian and that she thought he looked like someone who would show off his money by driving an expensive car. She also still seemed to be deliberately keeping her distance.

On the other side, though, there were moments when Nico felt something very different. When he caught her shifting her gaze as if she was disguising the fact she'd been watching him with at least interest, if not approval. Or when there was something about her body language that suggested she was not averse to being physically close to him. Was she actually having to force herself not to make eye contact right now?

Or, *oddio*…maybe that was wishful thinking?

Because, despite knowing that he would never allow any attraction to Frankie Moretti to come to anything, it was growing. Getting deeper as he noticed more and more things about her. Like her concern for Bruce being left in a vehicle that could become overheated. How kind she had been with that confused elderly patient they had gone to yesterday. The way she lit up with the adrenaline rush of every new call. And how hot was it that she rode a motorbike?

Surely he had his life under control well enough now that being friends with Frankie wouldn't present a problem? Was it possible that he could enjoy the sensation of attraction without it going any further?

'It's right over the road from the bush reserve.'

'What? Sorry...' Nico blinked. 'What's that expression? I was...miles away...'

'Mmm...' There was a gleam of what looked like amusement in Frankie's dark eyes—as if she knew precisely in what direction he had just strayed. 'I was just saying that I've seen a "For Rent" sign on a place I run past on my way to the reserve. It's a hand-painted sign and it's been there for weeks, so it's either some mansion that's way too expensive for the market and the owners are too tight to pay for a proper sign, or it's so rundown it's uninhabitable, which is more likely. It's hidden by trees so I have no idea what it looks like.' Frankie reached for her pager as it sounded. 'Mind you, if it is rundown, the landlord probably wouldn't mind you having a dog. Might be worth having a look?'

'Absolutely.' Nico was reading the message on his own pager as more information came over their radios. Resources were being directed urgently to a serious traffic incident on a motorway involving a truck and several cars. He was on his feet by the time he finished reading the initial information but he turned to catch Frankie's gaze. 'After work?'

'Sure.' But Frankie's tone was offhand now. She was focused on the challenge ahead of them.

So was Nico, but as he took his seat in the helicopter and flipped his microphone down so he could communicate with his crewmates he couldn't resist a glance at Frankie's face. She didn't notice. She was focused on the screen of her tablet, gathering as much information as she could about what they were heading towards.

And Nico knew he might be in trouble if he didn't gain control very soon. Not simply because he was being distracted, if only for a heartbeat, from what he should be focused on, but because Frankie's passion for the work she did—that he understood so well it was automatically a deep connection between them—was just as sexy as everything else about this woman.

It was the kind of scene that road traffic management authorities dreaded. Multiple lanes of the major motorway leading into Australia's most populated city were blocked in both directions—by the accident on one side and, on the other, by the traffic slowing as people stared in horror at the carnage, causing a chain reaction of braking or even running into the back of other vehicles until all movement stopped.

Numerous police vehicles, fire trucks and ambulances were either on scene or fighting to get through the traffic jam but, fortunately, it was far enough out of the city for farmland to provide easy landing for more than one rescue helicopter. Mozzie stayed with the aircraft. Frankie, Nico and Ricky slipped backpacks on and picked up other gear like a defibrillator and suction unit. They headed for what looked a triage area that had been established near a police command vehicle and found an ambulance scene commander updating a whiteboard with the number of patients and the status of their condition.

'We've got the fire service extracting a category two patient with a spinal injury. He's got a paramedic with him who's keeping him immobilised. The driver of that vehicle is category zero. We've got two category threes in the back of an ambulance that's about to transport them and some non-urgent minor injuries that are still being assessed.' He indicated the area behind him in the triage tent where several people were seated and being attended to.

'We can leave our crewman, Ricky, here to help with that until we know where we'll be most useful,' Frankie said.

'Thanks. There's a category one with a head injury currently being loaded into the other chopper but where we need you guys is over there…' He pointed to a cluster of people almost hidden by the truck trailer that was leaning at an ominous angle. 'There was a motorbike that got caught up in the middle of this mess. Young guy who's conscious but the crew with him has just upgraded him from a category three to a two. His blood pressure's dropping.'

Frankie nodded. The lower the category number, the more serious condition the patient was in. This patient had been initially assessed as someone who had a potentially life-threatening condition and needed treatment within thirty minutes to someone with an imminently life-threating condition who needed treatment within ten minutes. The category one who was in the helicopter lifting off the ground as Frankie and Nico went towards the truck was critically ill or in cardiac arrest and a category zero was dead.

Nico increased his pace to step sideways in front of Frankie but she had to slow down to not bump into him and she could feel herself frowning. Why was he changing direction to walk away from the patient they were about to reach?

'Hey...' Nico's call was loud enough to attract the attention of a fire officer who was watching his crew using pneumatic cutting gear to get into a car. Frankie could see a paramedic in the back seat of the vehicle, holding the front passenger's head still, under a plastic sheet to protect both himself and the patient in the front seat from shattering glass.

'What's up, buddy?'

'How stable is this truck trailer? And are there any dangerous goods inside it?'

'It's a load from a grocery warehouse. No chemicals. And it's been checked. It's not about to tip over on you lot.'

Nico nodded. He was looking up as he moved forward again. Scanning for potential hazards like a damaged power line? Frankie realised she'd almost made a rookie mistake of assuming that the crew already there would have cleared the scene for hazards. Nico was being cautious but he was alert to anything that could put them in danger. He was doing his best to keep her safe and Frankie's level of trust in her partner just went up a notch. He had her back. At another time she might well have his, if he forgot a step in a protocol or found himself needing assistance with a procedure.

Because that was what partners did. In a good partnership they not only filled any gaps in the other's performance but they enabled each other to do better than they could have done on their own.

Working with Jenny had been great but Frankie knew, deep down, that working with Nico already had the potential to be even better. More challenging.

More satisfying.

She took a deep breath as they arrived beside a man lying

on the gravel of the motorway verge, having his clothing cut clear of his legs by two ambulance officers that looked young enough to be new on the job. Both legs were lying in an odd position with the feet turned outwards.

'Bilateral external rotation,' Frankie said quietly to Nico as she slipped off the straps of her backpack.

'But no obvious deformation from fractures.'

They shared a glance. They knew that this patient's condition had deteriorated due to a falling blood pressure and the most likely cause for that in this situation was blood loss. Internal, because there was no sign of blood on the road or his clothing. And the most likely cause of that blood loss, given the way his legs were lying, was a fractured pelvis—an injury that could potentially be fatal within a short period of time.

'Hiya…' Frankie crouched near the head of a very pale young man whose helmet had already been removed. 'My name's Frankie and I've got Nico with me. We're going to help the crew here to get you sorted and then we're going to get you into hospital just as quickly as we can. Is that okay with you?'

He gave a single nod. 'It hurts…'

'The whistle isn't helping enough?' Frankie could see he was clutching a 'green whistle' which delivered the pain-relieving drug Methoxyflurane.

'No…'

'We'll do something about that very soon. I just need to find out a bit more about you.' Frankie put a hand on his wrist to check for a radial pulse, but looked up to find the junior paramedics looking relieved. 'Tell me what you've found so far,' she invited.

She had time to collect any information on the latest vital signs that had been recorded because, in her peripheral vision, she could see that Nico had also noticed that no IV access had been obtained. He was collecting everything he needed to put a line in, administer effective pain relief and get some fluids running to try and stabilise the blood pressure. He had located the pelvic splint pack as well so they could slip the belt around the injured biker's hips and tighten it enough to keep the pelvis stable and hopefully control any internal blood loss.

Frankie felt the stress levels, that were always there in this first assessment of a potentially critically injured patient, easing in a way that meant they were not about to undermine her confidence in the job she was about to do. With a noticeable—and welcome—shift, she felt a new kind of confidence in what she was capable of doing, knowing that she had someone like Nico working with her. Backing her up.

Keeping her safe. Again…

CHAPTER FOUR

THE ORIGIN OF the piece of wood at the end of the driveway that had the words 'For Rent' and a mobile phone number painted on it became obvious as Frankie and Nico got far enough to see what lay behind the trees.

The ancient beach house was falling apart and the plank of wood that had been used for the sign had no doubt once been part of the collapsed garden shed or car port near the house. The paint peeling off the sides of the house was pale blue and it was a simple box shape of a square window on either side of a front door, like a child's drawing. The corrugated iron roof was rusty and the veranda sagged in the middle but when they ventured cautiously up the steps to peer through the grimy glass of the windows, the boards of the veranda felt sturdy enough and the empty room looked intact and, more importantly, weatherproof.

And when they turned back and caught a glimpse of the sea through the small forest of gum tree trunks, with the pink glow of a sunset just beginning, they both caught a breath.

'Oh…wow…' Frankie murmured. 'Nico…this is gorgeous.' Her breath escaped in a huff of laughter. 'Apart from the house, of course.'

But when they were walking away and she took another

glance over her shoulder at this little dwelling, Frankie's imagination was captured. She could see it renovated. Freshly painted, with white wicker chairs on the veranda. The front door was open and she could imagine the laughter of excited children getting ready to run down to the reserve to play or to go to the pool for a swim. She could imagine living in this house. With her own family. Sitting on that veranda, watching the sun going down, with the father of those children sitting beside her, holding her hand…

A man who had dark hair and even darker eyes? Like Nico?

It would be…

Well…perfect. Like any good fantasy.

Without any basis in reality at all, of course, which was why it was a fantasy. She really had to stop having day-dreams like this, but they'd been happening almost ever since she'd first been aware of her attraction to Nico. If they got any worse they could be a threat to their working relationship but, fortunately, this particular bubble of that flight of fancy vanished almost as soon as it had appeared. Nico hadn't even noticed that Frankie was momentarily distracted as he paused to follow the direction of her gaze.

'I would need to see more inside,' he said. 'And find out if it has running water and electricity. Or maybe that doesn't matter so much. If it's not too expensive. It might work for now, even if it was just a place to park my van without the rules of a camping ground about dogs. I could swim in the sea to shower if I had to. And I have somewhere to cook already with my gas stove.'

'Oh, no…' Frankie's eyes widened. 'It's Friday, isn't it?'

'Ah…yes…' Nico lifted an eyebrow. 'Do you have somewhere you need to be?'

Frankie nodded. 'Home. We have a thing in our share house where we all take a turn to cook on a Friday night and everyone who isn't working comes home for dinner. You talking about cooking just reminded me that it's my turn.' She turned away from the view. She even walked a few steps away from Nico but then she turned her head. 'You're welcome to come. I always make way too much food. We never quite know who's coming or bringing someone home with them.'

'Ah…no… I need to look after Bruce. Maybe I will take him down to see the reserve. A soak in seawater might be good for his leg.'

'He's welcome too.'

Suddenly—for a reason Frankie had no intention of trying to analyse—she really wanted to cook for Nico. Italian food. 'I'm making pasta *alla gricia*,' she told him.

Nico looked as if she'd just cast a magic spell on him. 'How did you know?' he demanded.

'Know what?'

'That it's my absolute favourite.' He licked his lips. 'Do you use spaghetti or *rigatori*?'

'*Rigatori*, of course. I'd make my own but the shop I go to for the *guanciale* makes fresh pasta every day. And they deliver. There will be a box of ingredients on my doorstep, which is only five minutes' drive away from here.' Frankie offered Nico a smile as she raised her eyebrows. 'Are you sure I can't tempt you?'

Oh…my… The smouldering look in Nico's eyes, that looked completely black in this fading light, made Frankie's heart skip a beat and then race to catch up as she recognised the *double entendre* she had inadvertently delivered. Would he look like this if she was trying to tempt him to do something quite different than eating her homecooked food? She had to clear her throat as she cut the eye contact. It had already gone on too long.

'I mean…we've survived this week working together and we have our days off starting tomorrow. That's something to celebrate, isn't it? If I know my housemates, there'll be a stack of cold beers in the fridge and…hey…why don't you take a photo of the sign at the end of the drive and you can ring the owner. You might even be able to arrange to look inside the place while you're on this side of the bay and it could save you a long drive tomorrow.'

Nico raised his hands in a gesture of surrender as he walked towards her. Frankie began heading down the driveway again as if this was no big deal, but he caught up with her in a few long strides. He tipped his head towards her and she could hear the smile in his voice. His lips were close enough to her ear to be almost able to *feel* his voice—in a shiver that went straight to Frankie's bones.

'You had me at pasta *alla gricia*,' he said.

Frankie found herself feeling very uncharacteristically nervous during that five-minute ride home with Nico following her in his van.

Inviting Nico to dinner was not exactly keeping a professional distance and, even though the jury might have resoundingly offered the verdict that he was going to more than fit in with the rest of the crew on Red Watch, there was still that personal judgement that Frankie was struggling with.

Or, if she was honest, that personal *attraction* that was giving her grief.

Part of her—something that was probably being directed by her body rather than her brain—was rather hoping that all her housemates had taken on extra shifts at their workplaces or had received offers they couldn't refuse, like free tickets to some not-to-be-missed rock concert or something, because that would mean it would be just her and Nico.

Alone. Cooking and eating the food they both loved. Cementing another connection thanks to a shared heritage.

The part of her that was under instruction from her brain, however, was very relieved to find that everybody was at home or on their way. She left Nico in his van to get changed out of his uniform and grabbed the clothes that were lying on the end of her bed so that she didn't give herself time to even think about putting on something—like a dress—that would make her housemates think this was anything more than simply inviting a new colleague for dinner. She was in her denim cut-offs with a soft top that was knotted at the hem on one side and hadn't bothered putting anything on her feet, when Nico came in wearing a pair of black jeans and a tee shirt that was so ancient the image of the Italian flag on the front was cracked and faded. This was good, Frankie decided. Ordinary clothes. She had that tingle well under control.

Until she looked down to see Bruce approaching, carefully using only three legs, and noticed that Nico, like herself, had bare feet and, oh, boy...that tingle had moved to a whole new level. It was more like a spear of sensation, centred deep in her belly but firing outwards so fast it had reached her toes before she could blink. A sensation that was actually painful but in a rather delicious way.

To avoid thinking that she might be in a spot of trouble as far as staying firmly in control of her attraction to Nico, Frankie took the box of ingredients that had been put on the kitchen table to the bench. She opened cupboards then, to find the enormous pot she used to cook pasta and another one for making the sauce. Then she collected a chopping board, sharp knife and grater, just throwing an occasional smile over her shoulder, casually introducing everyone to each other as the housemates gathered in this large kitchen area.

'Nico, this is Justin—he's a paramedic based in Miranda and that's his girlfriend Janine. Guys, this is Nico and that's Bruce. I told you about rescuing him off the cliff the other night, didn't I?'

Suzie, a theatre nurse at St Mary's, was already on the floor giving Bruce some love when the final housemate, Derek, arrived home and headed straight for the fridge.

'What a day,' he said. 'Who else wants a beer?'

The enthusiastic chorus of assent suggested that Nico had instantly become a part of this group of friendly, intelligent people that he had plenty in common with. He even recognised Derek.

'I've seen you somewhere before, haven't I?'

'On the roof of St Mary's.' Derek nodded. 'When you brought that guy in who'd broken his ankle and then had a cardiac arrest on the way back.'

Nico nodded as he accepted the icy-cold lager with

a wedge of lime stuffed into the neck of the bottle. 'Of course...you don't know what happened to him, do you?'

'He went to the Cath lab, got three stents and got discharged with minimal myocardial damage, I believe. He went home with a cast on his leg, a pair of crutches and some advice about lifestyle changes. You did a good job.' Derek made a face. 'Don't get the wrong idea—I don't normally stalk everyone who comes through our department but I know how much Frankie appreciates a follow-up.'

'I do,' Frankie agreed. 'And I appreciate my friends working in the right places.' She was slicing up the *guanciale* with its stripe of pink meat between layers of fat, putting it into a saucepan to render over a low heat.

'That smells *so* good.' Suzie got up to peer over Frankie's shoulder. 'What is it? Salami? Pancetta?' She threw a glance at Nico. 'We love it when it's Frankie's turn to cook.'

'It's a type of salami made from pig cheeks,' Frankie said. 'It's stronger than pancetta. Spiced with black pepper and chilli.'

Nico had moved closer as well. 'And that's *Pecorino Romano*.'

'Stinky cheese,' Justin declared. 'We've had that before. It's made from sheep's milk, isn't it?'

'Oh, gross...' Janine made a face. 'Don't tell me anything else.'

'You'll love it,' Nico assured her. 'But if you don't, I can help. It's the favourite thing my *nonna* used to cook for us when I was a kid.'

'What part of Italy do you come from, Nico?' Suzie asked. 'And what made you come to Sydney?'

'What made you want to work with Frankie?' Derek

shook his head. 'Did no one warn you how bossy she can be?'

'Hey…' Frankie lifted her hand in protest, still holding her sharp knife. 'I'm the one slaving over a hot stove, here.'

Everyone noticed the way that Nico stiffened and took a swift step backwards as if he was feigning horror. Bruce had to hop, keeping his injured leg off the floor, but he was at Nico's side instantly, his alarmed gaze fixed on Frankie.

There was a shout of laughter in the room. 'She might be bossy,' Derek said, 'but she's quite safe with knives.'

'As far as we know,' Justin offered.

Nico looked embarrassed now. Frankie put the knife down and focused on her cooking but there was still a beat of something awkward in the room. Instinct suggested that there had been something more than the pretence of fear in Nico's eyes. Had he found himself in a situation when he'd been under threat, perhaps? When he'd been truly afraid?

Maybe that thought could have undermined the sheer masculinity of the man but, instead, the hint of something softer—as compelling as vulnerability, perhaps—only drew Frankie towards him on a different but no less powerful level. The urge to offer protection felt like a physical squeeze on her heart.

'Come outside,' Suzie suggested. 'It's cooler under the tree. We can drag some bean chairs from the lounge onto the lawn and have dinner out there.'

It was one of those great nights that had an alchemy to make it something special. The solar fairy lights wound through the branches of the big tree on the lawn were shining and there was a contented silence as everyone tucked into the bowls of steaming, fragrant pasta.

She was watching Nico as he took his first bite and caught her breath as she watched him close his eyes with the pleasure of filling his mouth with that *al dente* pasta in its simple creamy sauce of spicy meat and cheese. Food that *she* had cooked. And then he licked some sauce off his lips with his eyes still closed and Frankie found her glow of pride being overtaken by sheer physical desire. There was something else in that mix as well. Something nice that came from providing food. Caring for someone… Something that was on the same level as knowing that someone could be vulnerable? Being able to nurture as well as protect?

By the time they'd all eaten their fill of the delicious meal Frankie had created, Nico was definitely part of the group. They all had the common interest of working in the medical world and it was easy to swap stories they could all appreciate. When it degenerated into a competition of who had seen the case of the strangest foreign objects people had swallowed they were in fits of laughter.

'Teeth,' Derek told them. 'Three of them.'

'Well, three is a little excessive,' Justin agreed. 'But it's not that unusual to swallow a tooth.'

'These weren't his own,' Derek said.

'Oops…' Frankie was lying on the grass, enjoying the fairy lights above her. She propped herself up on one elbow when Nico offered a story.

'I did my paramedic training in Milan,' he told them, 'and, I kid you not, one of the jobs on my very first day on the road was somebody who had swallowed the remote control for the television. He'd been having an argument with his wife about what programme to watch. When we arrived, she was trying to punch him in the stomach to change the channel. He was so drunk he thought it was funny.'

Frankie thought it was funny too, but she was only smiling rather than laughing aloud.

Because it was dark enough for nobody to notice that her gaze was lingering on Nico and her mind had gone wandering again. She loved this kind of social occasion. Being in a group of people. Being in a couple within that group was even better, because when it broke up you still weren't alone.

Frankie had been brought up in a big Italian community in Melbourne but she'd been an only child, because her mother had never remarried after her father died. She'd been far more inclined to be out on the streets trying to join in the boys' games of football than to be inside her own house and she'd watched in envy as extended families celebrated the arrival of every new baby. It had felt like she was the only one without siblings and that was when the seeds of her plan to create a big family of her own one day were planted.

Not having a father wasn't as bad as not having siblings because she was showered with love from her mother and grandmother and even at a young age she could see that the males were dominant enough in her community to be intimidating. The children were disciplined, sometimes strictly, and the women were mostly expected to adhere to the traditional roles of caring for the children, keeping house and cooking the food. When the local boys who wanted nothing more than to be seen as 'Italian stallions' assumed Frankie would like nothing more than to date them and, one day, marry one of them, the seeds of rebellion had really been sown. Francesca Moretti was going to be her own woman and forge her own destiny.

It didn't mean she didn't want a whole bunch of kids, mind you—enough that they would never be lonely—but it would be with someone who would be an equal partner. Even the painful wakes of broken relationships hadn't been enough to dent the dream of creating that big, loving family.

A family that would always gather to share food like they were doing tonight, to celebrate every good thing in life but also gather to offer comfort for the not so good things. She was thirty-four years old and she still hadn't found the relationship that was even close to a foundation strong enough to build a family on.

'Who wants coffee?' Derek asked. 'I'll make it.'

'I'll help.' Nico got up when everyone agreed that it would make a good end to the dinner. He also helped to collect the empty bowls and used cutlery and Frankie held hers up as he came her way.

'Thank you. It's Brownie points if you do the dishes around here.'

'Of course,' Nico said. 'You cooked, you don't get to clean up. But it's me who should be thanking *you*.' He was smiling down at her. '*Grazie mille*, Frankie.' He gave a chef's kiss. '*È stato delizioso.*'

Maybe it was hearing him speak in the lilting language of her heritage. Or that they'd been eating the kind of food that was uniquely Italian and how much Nico had loved it had made her feel so proud. So…happy.

Or perhaps it was because she'd just been thinking of family and children and the yearning to fill in the gaps of what had been missing in her own childhood. Quite possibly, it was as simple as watching the most attractive man she'd ever met in her life walking away with his hands full of dirty dishes.

Whatever it was, her black and white rules were getting smudged into an increasingly indistinct greyness. The rule about never dating Italian men, for one. Even the one about never dating someone she was working closely with might not be as ironclad as she'd thought.

By the time Nico was back and they were all sipping coffee and polishing off a box of chocolates Suzie had contributed, Frankie was almost ready to make a momentous decision.

She was actually prepared to break yet another one of her rules. The lesser known rule about not being the one to ask someone out on a date. Nobody would ever guess that the confidence Frankie could display in every other aspect of her life was totally lacking when it came to feeling desirable. She'd been discarded in favour of other women too many times by those blond, blue-eyed Aussie surfer dudes. Even the one she'd been in such a long-term relationship with she had been sure that he would end up being the father of her children.

But... Nico was different. And, being Italian, he probably wanted children as much as she did. She knew he was older than her by a few years. The timing could be as perfect as everything else.

Maybe the stars were finally aligning themselves.

Or was it another fantasy that she might have found the 'one'? The holy grail of romance that was too big to be bound by any rules.

It was too good to be true, of course, but then Frankie

remembered that smouldering look when she'd asked if she could tempt him and she knew she had to find the courage to at least try and find out or she might regret it for ever.

Bruce was now lying on the lawn beside him, his head on Nico's knee, looking up at him as his ears were being softly rubbed.

'He knows you rescued him,' Suzie said. 'He adores you, doesn't he?'

'We belong together,' Nico said. 'I never knew it was a dog that was missing from my life, you know?'

Justin laughed. 'You've got yourself a fur kid.'

'A what?' Nico seemed to be unfamiliar with the expression.

'It's what people call their pets when they're substitute children,' Derek explained. 'They're the chosen kids but they're covered in fur.'

'You can have both,' Frankie put in. 'The best families have real kids *and* a dog.'

'Dogs are so much easier.' Justin was laughing. 'You can leave them home alone when you want to go out and have a good time. They kind of frown on you doing that with the human kids.'

'True…' Nico nodded. 'Another good reason why a fur kid is certainly the only sort of child I will ever have.'

Frankie blinked. This wasn't a part of the script for her perfect fantasy coming to life. 'You don't want real kids?'

'Not on my own, no…'

Frankie focused on the mug of coffee in her hand but didn't drink any because she was holding her breath. Waiting for someone else to break the silence?

Suzie obliged. 'No problem. You just need to find the person who wants a real kid as well as a fur kid.'

'A wife?' Nico's voice was quiet. 'No, thank you. Been there, done that.' His next quiet words that almost sounded like he was thinking aloud fell into a new, slightly shocked silence. *'Il gatto scottato teme l'acqua fredda.'*

'Huh?' Janine was staring at him. 'What does that mean?'

It was Frankie who translated. 'Literally, it means the scalded cat fears cold water.'

It felt remarkably as if she had just been doused in icy cold water herself. Or maybe it was more like being hit with something much more solid, because she was experiencing the sensation of being completely crushed. Derek was still looking bemused.

'The equivalent in English would probably be once bitten, twice shy,' she added.

And, in this context, someone whose marriage had been so bad it would never happen again.

'Ah...' The murmur from more than one person was sympathetic.

'You just need to find the right woman, mate,' Justin said. He smiled at Janine. 'That can change everything.'

Nico was also smiling but he was shaking his head. 'It's time I took my fur child home,' he said. 'Thank you all very much for having me. If I end up living down the road, I will return the invitation.' He lifted a hand in Frankie's direction. 'Enjoy your days off,' he said. 'I'll see you at work again next week.'

At work.

As a colleague.

And that was all Nico was ever going to be, despite any brave ideas on Frankie's part to ask him out.

She had heard the undertone in Nico's voice when he'd muttered that expression in his first language. There had been an indisputable finality about his words when he said he had no desire to repeat what had clearly been a disastrous marriage. That he had no desire to have human children either.

Which meant that the only kind of relationship Nico would want would be a no-strings 'friends with benefits' kind of arrangement and that was not something Frankie would ever choose. Not at this stage in her life, anyway. It hadn't mattered so much a decade ago, but it was probably what too many past boyfriends had assumed they had with her so it had been all too easy for them to move on and Frankie's heart had been broken too often. She didn't have any more time to waste on dead ends. She needed more in her life.

She needed a family.

But Nico Romano was not going to be the man to be a part of that dream.

And that was quite astonishingly disappointing. Weirdly, it felt almost as heartbreaking as she remembered the failure of actual romances to have been.

No. It was more than weird. It was ridiculous. As Frankie watched Nico's van disappear into the night, she made a new vow. She had four days off and she was going to use every one of them to push a 'reset' button. By the time she was back at work she might even be ready to laugh at herself for the stupid fantasies she'd been having about a new colleague.

She had to get over it, didn't she? Frankie wasn't about to follow her friend Jenny's example and hide away in some sleepy little country town to escape. No.

Nico had the right idea about such challenges in life. The way through this was to keep herself too busy to have time to think about it.

CHAPTER FIVE

FRANKIE WAS NOT HAPPY.

Everything had seemed normal when Nico had arrived back at the South Sydney Air Rescue base this morning. She'd even looked pleased to hear his news that he had signed a lease for the beach house property in her neighbourhood.

'It has electricity. A bathroom, even. No furniture, but I won't need much.'

'Have you been online?' Frankie asked. 'You should find everything you need for next to nothing there.'

'*Sì…*' Nico had already been online to search the most popular digital marketplace. 'I have already picked up a fridge. When I find the extra kitchen things, I'll be able to make dinner for you and your housemates. I enjoyed Friday night a lot.'

Frankie smiled but her gaze slid away from his almost instantly. 'You don't need to do that,' she said. 'And it's pretty difficult to get us all in the same place on the same night. Friday was a bit of a fluke.'

Nico frowned. He could sense something wasn't quite right. Was it because he wasn't understanding well enough?

'A fluke? Isn't that a musical instrument?'

'That's a *flute*.'

This time, when Frankie smiled, Nico knew what had felt wrong. This smile was genuine, not simply polite. And… it was a gorgeous smile. He could actually *feel* it as much as he could see it. In his gut somewhere. Or perhaps it was in his heart.

'A fluke is something that happens by luck rather than good management,' Frankie was explaining. 'A *colpo di fortuna*, perhaps? Sorry, my Italian is very rusty. It's obviously time I went home to visit my *nonna*.'

She'd understood well enough to translate the saying about the scalded cat that he hadn't actually meant to say aloud the other night, but Nico was still processing the fact that she had initially given him a smile that was polite enough to be distant. Impersonal.

It shouldn't bother him. But it did. It was how Frankie had been around him when he'd first arrived. Before they'd worked together long enough to know they could trust each other professionally. Before she'd cooked that amazing meal and he'd sat under a tree with fairy lights through its branches amidst the laughter of people who had happily included him as part of their group. An evening where Nico had felt more like he could simply be himself than he could remember feeling safe to be in such a long time it felt like for ever.

He tried to shrug off the setback. It shouldn't matter if they weren't going to be good friends.

Except it did.

He liked Frankie.

He *really* liked her. He would very much like to be part of her circle of friends. He wanted to be able to be in her company away from work and share a meal again. To hear her laughter and get to know her. She was an Australian-born Italian but how similar were their backgrounds? Was she as close to her *nonna* as he had been to his? Did she have a big, noisy, nosy family like he did? Was he going to make Frankie even less happy if he asked a personal question or two? It was worth finding out.

'Where's home?' he asked.

'Melbourne.'

'And that's where your whole family lives?'

'Just my *nonna*. And my mother.' Frankie shrugged. 'But that is my whole family, yes. My father died when I was too young to remember so my mother moved back to be with *her* mother.'

'No brothers or sisters?'

'Nope.' The word was clipped and Nico got the impression that was the end of the conversation. It was his turn to shrug. 'Maybe you were lucky,' he told her. 'I have four sisters and they were always fighting with each other.'

She only looked directly at him for a split-second but it was enough for Nico to see something in Frankie's eyes that was...what was it? Sadness? Had he stumbled on something private, like a past tragedy in her family? Nico knew about how important it could be to keep some things private. He opened his mouth to apologise for telling her she was lucky not to have brothers or sisters, but Frankie was making a sound that was vaguely dismissive and then she wandered away to stare out of the huge windows that overlooked the helipad. Mozzie and Ricky were busy with the aircraft. Going through an equipment checklist, perhaps?

Was Frankie creating distance in the hope that he wouldn't ask her any more personal questions? Wishing for a call-out that would put them into a professional space that would make it totally inappropriate to pry into her private life?

If so, she got her wish. Nico could feel his pager vibrating on his belt and the sharp tone of its beeping. At the same time, Colin's voice came through the loudspeaker system.

'Tango Papa Bravo. Code One. Two-vehicle MVA on the M31, vicinity of Yanderra. GPS coordinates coming through. Police and ambulance in attendance.'

Frankie was already heading through the door on the way downstairs to the helipad. She hadn't waited to hold it open for Nico.

It kind of looked like she was running away from him.

And the fact that it bothered him this much was a warning that he knew he needed to take heed of.

He could do the distant thing as well as she could if that was what it was going to take to make her feel safe enough to drop her defences.

Motor vehicle accidents were an almost routine deployment for Air Rescue, especially when they were in semi-rural areas with a long transport time to a hospital that had major trauma capability and on motorways with their higher speed limits that meant that collisions were much more likely to involve serious injuries.

Seeing the dents in a car roof that indicated the vehicle had rolled and that the engine of the second car was lying in the centre of a motorway lane were early indications that the mechanism of injury was significant so the victims had a high chance of serious injuries. There was an ambulance, a rapid response vehicle, police and fire service personnel on scene.

Frankie knew the critical care paramedic who'd arrived on scene in his rapid response vehicle and was currently kneeling at the head of a female patient, lying on the ground beside the car that had been sideswiped with such ferocity it had lost its engine and a front wheel.

'Hey, Tom.' Frankie crouched beside him. 'This is the patient you've called rapid transport for, yes?'

Tom nodded. 'I've just intubated her to protect her airway.' He squeezed the bag in his hand, watching the chest rise. 'She was unconscious on arrival with a GCS of three. Airbags were deployed but I'm thinking there must have been something loose that hit her head. She's got unequal pupils, bleeding from her ears and this bruising coming up around her eyes suggests a basal skull fracture. She's also got a widening pulse pressure so the sooner she gets to ED the better. A ten-minute flight time is a hell of a lot better than at least forty-five minutes by road.'

'Let's load and go, then. We'll get her hooked up to our portable ventilator as soon as we get her onboard.' Frankie looked up to signal Ricky that the scoop stretcher was needed. Behind him, she could see Nico kneeling in front of a small girl who was sitting on the lowered back steps of the ambulance. She was holding a doll in one hand and was crying. Frankie swallowed hard. 'There were children in the car?'

'Just the one,' Tom told her. 'Her name's Amelia and she's nearly four years old. She was in a good quality car seat in the back and appears uninjured, but if you've got room to take her with her mum that would be ideal. Nobody's been able to contact the dad yet.'

'We can do that.' Frankie nodded.

'Great. When they find Dad, they can send him straight to St Mary's. We haven't told Amelia how badly hurt Mum might be. She thinks she's just having a bit of a sleep because she's tired.'

'What about the other vehicle involved?' Frankie had more than enough medical assistance with the patient she'd headed for, but had Nico been right to stop to talk with a child who was already with a ground crew paramedic rather than going to the vehicle that had flipped?

'Teenage driver.' Tom blew out a huff of breath. 'Extricated himself and appears okay. He's refused medical attention, probably due to his alcohol level. Must have been some night last night, that's all I can say. The police are dealing with him.'

Ricky had separated the two sections of the scoop stretcher. Tom continued to look after the airway and breathing for their patient as Frankie helped a paramedic log roll her just enough to slide one section beneath her body. She pushed aside clothing that had already been cut and ran her hand down the spine before they lowered her onto the stretcher.

'No obvious spinal injury.'

They repeated the process on the other side, clicked the scoop stretcher together and lifted it onto the air mattress on top of the helicopter stretcher. Ricky placed the padded blocks on either side of the patient's head, ready to tape them into position to add extra immobilisation.

'Loosen the collar as soon as that's taped,' Frankie reminded him. 'And we want a slight thirty-degree up-tilt on her head to improved venous drainage.'

Another sideways glance revealed Nico still with the child. It looked like he was simply talking to Amelia but Frankie was quite confident that he would be doing another assessment of whether or not she was injured. He'd be watching and listening to any signs or symptoms that her breathing might be affected, looking at skin colour and any obvious bruising, listening to her speech to see how oriented and alert she was and, even though it was usually the quietest children who had the most serious injuries, that crying could be due to significant pain.

Nico's face did look as if he'd found out something very concerning but, as she and Ricky got closer with the stretcher, Frankie could see that the little girl was only holding the body of her fashion doll in one hand with nothing more than a plastic bobble on top of its neck. In her other hand she was holding a head with improbably long, curly blonde hair and the little girl looked distraught. Nico looked up and nodded as he registered that they were on the move to load and go as soon as possible.

'Is Amelia coming with us?'

'Yes.'

'Come on, *cara*. Let's go with Mummy.'

'But I want you…to fix Princess Pixie,' Amelia wailed.

'The hospital is the best place for anyone who has hurt their head,' Nico said. 'For mummies and princesses. But you know what?'

'What?'

'I might be able to operate on Princess Pixie on the way.' Nico held out his hand and Frankie watched as Amelia didn't hesitate to respond. She held up her arms, her face still crumpled in grief for her beloved doll, no doubt mixed with shock from the accident and confusion and fear for her mother. Nico scooped the child up and she buried her face against his neck as he strode alongside the stretcher.

And Frankie looked at those small arms wound around Nico's neck and the cloud of still baby-soft hair covering the head snuggled against his shoulder and her heart just melted.

Did he have any idea what a wonderful father he could be? He clearly had the gift of winning a frightened child's trust and Frankie knew how hard that could be. Children—and dogs, for that matter—had an intuition about people and Nico was one of the good guys. It was kind of heart-breaking if a bad marriage had put him off ever creating a family of his own.

But it was none of Frankie's business and allowing her heart to be melted was not helping her consolidate the new boundaries she had put in place in the last few days to prevent the possibility of stepping anywhere near that dead end street on a relationship map. Being in the friend zone didn't include getting misty-eyed over seeing a man being so charming to a small child.

She focused completely on monitoring Amelia's mother on the short flight to St Mary's and their patient was stable enough for her not to need assistance for the moment, which meant that both Nico and Ricky had the chance to look after Amelia. A glance behind her showed Nico lifting one side of the headphones Amelia was wearing so she could hear him over the noise of the rotors. Frankie could hear what he was saying through the headphones in her helmet.

'Can you give me the head, please, Nurse Amelia? I think I'm ready for the reattachment surgery. There…'

Frankie glanced behind her to see Nico pushing the doll's head back onto the bobble.

'*Va meglio*… That's better. As good as new…'

A chuckle of laughter came from Ricky. 'First successful recapitation I've seen. Good job, team.'

'I think she needs a bandage,' Nico said. 'What do you think, Nurse Amelia?'

'Mummy gives me a sticky plaster when I get an ouch.' Amelia was sitting so close to Nico that Frankie could hear her voice via Nico's microphone.

'Ricky?' There was suppressed laughter in Nico's voice. 'Do we happen to have a sticky plaster for ouches in our supplies?'

'I think I can probably find one.'

So the handover on the roof of St Mary's involved not only a human with a head injury but a doll who had enough of a bandage around its neck to look like it was also wearing a cervical collar. When Frankie saw Amelia looking over the shoulder of the nurse who was carrying her in the wake of her mother's stretcher, so that she could keep her gaze fixed on Nico, she knew she was going to have to work a bit harder on those boundaries.

What was it about men who were gentle with children or loved their dogs that was so sexy? Was it because it suggested that they would also look after the woman in their life with the same level of care? Physical sex appeal was one thing but passion with a background of an ability to care— and protect—was a whole different planet of attractiveness.

Mr Perfect was making it a lot harder than she had anticipated to get over her attraction.

Hot, humid end-of-summer nights made it harder to sleep.

Lying awake made it harder not to think about Nico.

It was, however, getting easier to work with him as they began their next four-day roster together on Red Watch. Nico was settling in, both to his new house and his new job. Bruce was also settling into his new life. He came to work with Nico and lay quietly in a corner of the staff area or a hangar or under the table at mealtimes. The dog's leg was healing well, although he was still walking with a limp and had perfected the cute trick of holding his front paw up as if it was hurting when he wanted attention from Nico.

'Have you heard yet whether there's any family who might want to take Bruce on?' Frankie hadn't missed the way Nico was sharing his lunch by slipping scraps of food under the table to Bruce.

'No.' Nico was fondling Bruce's ear now. 'I think I'm afraid to ask. I would miss him very much if someone comes forward.'

'I could ask Jen,' Frankie offered. 'I imagine she's feeling the same way about Stumpy by now.'

'Maybe it wasn't a new life she needed at all,' Mozzie put in. 'Maybe she just needed a dog in her life instead of dating a bastard.' He glanced up. 'Who are *you* dating at the moment, Frankie? What happened to that hotshot surgeon you brought to the Christmas do last year?'

'Long gone.' Frankie pasted a smile on her face. 'Turned out he preferred the girlfriend he had before me so he went back to her. Actually, I don't think he ever broke up with her. He was just, you know, thinking that the grass might be greener on the other side of the fence.'

Mozzie grunted. 'We'll put him on the bastard list too, then.' His gaze shifted from Frankie to Nico and then back again and he wasn't doing a very good job of hiding a smile or looking like he was having a 'light bulb' moment.

'Oh, come on, Mozzie.' Frankie's tone was sharper than she had intended but she was wincing internally. This was hitting a little too close to home. 'You know that's not going to happen. I'm happily single right now.'

'So am I.' Nico sounded alarmed.

'And surely you haven't forgotten the pact we all made about not dating colleagues?' Frankie was not about to embarrass Nico—or herself—any further. 'You weren't even on the same watch as that paramedic you were dating when I first arrived here and you still threatened to resign and go and work as a crop duster in the outback when it all turned to custard.'

Mozzie grimaced at the bad memory. 'Fair call,' he muttered. 'Right... I'm going outside. My bubble needs washing.'

'And I need to call Jen.' Frankie followed him. She might as well get a bit of fresh air while she made her call and, hopefully, any awkwardness that Mozzie had sparked by the implied suggestion that she and Nico dated each other would be completely forgotten by the time she was finished.

Her call was answered almost immediately.

'Jen?'

'Hey...'

There was something in Jenny's tone that made Frankie pause. 'You busy?'

'Sort of…'

'You sound half asleep. You're not at work?'

'Um…no… Is this urgent?' Jen asked. 'Can I call you back?'

Okay. Frankie had a good idea of what was going on with her friend right now. 'You're with someone,' she said. 'Aren't you?'

'*Frankie…*' The tone was a warning.

'Hey… I'm going.' Frankie was grinning. 'But you have to ring and tell me everything. I wanted to talk dog but it can wait.' She shook her head. 'Eight o'clock in the morning, huh?'

Her grin was subsiding into a smile but it felt like it was only her face involved now. Inside, she had to admit she was feeling a bit…left out?

Envious?

Lonely, even?

'There's no urgency,' she told Jenny. 'I just had a moment and thought I'd check in. Now I'm very glad I did. You go, girl—right back to what you were doing.'

Frankie swiped her screen to end the call. She didn't move from where she was standing, however. She watched Mozzie hosing the bubble-shaped windows on the front of their helicopter to get the dust off and then using a soapy cloth to give them a thorough wash.

She still felt out of sorts. Who was Jenny with? That guy called Rob she had mentioned the night that they'd rescued Bruce? But that was only a couple of weeks ago. Frankie was about to decide it was a bit quick to be jumping into bed with someone, but she had no right to judge her friend, did she? If she'd been offered the chance to get that close to Nico, would she have turned it down?

She couldn't push the thought away quite fast enough to avoid answering her own question. Thank goodness Nico hadn't been remotely interested because Frankie knew perfectly well that an offer like that would have been irresistible.

It was getting easier to keep his distance from Frankie.

After that awkward suggestion from Mozzie that he and Frankie might be interested in each other as more than colleagues, his crew pilot was now finding it fun to try and set him up on blind dates with every single woman associated with South Sydney Air Rescue. And anyone else he knew. Like someone called Donna who worked in the Emergency Response Centre.

'She's cute. In her mid-forties but looks after herself. How old are you, Nico?'

'Thirty-eight.'

'Nothing wrong with dating an older woman. Shall I set it up?'

'*No.*' This wasn't funny any longer. 'Stop, Mozzie. I can find my own woman. If I wanted one at the moment, which I *don't*. I'm too busy. With my job and my new house and looking after my dog.'

My dog. Because it looked as though no one was coming forward to claim Bruce, and Nico was more than happy about that. He was also very happy in the place he'd found to live with Bruce. He could carry his paddleboard down to the sea, through the reserve to where he'd found a place where the cliff was low enough to be easy to navigate a few steps and there was a tiny beach where Bruce could sit in a shady spot. The exercise was helping his leg now and Nico was hoping that Bruce might be persuaded to go swimming one day soon, which might be even better than a shower with the hose at work to keep him clean.

The best time to head for the sea was after work, with summer evenings still staying light enough to get home even well after a sunset at about seven-thirty p.m. Today was the best yet, with a sunset not far away that was promising to light up the sky in glowing shades of red as Nico paddled back towards what he was coming to think of as *his* beach.

Seeing someone climbing down the few steps to the shore was a bit of a shock, to be honest. And, even more surprising, was that Bruce didn't seem bothered. Surely he wasn't actually wagging his tail?

A strong push with his paddle and his board shot forward. It was someone wearing tiny shorts that made her legs look impossibly long and a sports top that doubled as a bra, leaving her midriff bare, and she had running shoes on her feet. Nico didn't need to see the long, dark braid swinging as she bent down to pat Bruce to know who this was.

'Frankie…'

She looked up at his call, straightened and watched as he came back to shore, dropping to kneel on his board and then put one foot down as he felt the sand beneath it.

'I saw Bruce when I was running on the track up there. I thought he might have wandered off by himself and got lost.' She had her hands in the air, as if she needed to emphasise what she was saying. 'I should have known he wouldn't have let you out of his sight.'

Nico was standing beside his board now. 'Perfect timing,' he said.

'Why?'

'Didn't you say you'd always wanted to try a SUP? Now's your chance. There's just enough daylight left.'

'But I'm not wearing my togs. I might fall in and get soaked.'

Oh…there was a thought. But Nico tried to push it aside.

'I'm not wet. See?' His shorts and tee shirt were, indeed, bone-dry. 'You might be a natural and not fall off. But, if you do, it's not far to run home, is it? And it's been such a hot day…'

Frankie looked at him. She looked at the paddle and the board he was holding and then she looked past him to the boats floating on the calm water. The horizon was a glow of pink that was reflecting on the water and Nico knew that she was tempted.

He gave her his most encouraging smile. 'You'll love it,' he said. 'I promise…'

Frankie shrugged. 'Why not? Just a quick go before it gets dark.' She was tugging off her shoes. 'You're right, it's not that far to get home if I get wet.'

Within seconds she was standing in the water beside him. Close enough to feel the warmth of her skin.

'See this, in the middle of the board? It's the carry handle. When you get on, you need to kneel on either side of the handle so that your weight is evenly over the centre line.'

The board wobbled ominously as Frankie climbed on and she gave a surprised squeak. 'I'm going to fall in…'

'No. I've got you.' Nico was steadying the board. He

handed the paddle to Frankie. 'Try paddling on your knees to start with.'

Frankie wobbled but then managed a stroke and then another. 'I can do it,' she said delightedly. 'Can I stand up now?'

Nico was standing in water deep enough to be soaking the bottom of his shorts but he wasn't close enough to help Frankie if she fell in.

'You can swim, can't you?'

'I'm not going to fall in. I've got this.' Frankie's grin was wide. 'Just tell me how to do it.'

'Okay.' Nico's hand gesture was one of surrender. 'Put the paddle in front of you across the board and put your hands on it. Put your feet where your knees were and then stand up.'

Frankie wobbled alarmingly this time but managed to stay upright.

'Put your paddle in the water. No…don't look down. You need to look at the horizon—something stable. Start paddling…'

But Frankie was still looking down and she lost her balance and fell into the water with a splash that was big enough to make Bruce bark.

Oh, no… Nico had made a promise that he might have just broken. Frankie might be really annoyed by this un-scheduled dunking in cool seawater.

But she was laughing as she surfaced. Nico was wad-ing in a little further to catch the end of the board so he ended up right beside Frankie as she shook the water from her eyes.

'Oops,' she said.

Nico didn't say anything. The light was changing fast around them, as if a dimmer switch had been turned, and he was looking at Frankie's face, with the glow of sunset colours behind it which softened her features and made her smile even more striking. And those eyes...

Dio mio, but she had to be the most beautiful woman Nico had ever seen.

'I'd better get out,' Frankie said. She took a step towards the shore but must have caught her foot on a rock because she stumbled in the waist-deep water and would have fallen in again if Nico hadn't put his hand out for her to catch.

And there they were...standing in the sea with the sun setting around them and...they were touching each other. Frankie was only holding his hand but he could feel the heat from her skin touching his reaching every cell in his body.

Nico felt as if he had rocks beneath *his* feet now. That he was about to fall even though he knew perfectly well he wasn't moving a muscle. He couldn't move. He couldn't look away from Frankie's eyes. And she wasn't moving either.

The paddleboard was drifting towards the shore with the tiny ripple of movement on the surface of the water, but it could have been drifting out to sea right now and Nico wouldn't have even noticed.

Because he was moving now.

Or Frankie was.

It didn't matter who had initiated this because it felt completely inevitable. This had always been going to happen.

This kiss...that felt like it had the power to turn his world inside out and upside down from the instant Nico's lips touched Frankie's.

CHAPTER SIX

OH, DEAR LORD...

Frankie put her foot down to steady her bike as she parked it, turned the engine off and pushed her kickstand into place. As she moved to swing her leg over the seat, cowboy style, to dismount, she could see it in her rear-view mirror.

The red and white Kombi van.

Was Nico still inside his vehicle, which would mean their paths would cross in a matter of seconds? Was he taking Bruce for a walk on the grass to make sure he'd be okay inside for a few hours if necessary or was he already in the building? Having a coffee with Mozzie and Ricky, perhaps, and saying, yeah...it hadn't been a bad night at all, thanks.

Frankie could feel herself cringing.

It was going to be impossible to make eye contact with Nico this morning, wasn't it?

Not because anything horribly awkward or embarrassing had happened.

Oh, no...

Quite the opposite.

Even that kiss had been like no other Frankie had ever experienced. *Ever*...

That first touch had been simply that. No more than a

touch. Soft. Brief. Over before it really happened and there'd been that moment of...shock, almost, because it *had* happened. And then, like the afternote of tasting an amazing wine, Frankie had realised that this was different. She was ready for the next brief touch of their lips. And she couldn't wait for the one after that. She'd welcomed the way Nico cradled her head and angled it so that he could explore her mouth with his tongue and Frankie lost all concept of time at that point. She had forgotten she was standing waist-deep in chilly seawater because the heat that this kiss was generating made it irrelevant.

Until she'd shivered. And Nico said it was time to get out.

He said it was not only cold but it was almost dark and he didn't want her to get hypothermia, so she'd better come and dry out at his place before she went home, but they both knew that wasn't the reason she would be going home with him. The sexual tension in the air all around them was so huge, it felt solid. Hard to breathe, even. Had Nico spent that whole, short walk back to his house trying to talk himself out of it? Finding all the reasons, like Frankie was trying so hard to do, why it would be a very bad idea?

Had he worried, like Frankie had, about how awkward it might be arriving at work this morning? She closed her eyes as she eased her helmet off, opening one of the large hard shell panniers on the back of her bike to store it. And then she unfastened the button on her protective overtrousers and pushed them down to take them off.

As she did so, another kaleidoscope of memories cascaded through her head. And her body...

Peeling off those wet shorts.

Loosening her braid to squeeze water out of it with the towel Nico provided.

Lifting her arms so that Nico could peel off the sports top that was still soaked enough to make the skin on her breasts feel icy cold. Or was it just the contrast of the heat of Nico's mouth and tongue that made her skin erupt in goose pimples and her nipples as hard as stone?

Frankie locked her pannier. She took a slow, deep breath, trying to find the courage to turn and walk into her place of work.

She could do this.

She had no choice.

It wasn't as if it was a 'thing'. They both knew that. There had been a moment, when they arrived at Nico's front door, when either of them could have stopped it happening.

'*Do you want to come in?*' he'd asked softly.

She'd tried, and failed, to take a breath. '*I shouldn't.*'

'You don't have to.'

'*But I want to.*' The admission was torn out of her.

'Me too.'

'*It might make things weird at work.*'

'*It won't. Not if we don't let it.*'

Frankie knew that Nico was watching the way she was biting her bottom lip. She was lost the moment she saw the tip of his tongue touching his own lip, but she had to make sure they understood each other.

'*This can't become...you know...a "thing".*'

'*I don't do "things".*' Nico's smile was wicked. '*This is just for tonight.*'

'*Just this once...?*'

'*Just this once.*'

They had done nothing to be ashamed of. She and Nico were both single, responsible adults and it had been totally consensual sex.

Except...

Oh, help... Frankie swallowed hard. Except she'd done things she'd never dreamed of doing before. It had been the wildest, *sexiest* sex she'd ever had. She was going to blush the moment she saw Nico, wasn't she? Everybody would guess what had happened last night and they'd both get teased mercilessly. It wouldn't matter that she and Nico had talked about this in the aftermath of that passionate encounter and they'd been firmly in agreement.

'We can't tell anybody.'

Nico had driven Frankie home but stopped far enough away from her house that his van wouldn't have been seen.

'No. Mozzie would claim it was all his idea that we started dating.'

'We're not dating.'

'No...it was just sex...'

'Really? "Just" sex?' Nico's raised eyebrow was teasing.

'No...it was the best sex ever.'

'Yeah... I thought so too. And maybe it's a good thing we broke the rules. We can stop wondering what it would be like now.'

Maybe Nico could stop wondering. Frankie thought it might be even more distracting now that she knew how good it was. There was still no sign of Nico so she walked inside.

'Morning, Frankie.' Colin smiled at her but didn't stop as he headed for his office carrying a stack of paperwork from the direction of the printer.

Mozzie was beside the stove in the kitchen area. 'You're just in time,' he told her. 'Want a bacon butty? Not you,' he added, looking down to where Bruce was lying right beside his foot. Bruce thumped his tail on the floor and Mozzie shook his head. 'So he wants to be my friend now,' he said sadly. 'Cupboard love, that's all it is.'

Frankie remembered the accusing look Bruce had given her when he'd been shut out of the bedroom last night. It was just as well dogs couldn't talk, wasn't it?

Nico and Ricky were both sitting at the table, eating the sandwiches Mozzie was creating. Nico had his mouth too full to speak but he caught Frankie's gaze for a heart-beat and she could actually feel her level of stress drop-ping rapidly.

We've got this, his look told her in less than a second. *It's not a problem.*

'They smell so good,' Frankie said to Mozzie. 'I'd love one if you've got enough for an extra.'

'Always enough for you.' Mozzie had a wad of crispy curls of bacon in the tongs he was holding. 'Grab a piece of bread.'

Colin poked his head out of his office as she took her first, delicious bite of the unexpected breakfast.

'If you get any downtime today,' he said, 'the storeroom needs a bit of a tidy and a stock count for the disposables. I've got to get an order in tomorrow.'

'Sure.' Ricky nodded. 'Be good for Nico to get another look at everything we keep in there.'

Nico nodded, swallowing the last bite of his sandwich. 'I'm getting used to the system here. I really like the way you organise things with colour codes, like the main medical kits and the trauma and paediatric bags. It's so much easier to find and grab when we need to move fast.'

'We know that everything on board is intact because one of my jobs is to make sure it's checked and replaced after every call whenever possible,' Ricky said. 'What we don't want is to find we're low on anything in the storeroom, like airway or IV kit supplies.'

Frankie was just listening, enjoying her sandwich. Enjoying even more this feeling of normality. She should have known she could trust Nico. She'd certainly trusted him last night…

She had to keep her eyes fixed on her sandwich at that point, pretending to poke a fragment of bacon that was threatening to escape back inside the bread. Because she didn't dare look up and catch Nico's gaze. Not when another round of flashbacks was occupying her brain. So fast they were a blur and yet every instant was recorded in all its glory and every sense, dominated by touch. And taste.

And that feeling of sheer freedom. No inhibition. *Passion*…

There was no way Frankie could take another bite. Not while she could see herself on top of Nico. On *top*…straddling him—her loose hair puddling on his chest as she leaned down to try and kiss him without breaking their rhythm. When she could feel that iron strength in his hands and arms as he flipped her over to reverse their positions and she lifted her legs to wrap them around his waist and let him fill a space she'd never known existed…

'Something wrong with that butty?' Mozzie's tone was surprised. 'Not like you not to devour your food, Frankie.'

'It's so good, I just wanted to make it last a bit longer.'

Frankie's gaze grazed Nico's on its way to catch Mozzie's and reassure him about his cooking abilities.

Just the lightest touch of eye contact but she knew that *he* knew what she was thinking about. That he'd caught the subtext in her comment.

That the sex had been so good, maybe that could last a bit longer as well? That 'just this once' could be repeated?

If so, they would have to keep it secret, which could be tricky now that they knew too much about each other. Nico knew about that unique birthmark Frankie had on her butt cheek that was shaped remarkably like a frog. Frankie knew that Nico had been a daredevil in his teenage years and collected a few scars in hidden places from stupid exploits he probably wouldn't want his colleagues to know about. He hadn't wanted to tell even Frankie about them. Maybe she'd been right about him having a terrifying encounter with someone wielding a knife and she could understand that he wouldn't want to talk about it. Her curiosity had grown, however, as she'd slowly traced the damaged skin on one of his shoulders with her fingertips and perhaps Nico had realised that she wanted to ask questions that he really didn't want to answer. It had certainly been what had finally broken the mood last night and sent Frankie back home, in still damp clothes, for an extremely late dinner.

More importantly, if anything else happened between them, it would have to be a secret so that it wouldn't impinge in any way on their professional relationship. Nico had been confident that they could prevent it getting weird and, so far, that seemed to be working but could the boundary between work and play be solid enough if it happened again?

Did Frankie really *want* it to happen again?

It might have been the best sex ever, but that was all it was.

Nico was happily single and wanted to stay that way for ever.

Frankie was also single, but only until she met the right man to fall in love with. The one who would want to be with her for ever and help create the family that was what Frankie wanted so much in her life. But maybe this had been meant to happen—just for a while.

Because Frankie was beginning to realise it might be a good idea to loosen rules that might have been holding her back without her even knowing.

She could learn to let go of those restrictions she had placed on the type of man she wanted to be with, and that had to be a good thing.

And she was already learning things about herself that were quite the revelation. Sex would never be the same and…that was a good thing too, as long as she didn't allow herself to fall in love with Nico, because that would change *too* much. It might make it impossible to settle for less than the things that were perfect about him and that might mean she would lose the opportunity to find a partner who was ready to settle down and create the family she dreamed of having. In the worst-case scenario, she could fall so deeply in love that she was ready to give up the dream of marriage and children, only to regret it later, when it was too late to do anything about it. And that might ruin her life.

No. That wasn't going to happen. Last night had been empowering in more ways than sexually. Frankie was capable of more than she'd ever given herself credit for, wasn't she?

This time, she deliberately let her gaze catch Nico's.

You're right, she communicated silently. *We have got this.*

She knew the answer to that other question too.

Yeah…she really wanted it to happen again. At least once more, anyway…

Nico let his breath out without having realised he'd been holding it.

He'd wondered how it would be with Frankie this morning but he could finally relax, knowing that it wasn't going to be a big deal.

What had happened had happened and the sex had been astonishingly good, but he wasn't about to start dating Frankie. He wasn't about to start 'dating' anyone. Not if it meant that a relationship might be seen as more than friendship and that expectations would be created. That was never going to happen.

The kind of trust that required had been broken irreparably.

He had got the distinct feeling, thanks to that look she'd given him after saying that her sandwich was so good she wanted it to last longer, that Frankie might be up for indulging in another one-off encounter some time but if avoiding sparking any kind of expectation meant that would never happen, so be it.

But… *Dio mio*…how good had that sex been?

He knew that kind of passion was playing with fire, but he also knew how badly burnt you could get if you let it get out of control, in more ways than the obvious. And he knew himself well enough to know he was more than capable of keeping himself safe.

He wasn't concerned about any awkwardness between himself and Frankie after that reassuring glance she'd just given him. The fact that they could communicate so well with no more than a glance was a worry, however. Would it be added to the physical attraction of this woman, that had not exactly been dampened by last night's adventure, and interfere with his focus on his job? Even as the thought formed, a call came in for a Priority One response, meaning there was an immediate threat to life.

Within seconds, the whole team was standing in front of an aerial map that covered an entire wall of this huge room, and Nico knew that he had nothing to worry about. The mission they were about to embark on was the only thing filling his mind.

'Somewhere around here.' Colin pointed to a green patch on the edge of one of the national parks south of Sydney. 'Someone saw him come down. No one's found exactly where it's landed yet, but local emergency response is heading in that direction.'

'That's around Wallaby Flats,' Mozzie said. 'I know it. You could find a decent area to land if you were in trouble and there are plenty of forestry tracks that will cater for large vehicles like a fire truck.'

'And it was a microlight, not a hang-glider?'

'Yep.' Colin's face was grim. 'It would be travelling faster.'

'And landing a lot harder,' Frankie added. 'Let's go...'

The air rescue crew received an update en route to the scene. The location had been found and an ambulance and fire truck had arrived. The pilot of the microlight plane was conscious but trapped in the wreckage of the aircraft and the only injuries found on a primary survey were a compound fracture of his left tibia and a painful, bruised neck after being caught by one of the wires supporting the wing structure that had snapped on impact.

Frankie caught Nico's gaze at that information and they didn't need to say anything aloud. They both knew that a neck injury was a huge red flag. If the injury was associated with swelling and bleeding, they could find themselves dealing with an airway emergency and that was something that was far more likely to be fatal than a broken leg. The A for airway was the first part of the ABC of first response for a very good reason.

They didn't play a secret game of rock, paper, scissors to see who was going to take the lead on this case. Frankie was ahead of Nico as they ducked beneath the helicopter's rotors as soon as they touched down and the first to reach the mangled metal with the only recognisable part of the plane being its nose and front wheel pointing up from the ground.

'We got him free about five minutes ago,' a fire officer told Frankie.

'We got an IV line in while he was still trapped.' The land crew paramedic looked up from where he and his partner were splinting the broken bone in his lower leg. 'He's had five milligrams of morphine.'

'Hey...' Frankie crouched beside the young man. 'I'm Frankie and I've got Nico and Ricky with me. What's your name?'

'Levi.'

'Great name...' Frankie smiled but she was watching him carefully. His respiration rate was high and his voice sounded very hoarse. 'Are you having any trouble breathing at the moment, Levi?'

'Yeah…my neck hurts…' He coughed, groaned and then wiped his mouth, leaving a streak of blood on the sleeve of the flight suit he was wearing.

Frankie unhooked the stethoscope around her neck. 'I'm going to listen to your breathing, Levi.' She looked up at Nico. 'Can you get some monitor leads on, please? I'd like a full set of current vitals as well. An SpO2 ASAP would be great.'

Levi became increasingly anxious as they worked on him to attach monitor electrodes and get an ECG trace showing on the monitor screen.

'I can't breathe,' he told them. 'It really hurts.'

Frankie examined his neck but even a gentle palpation was enough to make him groan in agony. She could feel the slight crunching of crepitus over his laryngeal structures, which suggested damage—possibly a fracture—to his larynx. This was certainly not a patient they wanted to be intubating in the air if he went into a respiratory arrest because, with the neck trauma, it could be a very difficult airway to secure. If an endotracheal intubation and using a supraglottic device failed, they would have to try a surgical airway.

'How far are we from the nearest hospital by road?' she asked.

'Thirty minutes.'

It had taken them ten minutes to get here by air and it was only a minute or two further than the base to get to the helipad on the roof of St Mary's.

Levi's rate of breathing was increasing and, more worryingly, the level of oxygen in his blood was dropping to a dangerous level of less than ninety percent even with a high flow of oxygen going through his mask. He looked pale and unwell.

Frankie moved to crouch beside her opened kit. Nico was opening the kit he'd carried from the helicopter and he was clearly one step ahead of her in anticipating what they might need at any minute. He had an airway set, including a video laryngoscope, which could help get a tube past anatomical changes due to trauma, endotracheal tubes, bougie wires, laryngeal mask airways and a pouch containing all the drugs they would need to sedate and paralyse a patient for a rapid sequence intubation.

Frankie spoke so that only Nico could hear her. 'An attempt to intubate carries a risk,' she said. 'If there's trauma that prevents passing the tube, even one attempt, let alone more, could exacerbate the damage and close the airway completely so a backup of an LMA won't be viable.'

'And trauma could make a cricothyrotomy impossible,' Nico added quietly. 'What do you want to do, Frankie? Transport him by road?'

'Frankie?' Ricky was closest to their patient at the moment. He sounded calm but she could hear the warning in his tone. Levi's condition was deteriorating.

It was Nico who turned first and, seamlessly, Frankie moved to assist him rather than lead as they dealt with Levi's imminent respiratory arrest. She drew up drugs and ticked off the RSI checklist as Nico administered the anaesthetic and then prepared to get a tube in to secure the airway as quickly as possible.

'I'll use a smaller tracheal tube, thanks,' he told Frankie. 'Six-millimetre. And no cricoid pressure.'

Frankie could see the intense focus on Nico's face as he crouched over Levi's head and peered at the screen on the video laryngoscope as he inserted the blade.

'It's a mess,' he said. 'I'll have one go, as gently as I can. Is the surgical airway kit good to go?'

'Yes.' Frankie had it open beside her and when Nico sat back on his heels and picked up the bag valve mask to ventilate manually and reoxygenate when his attempt had failed, his glance and nod towards her made her take the lead again to perform the procedure that could well be the last chance for them to get Levi to hospital alive. The clock was ticking and it needed to be done as quickly as possible. Within a minute, preferably.

She tipped disinfectant over his neck after Nico had positioned him with his neck extended and padding to arch his shoulders backwards. She held the larynx as carefully as she could with one hand while she made a midline incision into the skin, subcutaneous tissue and cricothyroid membrane, sending up a silent plea that there wouldn't be any major damage at a lower level in the trachea.

Using a bougie wire, she guided an endotracheal tube in place and then inflated the cuff and secured it. Nico was ready to attach and squeeze the bag valve mask to watch for inflation of the lungs on both sides, which would indicate a successful placement. Listening with a stethoscope was next on the checklist and then they could hook the tube up to their portable ventilator and, if they were happy with how stable Levi was and with the help of all the expert personnel still on scene, they could take off within a matter of minutes and get him to where he needed to be—in a well-equipped emergency department with an operating theatre on standby.

It wasn't until much later, when Frankie and Nico had their kits open in the back of the helicopter and they were replacing every item and drug that had been used, that she realised she hadn't given a single thought to Nico as anything but a professional colleague.

The best she'd ever had.

Roles, especially in procedures like airway management, were usually assigned and kept to in order to avoid confusion or wasted time on scene, but working with Nico was almost like working with another version of herself and they could communicate so easily that it felt natural to cross boundaries and simply work together to do what was needed.

They were a perfect match.

And it was only then that the first *un*professional thought Frankie had had since that shared breakfast entered her mind.

That perhaps they were a perfect match in bed as well as working together?

She waited for that thought to lead to an uncontrolled montage of flashbacks to their night together that could have left her totally distracted, but it didn't happen. Quite the opposite, in fact, and it was a relief that she could just move them to one side—to be revisited later, but only if she chose to do that.

'We need more size six endotracheal tubes for both the airway and the surgical kits,' she told Nico.

'Onto it.' Nico had the drug kit open. 'How good was it to hear that Levi's stable in ICU now? Do you think we could go and see him the next time we're at St Mary's?'

'I think we should.' Frankie nodded. 'It was good to know he's made it through. Looked a bit dodgy there for a while, didn't it?'

She was smiling as she turned back to their task. They had dealt with a very challenging case today and had, undoubtedly, saved a life.

Which meant they *did* also have this situation between them under control. They weren't about to start 'dating', but their unexpected attraction to each other that had led to sex hadn't interfered at all with their ability to work together.

Which meant there was no reason not to allow it to happen again, was there?

If Nico wanted it to happen again, of course.

As much as she did...

CHAPTER SEVEN

THERE WASN'T GOING to be any kind of Indian summer on the east coast of Australia this year.

As autumn gained momentum over the next few days, it seemed like it was already raining far more than usual. Surface flooding was enough to be intermittently cutting access on some inland roads, which meant air rescue helicopters were needed at times to transfer patients who would normally have travelled to hospital by ambulance or their own vehicles.

Red Watch was being kept busy with extra calls using up any downtime between emergencies. Rain wasn't enough to stop the SSAR helicopters flying, unless it was a storm with the potential for hail or lightning which could cause millions of dollars' worth of damage on top of making a flight challenging enough to be dangerous. Mozzie was keeping a very close eye on all the aviation weather maps and detailed forecasts and information coming in from other pilots of both fixed wing planes and helicopters.

'This isn't going away any time soon,' he grumbled during their lunch break. 'The long-term forecast for the rest of March is awful. We'd better start digging our gumboots out. I'm going to go and put new windscreen wipers on the chopper. I can sense an imminent summons for an air taxi to get over the puddles.'

'You might be able to paddleboard to work soon,' Frankie told Nico as both Mozzie and Ricky wandered off. 'You could teach Bruce to sit on the end of the board.'

'Funny you should say that. He swam out to meet me when I was coming back to shore last night. He did his best to get on the board, but ended up tipping me into the water.'

Frankie laughed but made the mistake of holding Nico's gaze a heartbeat too long and she knew they were both remembering her falling off the board and what had happened afterwards.

Only two days ago.

But it felt like for ever.

Who was going to make the first move? Was Frankie brave enough to test the water, so to speak, and see what Nico's response might be?

Yeah… That curl of desire deep in her belly was quite enough of an encouraging push.

'Let me know next time you're going down to that beach. I wouldn't mind having another go myself.' Frankie could feel her cheeks getting warm. 'At paddleboarding,' she added hurriedly.

Nico's eyes had a glint that suggested he was silently laughing at her. 'I'll probably go tonight because Bruce loves his walk, but it's still going to be raining.'

Frankie shrugged. 'It's not that cold. And I'd probably fall in again and get wet anyway.'

'Fair call.' Nico lowered his voice even though they were currently alone in the staff area. 'I might know a good way to warm up too.' One of Nico's eyebrows moved just enough for Frankie to know that he knew exactly what was on Frankie's mind. And that he was happy that she'd made the first move. It wasn't going to stop him teasing her, however. 'A hot shower,' he said. 'Or something hot to eat. I still owe you dinner, don't I?'

'But can you actually cook?' It was Frankie's turn to raise her eyebrows. 'I can't remember any Italian men in my neighbourhood even setting foot in a kitchen. They weren't likely to be able to cook anything other than a prawn or a steak on a barbecue.'

Nico made a very Italian movement with his hand to dismiss the insult. 'My *mamma* and my sisters were determined to teach me. My best dishes are lasagne, chicken parmigiana, calzone, risotto and gnocchi.'

'Do you make your own gnocchi?' Frankie was remembering asking Nico to dinner at her house that night. When they were talking about pasta *alla gricia*.

'*Certamente.*' Nico looked offended again by the suggestion that he might buy the gnocchi ready-made.

'And the sauce?'

'Butter and sage. *Cos'altro*?'

'What else, indeed? Frankie used the tip of her tongue to moisten her bottom lip. 'You're making me feel hungry and I've only just eaten my lunch.'

The glint in Nico's eyes was positively wicked now. 'So I can I tempt you?'

So she wasn't the only one remembering that night. The reference to temptation was definitely on another level now, however.

Because they both knew where that temptation would leave them. And how satisfying it could be.

But... Frankie found herself swallowing hard. 'I like working with you,' she said quietly. 'I really don't want that to get weird.'

'We're talking about dinner,' Nico said calmly. 'About being friends? We both know that's all it is, don't we?'

The boundaries were right there. Frankie could touch them and it felt...safe...

'Dinner,' she echoed, nodding. 'And friends... Okay...'

And if that was all it turned out to be, that really was okay. If it turned out that the sex was so good they both wanted to go there again, that would be okay too. More than okay.

Frankie turned away before Nico could see her smile, but she knew he could hear her murmur.

'Maybe just this once.'

There was a break in the weather that evening but the plan for Frankie to have another paddleboarding lesson didn't quite happen.

Nico was putting potatoes in the oven to bake when she arrived at the beach house.

'We've got at least an hour before they're cooked enough for me to scoop them out to make the gnocchi,' he told her. 'Plenty of time before it gets dark.'

'Mmm...' Frankie had picked up a leafy bunch from the bench beside him and held it to her nose. 'Fresh sage...' But the mention of daylight ending had reminded her of why she had wanted to be here so much, and it had very little to do with eating dinner.

It seemed that Nico had caught her thought. He took the bunch of sage from her hand and put it to one side. As she turned towards him he lifted his hand and touched her cheek with his fingertips, slowly tracing the shape of her face until he could drag his thumb across her bottom lip. Whatever heat the oven beside her was generating in order to bake those potatoes was insignificant to the fire Nico had just ignited and he knew it.

Or maybe he was feeling it just as much as she was. Frankie closed her eyes as she saw him begin to tilt his head, his gaze fixed on her mouth, but she tipped her head back a little to prolong this delicious anticipation and then felt his lips against her neck. On that point where her pulse would be felt so easily so Nico would know exactly the effect he was having on her body. When he finally claimed her mouth with his own, Frankie wrapped her arms around his neck and Nico lifted her against him. She wrapped her legs around his body and he carried her like that, into his bedroom, kicking the door shut behind him to ban Bruce from being a witness to what was about to happen in that room.

They had at least an hour, but it seemed to be over in a blink of time. Oddly, however, it also felt as if time had stopped completely from the moment Nico touched her body so intimately, his lips still covering hers until, eventually, they were lying curled up as closely as possible in his bed, waiting to catch their breath and let their heart rates get back to normal.

It was Nico who untangled himself with a sound of reluctance. 'I need to turn the oven off,' he said. 'Don't move...'

Frankie only moved enough to sit up against the pillows and pull up a sheet to cover herself. Nico came back with a bottle of wine, two glasses and Bruce padding behind him.

'We need to wait for the potatoes to cool down or I'll

burn my fingers scooping out the insides,' he said. 'So I thought we may as well be comfortable, seeing as I haven't got any chairs to sit on yet.'

Sitting in bed, sipping an excellent red wine, with Bruce happily asleep on the floor beside them was intimate in a completely different way than their lovemaking had been, but Frankie knew it was something she would also remember for the rest of her life. She leaned her head against Nico's shoulder, letting her breath out in a contented sigh—completely in the moment, without any thought to her past or what the future held—feeling as safe and happy as anyone could dream of being.

'It's been a good day,' she said softly. 'Despite being too much of a flying taxi.'

'The best part is still to come,' Nico said. 'You haven't tried my gnocchi yet.'

Frankie laughed. As if Nico could provide anything better than what he'd just given her. She had something she'd been saving to give him too, and now seemed the perfect time.

'You remember the call we had to Willhua today? When we had to delay the transfer of that woman to Sydney because we got caught in that storm?'

'Of course. You deserted us to go and have coffee with your friend, Jenny.'

'I did. And I was waiting for a break to tell you about it, but we got so busy I kind of forgot and then I thought I'd keep it as a nice surprise.'

'Tell me,' Nico demanded. 'The suspense is killing me.'

'You know Jen's been looking after Bruce's mate, Stumpy?'

'*Sì...*'

'Well, she told me that they haven't found a single relative or friend of Charlie's so nobody's going to claim them. You get to keep Bruce, if you want to.'

Nico was smiling. 'Of course I want to,' he said. 'You're right. Today *is* a very good day.'

She could taste the wine on his lips as he kissed her.

'I'm glad you're happy.'

'Jenny must be happy too. She will keep Stumpy?'

'Yes...'

'You don't sound so happy about that.'

'Oh, I'm delighted that the dogs have found forever homes with people who love them. I'm just a bit worried about Jenny, that's all. I think she's met someone she really likes, but she's running away from him.'

'Why would she do that?'

'Do you know the reason why she resigned from her job with us?'

'Mozzie and Ricky were telling me about it while we were waiting for the storm to pass,' Nico admitted. 'She was in a relationship with the CEO of the SSAR and then found out he was married.'

'Yeah... She was so humiliated, she put in her resignation almost immediately. A bit prematurely, I thought, because he's gone off to work in New York now. But, what the real kicker is, she's found out this new guy she likes—Rob—is also married.'

'No wonder she's running away, then.' Nico sounded disgusted. 'I would as well. No... I wouldn't be stupid enough to get in too deep, too soon and let history repeat itself.' He drained his wine glass. 'I wouldn't get in at all. Once was more than enough.'

Frankie bit her lip, thinking about his reference to the scalded cat who feared even cold water.

'It's not the same,' she said quietly. 'Rob's married, but his wife's on life support. She's been brain dead for years.'

'Oh...' Nico nodded slowly. 'That is different. But...it's only been a couple of weeks, hasn't it? It's too soon for it to mean too much. That's...*cerca di guai*.'

'Asking for trouble,' Frankie echoed. 'Yeah, I guess...'

Wanting to change the subject now, she lifted her head to catch Nico's gaze but her attention was caught by the rippled patch of skin on his shoulder, high enough to be hidden by a short shirt sleeve, that was one of the scars she had noticed before.

'Tell me again,' she said. 'Was this the one from your mountain biking accident or the one from the time the sky-rocket exploded?'

Nico snorted. 'I think it was the time the shark bit me.'

'Of course it was.' Frankie was smiling now, her worries about her friend fading, at least for now.

'It's time to get up,' Nico announced, acting on his words by rolling away from Frankie to put his feet on the floor and stand up. Bruce was on his feet too, his big fluffy tail waving approvingly.

Frankie's smile was fading as she watched Nico pull on his board shorts and then a tee shirt that effectively covered the imperfections that marred his smooth olive skin. The shark bite was a highly unlikely explanation. Exploding fireworks were just as unlikely but...that patch on his shoulder did look like the kind of scar a nasty burn could leave behind.

Whatever... Nico might make jokes, but Frankie knew

he didn't want to talk about it. It was part of his past. Like his marriage?

She could respect that. The last thing Frankie wanted to do was to push boundaries that could rebound and push her away from Nico. And if he wanted to protect himself, for whatever reason, by making light of past injuries, that was fine too. An air of mystery was just another dollop of sexiness, wasn't it?

By the time Frankie was dressed and had done her best to tidy her tangled mane of hair, Nico had scooped out and mashed the still steaming insides of the baked potatoes and was making dough by adding flour. He certainly knew what he was doing. Frankie leaned on the counter beside him and watched the deft movements of his hands as he brought the dough together and then took parts of it to roll into snakes to cut into small tubular pieces. The really impressive skill was the way he used the tines of a fork to shape the gnocchi ready to drop them into a pan of boiling water.

'They need the ridges,' he explained, when he caught Frankie watching him. 'It makes them hold the sauce better. My sister Rosa taught me that.'

'Good for her,' Frankie said approvingly. 'Maybe the undesirable gender roles I grew up with will start changing if there are more women like your sisters.'

'You love Italian food, but you don't like Italian men.' Nico's sideways glance was curious.

'I like you,' Frankie said lightly.

'Because I can cook?'

'Yes.' Frankie lifted her hands, her palms facing upwards. 'And it may be that I've been misjudging other Italian men because I've based my opinion on a previous generation and I will take that into account in the future. It has been a long time since I decided I didn't like Italian boys.'

'What did they do to you?'

'They wouldn't let me play football in the street with them and it was all I wanted to do when I was ten years old. They told me to go home because I was only a *girl*.'

Nico laughed. 'I bet they changed their mind about playing with you when you were older.'

'That was even worse.' Frankie's hand gestures were sharper now. 'It was all wolf whistles and honking car horns and shouts of "*Bella*, come out with us…". And eyes everywhere, blatantly undressing me. By the time I was old enough to be allowed out, I had sworn I would never date an Italian boy.'

Nico put the last gnocchi into the boiling water. His hand was still covered in flour when he cupped Frankie's chin and leaned in to place a slow, sexy kiss on her lips. 'It's just as well we're not dating, then, isn't it?' he murmured.

'Just as well.' Frankie still had her eyes closed. She opened them to find Nico smiling at her.

'I will play football with you if you wish,' he offered. He put a large slice of butter into a pan to melt.

Frankie laughed, but his words touched a part of her heart that she hadn't thought about for many, many years. That part that had been so lonely when she was an only child. When she'd wanted so desperately to be allowed to join those football games. There had been girls to hang around with, but little Frankie had had no interest in dolls or make-up or, later, hanging around in shopping malls to look at clothes or jewellery and talk about nothing but boys.

She watched Nico chop the sage leaves to go into the butter. Mr Perfect.

He wasn't just gorgeous to look at or so good at his job which had been enough for her to rethink her teenage vow and even believe that she could fall in love with Nico Romano. She now knew that he was the most passionate lover any woman could dream of. That he was kind to dogs and small girls and not-so-small girls. And he could cook. Frankie didn't need any more than the smell of the burnt butter and sage and the sight of soft, light gnocchi floating in the boiling water, ready to be served, to know that this dinner was going to be as perfect as everything else about Nico.

Almost everything else, she reminded herself.

Nico was the scalded cat. She could still hear the resolute tone of his voice when he'd said he would never get in too deep, too soon. That he would never get in at all, in fact. He was running just like Jenny was, but had he been doing it so long it had become an automatic part of his life? A part of who he was? Was it a rule he'd made that might need to be revised—like her antipathy to a man simply because of his nationality?

Perhaps Jenny was making the same mistake and allowing an admittedly justified prejudice to blind her to something that might, in fact, be completely different.

And maybe it *was* only two weeks since Jenny had met her man. But it was only two weeks since Frankie had met Nico and, if things were different, she could have been quite sure that she had found exactly what she hadn't known she was actually looking for. Two weeks wasn't too soon for it to mean something significant.

This—what she'd found so unexpectedly, with a man who shared her heritage—could have meant everything.

But Nico *had* been right about something else. Getting in so deep so soon was asking for trouble.

And Frankie had a horrible feeling she *was* in trouble. She hadn't meant it to happen but it was beginning to feel a lot like when she'd fallen off that paddleboard. She'd had no chance of stopping it happening.

So much for boundaries.

So much for brushing off how she felt about Nico as some sort of fantasy she could enjoy and then leave behind. Or believing that she could break the very sensible rule of not dating a colleague because of the potential fallout. Thinking that it might be good for her to learn to let go of the barriers she'd put in place in her own life, even.

Okay…they weren't 'dating'. Not officially, anyway. And maybe Nico was capable of being attracted enough to someone to be able to experience the kind of passionate lovemaking he'd introduced her to and not start falling in love with that person, but Frankie had overestimated her ability to control what was happening to both her body and her heart.

Somewhere, in the blink of time that two weeks represented in a lifetime, she might have already given too much of both her body and her heart to Nico Romano. How could she have believed she could stop herself falling in love with this man? The warning signs had been there right from the first moment she'd met him but, even then, she suspected it would have been too late to save herself.

It was just as well Nico had no idea how she felt about him because he'd made it very clear that it was the last thing he would want.

To her horror, Frankie could feel tears prickling at the back of her eyes. To hide them, she stooped to scratch behind Bruce's ears.

'You're a lucky dog,' she told him. 'And nobody's going to take you away because Nico loves you.'

Oh…this was already harder than she'd thought it would be.

This yearning to be loved by Nico herself, even when she knew it would never happen. It was so strong, it was actually a physical pain.

'And you're going to love this…' Nico was holding out a bowl with a generous serving of his gnocchi and sauce. 'You have a choice,' he told her.

Did she?

Frankie didn't feel like she had a choice at all. If she did, she would have been sensible and not allowed herself to get in too deep, too soon, with Nico. She wouldn't be here now, making things harder for herself by sinking even further into these feelings. She knew perfectly well that, at some point, she was going to have to deal with another broken heart but, when the only choice was whether to do that now or put it off as long as possible so that she could enjoy every moment of being with Nico while it lasted, it was a no-brainer. She wanted this.

No… It felt more like she *needed* it.

Like oxygen. Or light. And food… Inhaling the familiar aroma of the sage was a way back to the present and being able to shut down her line of thought.

'I promise I will find a table and chairs or a couch before you come to have dinner next time,' Nico said as Frankie accepted the bowl. 'For now, we can sit in the van to eat, on the steps of the veranda, although we might get rained on, or we can go back to bed.'

'The veranda,' Frankie decided. 'The van if it starts raining.'

Definitely not the bed. She might end up with those tears actually escaping.

Frankie might not have a choice she was capable of making about whether or not to be with Nico but, if she wanted it to last for even one more 'just this once', she had to make sure he wasn't aware of how she felt. Instinct told her that if he knew, he would run a lot further and faster than Jenny was running away from Rob. So fast, Frankie would lose sight of him instantly.

Not in a physical sense, because they would still have to work together, but she would never see the glimpses of the intimate connection they'd made in those shared, meaningful glances or a secret code running beneath an innocuous comment. They'd probably never play rock, paper, scissors again to decide who would lead the assessment and treatment of a patient. Was it possible that it could be so uncomfortable that one of them would end up requesting a transfer to a different watch, or even move on to a new job?

No. It was within Frankie's power to not let that happen and it wasn't as if she'd never had any practice. Those boys who had refused to let her play football with them had never known how bad it had made her feel. She could remember the way she'd tossed her hair and walked away with a smile on her face.

I don't care... I've got better things to do today, anyway...

And hadn't Nico all but promised there would be a 'next time'—when he had chairs or a couch for them to sit on?

Frankie didn't need to think about anything other than how good it was to be here right now. She certainly didn't need to cry about something that hadn't even happened yet.

Maybe it wouldn't happen for a very long time. Long enough for Nico to realise that he could safely break his own rules, perhaps?

Suddenly, it was easy to smile at Nico. *'Deliziosa,'* she said, having swallowed her first bite of the meal he'd prepared with such care. 'I *do* love this. *Grazie molte...'*

Life couldn't get any better than this, could it?

A few days later, Nico felt like his heart was filling to the point of being in danger of bursting as he looked down to where his dog was sitting, proud and tall, on the front of his paddleboard—like one of those carved wooden figures that used to be on oceangoing ships to give protection to its crew and safeguard their homeward journey.

Bruce was wearing the bright orange canine life jacket Nico had sourced online. The handles on the top had solved the problem of the large dog tipping him off by trying to scramble on board. He'd quickly learned to stand or swim alongside and let Nico lift him out of the water. Because he trusted him. And the love, that was growing every day, went both ways. Bruce had become a whole lot more than simply a pet. He was another living being that was sharing his life. One who could be trusted a hundred percent to be loyal and loving and...and so happy to be with him because he thought Nico was perfect.

Well... Bruce was the perfect dog. How lucky was he that he was a part of Nico's life now and that nobody was going to try and take him away?

Nico had to shake his head to get rid of trickles of water coming from his hair and threatening to get into his eyes. Okay…maybe life could get a bit better with an improvement in the continuing unstable weather patterns, but neither he nor Bruce minded being out in the drizzle this evening, especially with the water so calm he could see their reflection as they moved past the moored boats on the way back to shore. He had old towels at home that he could dry Bruce with and a quick, hot shower would be just as effective for himself.

Or maybe he'd just use an old towel as well and wait until he could share that hot shower later this evening. With Frankie…

She was out shopping right now because it was her turn to cook. Nico put a bit more effort into his paddling until he could feel the muscles in his shoulders burning. He needed a bit more exercise because it seemed like he and Frankie had started competing to see who could create the most delicious Italian food. She was making Caprese pizza tonight. She'd promised homemade dough for a crispy base, soft mozzarella cheese, juicy tomatoes and fresh basil with a balsamic glaze that was one of her *nonna*'s closely guarded secrets.

Nico could actually hear his stomach growl.

Life *was* about to get a whole lot better. Because there would be amazing food. Quite probably even more amazing sex. And because, like Bruce was the perfect dog, Frankie was the perfect friend. She was loud and funny and warm, but she was also highly intelligent and extremely talented and so damned sexy but wasn't making any demands on him for any kind of commitment. They both knew this was never going to last. Nico didn't do deep. And he didn't do long-term. Frankie understood that. She'd known right from the start that he wasn't remotely interested in getting married again so, of course, this was never going to be anything serious.

Even saying 'just this once' had become a private joke but the truth was there, hiding in plain sight. It had to stop, but neither of them seemed to want it to stop quite yet because it was just too good? Maybe it should be worrying Nico that this was going on longer than maybe either of them had foreseen, but it was easy to reassure himself. They had, on more than one occasion, agreed that this was not a 'thing'. That they were not going to let it interfere with them being able to work together. The longer it went on for, the more important their friendship was also becoming.

Was Frankie confident that, when the time came, it would be easy to walk away?

Nico felt something like a chill run down his spine. Because it was getting colder out here on the water? Or were his thoughts veering towards considering something that was out of bounds. That, if things were different, he might have been able to be a man Frankie would choose to keep in her life.

But he wasn't that man. He couldn't be, no matter how much he might want to be, because he would always be haunted by the destruction the slow downward spiral of his marriage had wreaked over far too long a timespan. The echoes of Sofia's endless criticism that had proved how disappointing she'd found him would always be there. He had never been able to do anything right. He hadn't cared enough about her because he'd spent too much time with his family—alone, because Sofia had grown to hate disappearing into the crowd of big gatherings.

Sometimes, he could still feel a frisson of the humiliation in the way she had used affection as a reward and the withholding of it as a punishment and he never knew which side the spinning coin would land on. How many thousands of times had he heard about how unhappy he'd made her and how useless he was as a husband and a lover? That it was *his* fault she lost her temper so often? And how unforgettable had that vicious question been of how he could possibly think that anyone would ever want him to father their children?

Frankie didn't know anything about any of that and he wanted to keep it that way.

He'd found a career he was both passionate about and good at. He'd discovered that he was also far better at sex than Sofia had given him credit for.

And that was enough. He could never risk his heart again. Not when it felt like it had only just been glued back together properly.

Why would he even consider doing that when life felt *this* good just the way it was right now?

Getting home to the rundown beach house with his beloved Kombi van parked outside it at the end of the long drive was something else to be grateful for in this new life of his.

It felt like home.

It would feel even more like home when Frankie arrived with her bags full of fresh ingredients. It might be her turn to cook, but she was coming to his place to make the meal. Because they both knew that the passionate lovemaking they were both so into was not always quiet and they wanted to protect their privacy. Or was it that they both knew that if it became known, the people around them—friends, house-mates and colleagues— would make it a 'thing'. That maybe they would all think that he and Frankie were perfect for each other and, somehow, they would find out how wrong they were?

That Frankie would find out the shameful secret of just how appalling his marriage had been? How much of a fail-ure he'd been as a husband?

If they stopped this now, before they got any closer, she'd never need to find out. But Nico didn't want to stop. Not just yet. Not even if it was going to be so much harder when he had no choice.

Because it was the combination of having both Bruce and Frankie in his life that was making it so good. Between them, they were filling the gaps that had been there ever since he'd left his homeland and family behind.

It was no wonder that this little blue house felt like home when they were all here together. The Italian food was a bonus.

And the sex was the icing on that proverbial cake.

Oddio… Nico was starving now. For much more than simply food. He found himself closing his eyes to cope with the shaft of sheer desire that speared his gut when he heard the muted roar of a motorbike coming up his driveway.

CHAPTER EIGHT

RAIN FALLING ON the already sodden ground surrounding Sydney, especially inland and to the south, had nowhere to go so it lay on the surface of farmland and roads and got steadily deeper. River levels were rising and dams getting too full. There was talk of 'one in one hundred years' flooding events and of areas that were predicted to receive six months' worth of their annual rainfall in a matter of only days. Evacuations were happening to prevent people getting cut off and losing all normal services including health care but, even with the best intentions of heeding the warnings, there were some who found they'd left it too late to get out in time.

Like the woman in labour, two weeks earlier than expected, whose husband had begun driving her to her nearest hospital only to find a bridge had just been washed out and she was completely cut off. They went back to their farmhouse and called for help. The young farmer was able to use his dogs and clear a mob of sheep from a paddock high enough to not be covered in water and close enough for a helicopter to land so that Nico and Frankie got only moderately wet by the time they'd carried their equipment through the heavy rain and up the steps to the shelter of the wide veranda of a traditional square Australian farmhouse.

When they saw the woman walking down the hallway to greet them, it seemed like the plan for a quick load and go was on track. The labour suite in the nearest hospital would be the safest place for her to give birth and Mozzie hadn't shut down the helicopter in the expectation of an imminent take-off. Their patient's husband was right behind her, carrying a suitcase and another bag and, further down the hallway, was an older woman who was holding two small children by the hands.

'No, you can't go with Mummy,' Nico heard her say. 'But you can give her a kiss goodbye and we can watch the helicopter take off. Won't that be fun?'

'No...' One of the toddlers was crying. 'We want to go too...'

Nico had just changed his mind about this being a quick pick-up. Because he had just noticed a trail of drips on the polished wooden floorboards of the hallway.

But he was smiling at the woman. 'It's Shannon, isn't it? I'm Nico and this is Frankie. How far apart are your contractions now?'

'About six or seven minutes, I think. Ben's been timing them...'

Shannon's husband checked his watch. 'Last one was four and a half minutes ago. It lasted about sixty seconds. This is faster than it was with the twins.'

'And your waters broke a while ago?' Frankie asked. She was looking at the floor between Shannon's feet and Nico could see the way her face had gone still as she processed what she thought she might be seeing.

'That was why we started driving towards the hospital.' Ben nodded. 'Mum said the river was running high when she came over to look after the twins for us, but we couldn't believe our eyes when we got into the valley and the bridge was just…gone…'

'It was really scary,' Shannon said. 'Thank goodness you guys got here as fast as you did. I've got my bags ready. It's okay if Ben comes with me, isn't it?'

'Of course. But we'd like to check what's happening for you before we head out to the helicopter, if that's okay. Things like your blood pressure and the baby's heart rate.'

'I'd rather get going,' Ben said. 'We don't want to end up having a home birth. Not in this weather. We might be on a hill but we can't afford to be stranded with a newborn baby, not when he's already making his appearance too early.'

'And we need to know what we might be dealing with before we're in the air.' Nico kept his tone calm. 'How long have you been bleeding for, Shannon?'

'What?' Shannon looked down. 'Oh…that's just my waters, isn't it? I must need to change the pad I'm wearing.'

Nico stooped to touch the dark floorboards with his gloved finger. It was bright red when he held it up and both Shannon and Ben looked shocked.

'What's going on?' Ben demanded.

'That's what we need to find out.' Frankie put her hand on Shannon's arm, turning her back towards the interior of the house. 'Have you got somewhere close that you could lie down, Shannon? And some old towels we could cover a bed or couch with?'

Ben was still staring at them, his face pale. Shannon reached for his arm to steady herself as she bent forward. 'It's another one,' she groaned. 'Oh…this one really hurts…'

They couldn't ask Shannon to move until the contraction

was over. Nico estimated that it was only five minutes since the last one, it lasted a good ninety seconds and Shannon was still bleeding. He radioed Mozzie.

'You can shut down, mate,' he told him. 'I don't think we're going anywhere just yet. Come inside. We might need an extra set of hands. Could you bring some towels too?'

Ricky had been left behind because this was only supposed to be a patient transfer and they weren't sure how many passengers they might be dealing with. Shannon was trying to stifle a loud cry with the pain of her contraction and the two toddlers were shrieking, Ben almost tripped over one of the bags he'd dropped as he moved to put both his arms around his wife and the older woman looked as frightened as he did. A dog had appeared from nowhere and started barking at the spectacle and this whole scene had suddenly turned into a bit of a circus.

Frankie's housemates had jokingly warned him that she was bossy but he'd never seen her take charge quite like this.

'Okay, that contraction is easing, isn't it, Shannon? Try and slow your breathing a bit and save some of that energy. Ben? You and Nico get on either side of Shannon and help her lie down somewhere.' She turned her head to look through the nearest door. 'That couch is fine.' She turned back. 'Nana, take the little ones into the kitchen for the moment. And the dog too, please. Put the kettle on and make yourself a cup of tea.'

The instructions were rapid-fire and in a tone that was not to be argued with. The children and dog magically disappeared with their grandmother and the noise level faded as a door was closed. They managed to get Shannon near the door of the living room with the couch, but that was as far as she could move before another contraction started. She sank to the floor to get on her hands and knees and Nico's heart sank even further.

They needed to find out whether Shannon was bleeding enough for it to signify an obstetric emergency like a ruptured uterus or a placental abruption. They had to find out if the baby was in distress by monitoring its heart rate. They needed to get IV access to give fluids if Shannon's blood pressure was dropping. The tension was escalating to the point where Nico felt a knot forming in his gut. Of all the emergencies they could attend, an obstetric one was his greatest fear—because there were two lives at stake here.

Frankie wasn't showing anything like his own concern. She was crouched beside Shannon, with one hand on her wrist to take her pulse and the other rubbing her back. Between reassurance for Shannon, she was gathering as much information from Ben as possible.

'Have there been any problems at all with the pregnancy?

'When did you have the last ultrasound?

'Is it just one baby this time?

'Do you know what position the baby is in?'

The responses were all reassuring but Nico was starting to unpack all the gear that could be potentially vital, including a birthing and neonatal resuscitation kit.

Frankie still sounded completely in control. 'I need to have a look,' she told Shannon. 'I have a feeling your baby's not going to wait until hospital to make his arrival.'

'It's a girl,' Shannon wailed. 'Oh…it's starting again already. I need to push…'

'Hang on for just a sec.' Frankie was getting Shannon's clothing out of the way. 'Pant for me, love. Like you're blow-

ing out candles. You've done this before. You're an expert…'
She was panting herself to encourage Shannon as she knelt
behind her. 'Okay…' Her voice was still remarkably calm.
'Baby's crowning. I'm going to put a little bit of pressure on
her head so she doesn't arrive too quickly. Breathe through
this contraction and you can push with the next one.'

A minute or two later, Nico looked up from opening the
drug kit to draw up a dose of oxytocin, which would hopefully control the abnormal bleeding already happening and
reduce the risk of a postpartum haemorrhage. He could see
that the baby's head was presenting with the contraction. He
could also see that the umbilical cord was wrapped around
her neck, but even that didn't seem to faze Frankie.

'Stop pushing for a sec, Shannon. Pant again…' Frankie
slipped her finger under the cord and looped it over the
head. 'Okay…good to go. You're doing brilliantly… One
more push should do it.'

Frankie's movements were gentle and controlled as she
provided downwards traction to deliver the baby's anterior
shoulder and then upwards traction to help deliver the pos-
terior shoulder.

And then the baby was born, a small face already crumpled and arms raised as she took in her first breath to release a warbling cry. Ben had his arms around Shannon
to help her turn to meet their daughter and Frankie took
a clean towel from Mozzie, who'd just walked in the front
door, wrapped the baby and then lifted Shannon's shirt to
put the tiny girl on her mother's chest, skin to skin.

'Is that ten units of oxytocin?' Frankie smiled at Nico.
'Good job. We'll wait a couple of minutes before we cut the
cord. Can you do the first Apgar score?' She turned back to

their patient. 'I'm going to give you an injection of oxytocin into your thigh,' she told Shannon. 'Are you okay with that? It's going to help with the delivery of your placenta, which is important. It might also help you to not lose any more blood, which would be a good thing.'

Shannon nodded. She was in Ben's arms and they were both looking down at their newborn daughter, but the young mother was shivering violently.

'Mozzie? Could you go and find the *nonna* who's in the kitchen and get her to find a duvet or some blankets?' Nico caught Frankie's gaze. 'One minute Apgar score is five.'

The five-minute Apgar score was eight, which told them that this baby was doing well despite her precipitous birth. Ben was the one who cut the umbilical cord after Frankie had put the clamps on and the placenta arrived without any indication of bleeding that would cause concern. Wrapped in a puffy duvet, Shannon had stopped shivering.

'Shall I tell Nana that she can bring the boys in to meet their little sister?' Frankie was smiling. 'Then we'll get you all sorted for a trip into hospital.'

Ben's mother burst into tears and rushed out when Frankie opened the door, so she was the one left to cope with two small, excited boys. And the dog who was turning in joyous circles and barking enough to make Frankie shake her head. But she was laughing.

She came towards them with one toddler in her arms, perched on her hip, and holding the hand of the other twin. Nico stepped back to stand beside Mozzie as the whole family, including Frankie, clustered around to admire the new arrival.

And something was melting inside Nico's heart.

She looked so completely at home surrounded by adults, young children and a brand-new baby. Frankie was born to be a mother, wasn't she? The heart of a family like this. She was so calm and competent and she had so much love to give. Those were clearly happy tears she was brushing from her eyes as she cuddled the toddlers and let them look at their sister without getting *too* close. And then she took the baby from Shannon's arms so that Ben could help her into clean clothes and a warm puffer jacket as they started the preparations to take them to hospital for a thorough check. Nico and Mozzie were packing up the gear, but he couldn't help another glance over his shoulder to where Frankie had her head bent over the baby she'd delivered, closing her eyes to place a soft kiss on its head.

She'd look just like that when she was holding her own baby, he thought.

As if it was the most miraculous day of her life.

And Nico's heart was breaking.

Because he would feel like that as well, if she was holding *his* baby.

The yearning had never felt this powerful. So strong it felt like his heart was bleeding. A need that was never going to be realised, because he could never take even the first steps towards that dream when he knew what it was like to fall off the edge of the cliff he hadn't seen coming.

He wanted to take that first step in that moment, more than he'd ever wanted anything. He actually straightened, as if he was about to take a physical step towards Frankie at the same time, but then he froze.

He couldn't do it. His heart might have healed but the

glue that was holding the pieces together—that ability to trust—wasn't strong enough yet.

Maybe it never would be. And that meant that it was time to stop wasting Frankie's time. She should be with a man who could give her the joy of having her own baby, and she wasn't going to find him if he was hanging around as anything more than a friend.

But how could he do it without hurting Frankie?

Because that was something he wasn't sure he could bring himself to do. Their friendship was too important.

He cared about her too much.

No. He *loved* her that much…

There was something different about their lovemaking that evening.

Or was it that they were both overtired after a long day and some uncomfortable scenarios due to the bad weather? Neither of them had had the energy to cook a meal, but it was nearly eight o'clock by the time they'd completed the paperwork and restocking the kits and were able to head home. It was Frankie who'd offered to pick up some fish and chips while Nico gave Bruce a bit of a walk in what was left of the daylight.

Neither of them had been planning to go to bed together that night. Nico had a big old couch in his living room now and that was where they sat to share their dinner and a small glass of wine. They didn't even bother with plates or cutlery, but ate their meal from the paper opened on the couch between them.

'I'll have to ride home soon. It might be another big day tomorrow.'

Maybe it was the way Nico was looking at her that made Frankie lean close enough to kiss him, and it was then that she first noticed something different. The ignition point for passionate sex was the same but, for some reason, it felt like Nico was holding back from lighting it. The kiss was tender to the point of being almost heartbreaking.

'You okay?' she asked when she pulled away to catch a breath.

'Sure. Why wouldn't I be?'

Frankie shrugged. 'It's been a long day. A bit dodgy at times too. Don't know about you, but I was really scared about what was about to happen to Shannon.'

Nico nodded. 'I was too. What caused so much bleeding, do you think?'

'Her cervix might have dilated so abruptly that it broke a few blood vessels.' Frankie blew out a breath. 'I've never seen that much bleeding without it being something major. I had visions of her bleeding to death from a ruptured uterus or an abruption before we could get her to hospital.'

'You didn't look at all scared.' Nico's expression was impressed. 'You handled it *magnificamente*.'

'Thanks… You were pretty awesome yourself. I…' Frankie bit back the words she suddenly wanted to say about what she really thought of him. How she felt about him. Instead, she did her best to keep her expression, and her tone, as light as possible.

'I really like working with you, Nico…' She kissed him again, very lightly. 'I really like…*this*…'

He made a sound that could have been weariness. Or surrender? There was a note of distraction in it. Or maybe it was reluctance? Whatever it was, however, it had gone by the time Nico claimed her mouth properly and she could taste the rising level of desire for them both. One of them, and it might well have been Frankie, pushed the fish and chip wrappers off the couch and she saw the blur of Bruce grabbing a leftover piece of fish and heading for the veranda with his prize before he could be stopped.

Not that either of them had any intention of stopping Bruce from disappearing. Or stopping what they were doing as the kissing deepened and hands moved to shift clothing and gain access to skin. To stroke and touch with the certainty of knowing exactly what to do to increase that arousal to a deliciously unbearable peak.

But even then there was something…different enough about the way Nico was touching Frankie for her to be aware of it.

It wasn't different in a bad way. It might have been a lot less wild, but maybe that was being dictated by the limited space for two people on a couch. It was…*softer*, Frankie decided. The kind of sex that two people who knew each other so well could have if they were a bit tired or distracted but they still needed to be this close. Two people who really cared about each other.

Frankie lay in Nico's arms a little while later, her head— and her heart—filled with the thoughts she couldn't say aloud.

I love you…

I'm in love with you…

I never want this to stop…

The dreamy bridge between being alert and falling asleep was broken abruptly by the sound of an incoming video call from Nico's laptop that was open on the floor at one end of the couch.

'That might be my sister, Rosa.' He rolled away from Frankie and dragged on his shorts. 'I need to answer it. My mother wasn't so well the other day...' He glanced at his watch as he picked up his computer. 'It's nearly eleven p.m. here so that makes it lunchtime at home.'

Thankfully, Frankie wasn't completely undressed but she hastily did up the buttons on her shirt. How awkward would it be if Nico's sister spotted evidence of what they'd just been doing?

But Nico was walking away with the laptop screen— and its camera—facing only himself as he clicked to accept the call and the sudden joyous shouting from too many loud voices changed the atmosphere in this room so much that Bruce, who'd come back inside to check for any more leftover food, instantly headed for the open front door to escape again.

'Nico...' A woman was laughing and then speaking in Italian that was so fast Frankie had trouble keeping up. 'What time is it for you? Did we wake you up? Is it hot there? It's so hot here today...'

'Uncle Nico...' More than one child was shrieking in the background. 'We miss you...'

'I miss you too, *cara*. And you, Paolo, and you, Tommaso. Are you being good boys for your *mamma*?'

'No.' It was the laughing woman again. 'They are monsters, all of them. When are you coming to visit home again to help me tame them?'

'Soon, I hope. How is Mamma?'

'Much better. She's here too. And your other sisters,

but we all know I'm your favourite, yes?' There was increased volume in the background shouting. 'Okay, okay. Just wait... Nico, everybody wants to talk to you...'

Nico was leaning on the kitchen bench, his gaze fixed on the screen, but he looked up and nodded as Frankie waved and slipped out to give him time alone with his family. He blew her a kiss but, as Frankie paused to give Bruce a pat before she left, she took another glance back into the house.

Nico was laughing at something he was seeing now, but he almost looked as if he could burst into tears at any moment and Frankie knew she had just learned something new about this man she had fallen in love with.

He adored his family and they adored him.

The joy in the voices of those children as they'd greeted him reminded Frankie of how he'd been with that little girl and her broken doll.

How could he be so adamant that he never wanted a family of his own?

He would be as perfect a father as it was possible to be. A perfect husband and lover. He was already a precious son and brother and uncle.

Frankie kicked her bike into life and rode off into the rain, but it wasn't dampening her spirits one little bit.

Because it felt like there was hope. Given time, perhaps Nico would realise that, for whatever reason, he'd been lying to himself? And that he wanted exactly the same future that Frankie did?

With her...

CHAPTER NINE

EVERYBODY HAD HAD enough of the rain, especially when yet another deep low-pressure weather system headed straight towards New South Wales. After two days of this new front slowly passing through, there were worrying reports on the news of a potential catastrophe that kept Frankie's best friend, Jenny, constantly in her thoughts.

A good part of south Sydney's drinking water supply came from a huge man-made reservoir in hills about fifty kilometres inland from Willhua and the excessive amount of water it now contained was creating so much pressure that people feared the dam would burst and the ensuing flood would affect everything in its path as it roared down-hill towards the sea.

Towards Willhua. And Jenny.

In order to prevent the dam bursting, a release system was activated to lower the water level in the reservoir but, because the entire area was already so sodden that lower-lying areas were flooded, the enormous amount of extra water became a flash flood that turned into a situation that was quickly declared an evolving national disaster. Every resource—including local volunteers in the State Emergency Service, the Red Cross, military, fire, police and ambulance units and every helicopter and boat that could be made available—became part of the massive effort to protect people, livestock and properties.

There were heartbreaking scenes of people desperately trying to save their horses by risking swimming them through the floodwaters or trying to muster sheep or cattle to higher ground and there were lines of cars being guided to roads where the water was not yet deep enough to be dangerous, full of families and pets and whatever precious possessions they'd been able to grab before heading for community halls, churches or schools that were deemed safe and were already being run by volunteers who could provide dry clothing, hot food and access to medical care.

South Sydney Air Rescue was in the thick of it, having all available staff members brought in before first light to be briefed on the situation and rostered for shifts that would continue day and night until the disaster was under control. Bruce had been left in Nico's van because there were so many people milling around the base, but arrangements were made for someone to let him out if Nico couldn't get back to base often enough.

Being trained to operate a winch, Ricky got moved to another crew where they were short of a team member so it was just Mozzie, Nico and Frankie on board. They were allocated blocks of time when they would be available to fly depending on the weather, broken up by long breaks between the active spells. The dangers of the environment and the tasks they would be asked to do were high enough without allowing exhaustion and human error to exacerbate them.

The range of medical intervention needed ranged from full-on drama, going to the aid of a farmer who was in danger of bleeding to death from a partial amputation of his leg, having fallen into hidden farm machinery while trying to move stock to higher ground, to nothing more than reassurance and care in helping to relocate the confused and frightened residents of a retirement home that had water already several inches deep throughout the buildings.

A search and rescue mission for a car was needed when a driver had not heeded the stern warnings from authorities to stay out of any floodwaters. The vehicle had gone into what looked like only a big puddle, to get caught by an unseen current and swept into a torrent of water beside the road where the river was carving a new channel through rural land. It didn't take long for the Red Watch crew to spot the small hatchback that was caught in an island of tangled tree trunks and other debris and they stayed overhead to help the police and rescue teams locate the scene and then waited as they worked to get to the driver. If they couldn't get to the car, Frankie or Nico could go down on a winch line. If they could get to the car and the driver was injured, they could help with medical care and evacuation to hospital.

Both Frankie and Nico leaned out of the open door of the helicopter, watching the people in their high-vis gear and helmets gathering to attempt the rescue. They had a cable attached to the courageous police officer who battled the current of the river to get to the car, anchored by his colleagues. They watched as he smashed the window of the car and managed to prise the door open. They could see the elderly man in the driver's seat.

And they could hear the exchange between Mozzie and the SES team leader below.

'You can stand down, mate. He's deceased. Go somewhere you're really needed.'

'Roger that.' Mozzie's tone was grim. The death toll for
this disaster had just increased by one.

He'd no sooner radioed the control centre to say they
were headed back to base than another call came in.

'Sorry, guys. We know you're due for a break but you're
the closest we've got to a job that's been on the books for
too long now. East of Coledale. There's a whole family on
the roof of their farmhouse. Two adults and a six-year-old
child. They're on the top of the veranda because the roof's
too steep, but they've just told us the water's up to the gut-
tering and there's no one else that'll be available any time
soon by boat *or* air.'

Mozzie turned his head, knowing that Frankie and Nico
had heard the exchange. They both gave him a thumbs-up.
Maybe they needed the chance to help people who were
still alive before heading back to base and being unable to
help anyone for the next few hours.

'Send through the coordinates,' Mozzie told the dispatcher. 'We're on our way.'

They flew low, over a sea of murky brown water dotted with
the canopies of trees visible like oversized shrubs and just
the corrugated iron roofs of houses and outbuildings still
above the water level. It didn't take long to spot the group
of people huddled together on the very edge of a roof. A
woman was clinging to a young child. There was a plastic
pet crate beside them that had to contain a precious dog or
cat. A man stood up and waved his arms frantically to signal the approaching helicopter. He then crouched to try and

shelter his family as the helicopter hovered directly above them, with the downwash from the rotors rippling the water and tearing leaves from nearby trees.

Frankie had done the most recent winch job so it was theoretically Nico's turn to be winched down, but this rescue was going to be difficult.

Dangerous.

The urge to protect someone she loved was strong enough to make her turn towards Nico, with both her fist and her eyebrows raised, as an invitation to give her the chance to take the risks instead.

He held her gaze and he looked…almost angry?

'Don't even think about it,' he growled. 'There's no way I'd let you go down there.'

'I trust you,' Frankie said quietly. 'You'd keep me safe.'

But Nico was already checking his harness and attaching the hook.

'I'll bring the mum up first,' he said. 'Then the kid. I'll need a bag to put that crate in and I'll try and bring that up with the dad.'

'Clear to winch,' Mozzie confirmed only a minute or two later.

It was Frankie's job to operate the winch and keep Nico safe and she'd never felt the responsibility quite this sharply. Keeping Nico safe meant everything…

When he'd touched down on the roof and unhooked himself from the winch, Frankie's heart stopped for a moment as he slipped and fell on the wet corrugated iron. He slid towards the flat part of the roof over the veranda, where waves of the dirty water were breaking onto the iron. Frankie watched in horror as it seemed as if he was going to slide into that water and potentially get swept away to vanish without a trace and she knew, in that dreadful moment, that her life would never be the same without Nico Romano in it.

Even if it was only as a friend and colleague.

Losing him would be unbearable.

He managed to stop his slide in time for only his boots to hit the water. Frankie and Mozzie hovered and watched as Nico obviously had trouble persuading the mother to be the first person taken to safety. Maybe he told her that it would be far less terrifying for her child to be taken up to the helicopter if they knew that their mum was already there, waiting for them. And maybe he let them know, in no uncertain terms, that there was only a limited amount of daylight left and the wind was rising so the longer they left this rescue, the harder it would become.

Frankie could see the woman was following directions and keeping her arms down as she got near the skid, attached to Nico's harness. He grabbed the handle to steady himself and then got one foot in the helicopter door and one securely on the skid. Frankie could then get the woman safely inside the cabin and it was time to get Nico down again.

He leaned away from the skid to put all his weight into his harness and all his trust in Frankie's skill.

She held his gaze for a heartbeat before beginning to lower him again.

I've got this, she told him silently. *I'll keep you safe.*

And she did. It took another thirty minutes to get a small, terrified boy, his dad and an equally terrified Jack Russell terrier on board and then Mozzie headed towards the nearest evacuation centre, which happened to be a community hall close to Willhua hospital.

By all the rules set in place at the start of this frantic day, they should have gone straight back to base to stand down because they were already well over their allocated active time slot. But Frankie had been listening in mounting concern to an exchange on the radio that involved her friend Jenny. Apparently, when an ambulance was unable to reach a woman trapped by the floods who was in labour, she had kayaked in to the isolated farmhouse. She'd been there for hours and needed medical assistance for what she thought might become an obstetric emergency of an obstructed labour—a far more challenging situation than she and Nico had faced with the baby they'd delivered recently themselves.

Frankie came up with a solution and Mozzie was just as keen to break the rules.

'It won't take long,' he said. 'And it's our Jen we're talking about. We can't leave her in trouble. If that's okay with you, Nico?'

Frankie knew the look that she gave Nico was a very heartfelt plea and she'd never loved him more than when he smiled back at her. A smile that told her he understood exactly how important this was to her. That said he would help her try to reach for the moon, if that was what she wanted to do this much.

A smile that made her think that Nico did really care about her. Love her, even if he didn't realise it?

'Of course it is,' was all he said.

So Frankie left Nico to carry the little boy on one hip and the dog crate in his other hand, leading the parents away from the aircraft towards the waiting volunteers ready to take them into the hall and care for them. She ran into the hospital, relieved to find someone right at the entrance. Had he been watching the helicopter land?

'You're Dr Pierson, right?' Rob Pierson—the man that Jenny was so keen on?

'Right.'

'I'm Frankie. South Sydney Air Rescue. Friend of Jen's.' Frankie was speaking rapidly but there was no time to waste. She filled him in on Jenny's predicament and the fact that they were beyond their time allowance to take on the job themselves but they were prepared to push boundaries enough to get Jenny the extra medical help she needed.

'I'd have to take you down, in a harness attached to mine, but I'll make sure you're safe. Could you come?'

Frankie understood at least a part of why Rob Pierson agreed to take on the mission, despite being warned of the risks involved, because she'd seen his face when she'd told him that Jenny had put herself in danger to help someone else. She'd probably looked like that herself in that horrible moment when she'd faced the thought of losing Nico. Was her imagination running wild, or was this another man who might care enough to be in love, even if he didn't realise it himself yet?

She had to admire the man's courage even more when they arrived at the scene. It was dark now and the only safe place to put Rob down was a small patch of dry land now illuminated by the night sun beneath the helicopter.

'We're ready to move to the door.' Frankie checked the carabiner that attached Rob's harness to her own. 'You want me to go through things one more time?'

'No. I have it.'

'You're sure?'

'I'm sure.'

It took only minutes to take Rob and his gear down, unhook him and take the harness back and then Nico was operating the winch to bring Frankie back on board. She could see him waiting for her, a dark shape in the door of the helicopter as she came up through the blindingly bright light of the night sun, and all Frankie could think about was how this reminded her of the first time he'd winched her. When her arms were full of his now-beloved dog. When he'd promised to keep her safe…

Such a short time ago.

But her life was never going to be the same. And, even if this all ended in tears, she wouldn't have wanted to miss a moment of it.

They were totally exhausted by the time they arrived back on base.

'Go home. Get some sleep,' Colin ordered. 'The forecast's looking better for tomorrow, but even if the rain stops completely and the water starts receding we're going to be in for a majorly increased workload with the massive clean-up and restricted access. Unless it's impossible, I'm going to make sure you both get at least a day off tomorrow.'

'Has Bruce been okay?' Nico rubbed at his eyes, which felt gritty with fatigue.

'Sorry, mate, I haven't heard. I don't think anyone's had the chance to get out there for a while.'

Frankie kept up with his long strides towards the van but Nico could only think about Bruce. How long had he been shut in the van? Had he been without food or water or a toilet break? Did he think he'd been abandoned?

He certainly looked as if he was desperate to get to the grass at the edge of the car park. Nico let him go, knowing his favourite tree that he always used. He leaned inside the van to check that the water dish wasn't dry and that no accidents had occurred from being shut inside for too long.

And then he heard Frankie shouting. She was angry and her words were almost a shriek.

'*Bruce… No…* You stupid, *stupid* dog…'

Nico's blood ran cold. That tone. That abusive language. It wasn't Frankie he was listening to now.

It was a ghost from his past.

Sofia.

He wasn't the one who was about to suffer pain and humiliation, but it was someone he loved very much. Someone who depended on him for protection.

Bruce.

He couldn't let this happen. Nico took off, running towards the grassed area on the edge of the car park. Shouting at Frankie. Swearing at her, even. Telling her to get the hell away from his dog.

Good grief…

Mr Perfect had morphed into someone Frankie couldn't recognise. An angry man who was shouting at her as if she was doing something absolutely unforgivable.

She was not only shocked, Frankie was frightened.

So she defended herself. And shouted back.

'He was about to run onto the road. He could have been

killed. If you'd been looking after your dog I wouldn't have had to go anywhere near him.'

'You could have tried calling him. But you had to shout at him? *Hit* him?'

Frankie's indrawn breath was a gasp. 'I never *hit* him. I grabbed his collar, that's all.'

'I heard him howl.'

'So he got a fright. So did I, Nico.' But Frankie's anger was changing into something deeper. Something chilling. 'You *really* think I'd hit a dog? Any dog, let alone Bruce? Do I look like someone who would hurt anything on purpose?'

Nico was leaning down towards Bruce, who was looking as frightened as the first time Frankie had seen him, huddled on that cliff side near the wreck of that farm truck. 'As if you can tell what someone is capable of from the way they look,' he muttered. He was rubbing his dog's ears. 'It's okay, Bruce,' he said, his tone a world away from the one he'd just been using on Frankie. 'Everything's okay. Let's go home...'

It was a caring tone. Letting the dog know that he was loved. That he was going to be cared for. And Nico was walking away from Frankie without even a backwards glance.

How could she have almost convinced herself that Nico might be in love with her without realising it? He'd just attacked her verbally. Without even giving her a chance to defend herself. And now he was walking away?

It felt like history was repeating itself, with a twist she would never have seen coming. Maybe she was overreacting, but this had happened too many times before and it felt like it was happening again, even if, instead of another woman, Nico was choosing a relationship with a dog as more important than any connection he had with her.

Okay…she'd known it wasn't going to last, but hadn't they agreed that, when it ended, they would remain friends so that they could continue working together? This wasn't how friends treated each other and Frankie's heart was breaking.

She wasn't going to cry, though. Not here. Not in front of Nico.

So she tried to tap back into that anger of being accused of something she would never have done. The hurt that he would even think she was capable of doing.

'Nico?' Frankie knew her tone was an accusation. Had he not even heard her explanation? Was he not going to offer any kind of apology?

'Leave it, Frankie.' Nico still didn't turn around. He raised both his hands in the air in a gesture that could have been surrender. Or a warning not to come any closer? 'I don't want to talk about it.'

He sounded beyond exhausted.

Well, Frankie was exhausted too. And hurt. Something huge had just broken, in an unexpected and spectacular meltdown. and she couldn't make sense of how or why it had happened so suddenly.

Pushing Nico to keep talking now might only make things worse. It could take away any chance of repairing the damage. This was the downside of passion, wasn't it? A fight that was on the opposite side of the coin that had taught her just how amazing sex could be.

They both needed to sleep.

To calm down.

They might laugh about this one day. They might even say that it had been worth it because the make-up sex had been *so* good.

But Frankie couldn't even muster the hint of a smile right now. Or find a scrap of hope in the adage that tomorrow was another day and everything might look very different.

She could, instead, feel the first of what she knew might be many, many tears rolling down the side of her nose as she turned away.

CHAPTER TEN

TRUE TO HIS WORD, the base manager, Colin, stood Red Watch down to have a day's rest. The rain had stopped and there were patches of sunshine breaking through the cloud cover, but the enormous relief felt around the region was tempered by the continuous news coverage of people who were devastated by losing loved ones or who'd had their lives turned upside down, with homes and treasured possessions destroyed and pets missing, feared dead.

Frankie turned the news off. Despite utter exhaustion, she'd barely slept last night and couldn't face any more images of people stunned by the blow life had just dealt them. Her own heart felt as heavy as if she'd lost something tangible as well, but that only made her feel worse because she had no right to feel that way, did she?

In an effort to shake it off, Frankie put on her sports top and shorts and tied up the laces of her well-worn trainers and set off for a run, hoping that a few endorphins might make her feel at least slightly more awake if they weren't up to the task of lifting her mood.

Without thinking, she took her normal route towards and then through the reserve, and maybe she'd been running faster than usual or it was the fatigue was dragging her down and making it much harder than it should have been. Whatever it was, Frankie needed to stop for a second to catch her breath. It wasn't until she was leaning forward, with her hands on her knees, that she realised she'd stopped in the spot where she could see that tiny beach where she'd spotted Bruce sitting, waiting for Nico.

The evening of their first kiss.

The evening where an irresistible attraction had exploded into an encounter so passionate—so *different*—that Frankie's life was never going to be the same.

Just this once...

She'd known, right from that first time, that it was never going to become something significant. What she hadn't known was that falling in love with someone wasn't something that could be controlled. Maybe if you turned your back on it and walked away before anything had started, you might be able to stop yourself falling over that cliff, but that wasn't what Frankie had done, was it?

No…she'd done the exact opposite. She might as well have taken a running jump and hurled herself willingly over that cliff.

Had she, deep down, known that it couldn't be controlled? Had that given her hope that Nico might fall in love with her, even when he'd been perfectly open about never wanting a committed relationship again? Had she believed that she might be 'the one' who could dissolve the barriers he had around his heart?

Finally, Frankie felt like she was dragging enough oxygen into her lungs and she raised her head as she straightened. Her gaze caught the curve of the small beach again, but there was no loyal dog sitting on the sand, waiting. There was, however, a pair of shoes on top of a towel and, when Frankie looked out onto the water, she could see the solitary figure of a man on the paddleboard in the distance, with the silhouette of a large dog, sitting proudly upright on the front of the board.

The board was moving swiftly through calm water. Even from this distance, Frankie could sense the power coming from Nico's muscles. The effort he was putting into his paddling. As if he was trying to get away from something?

It reminded her, with a sharp pang, of the way Nico had put his hands up last night to create a barrier to prevent her trying to get any closer. He hadn't wanted to talk to her then and it was obvious he didn't want to talk to anyone right now either. This was a man seeking solitude.

A lone wolf.

With his dog.

The thought should have been enough to make Frankie smile but, instead, she could feel the sting of tears that she'd thought had run completely dry in the early hours of this morning.

She pushed herself to start running again.

If Nico needed to be alone right now, she could let him have that space.

Because, if you loved someone enough, you could put their needs ahead of your own?

Nico could feel the burn.

The muscles in his shoulders were about to go on strike unless he slowed down and his legs ached from keeping his balance, but he didn't want to stop. The pain was welcome, in fact, because it was providing a very effective distraction. If the pain wasn't there, he'd have to start thinking about something else.

About the way he'd overreacted last night, perhaps. Or the fact that he needed to apologise to Frankie.

And if he did that he'd have to explain why it had happened. He'd end up telling her the whole story, and he didn't want to do that. He never wanted to do that. Because she'd think less of him, and the shame of that would be unbearable. He'd managed to avoid it for so long now, it felt like he'd left it completely behind. That he'd never have to face even a look from someone that would have said what he'd known they would all think.

You just stood there and let it happen to you? What kind of man are you…?

A man with no self-respect, that's who. No kind of man at all… You're pathetic… That's why it happened in the first place…

She was right, your wife…it was your fault she was so unhappy. So angry…

No wonder you didn't want anyone to know…

No wonder you ran away…

You'll be running away for the rest of your life. Because that's how pathetic you are…

Nico paddled harder but he'd turned back to shore now because, if he'd kept going the way he was, he would have ended up right out to sea and that would have been dangerous—for Bruce even more than for himself—and the need to protect this beloved companion of his was strong enough to override anything else right now.

It was also a reminder that he needed to do more than apologise to Frankie. That his dog was sitting here on his board right now was quite probably due to the fact that she'd saved his life last night by stopping him getting anywhere near the traffic. Poor Bruce had been so excited to be released from the confinement of the van that he probably hadn't even noticed the direction he was running in.

How devastating would it have been to lose this companion that had become such an important part of his life? It had been thanks to Frankie that he had come home with Nico in the first place. She was the one who'd risked her own safety to get a large dog into a harness on the side of a cliff and get him up to the helicopter. The first day they'd ever worked together.

Bruce was a part of *their* story as much as he was now a part of Nico's life that he couldn't imagine being without. Okay, it was clearly past time for him to step back from being Frankie's lover, but hadn't they agreed that when that happened they'd stay friends and be able to work together? He was the one who was putting that at risk.

So he was the one who needed to do something about it.

'How 'bout we go for a walk later, Bruce?' he suggested aloud. 'We could walk around to Frankie's house. Just to say hello.'

And thank you.

And, somehow, to say sorry. Even if it meant telling her something that could change the way she felt about him for ever.

'Sorry, mate…she's not here. She took off for a bike ride.'

'Do you know when she might be back?'

Derek shook his head. 'No idea. Could be a while. I think she likes to blow the cobwebs away by stretching out on the open road sometimes. Sounds like you guys had a pretty rough day yesterday?'

Nico nodded. It *had* been a rough day. Not only because of the dangerous conditions and relentless workload but because it had ended on such a bad personal note. Finding Frankie wasn't at home and her housemates didn't have any idea when she might return felt like any window of opportunity for repairing the damage that had been done to their friendship was rapidly closing.

Frankie had every right to be angry with him.

And Nico had learned a very long time ago that it was a mistake to push an angry person into a conversation they were not ready to have. If she needed the time to go and ride that powerful motorbike as fast as possible in order to clear her head, there was nothing he could do about that.

Except hope like hell that she kept herself safe…

And that they could find a quiet moment at work tomorrow to put things right. Or to at least get a signal that they *could* be put right. Even a split second of connection would be enough. Like the way they could decide who took the lead in an assessment with an almost invisible game of rock, paper, scissors?

They had to run to get straight on board the helicopter within minutes of arriving for the shift the next day to respond to a Priority One call-out.

Frankie didn't even look to see if Nico wanted to play the deciding game. She had carefully avoided making eye contact as well. Because she couldn't afford to make this any harder than it already was. Derek had told her that Nico and Bruce had come to the house yesterday and she had guessed that he wanted to apologise. He'd probably wanted to confirm that their fling was over but suggest that they could still be friends and work well together.

She wasn't ready to talk about that.

It wasn't as if they had any choice about whether or not they kept working together right now. Maybe it was just as well that they were likely to get hammered with call-outs today. Along with the urgent missions to trauma or medical cases like this first job, there was still a waiting list of people needing evacuation from inaccessible areas and much-needed supplies that were being delivered to rural emergency services and more remote medical centres and hospitals.

It wasn't raining again yet but there was a heavy cloud cover which made everything grey and gloomy and there was still an ocean of dirty water beneath them and rivers that were angry torrents. The rising wind and the unexpected gusts that were jolting the aircraft meant that Mozzie was concentrating on his flying to the extent he probably didn't notice the lack of any conversation that wasn't strictly professional in the cabin of his helicopter.

Frankie could see where water levels had fallen in the small town they were flying over. Now there were piles of debris growing on mud-covered streets. Carpets were being pulled up and ruined furniture and fabrics moved to where they would be collected and disposed of. That was what the patient they were being called to see had been doing. He'd been dragging a mattress from a bed upstairs in his house and had fallen through sodden floorboards, hitting his head on an exposed brick chimney on the way.

It was a relief to know that Nico was as focused as she was on what lay ahead.

'He was knocked out but has now regained consciousness.' Nico was reading an update on his tablet. 'He's communicating but confused and has a laceration on his head that a local first responder's keeping pressure on.'

'The nearest hospital with neurosurgical and neuro intensive care facilities is going to be St Mary's. That's more than a ten-minute transport time.'

Which meant that intubating this patient would be a priority if his oxygen levels were too low or his level of consciousness was dropping. There were special considerations with a severe traumatic brain injury for maintaining a higher blood pressure and which drugs to use. Frankie spent a few seconds reminding herself of how to calculate a mean arterial pressure by adding the systolic pressure to twice the diastolic pressure and then dividing the sum by three. Nico looked as if he was doing something similar.

Yeah…it was a good thing that they had no choice about whether or not they worked together for now. This shared passion for their work and that ability they'd had right from the start to put anything personal aside might be exactly what was going to help Frankie deal with what felt like a bit of a disaster in her personal life. It might make her a better person, even. And being able to continue working with Nico would certainly make her a better paramedic.

Gerald, their sixty-eight-year-old patient, was lying amidst the carnage in his home that advertised a life in ruins, with sodden photograph albums and broken family treasures amongst the mud, and things had just got a whole lot worse for both Gerald and his family. His level of consciousness had dropped by the time the air rescue team arrived. He could open his eyes when asked to but he was only groaning rather than talking and wasn't following commands but only pulling away from something painful.

'GCS of eight,' Frankie estimated. It was a significant drop from the score of thirteen the local paramedic had given on arrival.

'And he's hypoxic.' Nico had clipped the saturation monitor to Gerald's finger. 'His oxygen level is below ninety percent. Let's get a non-rebreather mask on and, if that's not enough to get it up to at least ninety-five percent, he'll need some help with a bag valve mask before we secure his airway. Are you okay to cover that while I get an IV line in?'

Frankie was already attaching a mask to an oxygen cylinder. Getting Gerald's oxygen saturation up to more normal levels was the most important thing they could do to try and prevent the catastrophic brain damage that could result from an inadequate oxygen supply. They also had to try and get his blood pressure high enough to keep that oxygen circulating.

They hadn't needed to decide who was taking the lead in this case because their ability to work together seamlessly was still there. The minutes flew past as they worked to stabilise Gerald and try to minimise the effect that this serious injury was going to have on his future.

'I'm not happy with that level of oxygenation yet. The fluids are improving blood pressure but his saturation's still too low.'

'I agree.'

'The longer we put off intubation, the more hypoxic he's going to get.'

'Gerald?' Frankie leaned down so that her mouth was close to his ear. 'Can you open your eyes for me?'

There was no response.

'GSC is dropping.' Nico nodded. 'Let's get on with this.' He turned to the local paramedic. 'We need to clear any unnecessary gear to give us some space. Bring that suction unit closer and check that it's working.' He opened his drug kit and reached for syringes and ampoules of the medications needed to sedate and paralyse their patient.

Frankie hooked some nasal prongs around Gerald's ears but kept using the mask to pre-oxygenate him, trying to get his levels up enough to get him through the inevitable period when it would not be possible to supplement his oxygen while the tube was being placed in his trachea. She used rolled-up towels and a damp but serviceable pillow to put his head into the best position, with his ear in line with his sternal notch.

It was Nico who administered the drugs and then moved swiftly to insert the laryngoscope and the tube that would keep the airway safe for transport. Frankie was ready with the device to secure the tube in place, the ventilation bag with a PEEP valve attached and a stethoscope to hand to Nico so that he could check that the tube was in the right place.

It was. They both watched the lungs rise evenly when Frankie squeezed the bag and they both looked up to catch each other's gaze, their heads close together because they were both so intent on what they were doing.

And maybe the way Frankie found herself pulling in a deep breath was not just because they were over the first hurdle in getting this patient safely to the care he needed at St Mary's but because it felt just as natural as it always did when they were working together.

Nothing had changed. Professionally, anyway, and that had to be a good thing.

There were plenty of willing volunteers to help carry the stretcher to where Mozzie was waiting with the helicopter on the only recognisable patch of the town's rugby field.

There were more than just emergency department personnel waiting for them on the roof of St Mary's. Frankie's eyebrows rose as she saw a second stretcher being wheeled in their direction. She looked around but couldn't see another rescue helicopter waiting its turn to land.

'Didn't want to disturb you guys when you were so busy in the back,' Mozzie told her. 'We've been asked to take some gear to a rural hospital down south. They're low on dressings, splints and drugs. They've asked for backup defibrillator batteries and a charger as well. The local volunteer ambulance crew has borrowed the only ones they have. Shouldn't take too long. The main street's cleared for landing for us and someone will be waiting.'

'No worries.'

Both Nico and Frankie helped to load and secure the supplies in the back of the helicopter. There were enough of them to create a kind of wall between them and that felt like another small respite from an inevitable moment with Nico, when they couldn't shelter behind their professional relationship and had to face how much everything had changed between them on a personal basis. It was also kind of helpful that a rain squall was giving them a bit of turbulence. Frankie stared out of the window on her side, watching the ground beneath them get blurred by the sudden rain and not breaking the silence.

Until she saw something.

'Did you see that? In the river?'

'See what?'

'I thought I saw something white.' Oh, help…was Nico thinking the same thing that had just flashed through the back of her mind? That she'd said something very similar when she'd spotted where Bruce had been hidden on that cliff. Was she going to be ambushed by memories of their brief time together for the rest of her life?

'Something big,' she added hurriedly. 'It could have been the roof of a car…'

Mozzie was turning and the helicopter rocked with the gust of wind from the change of direction in the squally weather. 'Let's go back and take a quick look,' he said calmly.

This river was wide—a huge ribbon of brown water moving swiftly enough to create foaming waves around the edges of any debris caught in its path, like the huge island of tree trunks and branches that had accumulated around the remains of a washed-out bridge. Mozzie started there and flew upriver towards where they'd been a minute ago, but low enough now to be able to see just how fast this water was moving.

'Can't see anything,' Frankie said. 'Sorry…'

'It could well have been washed away by now. Or be underwater.'

'We'll go downriver—just for a kilometre or two. It might be caught on that wrecked bridge.'

Mozzie turned the helicopter again but, as he did so,

Frankie could feel the tail of the helicopter swing unexpectedly. She could actually feel the wind shear that was not only moving them horizontally but vertically. She knew they were probably too close to ground level for Mozzie to be able to correct for the sudden change in wind direction and velocity and she knew they were in trouble, but it all happened too fast for Mozzie to give them any warning. Too fast for Frankie to be terrified, even.

One instant they were flying above the river.

And the next they nosedived into the water at a speed that sent them below the surface to tip and roll as they were swept along in the current. Anything that hadn't been firmly secured in the cabin was now a danger and Frankie put her arms up over her face to protect herself from the boxes and plastic containers that were jolted free of the wall that had been between herself and Nico. She closed her eyes and waited then, because what was running through her mind with astonishing speed in those moments were the crash survival rules that had been drummed into all the participants during the classroom sessions of survival training.

Do not attempt to leave the aircraft until all movement has ceased.

Maintain orientation. Where is the door?

If in water, wait until all bubbles have cleared.

Let the aircraft fill with water. The door cannot be opened when it's under water pressure from the outside.

Release your harness. Open the door. Escape...

Frankie's thoughts were abruptly interrupted because they hit something.

Something solid enough to have stopped any movement

of the fuselage. Was it one of the bridge supports amongst that island of debris?

It was quite likely to have been a big tree branch that had smashed the bubble windscreen of the helicopter and, as the cabin began to rapidly fill with water, Frankie could see Mozzie struggling to release his harness. She saw him try to get a hand grip to turn and look back, but he was already being pulled through the shattered windscreen and into the current of the river and he disappeared almost instantly.

With that wall of supplies they'd been due to deliver now scattered and being dragged towards the front of the helicopter, Frankie could see, despite rapidly deteriorating visibility with water splashing on her visor and the darkness of whatever was surrounding them in the water, that Nico was trying to do what she was doing and release the clips on his harness.

They'd both done a HUET course—Helicopter Underwater Escape Training—where a specially designed deep swimming pool had a crane beside it that could raise and lower a metal cage that simulated the structure of a helicopter and its seating and door positions. Frankie had done a refresher course not long ago and it had been more advanced than the initial introduction, where she'd only been taught to escape a helicopter after it had been partially submerged and still vertical in the water and then again with the position changed to mimic an aircraft tipped onto its side. On this new course, she'd had the rather terrifying experience of being flipped upside down and then submerged, with a follow-up of doing it again wearing blackout goggles.

At least this hadn't happened at night or out at sea. And, even though they had been tipped and rolled, they had ended up not being fully upside down. But this was fast moving, dirty water around them and, although it felt like they were securely wedged and not about to start moving again any time soon, this was an alarmingly dangerous situation and…

And Nico was trying to get himself free with only one arm.

His other arm looked as if it was twisted and trapped between bent or broken parts of both the fuselage and the back of his seat.

Frankie was free now. She knew she had to make sure she maintained her orientation so that she knew exactly where the door was. She took a deep breath in the diminishing space that had any air available, but she was holding on tight to the handles and other solid structures. They were more protected from the current of the river in the cabin than Mozzie had been when the windscreen shattered but she wasn't going to risk being sucked in a direction she didn't want to go yet.

She wanted to go towards Nico.

Because it hadn't even occurred to Frankie to leave him behind in order to save herself.

CHAPTER ELEVEN

FEAR WAS BEING kept at bay by a level of determination to survive that was so powerful it made Frankie feel like she was capable of anything.

Even getting the door open, which took a great deal of physical strength.

Something else from that survival course was surfacing in her brain as she slid the door sideways. She'd been told that a big part of survival was a matter of this kind of determination. People could—and did—survive in the face of seemingly impossible challenges and her instructor had suggested that the real killers could be fear, a lack of confidence and an inability to problem solve.

Frankie wasn't lacking any of those factors. She'd decided to open the side door because that would give them an easier, faster exit than getting to the front of the helicopter to go out of the broken windscreen. She had already used the shears attached to her tool belt to hack through the safety harness where it was caught up in the gap where Nico's arm was trapped almost to his elbow and she thought he'd be able to pull himself free while she wrestled the door open.

The last space in the cabin was filling with water so time was running out. How long could she hold her breath? More or less than a minute?

How much was physical effort going to reduce that time limit by?

Nico was still trapped but his position was awkward enough to affect how hard he could pull. Frankie took hold of his arm with both hands to increase the force of the pressure but his arm didn't budge. And she could hear his cry of pain even underwater. He cut it short but even that must have stolen too much of the precious oxygen he was holding in his lungs.

Claws of fear were hooking themselves into Frankie.

For a tiny flicker of time that would haunt her for ever, she was convinced they were both going to die. Amazingly, even in the face of that fear there was something like...what was it...gratitude that she was with Nico? That her last moment of consciousness could be the awareness that she was with the man she loved *this* much?

And was it simply that Nico's eyes were a mirror for what had to be showing in her own?

No. Frankie might have been convinced that they were both about to die, but she was even more convinced that what she could see in Nico's eyes was a love for her that was just as powerful as the way she felt about him.

And that suddenly changed everything.

Frankie was not going to give up. She was going to fight to the end with everything she had. The fresh burst of adrenaline, or determination or whatever it was, gave her a strength she had no idea she possessed. She braced herself as she gripped Nico's arm again and when she pulled this time it was hard enough for her to feel a bone snapping beneath her hands, but even that sickening sensation only made her more determined.

Stronger.

And she could feel the movement. Breaking that bone had made it possible to change the angle of Nico's hand and wrist within whatever obstacle had trapped him, but she could feel him slumping as she pulled him clear. Frankie had to find even more strength to drag him towards the open door and then she had to try and use the last seconds of her own consciousness to remember which way she had to take them both to get to the surface of this water.

Which way was up?

Thank goodness she'd paid so much attention to that course because the final flashback might be the one that could save them both.

Blow out a breath. Bubbles always rise. Follow the bubbles...

So Frankie blew out the air she'd been holding in her lungs so long they felt ready to explode. And then, holding onto Nico as tightly as she could, she braced her feet against the fuselage of the helicopter and pushed hard enough to send them both into, but also up, through the swirling current of the deadly river.

She felt her head breaking the surface and tried to pull Nico's face clear of the water at the same time she was dragging in her first, painful gasp of air. She could feel her strength fading, however. There was no way she could keep them both above water if they got swept downriver. But staying where they were still meant they were in extreme danger. They could be hit at any second by another huge lump of debris.

But it felt as if natural forces were on their side now. The turbulent swirls and waves of the river surface were turning them, pushing them past the bent tip of a rotor blade showing above the surface and towards the island of tangled branches and tree trunks caught on the remains of the bridge structure. Some of the boxes and containers from the helicopter had added themselves to the mix and, although the small items were moving and some were getting sucked free, the rest of this artificial island felt more than solid enough to climb onto.

Best of all, Nico was conscious enough to help drag himself onto the pile. Pretty much inside it, in fact, because there was a kind of cave where huge pieces of this debris had crossed and caught and then other pieces had woven themselves around and over them. It was dense enough to cut a surprising amount of the noise from the rushing water outside and high enough to be out of range of the foaming waves of the rapids. Frankie had no idea how stable it might actually be but, for now, it felt safe. Solid. She was alive.

So was Nico...

He was sitting beside her, still dragging air into his lungs, and Frankie still hadn't let go of the tight hold she had on him.

She couldn't.

All Frankie could do was burst into tears.

'I broke your arm,' she sobbed. 'I'm *so* sorry, Nico.'

'It doesn't matter.' Nico's voice sounded raw. 'You saved my life, Frankie...'

He was holding her now, as tightly as Frankie was holding him. She might have got Nico out of the helicopter but they weren't out of the woods yet. What if this pile of debris broke apart and they were dragged back into the current and washed away? Like Mozzie had been?

Oh…there was an unbearable grief laced into that thought that Frankie couldn't afford to acknowledge yet. There was too much to try and deal with already. Too much to be frightened by. What if no one found them and they died of hypothermia? They were already wet and cold. The shelter of this odd cave might not be enough to save them, even if they were holding each other like this. Which had to be hurting Nico's arm.

But it *did* matter that she'd broken Nico's arm.

Frankie lifted her head so that she could look directly at Nico. She still had tears streaming down her face. 'I would never want to hurt you, Nico. How could I? I *love* you… I love you *so* much…'

Oh, God… Was that just river water trickling from inside his helmet or had she made Nico cry now? Because it was the last thing he wanted to hear her say?

'You didn't hurt me because you wanted to,' he said. 'You did it because you wanted to save me.'

Frankie nodded. 'Because I love you…' She pulled herself away from Nico, rubbing at her eyes to clear her blurred vision. 'And now I need to look after you. Let me see your arm.'

She must have dropped her shears when she'd hacked through that harness but the sleeve of Nico's flight suit was shredded anyway so she didn't need to cut his clothing clear to examine his arm. The skin around his forearm was grazed and, no doubt, badly bruised but it was the deformity in the bones of his wrist that was obviously the most serious injury. It was a classic fracture of the distal radius close to the wrist, with a dorsal angulation. A Colles fracture, often called a 'dinner fork' fracture because of the shape it made.

'Can you move your fingers? Can you feel me touching them?'

'I think so…yes…a little.' The grimace Nico made advertised how painful it was.

'It's impossible to assess your skin colour or capillary refill when you're this cold. I can hardly feel your radial pulse…'

'I'm alive. It's all good.' Nico was actually smiling at her and Frankie had to catch her breath and try to focus on what she was doing.

'Can you move your elbow?'

'Yes.'

'Does it hurt?'

'No.'

'I need to splint this arm.' Frankie looked around her. 'I wonder if there's anything useful in those boxes.' She had something positive to focus on now, and her mind was starting to feel like it was functioning properly again. 'I'm going to have a look. Don't move, Nico. And hold onto your arm.' She gently bent the broken limb so that it was across his chest and put his other hand close to the elbow to keep it still.

She found bandages and dressings in the first box she reached. They were completely sodden but they would still be useful. The cardboard, which could have made a great splint if it had been dry, was totally useless. But there were any number of branches around her and it wasn't hard to find some that were small enough to snap. The sound and feel of breaking them was a nasty reminder of how it had felt to break Nico's arm but she knew he was right. He wouldn't be alive now if she hadn't done something that dramatic. Neither of them would be, because she wouldn't have left him to die alone.

She made a ball out of wet gauze and put it in the palm of Nico's hand so that his fingers had support and wouldn't move and cause more pain and potentially more damage to any nerves or blood vessels affected by the fracture. She put sticks on either side of his arm from his elbow to beyond his fingers, holding them in place with one hand while she used her teeth to rip open the plastic covering of a crepe bandage so that she could bind the sticks together. She opened another bandage to secure Nico's arm across his body for even more support.

'Is that okay?'

'It's great. *Ben fatto, cara.*'

The praise for a job well done was heartbreaking, given that she had caused the injury herself, but Nico was smiling at her and Frankie could feel her face crumpling into lines that felt like...

Pure love, that was what it felt like.

And gratitude, that she'd allowed herself to break those stupid rules about both Italian men and the people she worked with. If she hadn't, she might never have discovered that a love like this actually existed. Something so huge, so astonishingly wonderful, that anything else in life was in the shadow of how brightly it shone.

It didn't feel like simply a reflection of what she was feeling that she could see in Nico's eyes this time. It felt like she was seeing a part of Nico she'd never been allowed to see before. Frankie knew, deep down, even if he never said anything, that Nico loved her and, weirdly, in the most dangerous situation she'd ever been in, Frankie had the sensation of feeling *safer* than she ever had before.

'*Dai, andiamo...*'

Let's go? Frankie's smile wobbled. They couldn't go anywhere, could they? Their only chance of survival was to stay on this temporary refuge of the debris island and hope like hell that they would get rescued.

'Are you sure your arm's feeling okay? That bandage isn't too tight, is it?'

'It's fine, *cara*.'

'I should have asked already, but have you ever fractured this arm before?'

Nico nodded. Frankie touched the top of his arm where it was exposed by the shredded sleeve of the flight suit and touched her fingers to the patch of rippled, damaged skin. A touch that sparked a kaleidoscope of memories and sensations and emotions that had been there every time they'd made love.

Because that was what it had been, right from the start, even though Frankie would have denied that as fiercely as Nico would have. It had never been simply about the sex, had it?

Nico's scars were like a physical form of the barrier that had been erected to hide what was really going on. The stories about how he'd got the scars were there as reinforcements. Frankie had respected those barriers, but what was the point of them now? What if this was the last time they would ever be together?

'Was it when you did this?' She tried to find her smile

again. 'The mountain biking accident? Or when the shark bit you?'

Nico shook his head again. Slowly. 'There was never a shark,' he admitted.

'I knew that.' Frankie was still doing her best to smile but Nico was holding her gaze and she felt a sudden chill run down her spine. 'You got burnt, didn't you? And it wasn't an exploding skyrocket.'

'No. I got too close to an iron.'

'And what was it that broke your arm the first time?'

'It got slammed in a door,' Nico said.

Nico had closed his eyes. Frankie could see the deep breath he dragged in. 'It's not the *what* that's the important thing,' he said. 'It's the *who*.' He opened his eyes to catch Frankie's gaze directly. 'It was Sofia who broke my arm. Who used the iron to burn me. Who did so many things to hurt me.'

There was nothing left of Frankie's smile. It felt like the blood was draining from her face. Making it freeze so that it was hard to move her lips. 'Who's Sofia?'

'She was my wife.'

There…

He'd said it.

In the craziest of situations, when it was still possible they weren't going to survive this and he could have taken his shameful secret to his grave, but the words had come out. He'd almost had to shout them, over the roar of the river around them and the crash of new debris that shook the small hole they'd found to hide in and…and it had almost felt like a cry of victory.

Of freedom.

He had to do it.

Because Frankie loved him.

Because she had risked her own life to save his.

But, most of all, because *he* loved *her*. Because he knew he could not only trust her with his life, he could trust her with his heart and soul. He could trust her not to ever want to hurt him. The complete opposite, in fact. He would never feel this safe with anybody else. Ever.

He'd known it all along. He just hadn't been brave enough to peel off that protective layer he'd encased himself in, so many years ago. Just in case that, if Frankie saw the truth, she wouldn't feel the same way about him.

Frankie was looking beyond shocked but, in a way, this was a good thing. She wasn't thinking about the danger they were still in. Or feeling scared that any rescue attempt might come too late. What Nico didn't want, however, was the mortification he could see filling her eyes. She had just broken his arm and she'd chosen to do it and, sure…it could have taken him back to that dark place of being in such an abusive relationship.

But it hadn't.

It had set him free.

'Don't,' he commanded. 'Don't ever think like that. I know you would never want to hurt anybody. Your whole life is about trying to stop people hurting. I knew you would never have hurt Bruce. I know you would never hurt me.' He touched Frankie's face with his fingers. 'I know you love me.'

Frankie's eyes were huge. So filled with emotion they looked black. 'How?' she asked. 'How do you know that?'

Nico touched his chest, just above where his splinted arm was secured across his body. Right over his heart.

'Because I can feel it,' he said. 'Here. And I know it's real because it feels the same as what's in here already. Because I love *you*, Frankie...'

Tears were spilling from those huge, dark eyes. 'I thought you might, but you never said anything so I couldn't tell you how *I* felt.'

'I couldn't say anything because I couldn't tell you the truth. I didn't want you to think it might have been because of how bad a husband I was.'

'Oh, my God... I know that's not true.' A poignant smile was breaking through those tears. 'I knew instantly how gentle and caring you are. I knew that from the moment I saw you holding Bruce in your arms for that ride back to base. I think that was the moment I started falling in love with you...'

Even with Frankie's great job of makeshift splinting, it hurt to use his good arm to pull her close but he couldn't have cared less. Nico had to kiss her. Because he'd seen the look in her eyes—that sheer amazement, followed by a kind of happiness that shouldn't have been possible given the danger they were in.

He'd also seen that the love was still there, even when he'd told her the worst about himself, and Nico could feel himself catching some of that joy, even though he was very aware of what was still threatening them. So aware that that kiss was fierce but only brief. He was monitoring the slightest movement in the pile of debris beneath them and the need to protect Frankie if it started breaking apart was paramount. If it was solid enough to support them until rescue came, it was the danger of hypothermia he needed to try and protect her from. All he could do was hold her as close as he could to his own body.

To wrap his arms—and his love—around her.

Frankie was still distracted from the danger. She almost sounded angry as she looked up at him again. Thanks to how dense this shelter they'd been lucky enough to find, he could hear her clearly when he bent his head.

'How long were you married for, Nico?'

'Too long,' he admitted. 'Five years. We were both too young but we were in love.'

Frankie shook her head. 'Nobody wants to hurt a person they love.'

'It wasn't like that at the beginning. I knew she had a bad temper. That she would shout and throw things and break them when she was angry. I thought the first time she hurt me had been an accident. I'd just got in the way of the broken bottle she threw. I wear my hair long to cover that scar.'

'Oh... *Nico*...' The pain in Frankie's voice made it crack. 'I don't understand how she could do that. How *anyone* could do that.'

'It didn't happen again for a long time, but then it did. And the more often it happened, the worse it got.'

'Didn't anybody else know?'

'I couldn't tell anyone.' Nico shook his head. 'You know how it is in Italy. The men are in control. If any hitting is done, it's done by the men. The *real* men.'

'No...' Frankie looked as fierce as she sounded. 'The *real* men are the ones who never do it in the first place. The ones who are strong enough to not hit back.' She was biting her bottom lip. 'How did you get away from her?'

'She said I couldn't leave. That she would tell everyone that I hurt *her* and she was only protecting herself. That I was stupid. The worst husband anyone could ever have… And then she would say how sorry she was. That she loved me. That she'd never do it again…'

'You were trapped…' The darkness in Frankie's eyes looked like anger.

'It was my sister Rosa who found out what was happening. I made her swear that she would keep it a secret and not go to the police, or even tell the rest of the family, but she would only do that if Sofia agreed to divorce me and disappear from my life. Sofia had no choice. My sister can be scary when she's protecting the people she loves.' He smiled at Frankie. 'Like you…' His heart felt like it was filling up to breaking point—in a good way.

'I'm scary?'

'I will never forget the expression on your face when you were fighting to get me free. You weren't going to give up, were you?'

Frankie's eyes were full of tears. 'Of course not. I felt like I was fighting for my own life as much as yours. I was so afraid I was going to lose you.'

'You'll never lose me,' Nico vowed. 'Because I give you my heart and you will have that for as long as you live, even if I'm not there to hold you… Like this…' He tightened his hold on Frankie, ignoring any pain in his arm.

'And mine is yours,' Frankie said. 'I didn't mean to give it to you because I knew you didn't want it, but…it happened anyway. I think it was always going to happen…'

'I want it,' Nico said. 'I've never wanted anything

as much as I want to be loved by you. And to love you back. Except…'

Frankie's eyes widened. 'Except what?'

'I really, really want to get out of here.'

And in that moment, as if the universe had been eavesdropping on this extraordinary conversation, there was a steady thump, thump, thump of sound above the noise of the rushing water outside this woven cave. A sound that got quickly louder until it was right above Nico and Frankie.

Hovering…

He pulled himself away from Frankie. Maybe the locator beacon that would have gone off automatically when they'd crashed had brought rescuers to this exact point or perhaps the bright red of their flight suits could be seen through gaps in the tangle of debris but he wasn't about to take any chances.

'Stay there,' he commanded.

He scrambled out of their shelter and pulled himself upright to wave with his uninjured arm. He could see the side door of the helicopter was open and someone was in his favourite position, clipped to an overhead anchor but leaning out, with one foot on the skid to balance themselves as they searched for their target.

He got a 'thumbs-up' signal in return and another head appeared in the doorway. It was impossible to be sure, but he thought it might be Ricky. Whoever it was, the wide grin on his face made their delight in finding survivors very obvious. Both faces disappeared back into the cabin at that point, but Nico knew that they were getting ready to send someone down on the winch line with an extra harness to take them up. One at a time.

He crouched to crawl back into the cave.

'*Dai, andiamo,*' he shouted over the noise of the river and the helicopter. 'Let's go… Put your helmet on properly again. You're going up first.'

But Frankie didn't move. She raised her eyebrows and held her hand up in a fist and Nico couldn't decide whether he needed to laugh or cry. She wanted to play rock, paper, scissors?

Maybe he needed to do both. But not yet. Not until he had the woman he loved so much in the safest place he could find.

'Not this time, *amore mio*,' he said. He held out his hand. 'This time it's my turn to look after you.'

CHAPTER TWELVE

'FRANKIE...OH, MY GOD... Colin didn't know where you'd been taken. I've rung every hospital in Sydney... How badly hurt are you? Can you talk? Why aren't you saying anything?'

'Because I can't get a word in?' Frankie gave a huff of laughter which hurt her ribs. She had bumps and bruises she hadn't even been aware of until she'd been brought into this emergency department to be thoroughly checked. 'I'm okay, Jen. So's Nico, thank goodness. Apart from a broken wrist which is being set for him right now in the fracture clinic.'

Jenny was crying now. 'And Ricky? What about Mozzie? I couldn't get through to anyone at the SSAR. Colin's message got relayed to me via Comms and they're overwhelmed by work. I couldn't keep pestering them.'

'Ricky wasn't with us. He was working with another crew who turned out to be the ones that came to rescue us.'

'And Mozzie?'

Frankie was also crying. 'We were so sure he hadn't made it. I'd actually seen him get sucked out of the chopper as soon as he got his harness off. We weren't completely underwater then and the current was wild.' She took in a breath to stop her voice wobbling. 'But he got swept down rapids and around a bend and got spotted by an SES crew

in an inflatable rescue boat. He's okay. He's up in the fracture clinic with Nico because he hurt his ankle but he got
wheeled in to see us when we arrived. It was Mozzie who
raised the alarm about the crash.'

'And you're sure you're okay?'

'I'm fine. Feeling exhausted but incredibly lucky to be
alive.' Incredibly lucky in more ways than simply having
survived, but there was all the time in the world to tell her
best friend about what had happened between herself and
Nico. For now, it was too amazing and new and life-chang-
ing to share. It was something precious and, huddled together in that short trip from the river to the closest hospital,
it had seemed like they'd made a tacit agreement that they
would keep it private as long as they could.

Because this was just between them.

Like the secret that Nico had shared with her because he
knew he could trust her. Completely.

For ever.

'What about you, Jen? I haven't had the chance to talk
to you since we dropped Rob in to help you when you were
trapped with that woman in labour. Did things work out
okay?'

'Couldn't have worked out better—and not just for the
mum and her gorgeous baby, who are both safe and well.'

'What… You mean…?' Frankie could feel the corners
of her mouth curling up.

'You were right. He is my Doc Pierson. My Rob…' The
tone of Jenny's voice made it obvious that she was smiling
too. 'I've found the person I want to be with for the rest of
my life. You're not going to tell me it's too soon to know,
are you?'

'No…' Through the gap in the curtain drawn around her bed, Frankie could see someone walking into the observation ward where she'd been left to rest, having been cleared of any major injury. Someone who had a cast on his arm and a way more professional-looking sling than a few loops of crepe bandage. 'I'm only going to tell you how very happy I am for you. But I need to go, Jen. Love you. Talk soon, yeah?'

'Oh, sorry…are you with someone?

But Frankie was already ending the call. She had put the cordless ward phone down on the locker beside her bed by the time Nico had come through the curtain and pulled it properly closed behind him.

Yes…

She was with someone.

She was going to be with him for the rest of her life.

She couldn't find any words to describe how happy she was feeling in this moment. All Frankie could do was to hold out her arms and invite Nico close enough to feel her heart beating. Close enough to give him the kind of kiss that might be able to let him know what she would say if she could find the right words.

'I need to go.' Reluctantly, Nico stood up after giving Frankie one last kiss. 'I got hold of Colin and he said Bruce is getting anxious. He's bringing some dry clothes from my locker and he's going to drive my van here to pick me up and then take us both home.'

'Both of us?' Frankie nodded. 'Is he bringing me some clothes too?'

'I think he meant me and Bruce.' But Nico was smiling.

'I could share my clothes with you, but there's only two seats in the front of the van.'

'So Colin can take a taxi back. I'll drive you. You need someone to keep an eye on you.' She was waving a hand in the air to emphasise her words. 'What if you've had a head injury they've missed? Bruce isn't going to be much help when you're lying on the floor unconscious, is he?'

Bossy Frankie was back. Talkative, loud and hand-waving Frankie was back. Normal life was resuming and Nico couldn't be happier about that.

It was never going to be the same life, of course. Too much had changed in the last few hours and Nico couldn't be happier about that either.

'I haven't got a head injury.' Nico leaned down to kiss Frankie again. 'And you need to rest. They want you to stay here overnight.'

'They want you to stay as well.'

'I can't. I have a fur child who needs me.'

Frankie couldn't argue with that but she was scowling.

'I'll come and get you in the morning,' Nico promised.

'With one arm? How?' Frankie was pushing back the blanket covering her and wriggling to get her legs over the side of the bed. 'Have you taught Bruce to drive?'

'No. But he's getting good at paddleboarding. Not that we'll be doing any of that for a while.' Nico was grinning now. He had a feeling he was losing this battle and he didn't actually mind at all. 'I think there's only one way to settle this argument, isn't there?'

Frankie's eyes lit up. 'You're on.' She stood up and held out a fist. 'One, two…three…'

They both kept a fist. The rock couldn't defeat another rock.

'Again,' Frankie ordered. 'One, two…three…'

They both had their middle and index fingers in a V shape. Scissors couldn't win over scissors.

They were holding each other's gaze as they tried for a third time. They both kept their hands flat. Paper was equal to paper.

They both laughed.

Frankie shook her head. 'Neither of us is going to win.'

But Nico smiled. 'I think it's because we've both already won, *amore mio*. We have each other.'

Frankie's smile was misty. 'I think you're right.'

She was leaning closer. Close enough for Nico to kiss her again and he was about to, when he saw the mischievous gleam in her eyes.

'So that means I can come home with you?'

'*Sì…*' Nico's lips were almost touching hers now. 'I don't want you to be anywhere else. Ever.'

'Good…' Frankie lips were brushing his so he could both hear and feel her murmured words. 'Neither do I.'

EPILOGUE

Three years later...

'BUDGE UP.'

'Budge up?' Rosa was laughing as she echoed Nico's command. *'Non capisco.'*

'I thought you wanted to speak English on your holiday. It means *spostati*. You need to move closer so I can get a photo of everybody to send home to the rest of the family.'

Rosa moved along the wooden bench on one side of the big table beneath the pergola that had a young grapevine doing its best to create some leafy shade in the Australian summer. She was close enough to put her arm around Frankie's shoulders and the sisters-in-law shared a fond smile. Rosa's husband, Giovanni, was encouraging their four children to gather and stand still but they were all performing in front of Nico.

'Take our photo,' they shouted. 'And when can we go to the beach again?'

'Don't ever go on holiday with children,' Rosa warned Frankie. 'It's total chaos.' And then she laughed again. 'Oops...too late.'

They were both still laughing as Nico took their photo, but Frankie wasn't looking at the camera. She had turned her head to look towards the end of the table, where her mother and *nonna* were sitting. Her *nonna* was holding the bundle that was her six-week-old son Paolo, who was the most perfect baby in the world. He even already looked like his *papà*.

Mr Perfect.

Not that anyone was perfect, of course, but this man that Frankie loved a little more with every extra day they got to spend together was as close as it got.

Their life was as close to perfect as anyone could hope for too.

They were still living in the little blue beach house that Nico had rented, but they owned it now and they were fixing it up and making it bigger when time and money allowed. One of the first things they'd done after they'd been lucky enough to buy the property was to build this outside courtyard with its paved floor and big, rustic wooden table and benches and the grapevine that would eventually make it a gorgeous, green outside room with lots of shade for summer.

Because this was a place for family to gather. The way the Romanos had in a similar courtyard when Frankie and Nico went back to Italy to get married nearly two years ago. The way their friends and family could gather when they came to visit. Jen and Rob had come just a week or two ago, with little Jacob and their adorable baby daughter Stephanie, who would be celebrating her first birthday soon. And Stumpy had been there too, of course. Bruce had been so happy to meet his old friend again and had shared the secret of where the best place to be was—under the big wooden table—especially when there were children on the benches who always dropped lots of food.

'We need a photo of Nico and Frankie,' Rosa declared. 'With Paolo. For Mamma.' She shook her head and sighed loudly. 'You'd think Paolo was her favourite grandchild, but we all know that I'm the family favourite so that makes my children the favourites too, doesn't it?'

Frankie caught Nico's gaze and shared a grin. Not that either of them would dare contradict Rosa, but they both knew that their baby was clearly the favourite. He was perfect, wasn't he?

She went to gently remove her son from her *nonna*'s arms and her grandmother gave her a knowing look as she relinquished the baby.

'I was right, wasn't I, Francesca?' she said. 'You just needed to find a nice Italian boy and settle down and have your own *bambino*. What took you so long?'

'I had to find the perfect man, Nonna.' Frankie smiled. 'I couldn't settle for anything less.'

And then she turned, with their precious baby in her arms, and walked towards Nico. The voices and laughter of their extended family were behind her as Giovanni prepared to take a photo of the new parents but all Frankie could see was the look in Nico's eyes.

The love that was becoming more and more like a physical touch as every step took her closer to this man she loved so much.

She would treasure the photo that was about to be taken. One day, when she was a *nonna* herself, she would be able to find it amongst so many other memories of the life she'd dreamed of having. She'd show it to Nico and they would smile at each other.

'What a wonderful day that was...'

'*Sì*. It was *perfetto*...'

* * * * *

COMING SOON!

We really hope you enjoyed reading this book. If you're looking for more romance be sure to head to the shops when new books are available on

Thursday 26ᵗʰ October

To see which titles are coming soon, please visit

millsandboon.co.uk/nextmonth

MILLS & BOON

MILLS & BOON ®

Coming next month

THE NURSE'S HOLIDAY SWAP
Ann McIntosh

Those penetrating hazel eyes locked on hers, searching and sending heat cascading through her veins.

"If you're in pain, you could go home. No one would blame you."

"Don't be silly," she replied. Her breath wanted to catch in her chest. He was so close his warmth and delicious scent touched her, making her heart beat erratically. "I...I'm fine. Besides, we're short staffed."

She didn't think he moved, but suddenly the moment seemed incredibly intimate.

"Well, if you have to leave, just let them know I said you could."

It suddenly occurred to her that with the way they were positioned, if she lifted her chin just a little, she'd be perfectly positioned for his kiss, and her heart went from thumping to racing.

What are you thinking?

Totally flustered, she forced her gaze down to her lap and away from the temptation he offered. Had she really been about to make a fool of herself with her boss? Imagining the warmth in his gaze was more than friendly concern?

Gathering her composure and giving her head a mental shake, she straightened, making her face impassive.

"Don't fuss." She made her voice as firm as she could, adding a bit of a shooing gesture with her right hand in emphasis. "Go back to work and I'll be out in a minute."

Javi's gaze dropped to where her bare legs poked out from beneath the drape, and she immediately felt naked.

Exposed.

Funny how when he was bandaging her up that hadn't even crossed her mind!

"Right," he said, abruptly turning for the door. "See you on the ward."

And it was only when the door closed behind him that she could breathe again.

Continue reading
THE NURSE'S HOLIDAY SWAP
Ann McIntosh

Available next month
www.millsandboon.co.uk